Acclaim for
Women of Myste
An Anthology

"Beyond the grave, temporarily in the grave, not grave at all . . . these stories explore the inconvenience of being dead, the allure of danger by night, ghostly visitations, lethal secrets, victims who richly deserve to die, victims who have no intention of dying, the propensity of gardens to be planted with more than flowers . . . Feast away!"

—Claire McNab
Author of the Detective Inspector Carol Ashton Mysteries,
the Denise Cleever Thrillers, and the Kylie Kendall
Private Eye Comedies

"When I first picked up the manuscript of *Women of Mystery,* my game plan was to skim a few stories until I found one that piqued my interest. Problem was, right off the bat I saw that skimming was impossible. Every single story I started held my attention until the very end—the mark of a winning mystery anthology, in my humble opinion.

Katherine V. Forrest has truly given me a gift. She has edited a series of short stories that allows me to do two of my favorite things at once: read about lesbians and read a good mystery. The stories span the spectrum from the lighthearted (and hilarious) to the dark and dangerous. All of them, however, are literate and sharply realized—no small accomplishment. If I'm allowed to state a favorite, it would have to be J. M. Redmann's 'The Intersection of Camp and St. Mary.' I adored the wit and the attitude. I can't remember a time when I've read a story that made me laugh so hard or feel so satisfied at the end.

I hope this anthology will prompt readers to explore other works by these clever, funny, and humane writers. And if anyone's interested in my vote, I'd like to see volume two of *Women of Mystery* sometime in the very near future."

—Ellen Hart
Five-time winner of the Lambda Literary Award
for Best Lesbian Mystery; Author of the Jane Lawless series
and the Sophie Greenway series

"This is by far the best collection of mystery stories by lesbian writers I have ever read. The writing is excellent throughout, the story lines truly innovative. The characters in these stories are refreshingly diverse and represent a variety of cultural, ethnic, socioeconomic, and political differences; their individuality is made real by a few bold strokes of the pen. Some stories are haunting (the political activist who is arrested for a brutal crime she did not commit), while others veer into magical realism (the lesbian who finds herself in the otherworld but discovers that she can still look in on this one). Some stories are wry and satirize the very genre they represent, while others are laugh-out-loud funny. The opening lines pull you in from the beginning ('I started to suspect she was a werewolf on our first date.'), and keep you there to the very end. I haven't had this much fun with lesbian mysteries in years and am already hoping for a second collection by the same editor and perhaps these same authors. This collection will stay with you long after you have put the book down."

—Evelyn Torton Beck
Editor of *Nice Jewish Girls:*
A Lesbian Anthology

"Recognizing myself as somewhat of a mystery-genre virgin, I was drawn into each of these stories. The prominence of lesbians became commonplace—perhaps distinguishing this collection from any other—allowing me to comfortably and engagingly move into the conflicts, challenges, and strange and eerie twists of the story lines as they evolved."

—Wendy Judith Cutler
Senior Instructor, Women's Studies Department,
Portland State University

Women of Mystery
An Anthology

Women of Mystery
An Anthology

Katherine V. Forrest
Editor

Alice Street Editions™
Harrington Park Press®
An Imprint of The Haworth Press, Inc.
New York • London • Oxford

For more information on this book or to order, visit
http://www.haworthpress.com/store/product.asp?sku=5371

or call 1-800-HAWORTH (800-429-6784) in the United States and Canada
or (607) 722-5857 outside the United States and Canada

or contact orders@HaworthPress.com

Published by

Alice Street Editions™, Harrington Park Press®, an imprint of The Haworth Press, Inc.,
10 Alice Street, Binghamton, NY 13904-1580.

PUBLISHER'S NOTE
This is a work of fiction. Names, characters, places, and incidents either are the products of the
author's imagination or are used fictitiously, and any resemblance to actual persons, living or
dead, business establishments, events, or locales is entirely coincidental.

Cover design by Jennifer M. Gaska.

Library of Congress Cataloging-in-Publication Data

Women of mystery : an anthology / Katherine V. Forrest, editor.
    p. cm.
  ISBN-13: 978-1-56023-543-9 (pbk. : alk. paper)
  ISBN-10: 1-56023-543-8 (pbk. : alk. paper)
   1. Lesbians—Fiction. 2. Women detectives—Fiction. 3. Detective and mystery stories,
American. 4. Lesbians' writings, American. I. Forrest, Katherine V., 1939-

PS648.L47W648 2005
813'.0872083526643—dc22

           2005007953

CONTENTS

Introduction
Judith P. Stelboum

As editor in chief of Alice Street Editions I am pleased to write the introduction to *Women of Mystery: An Anthology,* edited by the distinguished writer Katherine V. Forrest.

Alice Street Editions provides a voice for established as well as up-and-coming lesbian writers, reflecting the diversity of lesbian interests, ethnicities, ages, and class. This cutting-edge series of novels, memoirs, and nonfiction writing welcomes the opportunity to present controversial views, explore multicultural ideas, encourage debate, and inspire creativity from a variety of lesbian perspectives. Alice Street Editions hopes to make a significant contribution to the visibility and accessibility of lesbian writing through enlightening, illuminating, and provocative writing. Recognizing our own desires and ideas in print is life sustaining, acknowledging the reality of who we are, as well as our place in the world, individually and collectively.

This anthology initiates the first of its genre for Alice Street. Here we have mystery stories by lesbian writers featuring lesbian protagonists, lesbian murderers, and even a lesbian "werewolf." How lucky can we be to see such characters in any number of situations, each with its unique lesbian twists and turns? Finally we can sit down to a good read knowing that we don't have to look for that one lesbian character or that one lesbian reference.

Mysteries have always been popular reading. I did an informal survey asking people who like to read mystery stories why they enjoy them so much. Readers have said that they like the structure of the mystery story—imagining that the story must be carefully crafted, with the writer knowing the answer and then working back to create the plot, sometimes creating clues for the reader to guess the answers before the end of the story. For some, reading mysteries is like a treasure hunt. Good mysteries allow the reader to search for answers to a puzzle where red herrings have been placed in the path of discovery. In Victoria A. Brownworth's story, "Violation," the main character sits in prison, convicted of a gruesome crime, and thinks of her lesbian lover who, she assumes, is suffering as much as she is. The story told by the prisoner could be an elaboration of a line from an Emily Dickinson poem, "Tell all the Truth but tell it slant—Success in Circuit lies . . ."

Another avid fan of mysteries liked the problem solving involved, taking the clues and deciphering them as one would an Egyptian hieroglyphic. The better the translator/reader, the clearer the message as to "whodunit."

Many readers of mystery stories search for a sense of justice in the books. This grand concept, which we so seldom find realized in life, can be created in the pages of the mystery. The criminal is captured, punished, and the world is righted. Mystery devotees tell me that they thrive on this justice that reestablishes order to the world. It is no coincidence that a popular television series is titled *Law and Order*.

Other readers love understanding the psychology of the characters. There is a fascination with the psychosis of the criminal mind. Why would someone commit a criminal act? There are as many reasons as there are mysteries. Understanding the character and temperament of a deceased husband in Katherine V. Forrest's "A Leopard's Spots" leads to the inevitable solution of a complicated murder. It is this interest in fathoming human nature that has kept mystery writing in such demand for so many readers.

People who read mysteries say that they become active readers. They participate with the writer. The reader is looking for an adventure, and identifying with the sleuth has rewards. Sometimes the detective is just this side of the law, unorthodox, eccentric, and outside the mainstream. There is a long literary tradition of the wisecracking, cynical private investigator. "Murder on Chuckanut Drive" by Ouida Crozier is the classic problem-solving, clue-laden mystery in this mold.

People who don't enjoy mysteries may dislike the problem solving involved. They have no patience for the little clues and cannot wait until the denouement. Such readers quickly turn to the last few pages to get the answer before they begin to read at all. They are the constructionists. They want to see what's behind the curtain and are interested in the mechanics of the process. They are the ones who like to see how it's done with no surprises or suspense. Joan M. Drury's story, "The 'Sound' of Music," might satisfy even this reader because a murderer is caught by a technical reality.

The stories assembled in this collection by Katherine V. Forrest will satisfy all of the various requirements of mystery lovers, so enjoy the read.

The "Sound" of Music

Joan M. Drury

Most people tend to think being deaf is tragic when, in fact, sometimes it's a blessing. For instance, it's very peaceful for me at large gatherings of people because I can't hear everyone talking at once nor do I have to strain to hear the words from the person next to me. I am never assaulted, as one deaf comedian points out, by the likes of Howard Stern. And I never have to grit my teeth to survive the neighbor's teenaged son's abominable taste in music being played at intolerably loud levels.

Of course, I wouldn't even know about these things if I hadn't had other people describing such phenomena to me. I mean, how could *I* know that that large crowds of people are loud and disturbing to one's sense of equilibrium? (Actually, I don't really know what *loud* means. The distinction between loud and soft is lost on those of us who hear nothing.) Or that Howard Stern, once confined to a medium I can't receive, radio, is an egregiously annoying human being? Or that teenagers blast music at "deafening" levels, or, as far as that goes, even what constitutes abominable taste?

Music is an odd thing for those of us who dwell in the silent realm. Oh, it's true, sometimes I'll find my foot tapping because I'm in a room with a live band, and I'll feel the vibrations through the floor. But mostly I could care less about music. People seem to think I *should* miss it, but can I miss something I've never had? Honestly, I can't even *imagine* music—no context, you know—let alone pine for it.

Until DeeDee, that is. DeeDee is my current inamorata—a fine, dear, kind, intelligent, funny woman who happens to be a musician. Wouldn't you know? From the beginning, she couldn't bear the thought that I couldn't fully appreciate her work, her passion.

"But DeeDee," I signed, "if you were an accountant, I wouldn't know much about what you do for a living. It's okay if you're a musician and I can't imagine that. There are other ways we can connect." At which point I wriggled my eyebrows suggestively.

She frowned. "Nora, this is not like being an accountant. Music is not just a *job* to me. It's my obsession, my joy, my life!" I shrugged. "Will you let me try to figure a way to teach you?" she asked through the stutter of her fingers, with which I first fell in love. I shrugged again, unwilling to refuse such a loving, well-meaning offer while secretly thinking it was a waste of time.

We started with her baby grand. She put the lid down and placed my hands on it, then sat at the keys and struck them. After a few minutes, she stopped and signed. "Think of a small, rocky waterfall. The water is leaping from rock to rock, striking the sharp edges, then bouncing up into the sunlight—gathering the sparkle and rapture of the light into its fluid dance. That's how it sounds when fingers strike piano keys." Then she played some more. I could feel the vibrations through the warm, smooth wood of the piano and, thinking of the water frolicking down the wall of rocks, I could almost imagine the "sound" of a piano. I smiled, and DeeDee smiled back.

That was just the beginning. She took me to an orchestra's rehearsal. We stood by the instruments as she told me with her long, thin fingers—so agile on the piano keys, always stumbling when signing—in my hand, constantly talking to me, teaching music to the rest of my senses. This was one of the positive aspects of being deaf: we could have long, complicated conversations with one another and never disturb anyone around us.

"This is a drum. Think of the ocean: the slow, gradual roll of a coming wave, growing larger and larger; the smashing of those tons of water against the shore, shooting up into the air, rupturing the previous stillness of air and beach." We walked a couple of steps. "These are cymbals. Think of the Fourth of July. Fireworks! Explosions of dazzling lights in the dark sky. And here. String instruments—violin, cello, bass. This sound, if it's off just a little, can be so annoying but when it's right it's a perfect blend of . . ." She hesitated.

"Sweet and sour?" I suggested, getting into the swing of her efforts.

"Yes!" Her eyes sparkled with excitement. "Perfect! If it's too sour, you cringe." She demonstrated by scrunching her face in a bad-taste look and hunching her shoulders. "If it's too sweet, you want to spit it out." She made a spitting motion with her mouth. "But the perfect blend of the two . . ." We both smiled in appreciation of the concept. "And this is a flute." Again she hesitated, then signed, "Birds fluttering, cavorting in a birdbath." In this manner, she introduced me to all the instruments.

Then she began my education regarding kinds of music and specific performers. She put Nat King Cole on her stereo. "Mellow, dreamy music," DeeDee said as she glided around the room, her eyes closed. "Think of warm caramel being ladled over cold ice cream. The caramel is creamy, liquid silk." She opened her eyes. "What happens to that ice cream?" And then she answered herself. "It gets soft and mushy. It melts. The caramel is Cole's voice, and your soul is the ice cream."

"Gravel. Dusk. A smoky room. That's the blues," she said as she played The Uppity Blues Women. "And beat. How do I explain beat?" She tapped her fingers, over and over again on the coffee table. "Relentless, constant, rhythmic."

Then she put on Buddy Holly, the Beatles, Diana Ross and the Supremes. "Rock and Roll." She wouldn't sing but shout it, not so I could hear it, because I couldn't of course, but so I'd understand its largeness, its power. "Like blues kind of. Only more so—more beat, more smoky room, more dusk, more gravel."

On to Beethoven, Mozart, Dvorak. "Classical music captures the whole range of emotion and human experience," she signed as she put Schubert's Ninth on the CD player. "Every other kind of music just focuses on part of human feeling, part of human experience. But in classical, we have it all. Sadness. Despair. Exultation. Contentment. Fury. Terror." And her body mimicked all these feelings and experiences as she moved to the music.

"You know how the taste of a hot pepper in your mouth just detonates?" I would nod. "That's salsa. And . . ."

This went on for weeks. At first, I tried to explain to her how little this all meant to me. That it was like insisting that a paraplegic get up and walk. That it was close to being insulting. But she persisted, pointing out how much it meant to her. I finally decided, as flaws go, this was not a major one.

And gradually, I became more and more interested. I was curious to see what metaphors, what images she was going to employ next. It was like learning a new language. I learned about the aching, searing, ragged pain in Janis Joplin's voice and the gritty, fiery power of Jimi Hendrix. I leaned about the soft rain of Chopin's music and the light playfulness of Vivaldi.

"What about women's music?" I asked, knowing about performers like Meg Christian and Margie Adam and Alix Dobkin and others from the early days of 1970s feminism.

She screwed her mouth to one side, thinking. I waited patiently. Then she said, "Some of the women who do 'women's music' are incredible musicians, others are mediocre. Same as all musicians, actually. But the music—not too risky, not much of a stretch. It's a lot like folk music, which exists more for its lyrics, its evocation of culture than its musicality. Women's music is like that—more a cultural experience than a musical one. Important, in its own way." Then she gave me the lyrics to much of this music, and I could see how much it captured our history and politics and fervor and community—culture, just as DeeDee had said.

It wasn't long before I was showing off what an apt student I was by grabbing DeeDee's hand and signing, "Jazz," when I witnessed someone moving about in a disjointed manner. If she said "no," I'd sign, "Rock and roll! The blues!" until she'd laugh and tell me I was right. Swaying usually meant something DeeDee called "easy listening" or "elevator music," explaining to me that it was music akin to Jell-O. "No texture, no substance, little taste." A certain intensity of facial expression combined with tensing of muscles usually meant classical. So did balletlike dancing or conducting. Because I was a keen observer—that sharpening of the other senses that transpires when you don't have them all, you know—it didn't take me long to figure out what other people were hearing, if it was music.

This is how I learned about music, something I would never hear, never fully comprehend. And this was how I found myself in an odd situation to be of help in a murder investigation.

Because I'm a freelance copywriter and work at home, I'm very familiar with and accustomed to the people who populate my small world and their daily routines: the cleaning woman, Conchita, at the apartment across the courtyard who comes twice a week and always listens to the radio, dancing through her chores; the old woman, Mrs. Maguire, who takes her dachshund for a walk, rain or shine, snow or sleet, every two and a half hours, starting at eight in the morning; the mailman who comes just before noon every day and waves up at me if there's mail, because he knows I'm deaf and won't hear it if he rings our bell; the homeless wino who drifts between our front stoop and the one next door, hoping for a shower of coins; the scrawny, disheveled, yellow cat (DeeDee and I call her Kate Moss—you know, after that anorectic model) who goes from window to window, door to door, probably eating better than the well-groomed, beloved cats with owners.

And so it was one bright but brittle December morning. I had seen Conchita arrive, switch on the radio, and begin whirling through her work just after Mrs. Maguire returned from her first morning walk with her little dog in his red sweater that matched her red hat and mittens. I assumed she'd knitted them herself. When I took my ten-thirty break and walked to the corner to get myself a double latte, I'd stepped over our resident wino, parting with some change.

Mrs. Maguire was just coming back from her second walk of the day when I returned from the coffee shop, and I took a moment to lean over Mr. Red-Sweater and scratch his ears, while the old woman chattered at me. Or maybe at the dog, I was never sure. I always indicated to her that I was deaf, but I suspected—by the way she opened her mouth wider—that she merely talked louder. Lots of people did this, like maybe if they talked loudly enough—or if I concentrated hard enough—I might actually hear them. I didn't take it personally anymore, although it *is* personal, you know. It just isn't worth the emotional effort to be aggravated all the time.

Working at my window, I would glance out, often feeling like I was living in that Jimmy Stewart movie *Rear Window*. Kate Moss came by and gulped down the crumbs and a puddle of milk I'd left for her on the window sill. The mailman waved at me, so I took a break at noon and went down to get our mail. When I returned, I flipped through the mail, opened a couple of pieces, then made myself a sandwich and warmed up a cup of soup.

Later that day, in the early evening when DeeDee had returned from her day job in a music store and before she went to rehearsal, two police officers, whose identification introduced them as Detectives Albion and Yardley, stopped by to ask about Conchita. As they talked, DeeDee signed for them. I could read lips, but signing was quicker and more direct for me. And I didn't miss as many words and nuances. DeeDee was an accomplished signer now. Although her hands still had that endearing flutter I so adored when we first met, she was quick and thorough and did one other thing I particularly liked, kept up a steady barrage—when there was time—of personal commentary about the other speaker.

So I learned from her that the younger of the detectives, bulging in an ill-fitting suit and tie, spoke slowly and deliberately, as if maybe both of us—DeeDee and me—were a little dumb. The older cop, a woman with a grandmotherly look, evinced some impatience by barking out quick questions, seeming quite certain that neither of us was going to be of any help. That changed, of course, when I made it clear to them that I worked at home, had an excellent view of the apartment across the courtyard, and had seen Conchita that very morning.

The young man's face softened, even though he resembled some kind of stereotype of a Marine sergeant, when he told me that Conchita was dead, had been killed sometime today in that apartment. I felt the news like a blow, pulled away from them, withdrawing inside myself. Conchita dead? I turned and looked across the now-dark courtyard at the lights in the apartment, at people moving around in there. I pressed my hand against the cold glass and remembered her shoulders gyrating, remembered her twisting and turning, her joyful cleaning-dance.

DeeDee put her hand on my shoulder and fluttered sweetly in my palm, "I'm sorry, my love, but these officers need to ask you some questions." I nodded, still staring across the inky chasm, then turned back to the cops.

"What happened?" I asked, thinking of Mrs. Maguire waiting for a Conchita who was never going to show.

They relayed the information: she'd been raped and knifed. By some druggie, they assumed, since the place had been ransacked and some things of value were missing. I watched their faces closely. I don't know what it's like to hear a voice. Words that are signed can seem cold and dispassionate. I have to take all my clues from nonauditory messages. The woman's shoulders were bunched, as if in pain, and her face had become granitelike. *I'll bet she's been raped or had someone close to her raped,* I thought. The man was displaying less emotion, but there was a certain tightness to his mouth that convinced me he didn't take this lightly either.

I was looking back and forth from their faces to DeeDee's hands when I realized something about twelve o'clock had been signed. "Wait, wait," I stopped DeeDee. "What about this time? Twelve o'clock?"

She asked the detectives to repeat what they'd said and then conveyed to me that Conchita's watch had been smashed, and the hands were at twelve o'clock. I turned my head and stared with bewilderment for a minute out the window, then turned back to them, vigorously shaking my head.

"No," I insisted, "this is not true. Someone's deliberately messing with you."

"What do you mean?"

"She was still alive after noon."

It was their turn to be bewildered. "That's impossible," the man insisted. "Not only was her watch smashed at twelve, but one of the clocks in the apartment was also broken, at the same time."

I looked at him, wondering if he was stupid or just wanted this to be easy. "It wouldn't be hard," I signed, "to smash a watch and clock and set them both at a time you wanted."

"For what reason?" the female detective asked, but there was a shrewdness in her eyes that convinced me she knew the answer already.

I shrugged. "Presumably to help with an alibi?"

She nodded, her eyes intent. "How can you be so certain she was still alive after twelve?"

I related the daily routine here. I told them about the mailman, how he comes just before noon, how I went down and got the mail, went through it, then made myself some lunch—all of this taking some time, so I know it was after twelve, probably after twelve thirty by the time I was back at my desk and saw Conchita vacuuming and dancing.

"She always vacuums last, right before she leaves at one." Then I explained about Mrs. Maguire and her dog, how she walked to the bus stop with Conchita on her workdays because Conchita always finished by one o'clock. "Ask Mrs. Maguire," I said. "She'll tell you Conchita didn't show. She was killed between twelve and one, but closer to one. For *sure* after twelve thirty."

The man's eyebrows beetled skeptically. "That's all? Did you look at the clock when you saw her dancing?"

"No," I answered and felt uncertain, for a moment. Then I said to DeeDee, "Check the radio listing. She was listening to salsa music." I moved my shoulders a little, and DeeDee smiled.

She explained to the cops about my being able to identify music by the way a person moved to it while she looked at radio listings. "Here it is," she said, "Latin American music on KQXE between twelve thirty and one. Conchita was still alive after twelve thirty."

"But probably not by one," I added, "because she didn't join Mrs. Maguire." I felt an incredible sadness wash through me. All that vitality, all that elation gone.

DeeDee didn't go to rehearsal that night, stayed home to comfort me. She didn't know Conchita, had always been at work when she was in that apartment. Myself, I didn't really know Conchita either but felt like I did. Who I didn't know was the actual occupant of the apartment. I'd sometimes get a glimpse of him at night when he pulled the shades down and again in the morning when he opened them before leaving for work. Conchita was my only link with that place. Sometimes, when she was dancing and cleaning, she'd notice me at my window and wave to me, a wide grin on her face. I always waved back, smiling, too. And now she was dead. Viciously and tragically.

It was a couple of days before DeeDee called the precinct and asked for Detective Albion or Yardley. She got Yardley, the woman, who was enthusiastically voluble. "We got him!" she crowed. "And all because of your friend's information."

"Really?" DeeDee asked.

"Yes. It was the occupant of the apartment himself, a Daniel Spitz. Supposedly he came home from work at the end of the day, found Conchita's body, and called us. He was in the clear himself because he'd left his office just before noon, there were witnesses, and it was too far away for him to have reached the apartment by noon, the time we assumed she'd been killed because of the watch and the clock. But your friend's testimony put us to the wise, and we turned up the heat on him during questioning, telling him we knew she was alive after twelve thirty. Then we found blood traces on the soles of his shoes, and he collapsed, dropping his insistence on his innocence. But your girlfriend's information really did it! We probably would have continued assuming an unknown outsider and just left it at that, an open homicide. Probably wouldn't have checked his shoes or anything else so carefully. Tell her how much we appreciate her keen observations. And that thing with music? That's some trick!"

Yeah, I thought, *some trick,* as I looked across at the lifeless windows, wondering if Conchita had screamed, had called for help. Some trick.

Then I had DeeDee put salsa music on the CD player. She moved to it and described it to me. Exuberant. Vital. Explosive. Lively. Passionate. Spirited.

That's how I remembered Conchita and honored her life.

The Last Minute

Lisa Liel

Kara never felt the bullet hit her. What she did feel was more like a hammer blow to the side of her head that sent her reeling to her knees. So this is what they mean by seeing stars, she thought, blinking. There was a ringing in her ears, but that was fading, as were the stars and other shapes obscuring her vision. She closed her eyes for a long moment, then took a breath and opened them. The room still looked dim, but at least it was clear. She stood slowly, making sure she hadn't hurt herself, and looked around to see what had fallen on her. She froze. Standing where she had been just moments before was herself. Or rather, a statue of herself. Kara frowned. *Something isn't normal,* she thought. *That wasn't there before.*

She approached the statue and reached a tentative hand out to touch its face. As her hand passed through the surface, she uttered a little yelp and snatched it back. Kara stared. She hadn't felt a thing. She reached out again and touched the thing's arm. She felt the cloth of the blouse she had picked out that morning, but it was stiff as iron.

Is this a dream? she thought. Another thought nagged at her. It was like the movie *Ghost.* She was dead. *No.* She shook her head. *Things kept moving for him. They didn't freeze like that.* She realized how stupid that was and flushed. It was just a movie, after all. They might have guessed part of what happens when you die, just by coincidence, but more likely it was just a story. *And what a boring movie it would have been,* she thought with a half smile, *if no one in it could move except for Patrick Swayze.*

"Figured it out yet?" came a voice from behind her.

She spun around and backed up sharply, almost falling again. "Shit," she gasped, "you almost gave me a heart attack."

The woman leaning against the door shook her head, her eyes smiling. "Guess you didn't. A heart attack would be a little redundant."

Kara studied the newcomer. She was tall, maybe an inch taller than Kara's five-seven. Slender, with light brown hair that fell in soft curls to her shoulders. She wore blue jeans and a sweater and, Kara noted, she was very pretty.

The woman took a long stride toward Kara and held out her hand. "Elise," she said.

Kara returned the handshake, murmuring, "Fair Elise." She was immediately annoyed with herself. Aside from the lame pun on "Für Elise," this was quite possibly the dumbest situation in which to be flirting. Especially when she didn't even know . . . But from the pleased smile on Elise's face, she saw that there at least she hadn't been mistaken. She had always been good at sensing that. *The first person I meet in the next world,* she thought wryly, *and she's gay too. Maybe straight people go somewhere else?* Her eyes widened. Was this hell? Were all the fundamentalists right after all?

Elise shook her head and laughed, as if she could read Kara's mind. "There are straight people here too," she said.

Kara stared for a moment, and released Elise's hand. The woman had a firm grip. "Okay," she said slowly. "Since you seem to be up on what's going on here, mind telling me where exactly here is?"

"Here," Elise said, gesturing, "is the same place you were before you were shot."

"Shot?"

Elise pointed to the side of the Kara-statue's head. About a foot and a half away from the side of the statue's head, a bullet hung in the air, defying gravity.

Kara spun back to Elise with fear in her eyes. "Bullshit!" she blustered. "Who would want to shoot me?"

Elise shrugged. "I imagine you'd know better than I, don't you think?" She walked over to the bullet and took hold of it. She tried to wiggle it, but it wouldn't move. "Dead, you see? Anything living, plant, animal, whatever, is totally immaterial to us. And anything not living is tangible, but immobile."

Kara's thoughts raced. "Then how can we be breathing?" she demanded.

Elise shrugged again. "Maybe gases don't count," she suggested. "It doesn't matter much, because you can't make anything to take advantage of it. The only physical things we can affect are our clothes." She fingered her sweater. "Which I'm not sure aren't an illusion anyway. And other deaders."

Kara sat on the sofa. It was like a rock, totally unyielding. "Why don't you start from the beginning. For starters, why do you know so much?"

Elise thought about that for a moment. "Probably because I've been here all day. Such as days are here. As near as I can figure, we're in a sort of cut-rate afterlife. Maybe they had to trim the budget or something, but it's only a day long."

"A day long," Kara repeated blankly.

"It means that the only people around are people who died today, the ninth of November. It means that we can go anywhere we want physically, but timewise, we exist between one midnight and another. Come here." She took Kara's hand. Kara ignored the almost electric feel of Elise's hand on hers. Elise turned toward the window and focused. Kara felt a dragging motion, as if she were moving through a viscous fluid, though as far as she could tell, they weren't moving at all. After a moment, light began to glow through the window, and became brighter, until it was daytime outside. Elise continued this until the light began to dim and the room grew darker again.

"Come with me," she told Kara, leading her outside. The two walked out of Kara's apartment and down the three flights of stairs to the street. In the middle of the street, Elise stopped and held Kara's hand with her arm stretched out.

"What are you doing?" Kara asked, totally lost.

"Oh, this doesn't matter, just so long as we stay in contact. I just like the dramatic effect." She grinned disarmingly. She focused her eyes again, and this time, the scenery flashed, and they were standing in a subway station. Elise released Kara's hand and walked toward the track. She went up to one of the still figures waiting and put her hand on its back. She looked at Kara. "This is me. Was me," she corrected.

Kara walked around and saw that it was indeed Elise. She looked at the living Elise blankly. She shook her head. *The one that's not moving is the living one. The one I'm talking with is the dead one. Jesus.*

"Give me your hand again," Elise said. As before, she focused her eyes, only this time looking at her doppelgänger. After a moment, Kara noticed that people and things were moving. Slowly and with a dead silence that gave her the shivers, but they were moving. "Watch," Elise whispered.

Kara didn't know which way to look, but as she turned, she saw a teenaged boy with a Walkman shaking his head to the rhythm of whatever it was he was listening to and bopping toward them, eyes screwed shut and mouth moving with the music. Over the boy's shoulder, Kara saw a light as the D train started into the station. The silent Elise-statue, no longer a statue, had stepped toward the track and was leaning over to see if the train was coming. Kara saw what was coming and yelped. She moved toward the boy, but Elise pulled her back. A moment later, the boy had collided with the other Elise, who was falling in slow motion onto the tracks. Kara's throat tightened. She clutched at Elise and looked away. Elise stood rigid, watching as her previous self was mangled silently by the train.

They stood that way for a long moment. Then Elise said gently, "You're hurting me." Kara realized that she was gripping Elise's arms too tightly and released her. She started to look toward the track, but stopped herself. Everything was motionless again.

"Kara," she said vaguely.

"Excuse me?"

"My name is Kara."

"Kara Mia?" Elise asked playfully.

Kara jerked away from her, her eyes wide. "How—" she choked. "How can you joke after . . . watching . . ."

"After watching myself die?" Elise asked softly. She shrugged. "I've seen it before. There's only so many times you can watch something like that before it has all the emotional impact of a television rerun." Kara knew she was lying. She had felt Elise's tension during the accident.

"How do you travel like that?" Kara asked irrelevantly.

"You just focus on something and think about seeing it after, and you move forward. Or you think about seeing it before and you move backward. As far as places are concerned, you can walk. The only place you can jump to like I did before is to where your real self is. If you don't concentrate on staying in one place, then whenever you move forward or backward you get drawn behind your real self like a magnet."

Kara flinched both times Elise said "real self." She was real!

Grimly, she asked, "So I could jump back to my apartment? Where we were before?"

"Sure. So long as you were there now. Otherwise you'll jump to wherever you were. You can also move forward or backward in one place if you focus on staying in that place," she added.

"So . . . why . . ." Kara fumbled for words, her mind trying to take all of this in. "Why didn't we see you pop out when you fell just now?"

Elise shrugged. "Why don't we keep running into ourselves when we go to see the same event? I've watched myself fall there about a dozen times now, and I never see myself here watching." She cocked her head to the side thoughtfully. "I don't think we're moving in time, really. It's as if the other world is like a video that we can run forward and backward. A recording."

In a daze, Kara walked over to a bench and sat down heavily. *This is ridiculous,* she thought, as Elise sat down in the seat next to hers. *I don't know anyone who would want to kill me. And burglars don't just come in and shoot. Do they?* "Elise." She grabbed Elise's arm and said urgently, "I need to see who killed me. Will you help me?"

Elise's eyes twinkled. "Well . . ." Kara looked at her beseechingly. "Oh, all right," Elise laughed. "I was going to catch a movie, but I've never been all that hot on reading lips." Kara shook her head. She couldn't see how Elise could find any humor in this situation.

"Listen." Elise had turned serious. "You need to lighten up. If this is all the 'life' we have anymore, we might as well make the most of it. Being dead is bad enough without having to be depressed all the time."

"God!" Kara exploded. "You haven't been dead for a day, and it's like you don't care!"

"It's been a lot more than a day, Kara. It's been more like months. Time doesn't work the same here, remember? How do you think I know so much about moving around here? I mean, I'm bright—" She grinned. "But I'm not that bright." She took Kara's hand. "I've been roaming around here for all this time, but you're the first person I've seen pop out like that. I must have missed all the others."

"Where are all the others?"

"Around." Elise gestured vaguely. "Think about the number of people who died here within walking distance in one day. They can be anywhere or anywhen. You run into people now and then, but otherwise it's pretty lonely." She looked meaningfully at Kara, who was suddenly very conscious of the feel of Elise's hand on her own.

She pulled her hand free. "So I can jump back to my apartment?" she asked.

"Here, think about finding yourself," Elise explained. "That'll pull you to wherever you are now. Then you can follow yourself through the day until you're back getting shot." She grinned and Kara glared at her. "But keep contact with me, or I'll get left behind. It'll be difficult to connect again if that happens."

Kara hesitated, but Elise had been very helpful. *And,* she thought wryly, *in any other situation, I wouldn't need another reason to stick close to someone as attractive as she is.* She took Elise's hand again and thought of finding herself, and—

Flash

—she was in Julie's room. Along with her earlier self and Julie. Still in bed, but not asleep. "Shit," she breathed, yanking Elise into the hallway.

"Wha-at?" Elise laughed as Kara almost pulled her off balance.

Kara blushed deep red. "How the hell early were you at the subway?" she demanded.

"Early enough," Elise returned, amused. "Can't I go look?" she pleaded jokingly. "Pretty please? She's cute."

"Dammit, Elise! This is not a joke. Things have been rocky between me and Julie and they were finally starting to work out and now I . . . I . . ." She faltered, tears beginning to well up.

"Hey," Elise said gently, moving to hold Kara. Kara's tears turned to moans as she held onto Elise. She cried for long minutes, deep sobs of grief wracking her. They stayed that way until Kara cried herself out and her breathing had become calmer. Slowly, she disentangled herself from Elise and walked into the kitchen. She sat at the table and rested her chin in her hands, thinking. "Okay, I know what I'm going to do. If you want to come with, hang on."

She stood up and Elise put her hand on her arm. Kara looked at the clock hanging over the kitchen table. "When'd I leave?" she muttered. The clock began to advance slowly. "Let's see how fast this can go," she gritted, and the clock sped up until it was whirling. Blurred figures, presumably of Julie and living-Kara, flew in and around the kitchen and were gone. "Whoa, too fast," she said, and the hands stopped and began turning backwards.

"You don't have to do that."

Kara stopped her concentration. "Do what?"

"You don't have to move back. Just think yourself to wherever you are now and you can follow along until . . ." She shrugged. "Until you know."

Kara nodded. And then they were outside. Her earlier self was headed west, toward the subway. Kara furrowed her brow and the world went into a blur. She and Elise were yanked back and forth faster than they could see, buildings and walls and subway trains and tunnels whipping by dizzyingly. Elise gasped, and Kara told her, "Remember, we're staying still. Think of it as a three hundred and sixty degree movie. Or just close your eyes." Elise moaned and closed her eyes. Kara felt a small satisfaction. At least Elise wasn't laughing now.

The daylight faded, and Kara slowed down, long enough to get her bearings. They were just down the street from Kara's apartment. She remembered that she had gotten home from work late that night. She sped the world up again, and they drifted after Kara's double as she entered her apartment.

Kara watched herself heat up leftovers from the other night and eat. A chill passed through her as her earlier self sat down with the food to watch TV. She was alone that night because Julie was visiting her sister in Jersey. Would Julie have been shot as well if she'd been with Kara that night?

"I always fast-forward through the commercials when I'm watching tapes of shows," she commented to Elise without turning her head. "This is the first time I've actually been able to do it live. So to speak," she corrected. She remembered getting up in the middle of Letterman to fix some hot cocoa. That was the last thing she remembered before being hit on the head. *Shot,* she reminded herself. And there was Letterman now, grinning gap-toothedly out of the screen.

The world slowed down to normal speed. Kara turned to Elise. "I'm going to watch what happens, if you don't mind. I want to see if it was at least quick." Elise looked as if she wanted to say something, but thought better of it. As the two of them watched, doppel-Kara stood and turned to pick up her dishes to take them into the kitchen. And everything froze.

Kara stared at her double. Then at Elise. "What's going on?" she asked finally. "It won't go."

Elise walked to the frozen Kara-figure and bent over, craning her neck up to see the watch on the figure's wrist. "Your watch is wrong," she said.

"It's not wrong," Kara corrected automatically. "I keep it two minutes f—" She looked puzzled. "How do you know that?"

"Because it says 12:02. And as far as we're concerned, the world ends at midnight. You can't go past that."

"But . . ." Kara stared. "That means I'm not dead yet!"

Elise looked uncertain for a moment, then smiled. "Sure you are. You're here."

"No," Kara insisted, "don't you see? It hasn't happened yet. I can still prevent it." Her voice rose. "I can save myself, don't you see?" She started toward her motionless self and Elise grabbed her. Furiously, she yanked her arm free. "No!" Kara grabbed at the bullet hanging in the air. It refused to budge. "No! No! No!" she cried, hitting the bullet as hard as she could. She grabbed the bullet again, pulling with all her strength. Trying to pull it down, all she succeeded in doing was lifting herself up off the floor.

Elise looked at Kara hanging in the air. "Brava," she clapped approvingly.

Kara dropped to the floor, sobbing. "I am not dead yet. I'm not!"

Elise knelt and put her arm around Kara's shoulders. "Kara—" she began.

Kara jumped up. "Who did this?" she demanded angrily. She strode to the doorway and saw a man standing just to the side of the door, gun still aimed at his victim.

"Who are you, you bastard?" Kara slapped at the man and crashed into the side of the door as her hand passed through his face and she lost her balance. "Ow, shit!"

"You're lucky you didn't try to kick him in the balls," Elise observed. "You might have broken a toe. I tried pushing Mr. Bebop off the platform," she added helpfully. "No luck."

Kara stared at the man. "I don't know this guy," she said. "I don't think I've ever seen him before." She thought for a long moment. "I'm following him back. If you want to come with me, hold on."

Elise had barely touched Kara's arm when they were off. This time, Kara went more slowly, but going backward made it at least as disorienting. They passed through a bar, where the man had three drinks, and an afternoon showing of *Terminator 3*. "Definitely better in reverse," Elise quipped.

"Huh, watch this." Kara pointed to where the killer was headed. Or where he had come from, but was backing back into. The idea gave Kara a headache.

"A gun shop?"

Kara stopped the motion. "Think about it. He buys a gun, goes to a movie, has some drinks, and shows up in my apartment and shoots me. That sounds like it was pretty premeditated, don't you think?"

"But you say you don't know him."

"Never saw him before." Kara shook her head. "Why would a perfect stranger want to kill me? Unless maybe he thought I was someone else . . ."

"Let's go see," Elise suggested. "If it was a premeditated thing like you're suggesting, whatever set him off probably didn't happen all that long before he bought the gun."

Kara nodded and they followed him into the store. Sure enough, the gun he'd shot Kara with was back behind the counter before the killer backed out of the store. Kara and Elise floated after the man as he walked backward down the street. Kara began to get a strange look on her face as she saw where he was headed.

"No," she said slowly, shaking her head.

"What no?"

Kara said nothing as the killer entered the building on Eleventh Street. She stopped and stood still. Elise looked at her, puzzled.

"This is Julie's building." Kara stared bleakly.

"Um, Kara? There are dozens of apartments in this building."

Kara closed her eyes and thought. She looked again at her killer. "Okay, Mister Man. Take us to your leader." He walked backward toward the elevator, which opened at his approach. As he backed into it, Kara pulled Elise ahead and they got in before the door closed.

As they came to a stop, Kara looked at Elise.

"Her floor?"

Kara nodded. The doors opened, and the killer slapped at the button marked "Lobby" and backed out of the elevator. Kara followed him into the corridor, Elise trailing behind. Reaching behind her, Kara suddenly grabbed Elise's hand and zoomed backward in time far faster than either of them could see. When she stopped, there was her other self, walking down the hall toward the elevator on the way to work, oblivious to what the day held in store for her.

"I want to see this normally," Kara said coldly.

"Kara . . . ?" Elise said carefully.

"Shut up. You don't have to stay here if you don't want." She watched, unblinking, as living-Kara—*foolish-Kara!* she thought wildly, *sucker-Kara!*—entered the elevator and the doors closed. She set her jaw and sped the world up until the elevator door opened again and a man stepped out. It was the killer, all right. *Of course it is,* she thought grimly. *We know he was here.*

The man knocked on Julie's door and stood waiting. Julie opened the door and smiled at him. The two of them entered and the door shut. "Shit," muttered Kara, looking at the impenetrable door. She reversed the action until the door was open, and ducked past Julie.

She would have tried walking through her, but Julie's clothes blocked her way. Once inside, she let events move forward again.

Julie tilted her head up and kissed the man, and Kara's hand tightened until Elise gasped in pain. Kara stopped the action and released Elise's hand. "Bitch," she whispered. "Fucking, lying, unfaithful bitch!" she shouted. Then something broke in her. "Oh damn . . ." she breathed. "I thought . . ." She looked at Elise, begging with her eyes for this to be a mistake. "I thought everything was okay. I really did." She sagged and Elise took hold of her.

After a while, Elise asked, "Did you know she was bi?"

Kara nodded. "But she hasn't . . ." She trailed off. "Hasn't for years," she completed bleakly.

Elise looked at her sympathetically. "What do you want to do?"

Kara laughed bitterly. "Do? What's to do? The woman I love had me killed. I don't even exist anymore. Do?"

Elise said nothing.

After a moment, Kara looked into Elise's eyes. She nodded. "I have one idea, though," she said.

Julie and the man finished their kiss and walked down the hall to Julie's bedroom. The same room Kara and Julie had been in that morning. Kara watched as they undressed each other and moved to the bed.

Elise winced. "You don't have to do this, you know."

"Yes. I have to do this," Kara said desolately, her voice sounding as dead as she knew she was. She watched, unmoving, until the couple in the bed had finished. When they had closed their eyes and fallen asleep, she stopped the motion and pulled Elise out of the bedroom, down the hallway and into the living room.

She turned to Elise and placed her hands on the other woman's shoulders deliberately. "What do you want to do?" she asked. Elise looked at her questioningly. Kara pulled her close and kissed her. Elise pulled back and said carefully, "Are you sure . . . ?" Kara answered her with another kiss, and this time Elise responded.

They made love in Julie's living room, using their clothes, the only soft objects they had, as bedding.

Why? The question nagged at Kara as she lay spooning with Elise. Why kill her? Jesus, people break up all the time. What on earth would Julie have to gain from her death? If she'd decided to leave her for a man, why not just leave her? It made no sense.

"Penny for your thoughts," Elise murmured.

"I'm thinking about why I'm not falling asleep."

Elise sighed. "You're dead, sweetheart. The last time I slept was the night before I played chicken with a subway train. And it's been months for me subjectively, remember?" She shrugged. "I don't think we can sleep."

"Elise, why would she have him kill me, do you think? She can't possibly have hated me that much without having shown it at least a little."

Elise sat up, her legs crossed Indian-style. Resting her hand on Kara's side, she asked, "Does it really matter why? Kara," she said earnestly, "I'm not going to say anything against her, because that's not my place. But 'why' doesn't seem like much of a question. Maybe she was scared you'd make a fuss. Maybe she said something as a joke and Rambo in there took it seriously. Maybe . . ." She trailed off.

"Maybe, maybe, maybe," Kara said impatiently. "Come on." She stood up and started to get dressed. Elise followed suit. They went back into the bedroom. Julie and her lover were as Kara had left them. Kara stood with her hand on the small of Elise's back. Time moved forward. Julie woke and slipped out of bed.

"You're sure there's no way to lift objects here?" Kara asked, looking longingly at the heavy base of the lamp next to the bed and the unprotected head of her killer.

"Nohow," Elise answered.

"In *Ghost* . . ." Kara began.

"That was a movie, Kara. This is reality."

"Some reality," Kara said absently. "Let's see the end of this movie." She sped the action up and Julie came back in the room, moving very much like a character in an old silent movie. She jittered over to the side of the bed and shook the man awake. He grabbed her and tried to pull her into bed. Julie batted his hand away and moved to her dresser.

It was eerie watching them like this, Kara realized. She almost felt like an intruder, but she steeled herself. She wouldn't be here if that man hadn't killed her. She had a right to know why.

The man got out of bed and put his arms around Julie from behind. She turned and tried to break free. He kissed her and she shoved him away violently. Or did she?

"Too bad we can't hear what they're saying," Elise commented.

Kara stopped them. Shit, of course she could. She'd been fairly good at reading lips ever since she was little. She moved the action back to right before Jocko got out of the bed and started it again, this time at normal speed. She moved closer.

I told you you weren't no dyke, she could make out his words.

Julie laughed. *Don't bet on it, Brian.*

Brian came up behind Julie and put his arms around her. Kara had to move around them to see his lips move, because his face was so close to Julie. *Why don't you come with me this weekend?*

She turned. *Because I'm spending the weekend with Kara. I told you that.*

Elise moved closer to Kara. "What are they saying?" she whispered.

"Shh . . ." Kara waved her to silence. Brian kissed Julie and she shoved him away. *I told you that's enough,* she said angrily.

You're going to spend a weekend with a girlfriend, rather than with me?

Julie replied hotly, *I love her, you moron.*

Brian looked as if he'd been slapped. *You can't love her. You love me.*

Julie laughed derisively. *Love you?* Her eyes widened incredulously. *You were an itch, Brian. I scratched it. You don't mean anything. Now get out.* She pointed toward the door.

Julie's words hit Kara like a blow and she stopped the scene. She closed her eyes and took a deep breath. Elise asked hesitantly, "What's wrong?"

Kara shook her head. She was thinking back to a discussion with Julie, months before.

"Do you ever want to sleep with men?" Kara had asked.

Julie shrugged. "Sometimes. Does that bother you?"

"Honey, wanting is one thing. Actually," she said after a moment, "if you really feel like you need to scratch that kind of an itch, I don't think it would bother me. Sleep with another woman, though . . ." She glared with mock anger.

"Okay," Julie laughed. "Well, if I ever do feel that kind of itch, I'll clear it with you first."

Kara had pulled Julie toward her. "Babe, you do what you need to do. But if you do, and it means enough to you that you think I need to know, then I'll worry."

Now Kara looked at the still figure of Julie through tears. "She didn't do anything at all."

Elise looked confused. Kara pulled away and started Julie and Brian again. Brian had turned red and was advancing on Julie menacingly. *That bitch has you hypnotized,* he growled.

Julie backed away a step. *You better leave now, Brian,* she said angrily. *And in case you're curious, it's behavior like this that makes me prefer to be with a woman.*

Brian glared at her and strode out of the room. Kara and Elise followed and saw him leave the apartment. The door slammed silently behind him.

"She didn't?" Elise asked.

Kara shook her head. "No," she said quietly. "No, she didn't."

Elise looked sadly at Kara. "So what now? You know why he killed you. But it's over. There's nothing you can do about it."

Kara shut her eyes tightly. "You don't know that."

"But Kara," Elise said, shaking her head.

"You don't," Kara insisted. She thought. "Where's the nearest hospital?"

Elise looked at her blankly.

"I need to find someone who died today without getting shot up or mangled." She winced at her own words.

Elise looked uncertain. "There's St. Vincent's," she said. "That's not far from here."

"Let's go then." She held out her hand, but Elise hesitated. "What's the matter? Are you coming or what?" *You've been here for months, dammit,* she thought. *Why won't you let me try what I can?*

Elise sighed resignedly and took Kara's hand.

After a few false starts, they managed to work their way over to the hospital. Signs pointed to the emergency room entrance. They moved the world backward until they saw an ambulance arrive. Or rather, leave in reverse.

"Let's see what we have here." Kara moved to the back of the ambulance. The doors to the emergency room opened, and a pregnant and very live woman was carried back into the ambulance.

The next three ambulances also delivered live patients. But the one after that did not. Kara watched as the paramedics wheeled the stretcher in with the still form covered head to toe by a white sheet.

"Deader," Elise said callously. Kara made a face. They climbed into the ambulance before the doors closed, or rather, Kara thought, after the doors opened. She hated this backward view, so she sped it up until it was a blur, focusing on staying with the form under the sheet. Soon they were out of the ambulance and in a tall office building in the center of town. Kara gritted her teeth as they rose up through the floor. She slowed things down marginally, but it still looked as though she were using the scan rewind on her VCR.

They reached the floor that the dead person had apparently come from and zoomed down a hallway, turning dizzyingly at the corners. Finally, they came to stop in a large office with plush carpeting and a gorgeous view of the city. Kara kept the action moving until they saw the sheet pulled back to reveal an overweight man who appeared to be in his fifties. The paramedics jittered about him, dumped him on the floor, and ran backward out of the office. Kara couldn't help giggling at the sight. Not long after, the man began to twitch on the floor and soon was convulsing madly. He jerked back and forth, flew up into his chair and clutched his chest. Then he reached out and a pen flew off the desk into his hand and he began calmly to write.

Kara stopped the action and looked at Elise with raised eyebrows and a look of amusement. Then she grew serious. As funny as it had looked, she didn't imagine it had been much fun for the man.

Elise looked back at her. "Okay," she said. "Now what do we do?"

"Now, we wait."

"Wait for what?" Elise looked puzzled.

"How many times did you say you watched yourself get pushed off the platform?"

Elise frowned. "A dozen or so. Why?"

"I imagine most people here come to see their deaths periodically. So now we sit and wait for Mr. Businessman . . . excuse me: the late Mr. Businessman, to show up. He hasn't had as much time as you've had to work things out, but if it's been months for you, it's been at least weeks for him."

Elise nodded and they looked around for somewhere to sit. The office sofa looked well padded, but they knew that it would be hard as a rock. They settled for the carpet, which was worn enough that it wasn't a bed of nails. Kara didn't want to think about how it would have felt new.

Elise sat down, her knees touching Kara's. "Do you want to explain what you have in mind?"

Kara sighed. "The only thing I can think of," she said. "In *Ghost*—" Elise rolled her eyes, but Kara ignored her. "Remember how the dead people could jump into the bodies of live people?" Elise nodded. "I figure that if a person were to jump back into her own body exactly at the moment of death . . ."

"Oh, boy," Elise said sarcastically. "And wouldn't that be wonderful. I can just imagine it. I'd get to actually feel the train run over me." She snorted. "And then die again."

"Fine," Kara persisted, "but that's because the way you died didn't leave you any chance. This guy had a heart attack. Suppose he had a mild one, but it freaked him out so badly that his pulse went crazy and made it worse?" Elise shook her head uncomprehendingly. Kara leaned toward Elise and said intensely, "Think, Elise. This guy has had plenty of time to calm down. If he jumps back in, he'll still be having a heart attack, but if he can stay calm this time, it doesn't have to be fatal."

"And that will help you how?"

Kara sighed. "Elise, I'm not dead yet. I'm just not. If I can get back in time to move out of the way of that bullet . . ."

Elise made a sound of disgust. "Oh, right, Kara. Right. You're going to dodge a bullet. Gee," she went on caustically, "I didn't realize.

Why do you suppose the bullet didn't just bounce off you? Say, maybe it was a Kryptonite bullet, huh? D'ya think?"

Kara jumped up angrily and turned away from Elise, bumping into a figure that hadn't been there a moment before.

"Excuse me," the man said politely.

"Oh, shit." Kara stood still and let her anger drain out of her. "I'm sorry," she apologized. "I didn't see you there." Then she recognized him. "You're—" She pointed to the still figure behind the desk. "Him."

The man inclined his head. "That I am. Or was," he added lightly. "Russell Thomas." He held out his hand and Kara took it. "I'm Kara," she said, "and this is Elise," motioning to Elise.

Russell walked over and shook Elise's hand. "So," he said, looking at each of the women in turn, "what brings you here? Surely you don't need to have a loan approved?" He smiled with infectious good humor.

He sure seems at ease about being dead, Kara thought. *He may not be willing to go along with the idea.* "We want to try something," Kara said, ignoring Elise, who was shaking her head to indicate that it was no idea of hers. "If you're willing."

Russell raised an eyebrow. "Something new?" he asked. "Here? How marvelous." He seemed delighted.

"It may be a way to get back to there," Kara gestured at the office.

Russell didn't say anything. *Damn,* Kara thought. *I knew it.*

"Are you privy to some sort of secret information?" Russell asked finally.

"No," Kara explained. "It's just a theory." She explained to Russell the idea she had outlined to Elise only minutes earlier. He nodded once or twice while she was explaining the concept. When she had finished, he was silent again for a moment.

"Have you read 'The Langoliers'?" he asked.

"God!" Elise exploded.

Kara looked confused. "What are langoliers?" she asked.

"This is not *Ghost*!" Elise expostulated. "And it's not a Stephen King story either." She explained to Kara, "There's this story by Stephen King, where a plane full of people . . ." She trailed off and looked at Russell. "How would you explain it?"

"If you imagine that time is a wave, these people went through some kind of rift that left them behind that wave." Elise nodded. "So they're in this world," Russell continued, "much like ours, where there are objects, but no people. The langoliers are a kind of . . . celestial clean-up squad. They eat the remains of the world once time has passed it by. Conservationists." He smiled. "They're like big Pac-Man creatures, gobbling until nothing's left."

"None of which has anything to do with us," Elise shot at him.

Russell just shrugged. "I don't know that, and I don't imagine you do either, young lady." Elise glared. "But my point was only that it seems unlikely that we will be left here forever. If there is a way out, I would be willing to risk it."

"And if something happens?" Elise challenged.

Russell looked at her calmly. "I am a dead man, my dear. What on earth could happen to me that would be worse than that?"

Elise fell silent. Kara walked over to the Russell sitting at the desk. She waved her hand through the figure's head, which offered no resistance. "Alive," she pronounced. "All we have to do is find the exact moment it goes from immaterial to material. Right?" She looked at the other two, who nodded. "So," she continued, "Elise, Russell, hang on to me." They joined hands, and Kara began moving the scene forward. The Russell-figure jerked and dropped his pen. He clutched at his chest, and Kara stopped the motion. She touched the hand of the other Russell. It was solid.

"I don't recall any pain at all," Russell commented. "I imagine I died fairly quickly. All the flopping around must have been reflex action."

Something about that idea disturbed Kara, but the reason why eluded her. She moved them back very gradually, tapping at otherRussell's hand rhythmically. After a moment, her finger went through his hand and she stopped. "Come on, come on," she muttered. She pushed forward for the barest moment and tried again. Still nothing. Another moment—solid!

Kara turned to Russell. "Do you have any idea how to do this?"

Russell eyed the motionless form of his seated self. "Perhaps if you kind ladies were to help me up onto the desk, I could drop down into my . . . er, cadaver." He looked at Kara and Elise expectantly. Kara turned questioning eyes to Elise, who shrugged. They stood beside Russell, and helped him climb up on his desk. He stepped forward to stand before his double and looked back over his shoulder at Kara. "It may surprise you to hear that I rarely indulge in this type of physical activity."

Kara smiled back nervously. *Would this work? There had to be some way out.* She wasn't dead. She was sure of that. Not unless she gave up. "Hey, Russell," she said softly, "you might want to consider changing that once you're back."

Russell's mouth twitched in humor and he turned to face himself.

"Remember to stay calm," Kara reminded him.

Russell hit himself like a diver slicing through the water. Kara and Elise watched as his large form dropped through his other large form. There was something like a ripple in the air around him, and Russell was gone.

Kara waited a moment, and turned to Elise excitedly. Her eyes were glowing.

"I don't believe it," Elise said, amazed. Then she swallowed. "Are you still going to . . ."

"Try?" Kara finished for her. She took a deep breath. "I have to, Elise. Don't you see that?" She took Elise's hands.

Elise looked down, quietly. "Yeah," she said finally, looking up at Kara, eyes wet. "I guess I do." She laughed weakly and wiped at her eyes. "I guess I'd try too, if I wasn't spread all over the track like that."

Kara pulled Elise into a hug. "Thank you for understanding," she whispered.

Elise sniffled and broke away. "Damn," she said. "I wish I'd had a tissue in my pocket that morning." She smiled wanly. "I'm going to have to spend eternity wiping my nose on my sleeve."

"Gross," Kara complained, as Elise did just that. "Listen, I want to see what happened to Russell. Just to be sure."

Elise nodded and they joined hands. Kara nudged them forward very slowly, and they saw Russell's body jerk backward in the chair.

Funny, Kara thought. *I don't remember him doing that when we saw this before.* But as before, Russell dropped his pen and clutched his chest. He looked up at them, Kara could swear, with panic in his eyes as he began to convulse.

"Relax," Kara urged him in a low voice. "Oh, Russell, you have to stay calm."

But Russell couldn't hear her, and he was past paying attention in any case. He thrashed around wildly, managing to hit his intercom button before falling to the floor. His secretary opened the door and leaped back out in a panic, presumably to call 911. Kara and Elise stood helplessly watching, until with a great strain, Russell arched his back.

POP

With an audible sound, Russell flew out of his body onto the floor. He was gasping and moaning, and it took him several moments to stop convulsing.

"Russell, omigod." Kara ran to him and knelt at his side. "What happened?"

"I—I—oh, dear . . ." Russell closed his eyes, trying to bring himself under control. Kara looked up at Elise desperately, then back at Russell. "Don't talk," she told him. Russell took a deep breath and then another. As his respiration slowed he relaxed visibly. Finally he opened his eyes again.

"I think," he said hoarsely, "that I was better off dying without feeling it."

Kara asked again, insistently, "But what happened? We saw you go back—"

"And I tried to calm myself. I'm afraid years of sedentary life simply caught up with me. Kara," he explained, "sometimes it's just time." He coughed and sat up gingerly. "I'm truly sorry," he repeated.

Kara turned away. She didn't want him to see her tears. She was dead, she realized. Truly and finally dead. And all because of one asshole man who couldn't accept—

"No!" she jumped up, eyes blazing. "God damn no!" Elise looked at her, shocked. "I will not accept this! I will not allow that stinking scum to just . . ." she looked for a word, "extinguish me, like I'm nothing!" Spinning around, she moved back in time, sounds of protest from Russell and Elise cutting off suddenly as she left them behind.

She was so upset that she overshot at first, but she came back the second time to exactly where she wanted to be. Russell was sitting at his desk, pen in hand. She stood at the desk with the palms of her hands flat on it and stared at him. *Okay,* she thought. *Move, damn you.* She shifted very slightly forward, watching intently. Russell jerked backward in his chair and she stopped. Backing up, she watched it again.

"Yes!" she crowed. "You felt that!" She ran the scene backward and forward again. She was sure of what she was seeing. Russell's jump back into his body had moved him. Very slightly, but Kara knew he hadn't fallen back like that before they tried her experiment. Now, if only—

She closed her eyes and zoomed forward, past the people who came in and out of Russell's office in the wake of his death. Finally, she opened her eyes. Nothing was moving, even though she was still exerting the same forward pressure. Checking the clock on Russell's desk in the now deserted office, she saw it read 12:00.

"Right," she nodded. Concentrating on her own presence, she blinked, and was back in her apartment, a bullet inches away from her image. She moved to the bullet and stood behind it, sighting past the deadly piece of metal, trying to gauge where exactly it would hit her. The bullet had lost its shape, and it was hard to tell what angle it was moving at, but as near as she could figure, it was going to hit her just above her left ear, angling backward.

"Damn," she muttered. The thing would probably take the back of her head off. But . . . She breathed impatiently. There was no way to tell. If she were to shift forward and to the right by the barest fraction of an inch, the bullet might miss her. It might. If she had to move herself, she knew she'd never be able to get out of the way fast enough. Elise was right about that. But if her jumping in pushed her automatically, and if she were to jump from the right angle . . .

"Don't."

Kara spun around to see Elise. "How—"

"It was your idea," Elise told her. "I figured you'd come back to the last minute here eventually." She stepped toward Kara. "I thought I might have a longer wait, though."

"Don't try to stop me," Kara warned fiercely.

"Why are you doing this?"

Kara looked at Elise blankly.

"Think, Kara," Elise said calmly. "Please." She put her hands on Kara's shoulders and looked into her eyes. "What if it doesn't work? What do you have then? You'll have the chance very few people get to actually feel what it's like to have your head blown off." Kara winced. "And then you'll be in tomorrow. At the beginning of the day. Do you know how long I wandered around here without seeing another soul? Do you?" She was speaking calmly, but Kara could feel the sense of desperation welling up inside of her.

"But it might—"

"And even," Elise went on as if Kara hadn't spoken, "even if you manage not to die, you could still be hit. You could wind up brain-damaged. Or stuck in a wheelchair for the rest of your life, controlling it with a straw."

Kara flinched. She hadn't considered that possibility. *Life or death,* she had thought. *Win or lose.* She hadn't thought about how much she could lose even if she won. She looked at Elise, open, earnest, and serious, and it occurred to her that maybe there was something to be won even if she lost. She could do far worse than Elise. Even if she'd made love with her almost as an act of revenge against Julie, it had been good. If this didn't work, and even if everything went as she planned it . . .

She turned away from Elise. Could she and Julie make things work? *Oh, brilliant,* she thought. *As if that's all there is to life. But think,* she insisted. *Death, life, they were only words now. This was a kind of life, wasn't it?* If she and Elise could enjoy each other as they had, surely there were other possibilities in this new world. And Elise would certainly never leave her for a man.

It occurred to her that Brian would probably get caught. He didn't seem smart enough to get away with murdering her. And it was quite possible that the police would think Julie had been involved. If Kara had thought so . . .

But Julie's involvement wasn't her fault. It was Julie's own bad judgment. She was innocent, and she'd just have to convince the police of that.

A wave of sadness passed through her. *Is this you?* she asked herself. *Are you really going to just quit? Accept your death? Accept the end?*

Slowly, she turned back to Elise, pain in her eyes. Elise gazed at her and then nodded. "Yeah," she whispered. "I guess I knew that."

Kara took a deep breath. "Elise—"

Elise stepped backward. "Don't. I was wrong to ask." She crossed her arms and hugged herself as if she were cold. "You don't know how lonely it's been." She closed her eyes momentarily, then looked at Kara. "I hope you make it." She laughed sadly. "I'll never know if you did."

Kara couldn't think of a response.

Elise walked to Kara and kissed her lightly on the lips. "Good luck."

Kara looked at her through tear-filled eyes. "I'll always remember you," she promised. "And if this is like some kind of way station that you go to before moving on, I'll see you again some day. I promise."

Elise smiled. "I know you will," she said. "It doesn't look like anything ever stops you when you're determined."

Kara walked over to her motionless body. She faced herself at the angle that was necessary, and took a few steps backward. *Well,* she thought, *what am I waiting for?* She ran at herself, trying not to flinch as she neared what seemed to be a solid object.

Blam!

Kara went flying to the ground, off balance, as the loudest sound she had ever heard exploded next to her ear. *Focus!* she screamed at herself. She rolled with the fall and landed behind the stereo cabinet to the left of the door. She shoved the cabinet at Brian as he tried to position himself for a second shot.

"Brian!" she screamed as he dodged out of the way of the wheeled cabinet.

"What the hell—" He hesitated, shocked at her knowing his name, which was what she had hoped for, and his gun wavered. She ran across the room, diving behind the sofa just as another shot rang out.

"Bitch!" he bellowed. "Pervert bitch! I'll kill you!" He ran at her and she pulled books from the bookshelf behind her and began throwing them at him. He ducked, blocking the books with his right arm, which prevented him from taking aim at her again. But he was moving too fast, and he was furious, with a madman's strength. He leaped at her and held her with his left hand, trying to bring the gun down to strike her. She grabbed his wrist, trying to keep his hand from coming down, but she could feel how much stronger he was. *God!* she thought wildly. *Did I come back from the bloody dead just to have this gorilla beat me back to death?*

Frantically, she tried to knee him. Brian clamped his legs together and bent over to protect that tender area, losing his grip on Kara for a scant moment. She grabbed the bookshelf, pulling it down with all her strength.

It was almost as if she were back in that strange afterworld again, she thought, watching the shelf tip in slow motion, Brian reaching up to keep it from falling, fear in his eyes. Kara leaped over the back of the sofa as the shelf crashed down in the space between the sofa and the wall.

She crouched there, panting, terrified that Brian would crawl out and continue his attack. Some moments later, she climbed down and circled the sofa. Somehow, Brian had managed to jump backward. *Had he been a little slower,* Kara thought, seeing Brian's head poking out from the top of the shelf, neck at an impossible angle, *he might have made it. Good!* she thought viciously. *Let him think about that.*

Kara went to the telephone to call the police, then set the handset back in the cradle. She crossed the room and opened her desk drawer, taking out a piece of paper and a pen.

You lose, asshole, she wrote. *Everyone there comes back to where they died eventually, and you can come here and see this for the rest of eternity. Then it will be tomorrow, and I'll go on. You never will.* She looked at the note and thought about whether it was crueler than even Brian deserved. She shrugged. It was already written, she realized. There for him to see for as long as that otherworld lasted. Sighing, she put down the paper and called the police.

It was after four in the morning, and Kara was dead tired. She grimaced. Bad choice of words, that.

She looked again at the newspaper on the homicide detective's desk, which was open to page three. She read again, *The victim has been identified as Elise L. Parker, 26, of Manhattan. Witnesses reported that she appeared to have slipped off the platform just as the downtown D train was entering the station. Subway service was suspended in both directions for over an hour yesterday morning after the accident.*

Well, Elise, she thought, *you got more than just an obituary. Too bad you'll never see it.* She looked sadly at the picture accompanying the article.

The police detective had assured her, after seeing the marks on her front door where Brian had forced his way in and the bullets he'd fired at her, that it was an open-and-shut case of attempted murder. Now, as Kara walked down the hall toward the street exit, the door opened and two uniformed policemen walked in, followed by a familiar face.

"Julie," Kara breathed.

Julie walked quickly to Kara and pulled her into a hug. "Oh, God, Kara, are you okay?" She hugged her lover tightly and then took her hand as they left the station house.

"Listen, Kara . . ." Julie started. "That guy . . . the one who attacked you . . ."

"Yeah, Julie," Kara said quietly. "I know."

"How—"

"It doesn't matter."

"Kara." Julie turned to her. "I want to discuss things with you. I want so much for us to be together, but somehow we never talk. When I heard what happened, I absolutely freaked. You could have been killed." She looked earnestly at Kara. "We really need to work things out," she said. "Not keep putting them off until the last minute."

Kara laughed. "The last minute . . ." She shook her head. "I've spent enough time there lately, thank you very much." She touched Julie's face. "We'll make it work," she promised. "You're the best thing in my life. Believe me, even if he had killed me, I would have found a way to come back."

Julie smiled at that. "That's sweet of you to say," she told Kara, as they started home together.

Kara just smiled.

Elsie Riley
Martha Miller

Wednesday morning when Bertha Brannon, attorney at law, got off the elevator and started past Levine's Law Offices, the door was flung open, and there Elsie Riley, the only other woman of color on the third floor, stood before her.

Elsie was new. She'd taken the place of Myra Stewart, who had retired after working for the aging attorney for twenty-seven years. This new secretary had high cheekbones, bronze skin, and dark eyes. She wore a peach-colored silk suit and was carefully put together with a touch of mascara and lipstick, her black hair swept up to a crown of tight curls.

"Morning," said Bertha. She wanted to meet the woman, but today she had an appointment with a new client and had overslept.

"Mr. Levine is dead."

Bertha stopped. "Are you all right?" She tried to sound comforting while taking in the details.

Elsie Riley stepped back inside and nodded toward Levine's open office door. "He's in there."

Bertha crossed the waiting room. Through the doorway, sunlight slanted across Levine's opulent mahogany desktop. The dark wood contrasted with the matching alabaster carpet, draperies, and leather sofa. The old guy with his silver comb-over, liver-spotted forehead, and gold-rimmed spectacles looked as if he'd just lain down for a nap. His burgundy suspenders were as dark as aortic blood, and the sleeves on his white starched shirt were rolled up. Behind the desk, his gray suit jacket was draped over the back of the leather desk chair.

"Are you sure he's dead?"

Elsie Riley nodded, retreating slightly.

"I mean, did you check?"

"I-I checked." She pointed toward a cosmetic mirror on the couch arm.

"Have you called nine-one-one?"

Elsie shook her head no.

"Start there," said Bertha. "Go out to your desk and call. I think they'll send paramedics. Then call Mrs. Levine at home."

Elsie nodded and backed out of the room.

Bertha approached Levine and bent over his body. Had he felt bad and simply stretched out on the sofa for a moment? She touched his wrist. In addition to no pulse, his skin was cold. He'd been there for a while—probably all night. Surely his wife had noticed him gone, though Mrs. Levine *had* been a little forgetful of late. Actually, the old girl had been ill for quite some time. Bertha realized she knew very little about the elderly couple's habits.

Four years ago, when she had taken the small office in the back, Levine had been the first to welcome her. Over the years she'd learned that the old guy had a bad heart and a weakness for alcohol and sugar. She had considered him an ally when things were tough. Twice he had lent her rent money until her own client paid. And in the end it came to this—waiting with his body for the EMTs.

Bertha checked her watch and looked around the room. She had a *paying* client down the hall. Everything seemed in order. The old guy's desk was clean. Nothing had been disturbed. Across the room she noticed the door to the liquor cabinet ajar, but there was no empty, or half-empty, glass. An amber colored ashtray on the corner of his desk held Levine's trademark, a chewed up, unlit cigar.

Elsie appeared in the doorway dabbing her eyes with a cherry pink tissue. "I couldn't reach Mrs. Levine," she said. "Maybe a police officer can go out there."

"Where's Gussie Pratt?" Levine usually had an intern from the U of I law school. Pratt was the latest, a young redhead with wide hips and pale, freckled skin. Her white blouses were usually wrinkled. She glided in and out of court in a worn blazer and a longish skirt.

Elsie wrinkled her beautiful nose distastefully. "Library, I think. I just got here. I think she sleeps down there."

Bertha said, "Here's the thing, I have a client waiting. I've got to—"

Elsie sucked in her breath. "You're not going to leave?"

"The EMTs will be here soon. I'll send my secretary down to wait with you."

"That boy?" Elsie's brown eyes grew wide, her dislike for Gussie Pratt obviously subordinated.

"Alvin." Bertha nodded.

Elsie Riley bit her thumbnail as Bertha brushed past her and headed down the corridor toward Suite 310.

Alvin returned to the office around 9:30 a.m. "How'd it go with Mrs. Stark?"

Bertha looked up from a file she'd been going over for Juvenile Court that afternoon and said, "Child custody case."

Alvin smiled and rubbed his hands together. "Money."

"She hasn't got it."

Alvin nodded.

"So how'd it go down the hall?" asked Bertha.

"The ambulance," he said, "is taking Levine away. A police detective will be going out to the house to talk to Mrs. Levine."

Bertha turned to the window and watched the emergency vehicles below. She thought of her own grandmother, much older than Levine. What would that be like when the time came?

Alvin said, "You went to college with his son, right?"

"Ron. Yeah, we were there at the same time. Though I couldn't say we moved in the same circles."

"Why don't you call him? His mother will need him."

Bertha nodded. "See if you can find him in the Chicago Yellow Pages. He's a junior partner at Marcum, Brady, and Brown."

Before Alvin returned with the number, Gussie Pratt burst into Bertha's office. "Levine is dead," she said, and plopped down on a folding chair.

"I know."

Gussie seemed to examine Bertha's face. "Well," she said slowly, "something's wrong."

"What?"

Bertha didn't know Gussie all that well and would not have barged into her office, even though technically, as an attorney with her own practice, Bertha outranked her. They passed in the hall. They spoke in the elevator. Of course, death made people behave in strange ways, as if being alive gave them some kind of bond.

Gussie held up a hand and started counting on her fingers. "First, money is missing. Second, no one can reach the old lady. She hasn't picked up the phone all morning. I happen to know she's always at home watching *Animal Planet* this time of day. Third, I think some files are gone."

"Since when?"

"Will you please let me finish?"

Bertha looked away, annoyed, and saw Alvin standing in the doorway. She met his eyes and shook her head slightly. Alvin backed away, pulling the door closed. Had the frazzled woman's boss not died a couple of hours ago, Bertha might have been offended by her briskness. As it was, she took a deep breath and said, "Go on."

"It's that woman. That Miss Riley. Everything's gone to hell since she started."

"She found the body this morning."

Gussie leaned back in the chair and stretched out both feet. "So she says."

Bertha was puzzled. "She didn't find the body?"

"Oh," said Gussie. "I believe she found the body. I just don't think it was this morning."

Bertha squared her shoulders. "That's a serious accusation."

Gussie shrugged. "I suppose you think I've slipped a garter."

"I beg your pardon?"

"I'm nuts." Gussie's tone sharpened—her face flushed. "You think I'm nuts."

"I think this is very stressful for you," said Bertha. "Why don't you tell me exactly me what's going on?" Bertha remembered the expression on Elsie Riley's face earlier at the mention of Gussie Pratt. The two obviously didn't get along. As the latter sat before her, Bertha noticed Gussie's scuffed leather tennis shoes and unkempt hair.

"The day she started I knew she was trouble. *Miss* Gussie this. *Miss* Gussie that. Levine was smitten. For him, the woman could do no wrong. She actually convinced him to buy her a new office chair. Back problems, she said." Gussie looked around Bertha's office as if noticing it for the first time: the layer of dust on the bookshelf, the folding chair in which she sat, the four-drawer file cabinet, two drawers partially opened.

Bertha prodded, "Go on."

"Anyway, about the money. Mr. Levine never kept money in the safe that I knew of. But for one reason or another Miss Riley couldn't get to the bank yesterday." Gussie snorted. "Working late, I guess."

"Did she work late often?"

"A lot recently." Gussie leaned forward. "I hate to say this about a good man, but I think something, you know, romantic was going on."

Bertha tried to imagine the short old man and the tall, slender black woman in a clinch. To no avail. She shook her head. "Levine's too old."

"You don't know him very well, do you?" asked Gussie.

Bertha frowned. She thought she'd known Levine as well as Gussie Pratt had. Bertha said, "Tell me more about the money."

"Yesterday afternoon I was making like I wasn't there. I get so many interruptions. Damn woman answers the phone only half the time. If she's on a personal call, she lets the voice mail pick up. Seems like somebody always needs something. If I lay low, I have time to work on my thesis. So, I was in my office, with the door closed and the overhead light off going through database files when I heard them talking. A city developer had just come from a closing, and he paid Mr. Levine in cash. I heard him say to her, 'That's over sixty thousand in the safe. If you can't get to the bank tonight, I will send Gussie.' He never left cash in the safe. Anyway, I couldn't hear her response. But he didn't ask me to go."

"He didn't know you were there."

Gussie's face fell. "True."

"Maybe Miss Riley took the money to the bank."

"Is there a way to check?" asked Gussie. "I have his account number."

Bertha shook her head. "Especially not now that he's dead. Everything will be frozen until the widow takes some kind of action."

"How about that eight-hundred number for getting balances? The bank's computer surely doesn't know he's dead yet."

"You need a pin number to get that."

"I know all his pins and passwords. They're all the same: his birthday."

Bertha shook her head again. "No. It doesn't sound honest. I think you should give all this information to the police. Call them, go down there, whatever."

"You're not going to help me?" Gussie seemed startled, and then her eyes became pink slits. "It's because I'm white, isn't it?"

"What?"

"She's black and I'm white and you all stick together."

A tap at the door cut short Bertha's brilliant comeback. Alvin poked his head in. "Can I interrupt?"

Bertha's voice was flat. "What is it?"

"There's an officer out here talking to everyone in the building. There was a break-in at Levine's house. They found Mrs. Levine shot. She'd dead."

Gussie's mouth formed a small "O." She covered it quickly with her hand.

Though Bertha's temples were beginning to throb, she asked, "Will you bring a couple of chairs and both come in?"

Alvin came through the door followed by a young officer with bushy yellow eyebrows and a pink complexion. The officer removed his hat to reveal an almost white buzz cut against his pink skull. He waited while Alvin unfolded two more chairs. Officer Beeler introduced himself, and then added, "Homicide has two of us canvassing the building."

The officer asked the three of them several questions, and then went back to Levine's office with Gussie Pratt to have a look at the safe. Though Bertha had given Beeler the contact information for Levine's son, Ron, she picked up the phone as soon as she was alone.

"Marcum, Brady, and Brown," came a woman's hard Midwestern accent.

Bertha asked for Mr. Levine, and a Muzak version of an old Marvin Gaye song came on while she waited. She turned toward the windows. Outside, except for a couple of squad cars at the curb, everything looked normal. She tapped a pencil on the corner of the desk and tried to get her mind around all that had happened. Had Levine been lying there all night? Was some money missing? The deaths of the old couple had to be connected, but how? If Levine had been murdered too, why here, why wasn't he at home with his murdered wife?

"Ms. Brannon," a deep male voice came on the line, "how may I help you?"

"Ron Levine?"

"Yes."

"I'm sure you don't recognize my name, but I have an office in the Lambert Building. I'm down the hall from your father."

"I see . . ."

"There's been some trouble here this morning."

"With Dad? Is he all right?"

"No," Bertha said slowly. "No, your father was found in his office this morning, dead."

"My God."

"I'm sorry, there's—"

He wasn't listening. "Okay. I'll need to call home. I can be there this afternoon, as soon as I get a flight."

"Of course," said Bertha.

"Mother hasn't been well," he said quickly. "Has she been told?"

"No, she's . . ."

"I want to tell her. Thanks again." The line went dead.

She exhaled slowly and sat the phone back on her desk.

"That was short and sweet," said Alvin.

Bertha looked up. He was standing in the doorway again. "He's in shock," said Bertha.

Alvin crossed to the folding chair and sat down. "What's up with that Pratt woman?"

"Didn't you hear her? She claims that some money is missing. She thinks the secretary took it."

"What do you think?"

Bertha shrugged. "Who knows?"

"I spent over an hour and thirty minutes with that woman this morning. She hates Gussie Pratt, and I think the feeling is mutual."

Bertha nodded.

"Well," said Alvin, leaning forward. "Look at it this way—Gussie Pratt has been cheating Levine ever since she started working for him. She works on her thesis and bills clients for the time. She sleeps in the library and she hides out whenever she can. I've heard her talking in the break room. She's got a big mouth and I don't like her. As far as I know, Elsie Riley hasn't done one dishonest thing."

"You think Gussie is trying to hide something?"

Alvin shrugged. "This is pretty big stuff. Mrs. Levine has been murdered. I really can't figure how that fits into anything. But, I don't think Gussie Pratt is being honest. It's just not in her makeup, you know?"

The phone rang and Alvin hurried out to get it. Bertha leaned back in her chair and crossed her feet on a box of files beneath her desk. The hands on her battery-operated clock were pointing straight-up noon. The day already seemed like a long one, and she had court all afternoon.

When Bertha returned from lunch, Elsie Riley, under the supervision of a police officer, was locking the door to Levine's office. "How are you doing?" asked Bertha.

Elsie smiled and glanced toward the cop. "As well as can be expected, I suppose."

"Are you closing for the day?"

"They tell me that this is a crime scene now. I've called all of Mr. Levine's appointments and canceled them. I left instructions with the answering service. There's nothing else I can do in there. I'm going home to dust off my résumé and look at the want ads."

Bertha said, "You've had a bad day, finding a body and losing a job."

Elsie started toward the elevator and Bertha took a few steps with her.

"It's been stressful," said Elsie. "First the police and all their questions." She looked over her shoulder at the man in blue still standing across from Levine's office door. "Then Gussie Pratt, acting as if I'd killed him myself. She's got some bee in her bonnet about a bank deposit."

"She talked to me," said Bertha. "You made that deposit, didn't you?"

Elsie's face tightened. "There was no deposit, Miss Brannon. I don't know where she got the idea. I made the last deposit on Friday. Mr. Levine transferred some money from another business account, and along with four thousand in checks from the safe, he paid the bills. I mailed them myself."

"I see," said Bertha.

"Now if you'll excuse me," said Elsie Riley, punching the elevator button. "I'd like to get the hell out of here."

Late in the afternoon, when Bertha returned from Juvenile Court, Levine's office was dark and the police officer was nowhere in sight. Farther down the hall, she opened her outer office door and walked past a well-dressed man with a square jawline and black and silver hair. She nodded to the man then looked at Alvin.

Alvin stood, followed her into her office and said, "That's Ron Levine. I thought you knew him."

"Well, it's been a long time," said Bertha, uncertainly.

Alvin shrugged. "Should I send him in?"

Bertha nodded.

Ron Levine came through the door with his right hand outstretched. He introduced himself and immediately thanked her for calling him.

"I'm glad I could reach you. However, I didn't get a chance to tell you everything."

"Ms. Brannon," he said. "I've spent the past two hours at the police station. I think I know the worst."

Did he? Bertha wondered. She said, "I am so sorry."

"I need your help."

"Whatever I can do."

"Help me find the secretary. I want to feel her out on this business the Pratt woman brought up."

"Elsie Riley?" Bertha said softly.

Ron Levine hesitated, considering the name, and then simply nodded. "Do you know her?"

"Well, I talked to her this morning, of course. I saw her leave this afternoon. I suppose I could start in the phone book."

Levine leaned back in his chair and looked at his hands. "According to Ms. Pratt, there's some money missing from the office. It will take me a few days to verify that—by then she may be long gone."

"She claims that the last deposit she made was on Friday before she did the accounts payable—four thousand in checks and a balance transfer."

"So you talked to her?"

"Yes. Before she left today."

Ron hesitated and then said, "Brickler Construction may have paid him. Two weeks ago, Dad told me about the new account—told me Brickler wanted to deal in cash. He was worried that George Brickler, the old man, was laundering money again. He told me he was going to hire a detective to snoop around."

"And did he?"

Ron Levine shrugged. "I don't know, but the intern's story may be true. In fact, my mother and father may have died because Riley, or someone, wanted that money."

"Do you have a key to the office?" asked Bertha. "We could look around, maybe find your father's personnel files—"

"The office will be roped off—it's a crime scene," he said.

"It is. Nevertheless . . ."

Levine stood. "Come on, then. Let's look."

Inside the elder Levine's office, late afternoon shadows fell across the mahogany desktop, where the old man's suit jacket still hung on the back of his chair. The cool air reminded Bertha of the morning, of touching the old man's wrist, the cool, dead flesh. Bertha watched as Ron Levine searched the unlocked desk drawers for a key to the credenza. She looked around the office again and knelt to look in the liquor cabinet. An unopened bottle of blended scotch sat next to a half-empty fifth of Tanqueray. In the small, refrigerated section, the light fell on a club soda, an uncut lemon, and an empty ice bucket. Nothing remarkable.

"See anything?" Ron asked.

"Nothing here." She stood.

"Not in the cabinet—behind it."

Bertha looked at the space between the liquor cabinet and the wall and saw the safe.

Ron Levine rolled the cabinet aside and reached past her. Bertha touched his hand. "Wait. We can't be leaving prints everywhere." She looked around, spotted a box of tissues on the credenza and reached for one.

His fingers covered with a tissue, he deftly spun the dial back and forth, and then pulled a small square door open. The safe was empty.

Ron said, "I unlocked the credenza. Check the left drawer for personnel files while I phone the bank."

Bertha went behind the desk and sat in the old man's chair. The leather was rich and comfortable. She turned to the credenza and, using a tissue, pulled the drawer open.

"All I can get is a recording," said Ron. "I have a friend who manages operations. I'm going to walk over there. You have any luck?"

"Not yet."

"Keep at it; I'll be right back."

Bertha walked her fingers along the tops of the file folders. Toward the back she found the files in question and pulled out Elsie Riley's. The folder was thin, but not completely empty. Bertha swiveled around to the desktop. Something thudded against the chair. She looked down, then toward the dimly lit reception area. Ron had left Levine's door open, but the door to the hallway was closed and locked. She laid the file folder on the mahogany surface and flipped it open. A copy of Riley's W-4 form was the only item in the folder. On the reverse side of the form, Bertha found a phone number written in pencil.

She reached across Levine's desk for the phone and heard the soft thud again. It was definitely close to her.

This time Bertha turned and looked at the suit jacket that was draped across the back of the chair. Her movement caused the sound again. She patted the jacket down. In the breast pocket she found a cigar still in the cellophane. Her right hand traced the expensive cloth downward, and she knew immediately the hard shape pulling down on the side pocket was a gun. She reached for another tissue, shoved it in and retrieved a small-caliber, nickel-plated revolver. She could smell the gunpower. It had been recently fired.

"So, you've found it."

Bertha looked toward the doorway. The woman was silhouetted against the darkening outer office. She was dressed the same as earlier. A large leather bag was slung over her shoulder.

"This yours?" Bertha laid the gun on top of the open file.

"No. But I want it."

"If it's not yours," said Bertha, "and if you've done nothing wrong, then what do you need it for?"

"I promised Mr. Levine." She had locked eyes with Bertha and was moving toward her.

"Promised him what? I thought he was dead when you got here."

"That's not exactly true."

"You took the money, didn't you?"

The slender woman extended her hand. "Give me the gun, Bertha."

Bertha wondered how long Ron Levine would be at the bank. She glanced at the clock across the room. It was past 5:30. The teller windows would be closed, but if his friend worked in operations the man could be there for several more hours.

"Let's talk," Bertha said, stalling.

"I have a train to catch."

"Those trains are always late," said Bertha. "Give me a minute or two. I helped you this morning. You can help me now."

Elsie collapsed in an alabaster leather chair across from Bertha, her head propped up by her hand. She didn't look like a murderer—more like a frightened child.

Bertha said, "Whoever fired this gun killed Mrs. Levine, didn't they?"

Elsie nodded.

"Who was it?"

"Mr. Levine."

"Levine killed his wife?" But, as Bertha said it, she saw that it was probably the truth. The old lady had been sick and in pain for a long time. She wasn't going to get better. Levine loved her; of course he had killed her.

"I've got to get the weapon out of here," said Elsie. "I promised him."

Why hadn't the police found it? Bertha wondered. Of course, in the morning when they'd first come to the Lambert Building, they thought Levine had died of natural causes. So they hadn't thoroughly searched the room yet.

"How did you get involved in this?"

The dark woman met Bertha's eyes. "My mother worked for the Levines for several years. She cooked for that family almost all the time I was growing up. When she passed, Mr. Levine stepped in to help me. He didn't have to, but he is a good man. I couldn't find a job right out of college, so he put me on here. Now I won't even be able to use him as a reference."

"Go on," Bertha urged. "What about Mrs. Levine?"

"Until last week she could get up and around a little. Then she had another stroke. He said he tried to overmedicate her and she vomited. He just wanted to put her out of her pain."

"How did he end up dead?"

"He came in last night. I was just getting ready to leave. He came right out and told me what he'd done—told me he was going to call the police as soon as his attorney called him back."

"Then, how did he end up dead?" Bertha asked.

"I was waiting with him and he started looking sick. I've seen him take the nitro before and I asked him where it was. I swear—I saw the moment it occurred to him—to not take the nitro. I was fixin' to call the EMTs and he tore the phone out of my hand. Asked me to stay with him while he went. Said he didn't want to go on anyway. I told him to lie down, hoping it would ease up. But it didn't. He was talk-

ing, then he wasn't talking, then he was gone. So I waited for someone to come to work. You were first."

"Actually," said Bertha. "I was late this morning."

"Okay," Elsie admitted. "I had a few drinks—fell asleep. When I
woke I couldn't find the damn gun . . ."

"So, you were here all night?"

Elsie nodded.

"You looked awfully fresh this morning."

Elsie wrinkled her nose. "I fixed my makeup some. But I've been in
this suit since yesterday morning."

Bertha looked at Elsie Riley closely. On the best day of her life she
didn't look that fresh and wrinkle-free ten minutes after getting
dressed. No wonder Gussie Pratt hated Elsie Riley. Bertha took a
deep breath, and asked, "What about the money? Was there any
money?"

"It's a drop in the bucket compared to what the estate, his business,
and the insurance is worth. If they find out he killed his wife, all of
that could be tied up—maybe lost. He told me to take the gun so they
wouldn't know and take the money for myself to make a fresh start."

"But he didn't count on Gussie Pratt?"

"No." She shook her head. "And he died before he told me where
the gun was."

Bertha tried to size up Elsie Riley. Was she telling the truth, or was
there another truth that would be revealed? If Bertha let her have the
gun, and to be honest, she was considering it, what would happen if
Elsie Riley were lying?

They both stared at the gun that was still half covered with a tissue
on the desk.

The room was growing darker as the light from the western window faded. Bertha couldn't turn on the light—she wasn't supposed to
be there.

"If you know the family so well, why didn't Levine's son know
you?"

"What?"

"Levine's son, Ron," said Bertha. "He flew from Chicago."

"So soon?" Elsie considered this and then met Bertha's eyes. "He'll recognize my name eventually. I was a little girl when he lived with his parents."

Bertha remembered Ron Levine's hesitation when she'd said the secretary's name. "Why don't you wait for him? He'll be back soon. Explain it to him."

"Let me have the gun, Bertha," Elsie pleaded. "I have a train, remember?"

Bertha rolled Levine's desk chair back and stood. She reached for the rope to the blinds and saw Ron Levine exiting the bank across the street. The only thing she had to go on was her gut. She nodded. "Take it and get out of here."

Elsie reached across the desk and the gun disappeared in her bag. "Thank you."

"They will look for you, you know," said Bertha.

"Damn that Pratt woman," Elsie said between beautiful white teeth.

"And if you're lying, I'll hunt you down myself," Bertha said to the woman's back.

Then she was alone. Her hands shoved in her pockets, waiting for Ron Levine.

A Leopard's Spots

Katherine V. Forrest

"I know these events are very upsetting . . ." The deputy sheriff's tone was steeped in sympathy; a line between her gray-green eyes distinctly deepened. "May I know your names, please?"

Distraught as she was, Ruth Whitman nevertheless was interested that a small coastal California county would have a woman on its police force, and a bulky, middle-aged one at that.

A reedy voice came softly from beside her: "I'm Benjamin Dickinson. My friend here is Ruth Whitman."

"Dickinson and Whitman," the deputy repeated, writing in her notebook, her face still somber but the crease between her eyes lightening. "Like the poets."

"Last Halloween somebody did call me Emily," Dickinson offered. "But I was trying to be Eleanor Roosevelt."

Deputy Bannon cast a brief glance of amusement at him, then said, "Ms. Whitman, would you step outside with me? Mr. Dickinson, I'll be back in a few minutes."

"Everyone calls us by our last names," Whitman said. Catching Bannon's eye, she nodded meaningfully toward Dickinson.

This time Bannon's glance evaluated the grayish pallor in Benjamin Dickinson's face, the sag in his thin shoulders. She said to him, "On second thought, let's you and me have a brief chat."

Dickinson pulled his pea coat from the coat tree and donned it as he followed Bannon from the parlor of the Pinckney house out onto the porch.

Whitman sank heavily into the yielding depths of the brown corduroy sofa. Deferring to Dickinson as the first to be questioned had been an act of pure altruism. Grieved and heartsick over what had oc-

curred here, she was anxious to tell what little she knew and leave this
place; the superficial conversation with Bannon had in itself taxed her
reserves of strength. But she owed Dickinson extra consideration; he
had lost Roy to a heart attack less than a year ago, while her own loss
of Margaret was in its eighth year—a bereavement she felt no less
keenly, she was certain, than Dickinson suffered his more recent loss.

She leaned over to prop her elbows on her knees, rubbing her face
with both hands. For months death had hovered over this house, and
had now struck twice, turning it into a place of horror . . . with more
horror to come. Six friends had come here today, friends who were un-
dergoing the same police questioning as herself and Dickinson.
Which of the six was a murderer? And why?

Dickinson eased himself into the old-fashioned bench swing on the
porch. Bannon sat opposite him, gingerly arranging her bulk in a
flimsy canvas deck chair.

"I understand what's going on here." The swing creaked beneath
him as he looked out at the powder blue squad car parked in the lane.
"You've separated all of us because we're witnesses and you police
need to interview us individually."

Bannon contemplated the slight, elfin man, meeting his shrewd
blue eyes as he turned back to her. She said equably, "Sir, what's your
relationship with the victim?"

"She's—she was a friend. To all of us. A friend of long standing."

She nodded, and wrote in her notebook. "What brought you and
all the other people together here today?"

"The same activity that's always brought us together—except for
the past few months, of course. Our weekly poker—I mean card
game," he amended hastily.

Waving a hand, she said brusquely, "I don't care about any gam-
bling in a poker game, only Grace Pinckney's death. You said the
group hadn't met for the past few months. Why?"

"Ralph got a lot worse—"

"You're referring to Ralph Pinckney, the victim's deceased husband?"

"Yes. He had the upper hand on prostate cancer till he got a bad case of flu." Sighing, he sank back into the swing and crossed his arms to encourage more warmth from his jacket. "Fighting on one front is hard enough."

"I saw the obit in the *Clarion*—just last week, wasn't it? Ran the Hearth Insurance Company, isn't that right?"

"Yes." He raised his gaze to a sky milky with fog. "Poor Dan and Gene came up from San Jose for their father's funeral, and now they have to come right back and bury their stepmother . . ."

"A tragedy indeed," Bannon murmured. She asked softly, "What happened here today, Mr. Dickinson?"

Dickinson massaged his eyes with his fingertips. He did not want to talk about it. He did not want to remember.

Bannon put aside her notebook. She said, "Just tell me what you saw."

Whitman helped herself to her plaid wool jacket on the coat tree, tucked herself into a corner of the sofa, and pulled the jacket around her. The parlor, cozy as it appeared with its gold curtains and oval hooked rug and corduroy sofa, had grown colder on this chilly October day. The log fire Grace and Chris had built in the living room fireplace had long since burned low. Foggy sea air was permeating the house from doors opening and closing as the deputies and Doc Phillips went about their work.

She knew that the scenes of this day would remain imprinted in her mind like a series of engravings. Arriving here fifteen minutes late because of Dickinson's usual dithering, although she didn't blame him this time. Even though they'd all rallied around the Pinckneys as Ralph sank toward death, she herself had been reluctant to return to a house void of Ralph's presence, and Dickinson had too recently gone through his own tortures . . .

The round dining room table had been moved into the living room and set up for poker as usual, exactly the same as before, when a robustly alive Ralph presided over the game in jovial tyranny. The Andersons, Pete and Gladys, sat in their usual places at the table,

Fernando across from them; Grace had set out cheese and crackers, tortilla chips, and salsa, the wine glasses already in front of everyone, including Grace's special glass from the breakfront, which stood beside Chris's glass on the mantel. Chris coming in with the bottle of wine. Chris, so handsome in his blue turtleneck sweater and crisp jeans, had had the wine . . . And Chris had poured the wine.

Bannon was writing in her notebook. "So no one ate or drank anything till Christopher Fontaine brought in the wine. Are you certain it was Mr. Fontaine?"

Dickinson sighed. "Yes, it was Chris."

"Had the bottle been opened?"

"It had. The cork was still in it, but it'd been pulled."

"And who poured the wine?"

He admitted, reluctantly, "Chris."

"You seem very unhappy with the statements you're making," Bannon observed.

He closed his eyes for a moment, against the image of the disbelieving horror in Chris's chalk-white face when Doc Phillips had pronounced Grace dead. "I haven't known Chris that long," he said candidly. "None of us has. But he's a good man; he was here for Ralph all hours of the day and night."

"I understand he'd been Mr. Pinckney's private nurse."

Dickinson nodded. "Ralph couldn't manage to get himself out of bed at all some days, Grace couldn't really look after him, she needed someone."

"My brother-in-law had cancer," Bannon murmured. "It's a terrible thing."

Roy at least hadn't suffered, Dickinson thought, and he quoted the ancient words of the Latin poet Martial that had brought him a degree of solace: "'Life's not just being alive, but being well.'"

"Very true, Mr. Dickinson. So, Christopher Fontaine came in with the bottle of wine and poured glasses all around. What happened next?"

"We drank a ritual toast to our missing player. To Ralph."

Whitman was reliving the scene. All of them on their feet, awkwardly holding a long-stemmed glass of red wine, Fernando emotional as always, excusing the tears rolling down his cheeks by mumbling about his Latin heritage; Pete and Gladys holding hands, Gladys sniffling, the deep network of lines in Pete's face as he tried to conceal his own sentiment. An arm around Dickinson to give him physical as well as moral support to get through this moment, she and Dickinson had joined Grace and Chris who were standing at the mantel. All of them with their glasses raised. Grace in her white wool dress, looking younger and fresher than she had in months, saying, "To you, dear Ralph. I know you're watching, just like you promised."

Grace taking a ceremonial sip of the Brown Brothers cabernet, then placing the wineglass on the table; everyone gathering at the poker table, and Grace drinking more of her wine. Everyone knew she loved good red wine on the very rare occasions when she did take a drink. She dealt the first hand.

Then Grace uttering, "I feel dreadful," and getting up and staggering toward an armchair and collapsing into it in stark confirmation of that fact. Seconds later, a faint reddish mottling rising in her face: "I can't breathe—" Fingers at her swelling throat: "Oh God, it's penicillin—get Doc Phillips. Quick!"

Chris looking on in frozen, open-mouthed horror, then running for the phone; Dickinson springing into motion, rushing to her aid . . .

Bannon asked Dickinson, "So at first you had the victim sit up?"

"I was trying to help her breathe. My partner got pneumonia twice. He tended to hyperventilate . . ." He paused, bitterly aware of the irony that Roy's death had released him from reticence about his relationship with the man he had loved in secret for thirty-two years. "Doc Phillips got here in fifteen minutes but . . . she was gone." He looked out toward the shrouded ocean and shuddered in agonized memory of Chris's screams of desperation, Chris seizing Grace's shoulders as if he would shake the breath back into her. "I tried everything. CPR, everything—" Coughing, he broke off.

"Mr. Dickinson—"

He turned back to her. "I'm all right. Bad enough we couldn't save Grace, now we have Doc Phillips going around demanding which one of us gave her the penicillin that killed her."

Seeing Bannon's mouth tighten, he said, "Doc was upset. We were all upset. Hysterical, if you want to know the truth."

Bannon asked, "How did Grace come to know you, Mr. Dickinson?"

"Our profession. We're all ex-professors. We moved here to retire. Well, except for Ralph and Gladys and Fernando."

"So you're from out of town."

"Not very far. I taught at San Francisco State—so did Grace. Whitman was UCLA. Pete originally taught at Duke—"

"Beyond that, how would you characterize Grace's relationship with the other people here?"

An image of Whitman filled his mind: the fortitude in her slender, lined face, the wiry body that seemed possessed of a confident resilience, a tensile strength. How would he ever have managed this past year without that sturdiness to lean on? He decided that she could answer this deputy's question instead of him. He told Bannon, "As old Queen Bess once said, "I would not open windows into men's souls.' I won't, either."

Bannon shook her head. "Sir, I'm not asking you to open windows. I'm just looking for a few facts."

He did not reply. Bannon regarded him for several moments, then tucked her notebook into her shirt pocket. "Why don't I have a deputy drive you home. We can take down your official statement later, when you feel better."

"I came with Whitman, I'll leave with her." He added, "But I'd like to remain out here on the porch, if you don't mind."

As Bannon sat down beside her on the corduroy sofa, Whitman looked at the bronze name tag above the pocket of the deputy's khaki shirt. She asked, "Would you be any relation to Ann Bannon?"

Bannon shook her head, and Whitman shrugged; the allusion to the legendary author of classic lesbian novels of the fifties and sixties had been a mild litmus test as to whether Bannon was a member of the club.

Bannon repeated the question she had directed to Dickinson: "How would you characterize the victim's relationship with the people here?"

"We were all friends. Good friends. Fernando Cabrillo goes back the longest; he's known the Pinckneys for years. He's just devastated by this." Whitman remembered with anguish that during the fifteen or so minutes of Grace's dying, Fernando seemed to have aged twenty years. "He courted Grace after her first marriage, before she married Ralph."

"Did Mr. Cabrillo hold it against Ralph or Grace?"

Whitman's smile was brief and humorless. "Ralph was the one. He never said anything, mind you, but he gave the impression that he'd come galloping in to rescue a high-class Anglo woman from Fernando's Latino clutches."

Bannon grunted noncommittally. "If he felt that way about Mr. Cabrillo, it's odd he'd welcome him in his house."

"It was Grace who made us all welcome," Whitman said. "It never ever mattered to Grace that Fernando was Hispanic. Or about Dickinson and me, either."

Bannon said, "I hadn't noticed before that you and Mr. Dickinson were Hispanic."

Grinning, surprised by Bannon's mischievous humor, Whitman responded, "Ralph discovered there was some cachet in having a few friends . . . off the beaten track, shall we say. I think it was Walpole who said, 'It is charming to totter into vogue.' But I never thought I'd live to see the day when gay people . . . Anyway, Ralph indulged Grace's every whim, including the friends she chose. It kept her under his thumb, you see. He ran roughshod over the rest of us in a mocking, congenial sort of way. Ralph Pinckney was one of those bullies who mask it under bluff heartiness."

"I know the type. What can you tell me about the male nurse who looked after Mr. Pinckney?"

"Chris? Not much," she responded cautiously.

"Ms. Whitman, neither you nor Mr. Dickinson seem to welcome the subject of Christopher Fontaine."

Whitman decided that if Bannon did not obtain the information from her, it would surface from another, possibly malevolent source. "Let me put it this way. A lot of people wouldn't understand how bad a time Grace had with Ralph's illness, how Chris was an angel of deliverance. You can't imagine what an awful patient Ralph was."

"I think I can. My brother-in-law had cancer. The sicker he got, the more abusive he became—sarcastic, very bitter, and demanding."

Nodding, Whitman thought that he couldn't have been worse than Ralph Pinckney.

"It was an awful time for Sara, his wife," Bannon continued. "Toward the end, she met somebody who . . . consoled her." She looked expectantly at Whitman.

Warily, Whitman nodded.

"Is that what happened here, with Mr. Fontaine?"

Whitman said carefully, "Let me ask you this. Did your brother-in-law . . . object?"

"Charlie never knew. It would have killed him." Bannon chuckled in embarrassment. "Killed him sooner, I mean."

"Well, Ralph knew. And it didn't kill him."

"You don't mean he approved," Bannon said with clear incredulity.

"I mean it didn't kill him. He went ballistic, as the young people say. Ordered Chris out of the house, called Grace every horrible name you can imagine, accused all of us of betraying his friendship. Then not a week later he turns right around and says he owes everything good in his life to Grace and he's been selfish and stupid, and he hires Chris back and apologizes to the rest of us." She could still hear the amazement and relief in Grace's voice as she blurted out the news over the phone.

"Remarkable," Bannon said.

"You seem more than a little skeptical," Whitman observed.

"Somebody has to be, and it's part of my job. Did you ever discuss Mr. Fontaine with Ralph Pinckney?"

"Of course not. All I know is, he'd truly forgiven Grace. I think, at last, Ralph changed, and was trying to face his death with a little perspective and dignity. Or maybe I'd just like to believe there's such a thing as deathbed conversion."

"Maybe there is. But I couldn't prove it by my brother-in-law. He died the way he lived. He was a bastard to begin with; his cancer made him worse."

Lowering her notepad, Bannon looked around her, and Whitman followed her gaze, trying to see the house as Bannon would see it. A solidly built structure from the forties, with such homey graces as a porch and a large backyard with fruit trees, and simple, functional, comfortable furniture—Grace's taste, not Ralph's—he had leaned more to the ostentatious. A house filled with objects collected over the decades—in the living room alone, delft plates and pitchers, a framed map of California shaped from plaster, an art deco lamp, the carved boomerang from Australia . . .

"Mr. Fontaine and the victim aren't married."

Jarred back to the moment by Bannon's statement, Whitman retorted, "Certainly not. Ralph died only last week. I'm sure Chris and Grace hadn't even—" She broke off in embarrassment, then rushed on, "Grace would want an appropriate interval."

"Of course."

"So *why* would Chris do anything to Grace? He only needed to wait and he'd be married to her. They loved each other. You could see it. He's not Grace's heir . . ."

"How do you know? Have you seen her will?"

"No," Whitman responded. "But I know Grace."

"Look, Ms. Whitman. One of the six people who came here today killed Grace Pinckney. Christopher Fontaine served the victim the wine. If he didn't do this, then who did?"

Twenty minutes later, in the car, looking into Dickinson's grim face, Whitman said, "You heard."

"They've detained Chris," Dickinson said, gazing disconsolately out the windshield into the swirling, thickening fog. "Doc told me. I guess he told you, too."

Fingering her car keys, Whitman asked, "Could Chris do a thing like this?" She felt reluctant to leave this place, as if events would spin even further out of control in her absence.

He sighed. "No way. You saw how he was—"

"Yes. Utterly distraught." She added unwillingly, "How about Fernando? Grace married Ralph instead of him, then went on to someone else. And he's always been in love with her . . ."

Tears filled his eyes. "We all loved Grace."

Whitman started the Volvo, turned up the heater as Dickinson mumbled, "Pete and Gladys . . . Remember when Ralph hinted they were giving hand signals at poker?"

Whitman nodded. It had taken all of Grace's charm to convince them he was teasing. "Grace smoothed it over. Why would those two do anything to her?"

"I'm reaching here, Whitman," he said sharply. "Just trying to find any rational explanation. Chris opened the wine and served it. Who else could've slipped penicillin into it?"

Whitman pulled away from the curb. "Maybe Grace herself did," she said, not believing it for a moment.

"In front of Chris? All of us? You saw her—that woman fought for her life."

"Maybe she changed her mind. Maybe it was just a ghastly accident." Whitman scowled. "Look, Doc Phillips took care of Ralph and Grace—"

"So? He's the only doctor in town."

"Exactly."

Doc Phillips sat hunched over his desk, rolling his fountain pen between his thin fingers. "Grace's allergic reaction is called anaphylaxis," he explained in a resonant rumble. "Antibodies called immunoglobulin E, or IgE, cause blood vessels to leak and tissues to swell, blood pressure to drop—"

Whitman was not about to let him ramble on. "Why didn't she have epinephrine on hand to give herself an injection?"

His bushy eyebrows rose in apparent surprise at her knowledge. "Prescription-strength penicillin isn't a naturally occurring substance. People know when they ingest it, and it does have a smell. But a strong red wine would mask a small quantity of it, and that's all it would take. She did wear a MedicAlert bracelet . . ." He stared down at his desk.

"The bracelet didn't help her that time in the hospital when they gave her penicillin anyway," Whitman said tartly.

His head jerked up. "I apologize for my profession," he snapped. "Once in a while we do fall off our pedestals."

His lined face looked haggard, his white hair disheveled. Whitman understood his anger, understood that he had, in the space of a week, lost two long-time patients. She asked, "Who among our group have you given penicillin prescriptions to, Doc?"

"You know I can't divulge that information."

"Grace is dead," Dickinson argued, "and it seems—"

"But I prescribed penicillin for you, Whitman, last February."

As Whitman stared at him in outrage, Doc Phillips said, "Over the years I've prescribed penicillin for everyone in this whole town. Fontaine could easily get penicillin from a former patient. The truth is, the cops have all six of you under suspicion."

Doc Phillips tossed down his pen, laced his hands behind his head and leaned back wearily. "As far as I can see, nobody has any motive."

"Could Grace have done this to herself?"

"Sure. But I saw her just a few days ago—no sign of depression. Yes, she still felt guilty over Ralph finding out about her and Chris, but Ralph had given her his blessing. Chris's the odd man out, the one we know the least about. To be honest, if he did have something to do with this, then I have to wonder if he also hastened Ralph's death."

"Good heavens," Dickinson uttered.

"Doc," Whitman asked, "how much penicillin would it take for Grace—"

"Precious damn little. The more episodes, the higher the sensitivity. She'd had two serious exposures, one as a child, and the one in the hospital was damn near fatal. A minute amount would kill her unless she had an injection of epinephrine immediately."

"You know," Whitman said, "I've been thinking about something Deputy Bannon said to me. She was absolutely right." She got to her feet. "Thanks, Doc."

Dickinson leaped up and followed her out with more energy than Whitman had seen from him in almost a year. "I know who did this," he said.

Dickinson and Whitman marched into Seacrest's small, clapboard police substation. Deputy Bannon looked up from the report she was fastening into a folder. As the two of them seated themselves in the chairs matching her gray metal desk, she said with a trace of exasperation, "Have a seat."

"Thank you," Dickinson said, and plunged right in. "Of our poker group, only one of us had a real motive for killing Grace. The real killer had opportunity, too, access to penicillin—"

"All of you had easy access, and Christopher Fontaine served the wine," Bannon returned. "The victim was dealing with the death of her husband. It's possible she'd changed her mind about Fontaine and told him."

"Balderdash," Dickinson said.

"For the sake of argument, preposterous as it may be," Whitman said, "let's say Chris actually did kill Grace. How could he be stupid enough to incriminate himself in front of five other people?"

"Lots of criminals are stupid. It's why we catch them."

"Chris isn't stupid."

"Granting that," Bannon said easily, "Fontaine had access to penicillin, and we're taking a close look into his background and history with other patients. But," she conceded, comfortably shifting her bulk in her desk chair as she sat back, "I'll listen to anything you have to say."

"First of all," Dickinson said, "the real killer got the penicillin from treatments for the aftermath of the flu."

"Regardless of where your candidate got it, it had to get into the victim's glass."

"There were lots of hypodermics around, Chris gave Ralph injections—"

"No, Dickinson," Whitman said, placing a hand on his arm, "he didn't inject it into the bottle. Grace always used the same glass for special occasions. It was in her glass before the wine was even poured."

"For heaven's sake, Whitman," Dickinson protested, turning to her. "As soon as she took the glass out of the breakfront—"

"She wouldn't see anything. It wasn't visible. He coated the inside of the glass with liquid penicillin and put it back in the breakfront, ready for the next time she drank wine. She wouldn't even think to look for anything on her glass. Doc Phillips told us it would take the tiniest amount to kill her."

"If you're right, there's one way to find out," Dickinson said. "Test the bottle. Fingerprint the glass—"

"Ahem, you two junior detectives," Bannon said, "may I have your attention?" She tapped the report in front of her. "We cops aren't quite the dumb gumshoes you think we are."

"So what do your tests say?" Dickinson said eagerly.

"They're a confidential part of a police report." She held up both hands against their protests. "If there was no penicillin anywhere except in the victim's wineglass—and I'm not saying that's the case—it doesn't matter. It would only confirm that Fontaine simply dropped a pill into her glass."

"What about fingerprints?"

Bannon did not reply.

Looking into her face, Whitman crowed, "I'll stake my teacher's pension that somebody else's prints are on that glass . . ."

"A somebody not Christopher Fontaine," Dickinson exulted.

"Our reports are confidential," Bannon repeated firmly. "But I can tell you that we've released Mr. Fontaine." She looked from Whitman to Dickinson, and said slowly, "We'll file a case when we can demonstrate probable cause."

"There's probable cause, all right," Dickinson said, his face grim. "Sick as he was, that bastard got himself out of bed and over to that breakfront and poisoned her glass—"

"—and set up that obscene scenario where Grace would propose a toast to him," Whitman added vehemently, "and then—"

"—went off to his grave knowing Grace would die and all the rest of us would be under suspicion," Dickinson finished.

Bitterly, Whitman quoted Francis Bacon: "'Revenge triumphs over death.'" She said to Bannon, "You were so right when you said somebody had to be skeptical about Ralph Pinckney. He was a son of bitch, and he was a vengeful, murdering son of a bitch when he died."

Dickinson muttered, "'That I should after death invisibly return . . .'"

"Shakespeare?" Bannon asked, folding her arms across her ample chest.

"Whitman. Walt, I mean."

"Well, I'm a simple woman," Bannon said, "and all I know is, my scumbag of a brother-in-law got worse with his cancer, and leopards don't change their spots. But," she cautioned, "we're still checking out Mr. Fontaine."

Dickinson leaned forward, jabbing a finger at the report on Bannon's desk. "You can't seriously suspect anyone but Ralph Pinckney."

"We need to be careful. We need to check everything."

"You know the truth. I can tell by your face," Whitman said. "Ralph Pinckney spent the last days of his life figuring out the cruelest possible revenge on his wife and on his rival and on his friends. That's what you really believe."

"Believe," Bannon repeated. Fingering the report in front of her, she took in a deep breath and let it out unhurriedly.

Whitman knew she was making a crucial decision. Seacrest was not San Francisco nor Los Angeles, and police procedures would not be as formal here, but it was Bannon's choice as to how informal they could or should be.

"Well," Bannon said finally, "I think your theory might explain why, on that wineglass, up near the rim—where a person might hold it to carefully place it back in a cabinet—is a partial fingerprint belonging Ralph Pinckney."

Dickinson said to Whitman, "I told you."

"In all my years of police work," Bannon said as if Dickinson had not spoken, "I've never seen anything like this. The bottom line is, a man's committed murder from the grave. Unless you believe in God, he's got clean away with it."

Whitman and Dickinson stared at her.

"Think about it. The evidence is totally circumstantial. It rests on a single fingerprint and a leopard's spots."

Dickinson and Whitman exchanged glances, then Whitman said, "It's enough. It's probable cause."

"To the three of us, maybe. But not enough to file a case." Bannon spread her hands. "So, I guess if you believe in God, then, 'In His will is our peace.'"

Whitman guessed: "Francis Thompson?"

Bannon smiled ruefully. "Dante."

Let Sleeping Cats Lie
Jeane Harris

"I started to suspect she was a werewolf on our first date," Audrey told her best friend, Lauren, as they unwrapped their veggie sandwiches. They were having lunch at the San Diego Zoo near the Big Cat exhibit, where Audrey worked.

"Well, sure, makes sense," Lauren said sarcastically, nodding her unruly mop of brown curls. "Listen, Audrey. It's time to lay off the Stephen King again. Remember in high school after you read *Salem's Lot*? You thought everybody in town was a vampire. Or after *The Tommyknockers* and you told everybody there was an alien spacecraft buried in Nina Nelson's backyard?"

"Those things happened a long time ago. This is different," Audrey said fervently. "Believe me. There's just too much here that doesn't add up."

"I know . . . you told me," Lauren said. "She deliberately singled you out."

"Hey, now that part is true," Audrey said, brushing crumbs from her ugly brown uniform pants. "She stalked me for a week before she made her move."

Audrey had first noticed her soon-to-be lover, Elaine, one morning when she was hurrying along the walkway to the jaguars' cage. On her way she noticed a white van with the initials KWLF superimposed over a huge black and gold wolf with red eyes. As she neared the Big Cat house, she heard the deejay's voice.

"Hey, everybody! We're here at the world famous San Diego Zoo during Friends of the Zoo week. We've got lots of contests with great prizes—free hot dogs, Cokes, and balloons for the kiddies. Drop by our van at the Big Cat house—that's where they keep the lions, tigers, and . . . well, all the other big cats. Hey, get on down here. All your favorite jocks will be here, including everybody's number one wild woman—El Lobo. Yeah, dig it. This is KWLF—Kay-Wolf—and we'll be stalkin' ya all week long from the zoo."

The deejay's voice was relentless. Audrey tuned him out and walked faster.

Friends of the Zoo week was always intense. Thousands of people, most of them screaming kids who wanted to see the big cats, converged on the zoo. She had to get the cages clean before nine o'clock so the keepers could feed the cats before the crowds arrived. As she rounded the corner to the cat house, she suddenly halted in the shade of a huge rock beside the trail. She shivered, and the hair on the back of her neck stood up.

Even though there was no one else on the path, Audrey sensed that she was being watched. She looked around her—no one else appeared to be around. Then she heard a noise above her and looked up.

A woman was squatting on the top of a huge rock beside the pathway. Her arms hung down loosely between her parted legs, almost touching the rock. The brim of a baseball cap hid most of her hair, and though her face was in shadows, her mouth was slightly open and Audrey saw a gleam of white teeth.

Even though Audrey stood there, staring directly at her, the woman made no move, no noise, no acknowledgment at all of Audrey. She simply looked at her . . . dispassionately, Audrey thought later. Then to her surprise, the woman stood up until her head was blocking the sun, a bright nimbus around her head. She was extraordinarily tall. Audrey guessed she was at least six feet. Her legs were long and muscular. Audrey noticed that with the sun behind her, the fine, golden hair on her legs was visible.

Almost certainly a dyke, Audrey decided. Hairy legs were out of feminist fashion these days; they were even out of fashion for a lot of lesbians. A thought skittered across Audrey's mind that she barely registered at the time: whether the woman had fine golden hair all over her . . .

Audrey shook her head and returned to the task at hand. It was almost 9 a.m. and the keeper didn't like to be kept waiting, especially during Friends of the Zoo week. In addition to the screaming hordes of children, there were lots of big shots dropping in and the zoo couldn't afford to anger any potential benefactors.

The next time she saw the tall woman, Audrey was busy cleaning out the jaguar cages. Only after the cages were cleaned and the animals fed would the big cats be let out onto their grassy island that was surrounded by a moat. The keeper always fed the cats in their cages, so the people could watch them eat. If they gave the huge hunks of meat to the cats after they let them outside, they would go into the bushes or up a tree to eat. There were plenty of trees on the island for the jags to climb and hang out in.

She wore her dumb-looking brown uniform with the too long pants legs and the too big rubber boots. With her plastic garbage can, oversized dustpan, and broom, she knew she wasn't exactly hot looking. But as she scooped up the animals' waste and hosed down the cages, she still kept one eye out for any attractive lesbians who might be walking by. It was then she noticed the tall woman for the second time.

She was standing directly in front of the cage that Audrey had just finished cleaning. The woman wasn't looking at Audrey, though; she was staring into the jaguars' cage as though transfixed. Even from her vantage point, Audrey could see the woman's white-knuckled grip on the iron railing in front of the cage. She looked as if she were being electrocuted. What in the hell was so fascinating about the jaguars?

Suddenly, the woman turned and looked directly at Audrey. There was a fierce intensity to her stare. She frowned at the woman in order to let her know such intensity directed at someone you didn't know was inappropriate. To her amazement, the woman crooked her finger at Audrey, motioning her to come closer.

Audrey shrugged, holding out her broom and garbage can, as if say, "What can I do? I'm busy here."

In answer, the woman, whose face was still hidden by the cap, walked toward Audrey. Her walk was loose-limbed, graceful, like a dancer. She kept her eyes on Audrey while she walked, a slow grin spreading across her face, as if she already knew Audrey and was surprised but delighted to see her. The woman said in a friendly way,

"Hey, I think there's something going on over there in the jaguar cage you ought to see."

Audrey felt a surge of alarm. "What? Are they okay?" She dropped her dustpan with a clatter and quickly opened the side door of the cage. She covered the short distance in a few seconds.

What she saw made her face turn red with embarrassment. She felt, rather than saw, the woman standing next to her as she watched the two jaguars mating in the corner of the cage. Her face burning, Audrey heard the soft laughter of the woman who had moved even closer to her. The woman put her hand lightly in the middle of her back, to steady Audrey; then, as she spoke, Audrey felt the hand moving down, slowly, sensuously, to the top of her ass. She leaned very close to Audrey. She could feel the movement of her warm lips on the delicate parts of her ear, which she was sure, was also red.

The loudly purring male jaguar was on top of the female, holding her in position with his forepaws. His claws were barely extended, just enough to let the female know he was serious. He held her with his mouth by the nape of her neck. Every few moments he stopped his purring and screamed—a high, primitive sound. The female answered his frequent cries with screams of her own, her head flat on the concrete floor, her rump arched high in the air to meet the male's thrusts. Bloody scratches on her flanks were evidence that perhaps she had not been as willing at first as she appeared to be now. Despite her embarrassment, Audrey kept watching; she had never witnessed the jaguars mating before and she was weirdly fascinated.

Audrey finally turned her head to look at the woman and saw that her baseball cap had the words KWLF STAFF embossed on it.

"You work for that radio station," Audrey managed to say. Up close there was a tension that positively radiated from the woman, and she found herself trembling with the effort of standing close to her, simultaneously attracted and repulsed.

The woman's hair under the cap was deep tawny color, like that of a female lion. And she had never seen eyes like the woman's before. She had thought at first that they were hazel; but as she'd gazed into them, it was obvious that they were actually gold.

At the word "gold," Lauren put down her sandwich. "Gold?" she repeated dubiously.

"Like an animal. Look, I'm not dreaming this up, Lor. You remember—I told you before how I've always felt a little afraid of her."

"Afraid? I don't remember you saying you were afraid."

"Maybe not afraid exactly, not at first. But, definitely uneasy."

Her face had been lean and angular, her mouth full and richly sensuous. A mouth that begged to be kissed . . . or at least nibbled on. Audrey had found herself leaning into the woman's hip and responding to the hand nestled in the small of her back.

"Animals are so straightforward about what they want," the woman said softly to Audrey.

Audrey cleared her throat and managed to say, "Is that what you call it?"

"Absolutely," the woman purred. "They have no pretense, they don't lie, they just do . . ."

Audrey felt the hand on her back move down a little; now the heel of the woman's hand was actually resting on her butt.

"My name's Elaine," the woman said, moving her hand to Audrey's shoulder and patting her reassuringly.

"Audrey." She moved away then, away from the woman's hand and voice. "I work here . . . and I . . . uh, I have to get back to work." She shook her head to clear it. "I have work to do."

"Sure you do, so do I. But I'll be back to pick you up after you get off this afternoon," Elaine said. "We can go to dinner. I know a place you'll like."

"Dinner?" Audrey asked. "I don't know you . . . I can't . . . I was just . . ." She stopped and motioned vaguely to the cage she had been cleaning. Then she dropped her eyes. "I get off work at four thirty."

Elaine had smiled. "I know."

At this point in Audrey's recitation, Lauren interrupted again. "I still think you're lying about that part," she said flatly, taking a bite out of her sandwich. "It sounds like a line from a movie."

"Why is it so hard to believe?" Audrey asked.

"Because you lie all the time," Lauren said cheerfully. "Everybody knows that. You exaggerate, to make the story better, funnier, more dramatic. It's because you didn't get enough attention from your parents when you were little." She eyed Audrey suspiciously. "I suspect that's what you're doing right now with this werewolf business."

"Not this time. See, I should have known then—she was different. I'd never met anyone like her before."

Audrey truly hadn't ever known anyone like Elaine before. Her looks alone made her unusual.

Lauren interrupted again. "But you liked her?"

"Of course I liked her. But I knew something was wrong, almost from the beginning," Audrey said, as they watched the seals jostle one another for a fish the keeper was holding out, "I told you the next day how she took me to that steak house and she ate meat—ate it practically raw." She shuddered at the memory. "I know it had to be cold on the inside."

Lauren held up her hands. "Audrey, stop it. Just because we're vegetarians and Elaine likes to eat meat doesn't make her a werewolf. Stop a minute and listen to yourself."

"The meat's not the only thing—my God, there are a hundred others. What about her apartment? And that weird story she told me about her father and the jaguar woman?"

"I give up," Lauren said wearily, lacing her fingers behind her head and leaning back against the bench. "What about the apartment and the story she told you?"

"Well, the first night I saw her apartment I knew that her thing with wolves went way off the normal chart."

They had been dating for a few weeks. After a couple of beers at a lesbian bar in Imperial Beach, Elaine suggested that they go to her apartment. When they arrived Elaine turned on the radio and, saying she needed to use the bathroom, left Audrey in the living room.

Audrey had looked through the CDs and found recordings of wolves howling, *Peter and the Wolf,* and Leonard Bernstein playing at Wolftrap. Cris Williamson's *Wolf Moon* along with all of Kate Wolf's albums. There were also videos of werewolf movies—some Audrey had heard of, some titles in a foreign language that she didn't recognize.

The disc jockey's frantic voice diverted her attention: "Hey, this is Rick the Stick Summers and don't forget, it's a full moon tonight, kids, and you know what that means." CCR began wailing "Bad Moon Risin'."

"That's right, San Diego. Lock all the windows, bar all the doors, and load up your silver bullets 'cause tonight at midnight we turn her loose. The one, the only—El Lobo."

Then, a woman's voice—deep, low, growling—replaced the frantic deejay's. "I am on the prowl under the full moon. And the hunger is upon me."

Then she howled a bone-chilling cry of loneliness and sadness. Audrey felt the sound up and down her spine.

She switched off the radio as Elaine came back into the room. "God, that is such racist, sexist bullshit," Audrey said. "I can't believe you work at that radio station. Do you know that woman?"

Elaine looked at Audrey in surprise. "You don't like El Lobo?"

"I've never listened to El Lobo. I don't like top forty music. What do you do there, anyway?"

"I work on the technical end," Elaine said smoothly. "I'm an engineer." She paused. "She's actually a nice woman. I know her pretty well."

"I'm sorry," Audrey said, aware of the coolness in Elaine's voice. "I didn't mean to knock your job or anything. Hey, look who's talking, huh? Look what I do for a living. I clean up lion and bear shit." After an awkward silence, she said, "I guess you like wolves, huh?"

"Why?" Elaine said, arching an eyebrow. "Don't you?"

"I like wolves," Audrey said, trying to make her tone agreeable. "I don't know as much about them as you obviously do, but I like them okay." She motioned to the movies. "Where did you get all this shit about wolves?"

"Oh, that," Elaine said dismissively. "People send all kinds of wolf things to the station . . . they have to give it away to the employees . . . they don't have enough room for it."

"But you don't believe all that stuff do you?"

"What stuff?" Elaine asked.

"That stuff about werewolves. You know, full moon, silver bullets, people turning into wolves."

Elaine sat down beside Audrey on the couch. "Have I told you about my father?"

Audrey shook her head, puzzled by the sudden shift in topics. "You've never told me anything about your parents."

"My father's from one of the remotest areas of Brazil—along the Rio Negro, a tributary of the Amazon. Until he was twelve years old, he'd never seen anyone from outside his own village. One day he was checking his fish traps along the river and discovered a Brazilian air force officer who'd ejected from his plane. He was badly injured in the crash; his parachute hadn't opened completely.

"Anyway, my father's people nursed the officer for nearly a year till he was able to walk back to the river and wait for a boat to pick him up. This officer took an interest in my father. My father's father died when he was five and I think he kind of looked upon the officer as a father figure. For whatever reason, they formed a deep bond. Eventually the officer came back to the village and asked my father if he wanted to leave his village and go to school in Sao Paolo. My father accepted."

"Wow!" Audrey said. "Did your father ever go back?"

"Oh, yes," Elaine said. "My father came to the United States and went to medical school where he met my mother, who was a nurse. Eventually, after he completed his training, they returned to my father's village. My parents lived there for five years during my childhood. They provided medical care for the people who lived there.

"My father told me stories about his people and of course I was exposed to their culture during my childhood," Elaine continued. "The most interesting aspect of their culture, to me, is that they practice shape-shifting. During our stay I learned that my paternal grandmother was a powerful, respected woman because she could shape-shift into many kinds of predators and often provided food for the tribe."

Audrey stared at Elaine. "So I guess you do believe?"

Elaine smiled, her white incisors gleaming in the candlelight. "My father's people have a legend about jaguars. Would you like to hear it?"

"Uh, sure," Audrey said uncertainly. The apartment suddenly seemed darker than before and she felt a vague uneasiness, as if they were not alone. Which, she told herself, was ridiculous. Who else would be there? Lon Chaney? She smiled at the thought and began listening intently to Elaine.

"Jaguar woman lived in the village of jaguars deep in the jungle. She was a curious woman and was not interested in any of the jaguar men in her village. So she wandered until she came to a village where ordinary humans lived. She prowled the edge of the village, watching the people go about their daily tasks.

"One day she spied a beautiful woman bathing in the river. She wanted the woman in a way she had never wanted a man and knew that she had to have her. One day Jaguar woman changed herself into a human woman and waited by the river. Finally the human woman came down to the river for her bath and found Jaguar woman bathing there also. They began to talk and meet every day until the human woman had also fallen in love with Jaguar woman. It became their custom to meet at the river and after their baths to go into the jungle and make love together."

Audrey grinned and slid her arm around Elaine's shoulder. "I'm starting to like this story," she joked.

Elaine ignored her and went on with her story. "One day the woman came early to the river and saw Jaguar woman shift into a human form. She waited until after they had made love and then told Jaguar woman she could no longer be her lover. After that Jaguar woman prowled the outskirts of the village, growling and crying for her. Finally the people of the village could stand it no longer and they dragged the woman to the edge of the village and gave her to her jaguar lover. Jaguar woman fell upon the woman and devoured her so that she could keep the woman with her forever."

As Audrey trailed off in telling her story, Lauren wadded up her sandwich wrapper and threw it into the kangaroo-shaped trash barrel beside her. "Look, Audrey. My lunch hour's almost up. Could we cut to the chase? What exactly did you find so troubling about Elaine's story? I mean it sounds to me like the woman was trying to share part of her life with you."

"I don't know," Audrey mumbled. "You just had to be there. It was weird. I mean she never did tell me if she actually believed in werewolves. First she ate that raw steak and then she started telling me about people changing into animals. It was just weird."

"If she's so weird," Lauren asked, "how come you keep dating her?"

Audrey felt a blush creeping up her face and Lauren laughed uproariously and slapped her on the back.

"That good, huh?"

Audrey had never experienced anything like Elaine in bed. Audrey, who had had her share of lovers and was certainly not inexperienced when it came to women and sex, had never had sex like this. No one had ever brought sex toys to her before and shown her how much pleasure could be had using such playthings. She had never given herself to anyone with as much abandon as she gave herself to Elaine.

The first night Elaine made love to her, under a poster of a howling wolf silhouetted against a full moon, Audrey felt that there was something inside Elaine, something wild and savage, separate somehow and barely contained.

They had begun kissing on the couch in Elaine's front room, their lips and tongues frantically exploring each other's mouth. Elaine unbuttoned Audrey's shirt and gently pulled on her nipples. Audrey felt herself grow wet almost immediately and swung her leg over Elaine's lap and straddled her. Grinding her pelvis against Elaine's stomach, she lapped and bit at Elaine's mouth.

Soon they were peeling off each other's clothing and stumbling down the hallway into Elaine's bedroom where they collapsed onto the bed. Audrey had landed on her stomach and when she tried to roll over to resume kissing Elaine, Elaine held her shoulders to the bed.

"No," she whispered hoarsely, in a voice Audrey barely recognized. "I want you this way."

Audrey felt her underpants being removed and then the weight of Elaine's smooth, naked body settling onto her back. She lay there momentarily, unmoving and then as Audrey relaxed, Elaine pulled the hair away from her ear.

"Do you trust me?" she asked, kissing Audrey's earlobe.

"No," Audrey managed to say. "But I'll do anything you want."

"Good," Elaine growled. "That's the right answer." She lifted Audrey's hair from her neck and began gently biting the nape of her neck. The unaccustomed facedown position was exciting to Audrey. She felt totally in Elaine's power.

Elaine continued to bite and kiss her neck at the same time her hips moved against Audrey's backside. With each movement Elaine's coarse pubic hair ground into her butt and soon she was slick with Elaine's juices. Elaine began to pant in Audrey's ear, each breath a hoarse, gasping cry. Audrey reached down with her hand and parted her ass cheeks as Elaine ground herself against her harder and harder.

"I want you," Elaine panted in Audrey's ear.

In answer Audrey raised herself on all fours and shamelessly presented herself to Elaine who groaned as Audrey pressed back into her. "Come back here . . . come on." She grabbed Audrey around her waist and pulled her up against her pubic hair and ground into her. Audrey, excited beyond fear by Elaine's coaching, leaned back until she was practically sitting in Elaine's lap and leaned her head on Elaine's shoulder. Elaine's free hand was moving up and down her back and she felt Elaine's fingernails rake her back, burning welts across her shoulders.

Suddenly, Elaine stopped.

"What?" Audrey started.

Elaine held her by the shoulder and said, "Don't move. Don't turn around."

Audrey allowed herself to relax and slid forward, her face against the spread.

She heard Elaine open a drawer in her nightstand and then Elaine was back, with her hand on Audrey's shoulder.

"Just relax now," Elaine said, and then Audrey felt her part her ass cheeks. She was a little embarrassed, but then she felt Elaine rubbing something liquid—cool and slippery—onto her asshole and though this was entirely new to Audrey, it felt rather good.

"Hmmmmm," she responded to Elaine's finger, which was now circling and rubbing her asshole with a pleasing rhythm. Elaine continued to rub and circle with her finger, until finally Audrey felt Elaine's finger slip into her ass. She gasped and stopped moving.

"Don't stop moving," Elaine growled, pushing her finger deeper. "Just relax and move with me."

Audrey groaned, partly out of pain, partly out of pleasure. She had never experienced anything so intimate. Her face burned.

Elaine's lips moved across the back of her neck. "Does it hurt, baby?'

"Yes . . . no, I don't know," Audrey whimpered. "Do it some more."

"Come on, now. Give it to me. You know you want to."

Audrey felt Elaine's finger slip out of her asshole and then, almost immediately, replaced by what felt like two fingers.

She cried out in surprise and pain and from behind her Audrey could hear something that sounded like a big, overgrown house cat purring. She wanted to turn around and look but Elaine held her too tightly around the waist and by now the in and out of Elaine's fingers in her ass distracted her from anything else. Deeper and deeper her fingers slid into her and with each thrust Audrey felt something deep inside her begin to unfold and expand . . . almost as if a creature inside her was beginning to take wing and fly.

She started to thrust back as hard as Elaine thrust forward and soon she felt herself open . . . she felt orgasm coming, but it was unlike any she had ever felt—more powerful and deeper inside her.

Audrey began to cry and tremors shook her body. She began grinding herself against Elaine's fingers and buried her face in Elaine's neck. Elaine's other hand slipped in front and began stroking her clit. She felt her orgasm building and when it overtook her, she fell forward on the bed, abandoning herself to the fiery delicious sensation. She felt Elaine leaning over her, the weight of her body pressing her into the bed. Elaine began moaning, hurtling toward her own orgasm and soon Audrey found herself echoing Elaine's passionate cries.

Lauren stood in front of Audrey with her arms akimbo and a disgusted look on her face. "Yeah, I can see why you're so disturbed about this, Audrey. It's just terrible. You've met a beautiful woman and you're having the best sex you've ever had. That's really terrible. I feel for you."

"But there's more," Audrey protested. She reached out and pulled Lauren back down to the bench. "She's hairier sometimes than others."

"So sometimes she shaves and sometimes she doesn't," Lauren said patiently. "That's not—"

"No, it's more than that," Audrey interrupted. "I swear one night when we were making love; I swear I felt the hair on her neck growing longer. I saw her legs when she got up that night to get a drink. They were incredibly hairy. And they weren't before we went to bed. I noticed."

"Have you asked her about it?"

"Of course not," Audrey said. "What am I going to say? 'Oh, pardon me, dear. I noticed that you suddenly have a pelt'?"

"So what are you saying?" Lauren asked. "Do you actually think that the woman is a werewolf? That she sprouts hair and prowls around under the full moon?"

Audrey felt frustrated. "I know it sounds kind of far-fetched—but there's just too many weird things going on. I mean, aside from the eating raw meat, getting hairy in a matter of minutes, and the stories and books and records and poster—there's other stuff. Like how she gets up at night and disappears. I ask her about it and she says she got called into work. But it's regular. So I looked at the dates she got called in over the past few months—all on the full moon. Don't you think that's weird?"

Lauren looked at Audrey steadily. "No, Audrey, I don't think it's weird or strange or anything. I don't claim to know whether or not people can actually change into animals. Certainly no one I know has ever changed into an animal, at least not in front of me. But if you're asking if I think Elaine is a werewolf then the answer is absolutely not."

She stood up and tossed their soft-drink cups into the trash barrel. "And now, I have to go back to work. My advice to you is to go to Elaine's house tonight, make passionate love to her, and be happy you have a lover. If you really feel uneasy about it after that, I'd tell her all this stuff you've been thinking. She'll have some reasonable explanation for all these so-called oddities you've been obsessing about, you two will laugh about it, and that'll be the end of it."

She leaned down and kissed Audrey on the forehead. "Have an orgasm for me, okay? What the hell, have two."

When Audrey arrived at Elaine's apartment that night, Elaine answered the buzzer out of breath. "Hi, I'm in the bathroom. I'll unlock the door and buzz you in."

Audrey heard the shower when she entered the apartment and sat down on the couch to wait. Elaine stuck her head out of the bathroom. "I'll be just a minute," she said, wiping her hands on a towel. When she finally emerged, Audrey noticed that her hair was wet and there was a bandage on her left arm.

"What's wrong with your arm?"

"I cut myself at work today on a piece of equipment," Elaine explained. "I took a shower to try to wash away most of my day. It wasn't very pleasant." She sat down the couch beside Audrey and looked at her. "How was your day?"

Audrey took a deep breath and told Elaine about her meeting with Lauren at the zoo and everything they had said. She didn't know when she had decided to tell Elaine her suspicions or whether Elaine would laugh at her or throw her out. The story just tumbled out of her.

"And that's my story," Audrey finally said. "Pretty silly, huh?"

Elaine hadn't said a word during Audrey's story and continued her silence for a long time after Audrey finished, her expression quite serious. "Some people might think it's silly," Elaine said.

Audrey began to feel a little nervous. "I'd feel better about telling you now if you laughed or something. Told me my fears were childish . . ." She thought, *Just tell me you're not a werewolf.*

Elaine shook her head. "You have some questions about me and I intend to answer them. It's time I stopped hiding things from you.

I was a fool to think you wouldn't notice them. I'm sorry now that I lied to you."

Audrey's heart rate accelerated a little and she found herself leaning backward on the couch, away from Elaine, who stood over her and whose height suddenly seemed menacing.

"What kind of things?" Audrey asked, her voice quavering a little.

"Some of your questions will be answered by my first confession," Elaine said. "I'm not just an engineer at KWLF, as I told you at first."

Audrey looked past Elaine, measuring the distance from the couch to the front door of the apartment. She began cursing herself for not having this conversation with Elaine during the day. It was dark outside, throwing shadows in the deep corners of the room. She wished she could turn on the lights.

"You're not?"

"No, I lied about that."

"Okay." Audrey tried to keep her voice level and reasonable. "Well then, what do you do?"

"I'm El Lobo."

Elaine's words didn't sink in at first and Audrey looked puzzled. "El Lobo?"

"Yes, the disc jockey you said you didn't like," Elaine explained. "I was going to tell you the night we went out to dinner the first time, but you seemed to dislike her so much and you also seemed somewhat disgusted that I ate meat—it seemed like a lot to dislike on the first date and I just didn't want to create a worse impression."

"You're El Lobo?" Audrey repeated. She thought a moment and then began to smile. "That's why you leave sometimes at night."

"It's a gimmick," Elaine explained. "I actually do work at the station as an engineer, but a few nights a month, during the full moon, I'm El Lobo. The station started doing it a few years ago, during ratings weeks, just to get listeners but people liked it so much—now I do it every month.

"As for the hair—I have a hormonal condition. It's inherited through my father's family; apparently my grandmother also had it. I take medication that causes accelerated hair growth at certain times during the month." She smiled slightly. "It does strange things to my appetite too—I have a craving—which is why sometimes I like rare steak."

Audrey began to relax a little. "Like pregnant women who like pickles and ice cream, huh? Because their hormones are out of whack?"

Elaine nodded. "Yes, I guess so." She put her hand on Audrey's arm and squeezed it. As always, Audrey was awed and slightly aroused by the strength of her lover's grip.

"Do these hormones have an effect on your sex drive, too?" Audrey asked playfully.

Elaine smiled. "As a matter of fact, they do." She pulled Audrey to her and began kissing her neck.

"Hmmmmm," Audrey murmured. She pulled away from Elaine's embrace. "So I take it you're saying you're not a werewolf?"

Elaine held up her hand. "I swear I am not, nor have I ever been, nor will I ever be, a werewolf."

Audrey laughed and stood up. "Well, that's good enough for me. Why don't you go into the bedroom, take off your clothes, and we'll take that sex drive for a spin? I'm going to the bathroom."

There were watery droplets of blood in the sink where Elaine had rinsed her wound. Audrey noticed that she had left the gauze and tape out on the counter. She was opening the medicine chest to put them away when she caught the reflection of the wall in the shower in the mirror.

She shut the door of the medicine chest and pulled the shower curtain all the way open. There was watery blood in the shower; more than a little had collected around the drain. However, it looked as though something—probably a towel—had been used to clean up more blood on the tile walls.

Lots of blood.

Audrey looked around for the towel that Elaine had used. Audrey knew that Elaine kept a clothes basket in the bottom of the bathroom closet. She slowly opened the door.

The towel was right on top of the other clothes. It was soaked with blood. More blood than would have come from the small wound Audrey had seen.

But the bloody towel wasn't what caused Audrey to gasp in horror and shock.

She didn't know what a wolf's paw print looked like, but in her heart she knew that's what she was looking at.

Right there on the doorjamb, beside her hand.

Panic seized her. Her legs buckled, and she staggered backward into the sink. She had only one thought: to get out of the apartment before Elaine came for her.

Though she was terrified to do it, she turned off the light in the bathroom and stepped out into the hallway. Dark shadows lurked in the hallway, particularly at the end of the hall where Elaine's bedroom was. Audrey crept slowly and silently toward the living room, trying to avoid stumbling over anything.

When she heard the deep, menacing growl behind her, she turned.

Elaine was changing.

Her face was impossibly stretched into a long, catlike snout, and she was covered by golden fur, with jet black spots.

As Audrey gaped, Elaine's legs and arms began to twist and bulge and her hands changed into long, four-toed paws. Finally the Elaine-thing dropped to all fours.

When she spoke her voice sounded strange, as if her throat were being compressed. Audrey could barely make out the words.

"Going somewhere, my love?"

"You lied to me!" Audrey screamed. "You've lied to me all along. You are a werewolf."

"I didn't lie," the Elaine-thing said, and her whole body underwent a flowing, elemental change. The only things left of Elaine now were her lips and nose.

"I do have a hormonal condition passed on to me by my grand-mother. She was a shape-shifter too."

She moved out into the dim shadows of the living room and now Audrey could see all of her.

"You see?" The human lips moving in the animal's face were gro-tesque and terrifying. "I am not a werewolf."

Indeed, the last thing Audrey saw as the beast sprang across the room with inhuman grace and speed was the face of Jaguar Woman.

House Built of Sticks

J. L. Belrose

Rose had always been the chief suspect when candy went missing. "Not natural" is how Aunt Ethel described Rose's craving for sweets, reciting to the penny every dentist bill. Jason, I figured, was responsible when Auntie's jade earrings went missing. We all knew how he liked to impress his girlfriends with presents he couldn't afford to buy. But when Uncle Frank digs bones up in the backyard, I have no clues about that.

I'm sitting on the back porch step, lulled by the buzz of bees in the hollyhocks, keeping my legs together like Aunt Ethel says I have to, watching Frank as he jams a spade into the earth and rocks it back and forth to loosen tangles of grass roots before upending hunks of sod into a pile near the hedge. I'm waiting for Rose. Auntie's away, gone for the weekend, visiting her sister Kay in Toronto. Rose seems to know when the coast will be clear and that's when she comes back home to see me.

Frank's digging the goldfish pond Aunt Ethel has been saying for years she wants and he's doing it while she's away to surprise her. I could tell him it's a dumb idea. Auntie knows exactly how she wants things done and he should know that whatever he does won't be right. For starters, she doesn't want it in the back corner beside the hedge. But I don't say anything. He wouldn't listen to me anyway. Nobody figures kids know anything. He's wrong about that too, about me being a kid. I've turned into a woman.

Aunt Ethel says I should keep that a secret, that nice girls don't talk about such things, but I'm busting to tell Rose. And Nicole too, as soon as she gets back from summer camp. Nicole's my best friend. She'll probably tell me I have to prove it, jealous that I've started first when she's almost two years older. She'll have to stop telling me I'm too young to sneak out and hang with her and her other friends at the mall.

The first bone is a small one. "You remember anything about Rosie or Jason burying a dog back here?" Frank asks. I squint at him through the heavy afternoon sun and shake my head. Auntie has never allowed pets in the house; she has enough to do, she claims, keeping the house decent without an animal around making a mess. I've given up begging for a cat. I can't imagine Rose or Jason had ever been allowed to have a dog.

He reaches down, grunting like he always does when he bends over, then straightens up with a bigger bone, like a leg bone, in his hand. "This was farming country," he says to himself more than me. "It's likely a cow, horse maybe, went down and got covered over rather'n hauled off."

"I bet it's a dinosaur," I say and launch myself off the steps. I'm totally into dinosaurs.

Frank squats, grunting, and scratches soil away from what looks like a small gray boulder. I watch as a forehead and eyeholes become visible. Then, like he suddenly remembers I'm there, he turns on me. "You go upstairs," he orders. "You go to your room. Now."

I know not to argue. Not when he uses that voice. I back away a few steps, then turn and bolt across the lawn, up the porch steps, slam through the screen door into the house and vault up the stairs. The window in Jason's old room looks out over the backyard so I go in there and peek through a gap in the curtains. Frank is standing, looking down at the bones like he's never going to move, like he's stiffened with the arthritis and will stand there forever like a scarecrow. Finally, he picks up the spade and refills the hole.

It's dusk before he finishes replacing the chunks of sod, fitting them together like a ragged jigsaw and tramping them into place. The old plaid work shirt he's taken off and used for wiping sweat from his face is draped on the hedge and three empty beer bottles are nestled under the hedge. If he thinks Auntie won't notice the grass all messed and stamped down and the number of bottles gone empty in the beer carton hid under the basement stairs, I could tell him different.

I sit on the landing outside my room, cross-legged behind the polished oak railing, glimpsing him as he washes up, then clatters around in the kitchen below. I hope Rose isn't waiting till Saturday, or even Sunday, to come back. I love Rose more than anyone in the world. She has always looked after me, more like a sister than cousin. Not like my other cousin, Jason, who has never cared whether or not I existed. Rose is beautiful too, except for her teeth. She has black hair and brown eyes that everyone notices. I'm dark-haired too, like Rose, but my hair's more twisty, not smooth and shiny like hers. Jason has brown hair, the same as Aunt Ethel and Uncle Frank.

"You come down here now. Get your supper," Frank shouts.

It's potato salad and cold chicken Auntie has left fixed for us. I'm slid halfway onto my chair when Frank tells me, "I figured out about that fella buried in the backyard. He's an Indian. They had burial grounds all around these parts. You remember those arrowheads Jason used to find in Old Jackson's field? Or was that before you was born? Anyhow, it's best to leave these fellas in peace. In fact, it's the law. It's against the law to disturb old Indian bones. So there's no need to be telling anyone. Talking about it will only wake up the spirits and we don't want that. No sir, we don't want unhappy spirits wandering around. Do you understand?"

I nod. He has the sour, bleary smell of beer on him. Two more empty bottles sit on the counter beside the sink. I'm more afraid of him than of Indian spirits. I right off start planning how Nicole and I will get the spirit to talk to us. I get so busy in my head with what dance and chant we'll do I don't hear Rose until she shouts from the front hall. "Papa? Baby?"

I drop my chicken, not even wiping my hands before I bounce into the hall and into Rose's arms. "My God," she says, hugging me, "every time I see you you've grown. You're going to be tall. Taller even than me."

I want to tell her about the other thing too, about being a woman now, but I can't. Not with Frank coming up behind me. And . . . Rose isn't alone.

"This is Carole," she says. "A very special friend."

I want to ask Carole whether she's a man or a woman. Instead, I just look her over. Her hair is cropped short and she's wearing a blue denim shirt and blue jeans and boots and a black leather belt. I know, without being told, that Aunt Ethel wouldn't approve of Carole. There are things and people Auntie says aren't "normal," and Carole would be one of them.

Frank nods toward her without actually greeting her, then says to Rose, "Come in then. Have you heard from your brother? How he's doing?"

He cares more about Jason than anything else. If Rose notices he doesn't ask her how she's been, she doesn't let on. She places an arm around my shoulders, pulls me against her, and we bump each other into the kitchen.

"My dear brother got himself married last I heard," she says, "and they were headed for Banff with plans for getting into what he called 'the hospitality industry.' I think that means they'll be looking for work in a hotel or restaurant. Let's hope he didn't *borrow* anyone's car to get there."

Frank grunts in reply. He's always taken Jason's side in everything and we all know he's bad hurt that his favorite, his only son, never comes home or even calls. There's a photo on the bookshelf in the living room that shows Frank around Jason's age and a photo of Jason on the wall. Everyone who visits is asked to guess which is which, they're that much alike.

"Sit down," he tells me. "Finish your supper." Then, in a statement like he might say "it's raining" he says to Rose, "You got your teeth fixed."

I focus on her mouth. She smiles like I've never seen her smile before. Her top front teeth are whole and white. "Are those false teeth?" I ask her.

"No, baby. They're my own. They're capped."

Frank says, "That must have cost something."

Her smile shuts down. "If Mom'd had them fixed when I was younger I would have worked, I would have paid her back, every cent," she says.

I decide I don't like Carole. I don't know why Rose has to bother with her so much, moving a chair to the table for her and picking over the chicken, finding her the piece she'll most like. Then I find out Rose isn't even going to sleep with me in our room like she always has. She tells Frank, "Carole and I will use Jason's old room. The bed's bigger and more comfortable than the couch."

I see Frank flick his eyes in my direction in a signal to Rose. I wipe chicken grease and salad dressing off my plate with a crust of bread and pretend I'm not listening. But Rose doesn't let me play dumb. She places her hand on my arm, forcing me to look at her. Her eyes are bare and pleading. "You're old enough to understand, aren't you baby?"

I nod. I want to tell her to send Carole away, but I don't. I like that she's saying I'm old enough to understand. Everyone else treats me like a stupid kid.

I don't get any time alone with Rose. It comes to bedtime and I go without being told, wishing Nicole was home from camp. I imagine ways Carole might die, suddenly and tragically, and how I'd help Frank bury her in the backyard beside the Indian. Then Rose comes quietly into my room. "Laurie, honey," she whispers into the darkness, "Are you still awake?"

We rock in each other's arms. She says, "I miss you so much. I'm settled more now and I want you to come and stay with us sometimes. Would you like that?"

I'm not sure.

"I bled last week," I say.

"What?"

"You know . . . like a woman."

"No. That's not possible. You're too young."

"I'll be twelve soon," I remind her, wondering why she's crying. I scrunch over in bed as she settles in beside me. We snuggle and whisper in the dark like we used to when I was little. "I want so much for you," she tells me and asks about the new school I'll start in the Fall and if I have friends.

When I wake, sun is piercing my lace curtains and I'm alone. I find Rose in the kitchen, at the table with Carole, drinking coffee. She tells me, before I ask, that Uncle Frank has "gone fishing." That means he's gone somewhere, while Auntie's away, to drink beer with people she doesn't approve of. It means I'll have the whole day with Rose . . . and Carole.

After breakfast, Carole asks me, "Wanna toss a ball around?"

I bite my lip. Rose is washing dishes. Reluctantly, I follow Carole to the front veranda and wait as she goes to her car, opens the trunk, and digs out a baseball and a couple of gloves. She motions me to join her on the lawn. The glove's too big. She tosses the ball. I hold my hands out in front of me and shut my eyes. The ball hits me in the shoulder; a dull thud that surprises more than hurts.

"Are you okay?" she asks, rushing toward me. I hear concern in her voice, but her eyes are bewildered.

I adjust my skirt.

"Look, why don't you change? Get some jeans on," she says, "and we'll try this again. It's easy, honest. I'll show you how."

"I don't have jeans."

"You don't? Why not?" She's bewildered again.

"They're not ladylike," I say. This is what Auntie told me when I asked for a pair. Carole herself is wearing jeans so I don't say any more.

She strides to the car and holds the door open. "Come on," she says, "Get in. We'll run out to that mall I saw on the way into town and get you some."

I've been told all about never getting into cars with strangers. I look at Carole and I'm pretty sure she's one of the people I'm not supposed to trust. I back away, then dash for the veranda.

She follows slow and heavy. Rose steps out of the house as if she's been waiting behind the screen door. Carole plops down on the step and says to her, "That went well."

I position myself between them, facing Rose. "I have to tell you something," I say. Her gaze settles on me, but she doesn't answer. "It's private," I say. She doesn't move. I push her back, back toward the house, away from Carole.

She sighs. "I hoped you would understand."

I push her into the house. When we're alone in the hall, I say, "There's an Indian buried in the backyard."

She shakes her head.

"It's true. I saw it."

"Baby, I . . ."

"Have I ever ever lied to you about anything before?" I ask her.

"No . . . but . . ."

"I'll show you." I take her hand and lead her through the kitchen and out the back door and over the lawn to where the grass is trampled and seamed and traces of dark soil lay fresh near the hedge. I tell her the whole story.

"We don't say Indian. They're First Nation people," she tells me, then asks, "And why are you whispering?"

"Because Uncle Frank says talking about it will wake up the spirit."

I see I have her. She's interested more in me now than in Carole. All I have to do is keep talking. I say, "I bet Frank killed him. A long time ago. So long ago he forgot. Frank's not my real uncle anyway. I know that."

I have no idea why I said that. It came out of my mouth from nowhere. What's more surprising is that Rose doesn't argue with me. She stares at me, clouded and quiet, and I know I've stumbled somewhere close to the truth.

"I have a photo that shows Aunt Ethel getting married and it's not Uncle Frank. It's someone else," I tell her. "I've got it hidden upstairs. I'll show you."

She follows me into the house. I hope she won't ask how I came by the photo. I know snooping is a sin, like lying. I only did it because Nicole said I shouldn't believe Aunt Ethel's story about my mother, her youngest sister, leaving me on the front veranda one day, then disappearing. I only went through Auntie's things to see if I could find something, anything, about my parents.

Rose sits on my bed and watches solemnly as I pull my nightstand away from the wall and remove the envelope taped, like I saw in a TV show, to the back. I hand her the old black-and-white photo. In it, Aunt Ethel is posed in a white dress, holding flowers like a bride, and beside her, standing stiffly in a dark suit, is a tall man with very dark hair.

"Ohhh," Rose says and stares at the photo so long without speaking that I get scared. When she goes to the top of the stairs and calls Carole, I don't try to stop her. I know I've caused trouble or pain that's too big now for me to fix.

"Yeah?" Carole answers from below.

"We need you," Rose says, then comes back to me and sits down again on my bed. We listen to Carole's boots clump up the stairs and along the hall.

"God, woman, you look like you've seen a ghost," Carole says as she angles her bulk through my door.

Rose hands her the photo.

"Okay," Carole drawls, as if by stretching the word some brainwave will hit her before she's finished. It doesn't. "And what am I supposed to be seeing?" she asks.

"That's Mom," Rose says, "and maybe . . . my father."

Carole looks at Rose, then back to the photo. "Yeah," she says, "could be. There's some resemblance."

"She never told me. She let me grow up, all my life, thinking Papa . . . thinking Frank . . . was my father."

"Well, we don't really know, do we? Do you remember anything?"

"I'm not sure. As soon as I saw him, saw the photo, I thought I remembered, but I don't know. It's a memory, or memories, but they're all mixed up. I'm not sure what they mean."

"How old do you think you were?"

"Jason's five years younger than me and he's for sure Frank's son. If I do remember anything about this man in the photo, it would have to be from when I was four maybe or younger."

"Okay," Carole says in a take-charge voice. "When Frank comes home, ask him. Or we can stay until Ethel gets home, then you can ask her."

"No!" darts from my mouth.

"It's okay, baby," Rose soothes. "We won't say anything that gets you in trouble. I'll say I was cleaning or looking for keys or something and found the photo."

She takes a breath before she tells Carole, "There's something else. Laurie says there's a body buried in the backyard."

Carole lifts her eyebrows ready to laugh. Then she sees we're serious. She plonks her weight down on my small bedside chair, spreads her legs, and fastens her hands onto her knees and leans forward as if she realizes that talking sense into us is going to be a big job.

"It's bones," I say before she starts. "Not a body."

"I believe her," Rose says. "Laurie has never lied to me."

Carole leans back. "So you're thinking if somebody's been buried in the backyard, that it might be the guy in the photo, who's maybe your father? Correct?"

We don't answer. We just look at her.

"Whoa!" she says, lifting her thick hands, palms out in a stop sign toward Rose. "You're not going to suggest that I dig up the backyard now, are you?"

"Of course not," Rose answers, not even faintly amused. "We have to think what's the best way to handle this. We have to think about Laurie."

"Okay. Is there any reason we can't go get a hamburger and fries and think about it there?" Carole asks and claps her hands.

I'm looking at Rose and not expecting the noise. It startles me. Rose grabs me and hugs me, almost hauling me off my feet. "Hey," she says. "Doesn't that sound good? And ice cream?" Her voice is too brittle.

We descend the stairs, Carole first, Rose holding my hand. The stairs complain, like the walls sometimes do, even when it's not windy. Wood gasping to wood.

Carole heads for the car, but Rose stops her. "We can walk. This is a small town, remember? Just a five-minute stroll to the one and only main street. Then ten minutes one way and ten minutes the other. Supermarket at one end, hamburger place at the other end, four churches in between, and a cineplex in the middle."

"Thought we'd hit that mall outside town."

"Naw, I want to do the main street. I like reminding myself what I ran away from. And, anyhow, it'll let me show off my new teeth to people I grew up with."

I stay beside Rose which means, with the sidewalk narrowed in places and its old concrete heaved by a line of ancient maples, Carole has to walk alone, either ahead or behind. "These are big old places," she says about the houses with turrets and wraparound verandas. She pays for lunch, encourages us to get anything we want—both onion rings and fries, milkshakes and Cokes, nuggets and burgers—and doesn't complain when we can't eat it all. I know what they're doing. They're trying to make me forget about the bones and how much trouble I'm in because I've broken the most important rule in the house, the one about staying quiet and keeping secrets.

"How about a movie?" Carole asks me. "I think I saw *Spy Kids* was on."

"They're stupid," I say.

"Okay. What do you like?"

"Dinosaurs."

"Well, you're in luck. That was the other thing on."

By the time we get home, I have a bunch of dinosaur stickers from Carole and a book to put them in and I think I know why Rose likes her. Nothing makes her mad. Rose sits with me at the round oak table after dinner and reads out the descriptions from the book while I find the matching stickers. It's designed so you have to learn all the names and different species.

When Frank comes in he's tired and cranky and smells of beer. "You get upstairs to bed," he tells me.

He stumbles into the living room where Carole's watching TV, asks her who's playing, then sprawls on the couch. By the time I've got my stickers gathered and am climbing the stairs with my book, he's already snoring.

I can't sleep. My window's wide open but there's no air moving. I hear a murmur of voices outside and know that, down under my window, Rose and Carole are sitting on the veranda, talking. I pull aside my lace curtain and press my ear against the screen, but still can't make out any of their words.

I tiptoe to the top of the stairs. Frank's snores spread hollowly through the dark house. I sneak down step by step, out the back door, around the side of the house and then, slowly and silently spreading branches, pry my way into the bushes beside the veranda. I squat in the corner the veranda foundation forms with the house and pull my nightgown forward up between my legs to protect my privates from crawlers. A mosquito whines lazily around my head. I brush it away, afraid that swatting will make too much noise. I'm almost afraid to breathe in case they hear me.

"So what time do you want to leave tomorrow?" Carole asks.

"The first bus Mom might be on comes in at ten twenty so we should clear out by ten at the latest."

"Are you sure you don't want to wait and talk to her?"

"I'm sure."

I let my bum ease down until I'm sitting on the cool soil. Looking up, I see Carole's arm stretched along the veranda railing. She must be sitting on the bent-twig loveseat. Rose might be squeezed in beside her.

"I have to tell her," Rose says.

"Who? Laurie?"

"Yes. She wants to know. She's snooping around trying to find out. That's why she found the photo. She has a right to know. It's been wrong, all these years. Mom wouldn't let it be any other way, but I shouldn't have let her control me. I should have done things different for Laurie."

"You've done the best you knew how. Don't beat yourself up over it all."

"But it's wrong. It's wrong the way Laurie's being brought up."

"You turned out okay."

"But look how long it took me. It was hard. You don't know how hard it was to get away, to get some self-esteem, to open up to love someone. I don't want Laurie to go through that kind of pain and struggle."

"So tell her."

"I don't know how."

"You'll find the words."

"What do I say? 'Laurie, honey, when I was thirteen I wanted so badly to be loved and have friends that I let the first boy that paid attention to me have sex with me.'"

"No. You say, 'Laurie, honey, I'm your mother and it doesn't matter how or why. All that matters is that I love you and I've always loved you.'"

Rose? My mother? I know that can't be true. She isn't my mother. I don't understand why they're saying things that can't be true. Unless it's some kind of game they play with each other. It's a stupid game. They're stupid.

I hear Rose say, "She'll hate me," and I feel it happening. I do hate her. I hate her because she plays stupid games with Carole.

I crawl through the bushes not caring if they scratch. As soon as I'm around the side of the house I stand up and run to the back, in and up the stairs to my room. Frank's still snoring, but I don't care if he wakes up and sees me. I don't care about anything. I yank the blanket up from the foot of the bed and pull it over my head. If I suffocate and die from the heat, then they'll be sorry. I cry myself to sleep and then it's morning and Rose is sitting beside me on the bed. "Come on sleepy puss," she says. "Time to shine."

I pull away from her.

"Are you okay, baby?" she asks. "Do you feel warm?"

She reaches to touch my forehead, but I pull away again.

She looks puzzled. She says, "I want to talk to you about something."

"I don't want to talk," I say.

She's quiet a moment, then says, "You don't have to worry about anything here. I'm fixing it so you can come and stay with me and Carole. Would you like that?"

"No, I don't want to."

I roll away so my back's to her and pull the sheet up to my mouth.

"Is it your tummy? Too much junk food yesterday? Do you feel sick?"

I don't answer.

She sighs, then finally gets up and leaves my room. I decide to stay upstairs and watch from my window until I see them drive away. But, before that happens, Frank calls me down for my breakfast.

I'm two stairs from the bottom when I hear his voice in the kitchen. "What difference does it make?" he's asking like he feels hard done by. "I brung you up, didn't I? Right from when I met up with your mother and you were a little thing. Not many men would take that on with this old place, damn roof leaking and all that needed fixing. I treated you like my own, didn't I?"

"What difference!" Rose slings back at him. "I would have liked to know who my father was. My God, was that too much to ask?"

"And what good would it have done ya? He left you didn't he? You and your mother. He up and took off."

I can tell by the injured sound in his voice that he won't take much more from Rose. But she doesn't let go. She asks, "And how do you explain what you found out back? What about that?"

He doesn't answer. I'm afraid the silence means he's coming to look for me. Rose promised she wouldn't get me in trouble, but she's done it. He'll know it's me who told her about the bones. I expect him to yell for me, but all he finally says is, "Don't know nothing about that," and then it's quiet again.

Carole opens the front screen door from the outside and reaches in for the suitcase sitting in the hall. She sees me and starts to say something, so I move fast into the kitchen. There's a bowl of cereal set out for me on the table. I go straight to it, figuring no one will bother me if I'm sitting quiet eating my breakfast.

Frank is holding the photo and glancing and wavering around like he doesn't know what to do with it. Rose takes it away from him. Her voice is flat when she asks, "What was his name? Can you at least tell me that?"

"Ethel never wanted to talk about that time. There was things she wanted to forget and it was none of my business. No sir, none of my business," he says, scratching his stomach like he does when he's lying about his friends and what they do.

Rose shakes her head. It seems to make her whole body slump. She turns away from him, then swivels back to ask, "You're going to make that call though, right?"

Frank just grunts. That means the conversation is over and he's not going to talk anymore no matter what.

I stare down at my cereal as Rose comes toward me. "I'll be back real soon," she says to me.

I nod without looking up.

She kisses the top of my head from behind, rubs my shoulder, then takes off down the hall. The screen door bangs. I hear Carole ask, "Isn't Laurie coming?"

"She doesn't want to."

"Sure you don't want to stay?"

"I can't. She'll be okay."

"Right then. Let's get the show on the road."

I finish my cereal, tip the bowl up and drink the milk, already sorry I've been so mean to Rose. I run to the door thinking that maybe, just maybe, the car's still there, that maybe they've waited for me. But it's gone.

"Can I go over to Nicole's?" I ask Frank.

He stops thumbing through the phone book long enough to say, "She's away. You know that."

"Maybe she's home early," I say.

He's busy again and doesn't answer. The silence means I can do anything I want as long as I'm not bothering him. I change my mind about going to Nicole's. I go up to my room instead and work on my dinosaur book. Soon, too soon, Aunt Ethel's voice crackles through the house.

"I'm never going back there again. The woman's an imbecile. My own sister, a complete imbecile. Frank! What's this mess here then? Has this floor never been swept since I left? Laura! Where're you at? Laura!"

I follow the shiny oak banister down the stairs. She's in the kitchen. She hasn't been in Jason's room yet, hasn't found his bed used and soiled. And she hasn't been in the backyard yet, hasn't seen the grass hacked up. All that trouble is still to come.

"There you are," she says. "Don't just stand there dumber than a post. Bring the bag in off the veranda. It wouldn't have hurt you none to meet me at the bus, help carry a few things. Aunt Kay sent some cookies for you, although why I didn't just dump them I don't know. She's never been much of a cook. Frank! Where's that man at? Frank?"

I go to get the bag and see the cop car parked out front. Two cops are coming up our walk. One smiles at me. I back up. I'm halfway back down the hall toward the kitchen when Auntie sees me. "Laura! I told you to get that bag. I swear you get more useless every day."

The screen door rattles as the cop taps. Auntie squints past me up the hall, sees who it is and puts on her pleasant outside face. "Oh Robbie, is that you? You're Claire's son aren't you?" she asks, bustling to the door.

"This is business, Mrs. Duncan."

"What's it about then?" she asks.

I sidle backward up a few stairs, then stop and sit down, keeping my knees together like I'm supposed to and pulling my skirt down around my legs. The cop that smiled glances at me, then says, "Let's do this outside. Just a few questions, Mrs. Duncan. It might be easier if we go to the car."

"Oh, all right then. Morris up the street hasn't been complaining about that tree again, has he?" Auntie asks as she steps outside.

I scoot to my room and watch from my window. I see Auntie out by the cop car get more and more agitated as the cops talk to her. When Uncle Frank appears from around the back, she forgets she's outside where neighbors might hear and she yells at him. "Is this the thanks I get? Looking after you all these years, is this the thanks I get?" Her face is red. She looks like she wants to kill him. I'm some glad she's mad at him and not me.

One cop opens the back door of the cruiser and the other one guides her into the seat, shuts the door on her and stands there, his back to the door, arms crossed over his chest. The first cop goes to the trunk and lifts out a roll of yellow tape. He follows Uncle Frank to the side of the house. I rush into Jason's old room and look out his window in time to see Frank show the cop where the bones are buried. The cop ties one end of his tape around the mountain ash beside the shed, stretches it over to the hedge, down along the hedge, and back across to the tree, circling the burial place. The black letters on the yellow tape say POLICE LINE DO NOT CROSS.

I wish Nicole was home. I have so much to tell her. When I look out front again, the cops are gone. I listen for clues about what might be happening downstairs but the house is eerily silent. I edge down the stairs, one step at a time, until I see Uncle Frank sitting at the kitchen table, his head in his hands. I wait until I'm sure we're alone and he's not going to bother with me, then I get the bag from the veranda, find the package of cookies from Aunt Kay and pour myself some milk. They're chocolate chip, my favorite, better than the ones Aunt Ethel makes because there's more chocolate. I wish I had someone to talk to. I wish things were like they used to be before Rose left home and met Carole and got so stupid with her.

I go back upstairs but, even with my dinosaur book, I'm bored. Then, through my window, I see Carole's car pull up out front and park. I wait for Rose to come in and find me.

"Hi," she says. "You know, don't you? We think you might have done some eavesdropping last night and heard us talking. Did you?"

I nod.

She flops down on my bed. "I guess you're kind of disappointed, huh?"

I don't know what to say.

She says, "You showed me a picture in a magazine once and said it was your mother. The woman in the picture was very beautiful and she looked rich. I'm sorry, baby. I'm sorry it didn't turn out the way you dreamed it would."

I shrug. I'm getting more used to the idea of Rose being my mother. It doesn't seem so bad. "They took Auntie away," I say. "I think she's in jail."

"No, she's just being held for questioning right now."

"About the bones?"

"Yes, and we want you to come away with us before she gets back. Carole and I love each other and we want you to be part of our family. She'll be a good friend to you, if you let her. All you have to do is meet her halfway. Please. Won't you just give us a chance?"

She swings her legs off the bed and opens the shopping bag she's brought. She pulls out a pair of jeans. "We went to the mall and got these for you. I hope they fit. Try them on. Let's see."

The material feels stiff in my hands and strange on my legs. They're a bit big, but to me they're perfect. Then she takes a T-shirt out of the bag. "Carole chose this for you. Come on. Put it on."

It's pink and the silver glitter across the front says 100 PERCENT ANGEL.

She gives me a huge smile. "Go to the mirror. Look at yourself," she says. "No, wait." She picks up my brush and runs it through my hair, lifting and fluffing. "Now," she says. "Look at you."

I don't believe what I see. I look like someone else. Like someone in a magazine. Like the girls at school who are so pretty I can never say hello or anything. I can't stop looking at myself. Then I remember what Auntie says about pride and conceit, and turn away from the mirror. Auntie says pride is a sin. It cometh before a fall. With your head full of nonsense and your nose in the air, you don't see Satan's open pit in front of you until you've stepped off into hell.

"There's something else I think you'll like," Rose says. "We've got a cat. He's black and white and his name is Sock'em. I think we could talk Carole into getting a kitten. She had two cats but the older one got sick last year and died. I'm sure she'd let you pick the kitten and name it."

"Really?" I can't conceal my excitement. I'll do anything in the world for a kitten. Rose puts some of my socks and undies into the bag the jeans were in. I gather my dinosaur stuff and we're ready.

Rose stops as we pass the kitchen. Frank is still at the table. He hasn't moved. She says, "I'm leaving now, Papa. I'm taking Laurie."

He doesn't answer.

She goes to him. She places her hand on the back of the empty chair beside him as if she's going to pull it out and sit down, but she doesn't. She moves her hand to his shoulder. "You did the right thing," she tells him. "Thanks for helping us."

"Get out of here," he says. "Don't come back."

We're at the door before I hear him say, "Take care of yourselves."

I look into her face, expecting her to answer, but she doesn't. Instead, she winks at me and says, "Come on, kid. Let's get this show on the road."

Never Drop By

Diana McRae

Never drop by. Sane clients who need a private investigator call ahead. Only the bereft, the bipolar, and the bedraggled burst through the door of my private investigation firm and shout, "Can you help me?" Unlike nurses, therapists, and librarians, I never meant to go into a helping profession. I pictured myself fighting for truth and justice, a beacon of light in the murky netherworld of depraved criminal minds. Also, I wanted to earn decent money without getting bored. The money part doesn't always work out because I'm snobbish about what I do and don't do. If I wanted to do surveillance for major corporations or deliver subpoenas I'd be well-heeled, but I abstain unless I'm hard up.

I've acquired a reputation for taking quirky cases and my reputation now precedes me. My firm, Eliza Pirex Investigations—motto All the Muscle You Need—employs only me. I don't work well with others except for my long-time best friend Dennis and I even have reservations about him. Dennis suffers from sporadic despair; he wallows in dark waters. This condition goes with the territory, as any private investigator will tell you, but lately, he's been adding scotch to the water and that's not good.

Monday April 15th, tax day, I mail late hoping to avoid an audit. A client bursts through my door. She looks bereft, bedraggled, and, from her obvious state of serious agitation, possibly bipolar. I judge from her attire, Doc Martens and a flannel shirt, that she could be a Berkeley lesbian. If so, she hasn't been to the hairdresser in so long that people could mistake her for straight. Long, flyaway blonde hair streams in the wind. She wears no coat.

"Could you close the door?" I ask.

"Can you help me?" she exclaims and commences crying. I set about guessing her dilemma. Lost cat? Lost lover, wants her back? Lost her mind and believes self to be pursued by government agents? Lost on way to hairdresser and needs directions?

"I'm Eliza Pirex," I venture.

"I know. Amanda Corey," she returns, holding out her hand like an automaton. I shake the dead weight of her fingers.

"What can I do for you?" I ask, attempting to sound sprightly while passing her a box of Kleenex. I never know what to do when someone, other than one of my children, cries in front of me. The offer of tissue seems to help in this case.

"Lost something?" I inquire, in an effort to speed the interview along. Bad question. She sobs louder.

"Lost someone?" I inquire with sympathy. She nods. Oh, dear. Not that I'm squeamish but I try to stay away from lovers' quarrels. I don't enjoy tracking down and then meeting up with the person who went out for a pack of cigarettes and didn't come back. They're never nice to me. Never.

"Don't you think she, or he, will give you a buzz soon? You guys clearly have feelings for each other."

This suggestion stops her cold. She stares at me, innocent eyes filled with unshed tears. Little gasps issue forth.

"Where do you think she, or he, might have gone?" I ask, now aiming to sound uninvolved and practical.

"I don't know," she whispers. "I'm not religious."

"Pardon me," I say. I adopted this phrase from my ex-lover, Honor, who employs any number of near-meaningless politeisms. I find them useful beyond measure in just this sort of situation. I owe Honor a lot, this debt being the least.

"I don't have any conception of where people go when they die," my companion announces in a more resounding tone. "I'm into Native American spirituality but I just can't believe in the afterlife or in spirits going on. I can't help thinking that when you die, you might just be dead." Tears begin rolling down her cheeks again.

Death. I know how to handle death. For one thing, dead people never give you any aggravation. For another, I have to admit I'm callous enough to get excited. In my profession, the juicy cases involve a death. You've read Agatha Christie. The police close the case, calling the death a suicide. You prove that a seemingly innocuous cousin, hoping to inherit, planned a diabolical murder. He soaked the stew meat in yew berry juice. The suicide note was faked. He cracks and confesses when you present him with your findings. Drama on the grand scale.

"My family is religious to the point of fanaticism," my would-be client interjects. "I think their true-believer stuff pushed me in the opposite direction." She weeps again, out of grief or spiritual bankruptcy, I don't know which.

"Tell me what happened."

"We're the pits," she begins.

"Pardon me?" I say again and bite my tongue.

"I'm with a band called The Pits," she explains, sounding a bit wounded that I didn't recognize the name. "Because we don't shave them."

"Don't shave your—" I flounder.

"Pits," she replies with a sigh as if distracted from her troubles by how slow I am on the uptake.

"I'll have to catch your act some time," I tell her. I don't mind body hair on a performer.

"Thanks," she responds, mollified. Actors and singers probably appreciate a potential ticket buyer even in times of duress.

"May I ask who died?" I ask with due solemnity. Her patchy-green eyes fill with tears but she keeps her emotions under a tight rein this time.

"Kayla Cook, our drummer. She's been my best friend since kindergarten. The band is made up of Kayla, me, and Jennifer Waters. Kayla has been lovers with Jennifer since high school. They live— lived—in the guesthouse behind Kayla's parents' house."

"How did Kayla die?"

"The cabin behind the Cook house burned yesterday night. They found Kayla's body inside the wreckage. The coroner couldn't identify her at first. Her flesh burned away. Her jewelry, and Jennifer's, melted." A stifled moan escapes my client.

I marshal my professional reserve. If someone has to die, I'd rather that person not be a lesbian musician; it's too close to home. I swallow. I sometimes cry when other people cry but I try not to cry on the job.

"I'm sorry," I tell her. I really am sorry but I need to know why she's here. Is this a suspicious death? "What brings you here? Is there something that you want to investigate in relation to your friend's death? The police department's arson investigators are really good at their jobs. I can't duplicate their work. I don't have the resources."

"I think someone murdered Kayla," Amanda tells me. I had not expected this revelation. Amanda proceeds. "I need to know who killed her and why. I know they're going to find out that the fire was started intentionally but I don't trust the police to figure out that the fire was set to kill Kayla."

"What makes you think her death was a homicide?" I ask. I surreptitiously press the record key on the small device on my desktop designed for this purpose. Picking up a Dixon Ticonderoga pencil and pad, I set about taking notes, to look like I'm being thorough.

"The three of us, me and Kayla and Jennifer, are careful above and beyond the call of duty. We stay at cheap motels and we play crowded older buildings so we're paranoid about fire hazards. Jenn and Kayla had two smoke detectors and a carbon monoxide detector in their one-bedroom cottage. I'd believe that one detector malfunctioned but not three. The police asked if Kayla drank or did drugs. They assume she must have been unconscious when she died. Well, she didn't use anything. We sing to women about healthy living and we live what we preach." Amanda takes a deep, cleansing breath. "As for why I think someone killed her, that's easy. A whole bunch of people wanted to get rid of her." The young woman's eyes widen and flood with green tears.

"Who?" I inquire, startled again. Death can provoke all sorts of delusions. Still, Amanda speaks with what seems like convincing sanity despite her story of arson and murder. If she spoke like most of the crazies who drop by on a whim, I'd ignore her accusations against party or parties unknown, but instead I listen.

"Kayla's family, the Cooks, and their cult-member friends resented her existence. They wanted Kayla and Jennifer out of the cabin so they could use the place to host committee meetings."

"They would kill their daughter to free up a guest cottage?" I ask, shaking my head.

"You know Berkeley rent control. That would be the only way to evict your tenants if they're relatives. Also, Kayla's relationship with her parents and brother had become complicated. Their cult, The New Bay Area Bible Revivalists, denounces homosexuality. Most of the group doesn't know about the Cooks' lesbian daughter out in the backyard, behind the oak tree. It wouldn't go over well. My parents have joined the cult too. It's scary."

"I see," I tell her. "Think carefully. Is one of the Cooks, or one of the cult members, crazy enough to incinerate another human being?"

"I don't know. I think so, but the police told me I'm distraught over losing my friend. They say the fire was probably of 'unexplained origin' and Kayla's death an accident. They're going to test her bones to see if they reflect any prolonged drug use that would explain her failure to awaken. It's like she's on trial for burning to death." She draws a shuddering breath, brushing back her fine, straw-colored hair with long artistic fingers. "The police detective acted like I must be crazy to suspect the Cooks of having something to do with the fire. The Cooks have a hundred alibis for the time the fire broke out because they were attending a Bible meeting across town. Every fanatic at the gathering remembers seeing them, hearing them speak, or observing them in prayer. Mr. Cook started speaking in tongues. Very showy. The NBABRs think he was speaking ancient Hebrew. I bet he just started babbling Romanian and they didn't know the difference. He was an associate professor of Romanian at Cal Berkeley before he became a full-time zealot."

"How do you figure they set the fire in between speaking in tongues and praying and all?" I question her.

"I don't know," Amanda admits.

"Where was Kayla's partner, Jennifer?" I ask. The book on murder is that the spouse did it, so I have to ask. Amanda doesn't miss the implication, her green eyes go gray, but she supplies the answer without hesitation.

"Jennifer had been asked to speak at the Cooks' meeting that night to debate with the members about homosexual lifestyles. So, she can provide an alibi for them and the whole cult can provide an alibi for her. They jeered and heckled Jenn until she almost broke down. Jenn has a way with words, though. She asked the group to consider whether she might not be God's vessel come to save their souls but they still didn't listen. By the time Jenn got home, Kayla had been pronounced dead. Jenn's doctor has put her on medication, that's why she asked me to come see you alone. I have to speak with the Berkeley police after this, but Jenn's staying at my apartment if you'd like to talk with her."

"Is she well enough?"

"You're on our side, right? You believe Kayla might have been murdered? Jenn will be glad to see you."

I hope so. As a member of the non–warm-and-fuzzy element of the human race, I don't go out of my way to visit the newly bereaved. Professionalism, however, demands that I descend upon poor Jennifer Waters in this case and right away. I hope that the flames of tragedy haven't damped down her way with words.

Forty-five minutes later, Jennifer Waters meets me in a terry cloth bathrobe and asks to be called Jenn. She looks just like a Berkeley lesbian should—short, brown hair and brilliant blue eyes, definite-looking despite the pink at the tip of the nose from crying. If she's medicated, she wears it well. My condolences, by their very nature, fall short, but she accepts them. She motions me back into a large, sunny kitchen. "Kayla should be in Costa Rica," she murmurs, gliding over to pick up her cup of tea. "I don't know why she never took off on the plane."

"Why was she going to Costa Rica?"

"A consortium of environmental groups invited us, The Pits, to perform at a benefit. We couldn't afford for all of us to go so we decided that Kayla would represent the group. She sings—sang—the lead in most of our best numbers."

"Was she traveling with anyone?" I ask.

"No. I took her to the airport. I waited at the gate until they boarded her row. I kissed her good-bye and handed over her carry-on luggage and guitar. Then, I left for the NBABR gathering. When I heard about the fire, I thanked God that Kayla wasn't home. I never wanted her to go, for selfish reasons. We've barely spent a night apart since we met. I can't sleep without her." Jennifer's gleaming eyes fill with tears but she takes a deep breath and sits. I pull up a kitchen chair beside her.

"What might have caused her to get off the plane?" I ask, leaping to the salient issue while trying to overlook her distress.

"I have no idea." Jennifer shakes her head, brow furrowed in grief and mystification. "I saw her starting down the runway to the plane. She'd scheduled only one hour on the other end to get to the hall where she'd be performing. No way would she decide to take another flight and, if she did, she would have called me on my cell phone right away. I can't believe she's really dead and I don't believe she would have left the plane on her own."

"You can't be suggesting that someone kidnapped her off a loaded plane, an international flight surrounded by airport security? Even if that were the case, would the kidnapper take her to her own house to kill her and then set fire to the place? That doesn't make sense."

"The Cooks hate us," says Jennifer, her words deadly simple. "I don't know how they managed to stage the killing and the fire but I know they're behind Kayla's death. Can you prove how Kayla died, Eliza? I feel strangled. I need an explanation." She reaches over and takes my hand, her palm dry and her grip firm.

"I'll try to figure this out," I tell her. Amanda had been right; this young woman's words compelled me somehow. "I'll start with the Cooks and go from there. Will they see me voluntarily or do I have to spring myself on them?"

"I still have a lease on the property in the backyard," replies Jenn after considering my question. "I'm entitled to ask you to go back and check what remains there. The Cooks will come out to see what you're doing. Maybe you can get the information you need before they decide they hate you. Nothing personal, Eliza. They hate almost everybody, and gay people most of all."

On my way back to the front door, I glance out the window over the kitchen sink. Far away, a crescent of the San Francisco Bay shimmers, azure blue today. A sucker for a bay view, I trip on something as I pass the kitchen island in the center of the room. My foot lands in a puddle of slurped-upon water. Although I manage to land on my feet, a terrible roar follows and I throw up my hands to shield my face against whatever demon from hell might be hurtling toward me. Although I feel like a fool, the stolid gumshoe cowering under attack, I fear the boogey-monster that yanked Kayla off the plane and burned her to death will come for me.

"Woof," barks the monster. A dog. A bristly maned creature with a spiked collar faces me, angry that I spilled his water bowl. When I back away, I kick his food bowl and that doesn't help. "Grrrrrr," I hear. I can almost see the printed words coming out of his mouth like in a cartoon dog.

"Jenn," I call. I try to sound like a macho detective while praying that the dog's teeth don't sink into my calf. "Does this guy bite?"

"Never," says Jenn, running to the dog and grabbing his collar. "This is Peaches, our mascot. He's used to living at the cottage so he's out of sorts, and he's half rottweiler so you need to show him that you're boss." She takes the dog's ruff and presses him to the floor, ordering, "Down, Peaches," in a voice that brooks no disobedience.

Dog people possess a superior kind of authority, I reflect as Peaches lies down on the floor, panting submissively and gazing at Jennifer with adoration.

"Where was Peaches when the cabin burned?" I ask Jennifer.

"Peaches would have been inside the cottage, but he got loose somehow. I'm thankful that he at least was spared. The city's animal control people picked him up blocks from home, wild-eyed and freaked out. He's fine now, though."

"Was he Kayla's dog?"

"No. Kayla was a cat person. She put up with Peaches because Amanda and I are crazy about him. Kayla's family, the Cooks, love him to pieces too. I own him but the Cooks try to win him over. They lure him to their back door with raw meat. We're vegetarians. I think the real reason they never actually forced us out of the cabin is they didn't want to lose Peaches. Typical, huh? They reject their daughter, and every other gay person in the world, but they love the dog."

I bend down to pet the animal and he growls at me again. I put the hand in my pocket for protection. Peaches eyes me with malicious intent but doesn't dare make a move with his pack leader present.

"I'll go interview the Cooks," I tell Jennifer. "Once again, I'm very sorry for your loss. I hope I'm able to give you a full account of what happened to Kayla."

Jennifer nods, her face a picture of mute agony. Bending down, she strokes her dog for comfort.

Wending my way back through a living room sculpture garden composed of guitar stands and drum sets, I leave the surviving spouse. I hope the dog knows grief-counseling techniques. Most dogs do.

At first sight, Lila and Gene Cook look too Berkeley to be fundamentalist Christians. They wear old jeans and T-shirts. Only if you look close and see that the shirts read JESUS LIVES and WE'RE TOO BLESSED TO BE DEPRESSED would you realize that they probably aren't proponents of midwifery and public television. A light sweat breaks out, turning my palms slick.

"How's Peaches?" they demand when I tell them I've come from Amanda's place. Asking after the dog and not their daughter's partner strikes me as crass but I assure them that the dog looked fine.

They give me endless names of good Christian believers who can account for their whereabouts and their son's before, during, and after the fire and their daughter's death. They squeeze out some sniffles and clearings of the throat over their daughter's passing, which makes me view them a little more kindly. I ask if their adult son, Sean, can join us, and they tell me he's upstairs, prostrate with grief over his sister's terrible demise.

"And he's upset about Peaches moving over to that woman's house, that Amanda Corey," Lila adds. Her voice turns to a thin nasty whisper. "She's just as wicked as the other two." Lila's next sniff is censorious. There's a weird disconnect here. She seems to forget she's condemning her own dead child.

Gene continues for her. "We count ourselves lucky that one of our children walks the path of righteousness. Sean has never given us a moment of grief. Kayla never brought us anything but pain and humiliation, may she rest in peace."

I quiz them about what might have caused their daughter to exit the plane she'd boarded, but that seems to be a dead end. Kayla didn't even tell her parents she'd be out of town. Jennifer, after all, had remained in residence to take care of the dog, and Peaches' board and care would have been their only concern.

"What we really liked was when the whole damn band went on the road," interjects Gene Cook. "Excuse my language—I don't know what came over me. Anyway, they took good care of Peaches but we liked a chance to have him to ourselves. I bought that dog the best sirloin that Ernie's Butchers carries. The fat content in that stuff is nearly zero. You'd live forever if you ate nothing but that grade of ground meat every day."

I don't have the heart to point out that you'd become malnourished if you ate only fatless sirloin. Peaches' popularity starts to rankle. I stand in preparation for departure.

"I hope I'll be able to bring you some peace of mind by telling you what happened in Kayla's last hours," I tell them, and they nod. They don't appear overly concerned with how their daughter met her end, one way or the other. Poor Kayla! Living out there with only a 200-year-old oak to screen her from the eyes of a family who valued her far less than a dog!

Before I can leave, the hinges of a heavy door squeak and whine. A rumpled young man with dark stubble, who I presume to be Saint Sean, emerges from a bedroom door that opens into the dining room. His parents rush toward him with solicitude.

"Sean, darling, this lady will be investigating the cabin burning. Go get a mug of the good strong coffee I just made and then tell her everything about yesterday night."

Sean looks less than thrilled to find me in his home even though he doesn't know who I'm working for. I give him my credentials and wouldn't you know it? He still doesn't look thrilled.

"Jennifer Waters tells me that she put your sister on a plane to Costa Rica yesterday at SFO. Can you think of any reason that your sister would leave the plane and come back here?"

"No," answered Sean. "She forfeited the money for her ticket if she took her seat and then got off."

So, he knows something.

"You're sure about the airline's policy?"

"Sure. Kayla told me herself."

"Couldn't she get a refund if it was an emergency?" I press. Careful, I tell myself. A few more sips of coffee and he'll realize how much he doesn't like me.

"Your lover's dog acting sick does not constitute an emergency by airline standards," Sean states.

He blundered into revealing that easily. Reciting Bible passages and singing hymns have perhaps taken the edge off any natural mental agility.

"Was Peaches sick last night?" I press right away. "And if Kayla got off the plane to take care of the dog, how did you know?"

Sean looks pale with dismay and his parents turn to him in shock.

"Peaches sick?" cries Lila.

"Peaches turned out to be fine, Ma," says Sean. "I stopped by home last night to change clothes. I spilled Coca-Cola on my robe and pants. I didn't want to go up to the podium wet. When I got here, Peaches kept running around in circles and growling. He had foam on his mouth like a mad dog. I was so scared I called Sis on her cell phone. She was sitting on the plane but she got my call." He stops, and shakes his head patronizingly. "She should've turned off the phone on the plane but she never did play by the rules."

"Did you see your sister when she got back from the airport?" I ask. His face assumes a shifty appearance and I know he will lie to me.

"No. I had to leave right away. That's why I called Kayla. At first, she didn't want to come home at all. She didn't care much about Peaches. But I told her the dog had signs of rabies so she promised to check it out. It wasn't kindness to animals that brought her back. It was her feelings for That Woman, Jennifer. Jennifer was the one who really cared about Peaches." This guy might be stingier of spirit than his parents, if that were possible.

"You didn't try calling Jennifer from the church?" I ask.

"I did, but she didn't answer her cell and no one could find her. She disappeared for a while before she spoke. Then, she didn't do a good job winning over the congregation when she did show up. Our group knows the Bible inside and out. They quoted scripture to prove her wrong." His expression grew ever more pious and prim. "I gave her one of the old editions of our Bible with gold embossing on the cover and she left the Good Book in the men's bathroom of our church, on the back of the toilet!"

"What did you do with the dog after contacting Kayla?" I ask, choking back an inappropriate laugh. "Surely, you didn't leave that noble animal alone in a state of agitation."

"I couldn't help it!" Sean protests. "Amanda Corey wasn't home. For all I know," his furtive glance returned to my face, "Amanda's not so sorry to lose Kayla. Amanda gets to have Peaches at her house, not to mention getting a promotion to lead singer of The Pits. Kayla had it all, a career and a great dog."

I study him up close to make sure that his words aren't meant to be facetious. They aren't.

"If it doesn't turn out to be an accident, I suppose you think Jennifer or Amanda must have set the fire?" Gene says to me. "Since Jennifer had the opportunity in the interval before she spoke and Amanda had such good motives."

"How would Jennifer benefit from Kayla's death?" I inquire, puzzled. I refused to dignify the idea of Amanda as a suspect by repeating it.

"Renter's insurance," Lila answers, quickly, as if they'd prepared the answer.

"Did the forensics' guys test Jennifer's hands for traces of any flammable agent?" I ask.

"Was that what they were doing?" he asks. "They tested her, us, and Amanda. How soon do the results get back?"

"I'm not sure," I admit. "Soon, in this case."

The whole group looks uneasy. What do they know or suspect? "Anything you want to tell me?" I ask. They don't look terribly hostile. They've bonded with me in the strange fashion that people attach themselves to any sympathetic-seeming person when they've undergone a tragedy. Newspaper reporters, ministers, union reps, counselors, those who do this professionally use the bond to guide the bereaved to the shoals of hope. I want to guide this group to an island of honesty, despite the misguided trajectory of their lives.

"We held lighted candles at the meeting last night," says Lila. "Could that make the police think we lit the cabin on fire? We would never damage that place. We loved that little cabin and hoped to get those girls out. Besides, we wouldn't have risked Peaches getting trapped in a fire and injuring himself. Oh, and Kayla was our daughter, after all." Feeling despondent, I take my leave.

Back at my office, a few messages await on the machine. I never give out my cell phone number since I mostly don't want to be reached by anyone but my kids. The first message involves an old credit card fraud case. The credit card companies don't treat their customer-victims as well as they once did. So people turn to me. Myself, I handle defrauded cardholders with the utmost respect. When I play the second message I hear Jennifer Waters' beautiful contralto voice.

"The Cooks just called to warn me that you think I burned down the cottage with Kayla in it. Is that true? I loved her and she knew it. We had a better relationship than almost anyone I know. Please get back to me. Amanda promised you'd be smart and sympathetic and I got that impression of you. Please don't waste time by focusing on me." Peaches gave a few woofs toward the end of the message.

Why did I suspect that Peaches could have been better trained? Everyone in that dog's life seemed so infatuated with him that they might not have noticed if he needed Toughlove.

My slightly damp pants leg, the one that fell prey to Peaches' dog dish, reminds me of Sean's excuse for going home during Bible services. His clothes and robe, he said, had gotten wet. I sat down at my new desk chair, paid for by the credit card company's public service blunders, and think about dog lovers. Dog lovers, I guessed from my numerous experiences with cat lovers, could wax fanatic. Jennifer Waters did not strike me as fanatical, but the Cooks could be considered self-confessed fanatics. They loved Jesus, the New Testament, and Peaches, to excess. I call Jennifer back.

"Jenn," I say, over the phone, "I don't think you harmed Kayla. My intuition tells me that you two were as close as you say."

"Thank you," she answers with quiet dignity.

"I need an explanation for one thing, though," I tell her. I inform her why Kayla left the plane and went home. "What we don't know is how she became so deeply unconsciousness that she didn't rouse when she smelled smoke."

"That makes no sense," replied Jenn. "She slept incredibly light. If you're thinking that she took drugs or drank, I'm telling you, she didn't. Besides, if Sean told her that Peaches was sick, she would have taken him right to the after-hours veterinary clinic. This makes no sense."

"I agree. I'm going to figure this out, Jenn. This might not be much help, considering how major a loss you've suffered, but I'm going to clear your name and Kayla's."

I stare into space for a while, thinking. When no answers surface right on the spot, I decide to pick up my son, Jemmy, after school and drive him home—to my former house. His bus ride takes half an hour and he hates the stop-and-go progress down College Avenue. I can't keep him though. It's not my allotted time.

At the home I once shared with my lover, Honor, and our two children, I fix Jemmy some crackers, apple slices, and milk. I concentrate on the strengths and weaknesses of his basketball skills and those of every guy on his team. Jemmy shows me the new kitten, Feisty, that Honor allowed them to adopt. Feisty turns out to be a total pain in the butt. The kitten repeatedly lunges at my good, star-studded socks when I move my foot.

"Don't let Feisty's claws get stuck in your socks," warns Jemmy, "they could get broken."

My socks don't matter, I gather. That's when I realize what probably happened to Kayla Cook.

If I hadn't witnessed the total self-absorption of the Cook family, I would not have arrived at this theory, but the emotional integrity of my conjecture gives it credence.

I ask my buddy Dennis, luckily only two sheets to the wind, to call a contact at the county coroner's office and ask a specific question that can be answered with a yes or a no. Police officers don't mind talking to Dennis. I've ticked a lot of them off but he stays on their good side.

Dennis gets back to me with the news I expected. When they did the initial autopsy on Kayla Cook, they noted nicks in the skeletal frame, the ribs, and neck. These nicks could have come from a skiing or automobile injury.

Or, the nicks could have been made by a dog's canine teeth.

They send an officer over to pick up Peaches from Amanda Corey's house before the Cooks can get the wind up. Jenn accompanies him to the lock-up facility at the pound. I wonder how she'll feel when she realizes the police took Peaches into custody acting on a tip from me.

The Cooks, mostly Sean Cook, had circled the wagons around Peaches to shield the dog, but I couldn't let them get away with it. The way I figured, some of Sean's story would prove true. Peaches, what with people coming and going, had probably been acting erratic the night of Kayla's death. Sean came home and panicked over the dog's behavior. When he couldn't reach Jenn, who had visited a coffee shop to work on her speech, or Amanda, who went out with friends, he called his sister, not knowing she was already aboard her plane.

Being a good Samaritan, and not wanting Jenn and Amanda's dog to go untended, Kayla got off the plane and went home to take care of Peaches. Whatever the cause of the dog's frenzied behavior (maybe the dog just missed having all his admirers handy), Peaches attacked Kayla and either killed or wounded her when she came through the side gate of the property. She never should have dropped by her own house unannounced, I guess.

When Sean Cook returned from the meeting at the hall and discovered Peaches' transgressions, he knew he would need to act fast to keep the dog from death by injection at the city pound. He dragged his sister's body into the cabin and set the place on fire. We would all like to be sure that Kayla died before the flames consumed her. The autopsy comes back with no definite answer because the lungs are so degraded. Her brother, Sean, swears she wasn't breathing. Sean goes on record saying, "She should have approached Peaches carefully." He'd warned her, after all, that the dog was behaving strangely.

Sean Cook spills his guts because he assumes the arson investigators could nail him with forensic evidence. Funny thing, though, he'd used crumpled newspaper and a long-stemmed barbecue lighter to ignite the dry paper, so they might not have caught him. Until he broke down and blabbed, the evidence against him was pretty circumstantial. They're not sure what charges they'll bring against him, and the hearing process on the fate of Peaches drags on as well.

The Cooks will get their day in court. They turned out to have been spiriting Peaches away from the house for attack-dog training, against Jenn's wishes. According to them, Berkeley is crawling with heathens and they wanted protection. They loved Peaches so much that they taught him to maim and kill any barbarian folk who made so bold as to enter their yard. They couldn't get an ordinary watchdog. Peaches wouldn't have wanted to share his yard with a lesser deity.

"Oh, wow. You found the—" Amanda doesn't know what to say after that so she just pays her bill, shakes my hand, her green eyes looking straight into mine, and leaves my office. I pass Jenn on the street one day, but she's looking down as though scavenging for treasure.

So. The butler is off the hook. In this case, the dog did it. Not really, though. The dog became a threat to humanity because cold, uncaring human beings took away his innate ability to treat human beings as fellow members of the pack. The Cooks turned that dog into a carnivorous animal instead of a pet. I will regret Peaches' demise although not nearly to the extent I mourn the loss of Kayla Cook. Kayla's lovely voice floats out of CDs as though she is more alive than the rest of us.

The Pits give a memorial concert in Stern Grove. The Pits' new music, and their previous songs too, capture an old-time folksy gracefulness. Their unusual and original vocal and musical arrangements allure even the most jaded ear. I'm going to become a groupie. They're playing at Freight & Salvage next month and I'll be in the audience. The only thing they lack, they tell me, and the one missing element that they can't add to the mix ever again, is the sweetness of Kayla's melody line. Kayla Cook could sing like an angel, and when she played her ancient Martin guitar, your heart would take wing.

Yours, Eliza Pirex.

The Intersection of Camp and St. Mary

J. M. Redmann

"I need you to solve a mystery for me."

Alexis didn't believe in beginning a phone conversation with "hello" or "how are you," although she would occasionally affect a "where y'at, cher" like she had been born here in New Orleans instead of New Haven. They're both *new,* she had noted, adding that moving here when she was fourteen was close enough. Not in any South that I knew, and besides, both News were now old, and one was old industrial and the other was old French and there just is a difference. Her mother being a native of Chalmette didn't count either. (Chalmette is where the actual Battle of New Orleans took place, now a smudge of refineries, trailers, and jokes along the line of "How do you know someone is from Chalmette? Their tattoo is misspelled.")

"Lexy," I said. She hated it when I called her that, but it was my oh-so-subtle way of implying that I didn't appreciate her calling at 10:38 on a Friday night and asking the impossible from me. "Dwell with me in reality, I don't solve mysteries. Private eyes are in the phone book and the police can be reached at nine-one-one." It is most annoying when ex-lovers know you'll be home on a weekend night.

"You write them. You should have some practice at solving them."

"Write. Fiction. Make-believe."

"I have a sister."

"The evil twin. I knew it."

"Funny, Emma, funny," she said, clearly missing the humor. "Not a twin, she's five years older. Mom had her pre-wedlock and I'd like to find her."

This is one of the reasons we broke up—Alexis's habit of making statements and leaving me the job of ferreting out just what she wanted me to do. Of course, the main reason we broke up was that just after finally making the serious commitment of a U-Haul visit, she decided that New Orleans needed a feminist vegetarian restaurant. This is a city that considers fried pickles a vegetable, and lettuce and tomatoes are only used as something to sop up the juices on a roast beef, ham, cheese, and three other animal proteins po-boy. She didn't appreciate my helpful suggestion of changing hush puppies to hush pussies nor the idea that pralines could be made healthy by taking out the butter, sugar, and cream. It took her two hours in the kitchen to realize that left only pecans. Her too-literal streak also contributed to our break up. It wasn't really the restaurant, but her insistence that our eating had to be as pure as the driven snow peas. Every night I came home to another green concoction. She was trying out recipes for the restaurant. Most of them never made it to the menu. It didn't help that we had a loft bed and—okay, I'm a wimp—that I slept on the inside because I'm afraid of heights and that made it a long trip to the bathroom for me. Green wasn't a color that my digestive system liked, and it had a bad tendency to exit rather quickly one way or another. She claimed that we broke up because I didn't support her in her dream. My version is that I was driven over the edge from protein deficiency and nightmares of green bile.

"Did you hear what I said? I need to find my long-lost sister," Alexis prompted me.

Three months after we broke up, she decided that feminists could be carnivores after all and changed the menu to one tofu dish and fifty-two varieties of meat, including the fried oyster hamburger. My stomach still hasn't forgiven her for that betrayal.

"My hearing is perfect. It was only my digestive track that you left in shambles."

"Emma. Are you going to help me or not?"

"I'll be glad to assist you in any way I reasonably can. I know a good PI, she helped me when I was writing *The Intersection of North Bunny Friend and Desire*. Those are both actual New Orleans streets and Desire does bump the Bunny. Hey, we even have a Mystery Street—it's half a block long, making it a real mystery of a street."

"PIs are expensive."

Her Meat Woman restaurant was doing a booming business. I'm a reasonably successful writer, but she earned my best advance ever in one month. I sometimes make it to the midlist at the Girls, Books, and Boudin shop in New Iberia. And the boudin sausage does outsell me—three to one. Some of my titles include *Murder at the Nightlight Bar, I'll Be Cleaving You Always, Lost Otters, The Wire in the Mud, A Knave Talent, The Last Red Light Special, Robber's Whine, The Puce Place.*

"You want cheap or you want your sister?"

"She's really a half sister."

She wanted cheap. It was clearly bottom-line time. "Alexis, I'm a mystery writer. I sit in my room, stare at the wall, and make things up. I don't search for actual missing persons; I'm not a skip tracer."

"See? I don't even know what the word means. You do know a lot more about this than I do. I'll even throw in the filet mignon with braised oysters special."

"For me and a date?"

She thought for a moment then said, "It'd be worth it to see you with a date."

"Fuck you, Lexy." From that our conversation spiraled down into an agreement on my part to take this on.

Why did I consent to help her? My cynical side says that I'd do anything for filet mignon and oysters. My foolish side said I was a sucker for an impossible challenge. My realistic side didn't have an answer. That's never a good sign.

Alexis's mother blames me for her green period. She occasionally brought some of her experiments to the parental home and their digestive tracts appreciated it as much as mine did. Mrs. Parsons had barely managed to accept her daughter as a dyke, but at least there she could pretend that her daughter didn't actually have sex. She couldn't pretend that she didn't eat meat. And to be about as fair to her mother as I can, I suspect that Alexis was not above using me as a shield for her green concoctions. Her brother did once mention that Alexis got them to try something by saying how much I enjoyed it. Right. Only as a colonic.

So the next day, Alexis came over and I helped her with some questions to ask about the long-lost half sister.

"I can't ask my mother who she slept with before Dad!" was her response to the most obvious one.

"Lexy," I said, thinking my date would have to be a women's soccer team to get enough filet mignons to compensate me for my trouble, "if you want to find this woman, the more information we have, the better. Maybe she's been in contact with her father and he could lead you right to her."

"Sounds like fiction to me," she groused.

"Alexis. We're moving into a week of specials here, okay? Birth date. Eye color. Father. Who handled the adoption? Will your mother register to have her daughter contact her? Was it here in New Orleans or somewhere else? Any idea who the adoptive parents were? And did she have an orgasm when big sis was conceived?"

Alexis gasped at the idea of her mother having an orgasm, then recovered herself enough to grumble, "I hope so. She deserves something to put up with these questions." After about another fifteen minutes of torrentially expressed squeamishness about asking questions that touched on her mother's sex life, Alexis took the list of queries and trudged off. I was counting on Mother Parsons' answers putting an end to this search.

I was disappointed. Maternal instinct must run deeper than I'd ever seen, as Mrs. Parsons answered every question in great detail (although Alexis, the coward, did leave out the one about orgasms).

I looked at the information we had. It seemed a pitiful amount with which to find a human being in a haystack of humanity. Especially since I didn't know what the hell I was doing. Alexis had been astute enough to pick up some Bulldyke Burgers—half a pound of ground sirloin and a thick slab of cheese—from her restaurant on her way here. Food and sex always mellowed me out. Food, at least, was a good start. The sex part was going to take some work. Maybe after I finished with Lexy's list I'd swing by Rubyfruit's Rainbow, our local lesbian bar. And be once again reminded that being a semifamous lesbian writer wasn't exactly visible in the dim light of the bar, but there was enough illumination to show the gray in my hair and the beginnings of laugh lines that marked me as fortyish and obviously too old to dance let alone have sex. Maybe I'd go home instead and burp up some Bulldyke Burger for a real exciting evening.

What we knew about Sister X was that she was born on November 11, 1961, which made her two years older than I and five years beyond Alexis. Mom had been seventeen at the time and the father was the local football team's tight end. ("Not tight enough," Alexis opined, now able to make catty comments about her mother's sex life.) Tragically, at the age of nineteen, he had indulged in a long night of drinking on Bourbon Street and decided to soothe his hunger pangs with a Luck Dog hot dog, but had nodded out midwiener and choked to death. Alexis had snagged her mother's high school yearbooks and they had pictures of the deceased father. He looked like the same crew-cut nerd that Mrs. Parsons had ended up marrying. Maybe a little taller. They had whisked the baby away, not even letting Mrs. Parsons hold her, just telling her the baby was a girl, was healthy, and the usual pabulum about this being for the best for both of them.

Mrs. Parsons was willing to do all the registering things in case her daughter was looking for her. I had, I'm ashamed to say, cadged that information from my PI contact by claiming that I needed it for a book. Now I was stuck with having to write a book about searching for a missing person—and I had so wanted to do a gory serial killer for the next one.

I didn't know what to do beyond contacting the PI. Alexis looked at me like I was supposed to know. I took another bite of my Bulldyke Burger, then sopped up some ketchup with what I suggested she call Dildo Fries since they were big enough. Her manager, Trevor, and I have managed to tag them Silo Fries, and people got the picture without it bringing in the vice squad. The one he selected for the photo in the window did have some hush puppies arranged beside it in a suggestive manner. And Lexy wonders why she has such a steady base of gay boys coming in.

"What do we do now?" Alexis grilled me.

"We see if anything comes from the registries," I said.

"That could take forever!"

"And you've only got a lifetime. I feel your pain."

Alexis looked like she was about to snatch the last bite of burger from my malnourished hand. I was at least three years behind on my meat eating after my time with her. "Emmie," she said, using the diminutive that I hated, "if this were a book, what would you do next?"

"Listen to my agent when she would tell me it would never sell."

"How would your intrepid main character find my missing sister?"

"Intrepid is passé. I'm onto a new main character, no trepid at all." I managed to swallow the entire dildo fry, something few other dykes could do with an object that big, then said, "In a book, I'd have the main character seek shelter from a sudden cloudburst under a wrought iron balcony in the French Quarter. Along with her there would be several other shivering tourists. She'd notice one standing apart from the others, a handsome woman in her early forties, her hair left defiantly gray." When Alexis discovered meat, she also discovered hair coloring. "The woman would notice my character looking at her and quickly glance away. Being intrepid, my character would thread through the drenched tourists as they idly chatted about how 'it doesn't rain like this in Ohio, oh, no, not at all, 'cept that time in May when the cow got washed down the crick to the 7-Eleven parking lot.' She'd murmur, 'I'm sorry for staring, but you look like someone I know—a friend who is looking for her long-lost sister.' As she says this, my character can't help but notice that this woman has a confidence, and a perfect nose that makes her more attractive than the former lover who has enlisted her in this search." Alexis had gotten her father's nose instead of her mother's perfect one, a source of childhood trauma in her telling. "The woman, her confidence edging close to being haughty, would reply, 'A more interesting line than usual. What if I told you that I'm not adopted and, in any case, have only two brothers?' My character would give a slight smile and answer, 'Then I would know you were not the woman I am seeking and I would wish you an enjoyable, and drier, stay in the Big Easy.'"

"Drier? Why drier?" Alexis interrupted me. Her annoying literal streak at work again.

"There's a rainstorm; they're huddling under a leaky French Quarter balcony to get out of it," I reminded her. "And my character would turn up her collar as if about to head off into the rain and completely out of this woman's life when the woman would admit, 'But I was adopted. From here. I just wanted to come back and see a place I once lived. Without even knowing it.' She would hesitate and then softly ask, 'Your friend? What does she know about the woman she is seeking?' My character would answer, 'Only a birth date. That was all her mother was left with.' The woman would say, 'And what was that date?' and my character would answer, 'November 11, 1961.' A stunned look would come across the woman's face, she would reach out and grab my hand—my character's hand—and clasp it tightly, before letting out in a harsh whisper, 'That's the day I was born. Please take me to your friend. I think I need to meet her.' Still holding hands, they would venture out into the rain and into the future."

I ended the story here, thinking that perhaps I should give up the gory serial killer in favor of this missing person saga. I already had such a good beginning of an ending.

Alexis broke into my burst of creativity with, "So, what? I should hang out in rainstorms and hope I find someone with my mother's nose?"

"You asked me what would happen in the book. That's what would happen. Don't ask for reality from a fiction writer."

Alexis reached out and grabbed a Silo Fry that was on the way to my mouth. She took a bite out of it, then choked, reminding me of another reason we broke up.

After half a glass of water, she sputtered, "Damn it, Emma, I knew you wouldn't be able to help me. I should have known better than to come to you."

Why did her telling me what I had been trying to tell her piss me off? Taking the second Bulldyke Burger, claiming it was for her girlfriend Nona, whom I had never seen eat anything meatier than tuna salad, she left me in peace.

Except for the pissed-off part. Let it go, Emma, I told myself, you have a rewrite to do and a short story with a deadline of last week. I stared at the computer screen.

My PI friend was straight, married, and had, on several occasions, told me that she's always wanted to try it with a woman. I had, in a more polite fashion, told her that I was not a one-size-fits-all kind of lesbian. Plus, one night, after the third beer, she let out that her herpes was erupting again and between hers and her husband's they hadn't had sex in three weeks. She's also five-one and I don't find looking down at the tops of women's heads sexy.

Other than that she was cute, in a dyed-blonde way. Maybe we could go out together to the girls' bar, I'd use my fame to attract some women over to us, set her up, and she'd be grateful enough to do this one little impossible search for me.

Now you are writing fiction, I told myself.

I continued to stare at the computer screen. Inspiration hit. Unfortunately, it had nothing to do with the overdue short story. The girlfriend of a friend of a friend ran a support group for adults who were adopted as children. A long shot, but at least it would prove to me, if not Alexis, that I wasn't a total slouch.

So I called the friend who called her friend who called her girlfriend and evidently told her that some weirdo writer was writing a book about murdered adoptees. It took me about twenty minutes of explaining to rectify the mistranslations from my original request. She agreed to ask if anyone in the support group was born on November 11, 1961, although she sounded like she thought she'd be leading them to a lesbian serial killer. She almost hung up without getting my phone number.

Then it was back to staring at my computer screen. Alas, it seemed that I had used up my inspiration quota for the day on Alexis's quixotic quest. But I did win 77 percent on my FreeCell games.

Three days later I got a call from one of the group members. She just wanted to say that she loved my books and wanted to know if I'd "just read over a manuscript" she was working on. It wasn't a mystery, but an autobiographical piece of fiction about the interior life of a girl growing up on the West Bank (actually to the east—don't ask, it's New Orleans) and how hard it was that her family was so normal that she didn't have any real traumas to write about except for Fluffy, the cat, who had been run over because she was eighteen years old and couldn't be bothered to get up unless she was sure the car was going to move and so her father had gotten into the habit of honking the horn, but forgot one day, and Fluffy went to the great catnip farm in the sky. Oh, and it was 973 pages long.

Before claiming that I'd love to, but had just been diagnosed with the bubonic plague and was under strict quarantine for the next three years, I did ask a few questions. She was born in August and was four feet eleven. Two strikes and she was out. I did pass on to her the e-mail address of an author who not only wrote insipid books ("suddenly" three times in one paragraph, all her main characters were named either Kate or Megan—it was a major artistic stretch when she finally named one Kelly—and by the end of every book the main character had fallen in love forever, only to be broken up and unable to remember the woman's name by the next book) but thought that *assassin* and *reviewer* were synonymous. The woman thanked me profusely, said she loved this writer's books (so much for any discernment about my writing, which I had begun to think was her only redeeming feature) and promised to keep a lookout for November birthdays.

Four days later she did send a woman with a November birthday my way. Unfortunately (for my purpose, that is), she wasn't adopted. Somehow that pertinent detail had been lost. But this woman was nice, wasn't writing a book, and was five-seven. And had been with the same woman for the past eight years. She did offer to pass on any adopted Novembers and even suggested I try some of the online astrology groups. I could hit the Scorpio sites and see if I got lucky.

Four people offered to do my chart, three had manuscripts that they wanted me to look over, and one was sure we were fated to meet and she was just the girl to introduce me to the pleasures of spanking while chanting the attributes of my moon in Uranus.

I told her I had been with the same woman for the past eight years. With her, I finally had to change my e-mail address after I sent one final missive claiming that I had joined the Peace Corps and was on my way to Papua New Guinea.

Real detective stuff was hard work, much harder than staring at my computer screen and coming up with reasons why I could still play a few more games of FreeCell even though my short story was three weeks overdue.

I called my PI friend to see if she had any inspiring ideas for me, but it seemed that she and her husband had finally achieved a simultaneous clearing of their genital lesions. During the one time she answered the phone, I got three heavy breaths and a hasty promise to call later and no call later.

I took it as a sign that the fates were telling me to stick with being a writer and not a private dick—as well as to cut down on my consumption of red meat. No Bulldyke Burgers had passed my lips since the time Alexis had come by.

A bleak February settled in. It rained day after day, in that cold, dreary way New Orleans can manage in winter. I thought about calling Alexis and enlightening her about my enterprise on her behalf, but since I had produced nothing save a once-in-a-lifetime chance at learning astrological paddling, I didn't think that would impress her enough to even offer me a serving of Silo Fries unless I paid full price. And I had seen a picture of her and Nona looking happy and well-fed in not only the local gay paper, but also in the society page of *The Times-Picayune,* so I was in little mood to show my sorry and solitary ass in her vicinity.

It was this mood that brought that same sorry and solitary ass to a bar stool at Rubyfruit's Rainbow. I had no illusions; I was over forty, and probably most of the women in the bar considered heavy reading looking at a menu, so impressing them with my putative fame was useless. But at least it was a change from staring at the computer screen and the e-mail reminders that my short story was six weeks overdue. I could sit at the bar, watch the scenery for a while, tell anyone I knew that I was doing research, and have a beer. Or two. Or three.

The crowd was the usual bar crowd, most of them so young that I'd probably been having sex before they were born. That was a depressing thought, until I rationalized it to mean that I'd had way more sex than they did. I just didn't manage the critical thinking part: comparing how much sex I'd had when I was their age—did I even know what sex was when I was that young?—with how much sex they were managing just on the dance floor.

I turned away from the heavy kissing occurring next to the DJ booth, and instead confronted my reflection in the mirror behind the bar. By moving my head slightly I could align a vodka bottle with my nose. The mirror gave me a view to the door. I noticed her the minute she walked in. She was tall, with enough gray in her hair and lines on her face for me to know that she was closer to my age than anyone else in the bar. She glanced quickly around, then took off her raincoat and disappeared in the direction of the coatroom. I turned back to my beer. Something was familiar about the woman, yet I could swear I'd never seen her before. Maybe it was just my subconscious trying to suggest that I do something about my single life, and coming up with nothing better than the cliché, "Haven't I seen you somewhere before?"

I ordered another beer and turned my attention to the drag king show. It appeared that the next act would be delayed as the performer had dropped her mustache on the floor, and the bar cat had pounced on it and skedaddled under the stage. The emasculated drag king was trying to coax the cat out before the mustache totally resembled a slobbered on and dead mouse. The crowd was happily pointing out her lack of success with—as they, of course, were calling it—her pussy. Another group was discussing who had the bigger strap-on, with one side claiming to be purists who considered length alone and the other side advocating for a Pythagorean formula that incorporated diameter, curves and bumps, dolphin fins, lifelike throbbing veins, etc., and a third group saying it wasn't the silicone but the motion that counted.

I noticed the woman again, passing behind me. I made it a point to keep my head centered on the vodka bottle. *I am not so desperate that I'm going to be staring at a strange woman in a bar,* I told myself, while also noticing that the vodka I had aligned myself with was a cheap brand.

The barefaced drag king had been bumped and the next act, she of the Pythagorean argument, took the stage. Unfortunately her skills seemed to be more mathematical than performance, and she had so little stage presence that she was upstaged the entire time by the other performer who was still trying to get the cat out from under the stage. At the penultimate moment of her song, the cat finally decided to skitter out from the hand groping in her direction, mustache still in mouth. Kitty cat made her escape by going directly between the performing drag king's legs, careened off a stool that held two glasses of water, sending them both crashing to the floor, before disappearing, still with the mustache, out the back door. The performer looked like she was no longer lip-synching the words to "Me and Mrs. Jones," but instead mouthing something like "fucking, fucking, fucking cat."

With my attention still on the stage, I felt the brush of someone squeezing into the stool on the other side of me. "Scotch on the rocks, a splash of water," she said.

"If only she'd been singing 'What's New, Pussycat?' it would have been the highlight of the night," I commented as I turned away from the stage. The woman I had noticed earlier was sitting next to me.

I didn't realize how desperately I was hoping she would laugh until she did. Not everyone, as Alexis often pointed out, appreciated my sense of humor. *The third beer is a dangerous time, Emma,* I reminded myself. I was at that point one night when I convinced myself that riding a motorcycle and enjoying wrestling were interesting facets into a different culture instead of activities that I loathed. And I found myself waking up the next morning beside someone who thought that Pop-Tarts with ESPN in the background was a romantic brunch.

Be cool, be calm, yeah, she looks intelligent, but make sure she's sane before you consider anything other than a few passing comments, I admonished myself. At least that's what my brain said; everything below the waist had some different thoughts.

"Life upon the wicked stage," the woman replied.

She took her drink from the bartender and, I noticed, left a decent tip. Not cheap, that's a good thing. I took the opportunity to look at her while she was dealing with the barkeep. She did look familiar, but I also noted that she had the kind of looks that I tend to pay attention to. It wasn't even physical, more a sense of intelligence and maturity about her. Her hair was mixed gray and black, and she wore no makeup that I could see. There were more laugh lines than frown lines. She was tall, maybe even as tall as I am.

"I'm Emma," I said, putting out my hand.

She shook it, replying, "Jane. Two old-fashioned names. I was hoping you weren't a Tiffany or a Brittany."

I resisted saying that tired old cliché, "you look familiar." Instead I blurted out the next thing that came into my brain (that wasn't obscene), "You don't happen to be a private detective, do you?" Okay, not a great line, but still better than the other things rambling around my head, like "Do you come here often?" and "Do you ever have sex on the first date?"

"No, nothing so interesting. Why?"

I censored myself from answering that I needed a private dick. Instead I launched the story about Alexis and her long-lost half sister, making sure I called her my friend instead of my ex, as I've always thought that anyone who talks about her exes in the first five minutes—and we were under two here—was someone who needed a few more years of therapy before I might want to date them.

When I finished, Jane said, "That's all you really have? A birth date? Do you think you have any chance of finding this lost sister?" She actually sounded interested.

I considered for a moment, then had to admit, "No, I probably don't. I just hate to admit I can't do something even if I put all my effort into it."

She gave me a rueful smile and said, "I'm the same way. Work hard enough, think hard enough, and I should be able to do anything."

"You want to try finding Alexis's sister?" I inquired.

She shook her head, then nodded to the bartender, pointed to both her scotch and my beer. "Oddly enough, I was adopted. I've made a few attempts to find out who my birth parents were . . . but haven't gotten very far."

"How long have you been looking?"

"Off and on for about the past five years. Did a few of the things that you tried. No offers of spanking by astrological sign, though."

"Yeah, so what's your birth date?" I asked jokingly.

The bartender put the drinks in front of us. Jane waved away my hand as I reached for my wallet and paid for both of them. "You get the next round. I was born on November 11, 1961."

For a moment, I stared at her, then decided I was going to kill Alexis. Since I know damn well that things like this only happen in books and not in real life, I was astute enough to know I'd been set up and set up oh-so perfectly. I stared at her for a long moment and realized what was familiar about her was that she looked slightly like Alexis, except she was taller and had a nose that resembled Mrs. Parsons' perfect one. She did have Alexis's brow and lips and eyes almost the same color of blue. I could just see it—somehow they had met up, someone had noticed the resemblance, probably Nona since Alexis wasn't good at things like that and, after a few martinis (Alexis had decided that meateaters needed real drinks) they had come up with this plan.

"Is something the matter?" Jane asked—if that was even her real name.

I was trying to decide whether to play along or just call her on it right now. I sat for another moment, realizing how bitterly disappointed I was. I had thought I was talking to an interesting woman, someone with the hint of possibilities. Now I realized I was being taken in by a con artist, someone who had no real interest in me other than some stupid game.

"November 11, 1961. You're a good actor, I almost believe you. Tell Alexis it's not funny." I got up to leave.

Jane put her hand on my shoulder. "Wait, what's going on here? What's not funny?"

"That's the birth date. November 11, 1961. I'm not stupid. What's more likely? For me to stumble over Alexis's real sister in a bar or for Alexis to play some idiotic joke on me?"

"It's the same date?" she said, reaching out with her other hand so that she gripped both of my shoulders, almost pulling me to her, her hold was so fierce.

"Come on. Neither Tony, Emmy, nor Oscar know my name. Your performance is being wasted here in a lesbian bar."

"You don't understand. I was born on that date and I am adopted."

This woman should be playing opposite Meryl Streep, I thought. Despite knowing this had to be a joke, I was starting to believe her.

Or . . . Or she wasn't acting at all.

"November 11, 1961. It can't be," she said, her hands still on my shoulders.

"Can it be?" I said softly, only to her. And then, "Please be real," but that was mostly to myself. It wasn't Alexis who had set me up, but life.

"This can't be real," Jane murmured, staring intently at me, as if seeking answers in every fleeting emotion.

I put my hands lightly on her waist, to touch her back, to offer that comfort. If I was taken aback by this impossible turn to my until now intellectual quest, she had to be thunderstruck by this bizarre twist of fate.

Standing this close to her, I realized that she was about an inch taller than I. I've fallen in love with women for less reason. Then I told my brain that it had to function. If we fell in love, Mrs. Parsons would become my biological mother-in-law. Did I really want to go there again? "This has to be real. If it were fiction, no one would believe it," I told her. Then I had an idea, "Have you eaten yet? Your sister runs Meat Woman restaurant and she promised me the filet migon special if I found you."

Jane gave me a quick hug, as if sensing the moment needed it, but also realized that we couldn't just stand here like statues, her hands on my shoulders in a death grip, then pulled away. "It can be real, can't it?" she asked, with a smile that hung between incredulous and giddy.

"DNA. We can do DNA tests," I told her.

"Of course, that would be proof, wouldn't it?"

"You do have Alexis's eyes. And her mother's perfect nose. I need to warn you that she'll never forgive you for that."

"Now you tell me. A dysfunctional family."

"Hey, I'm the one with the sarcastic, black humor."

"You've got competition now, babe. I'm starving. You need to take me to dinner and introduce me to my sister." Jane grabbed my jacket off the bar stool where I had been sitting on it, then held it open for me.

"Don't forget your coat," I said as we were at the door. Which forced me to admit that I had noticed her when she came in. "I thought you looked familiar, okay?" I defended. "And you do. You look like Alexis."

"Yeah?" she challenged as we walked into the night. "Funny, I thought you looked familiar, too. But that was too cliché to say."

"Me?" It was about a four-block walk to Meat Woman. I headed us in the right direction.

"Emma Silverman, the mystery writer, I presume?"

"You recognized me? No one ever recognizes me. Especially in this town."

"I read books. I like yours a lot." She then spent the next two blocks giving me a very astute analysis of my books, including a mention of the flaws in structure in my first one, just enough for me to know that she wasn't going to merely gush.

It was all I could do to prevent myself from asking if she would be willing to have sex on the first quasi-date. Instead I managed, "Do you think you can tell Alexis with a straight face that we met under a balcony to get out of the rain?"

"If you ask me the right way."

Oh, hell. "Like this?" I very gently kissed her, just a soft touch of lips.

"Perfect," she said as we started walking again. She reached out and took my hand.

We just talked the rest of the way to the restaurant, an easy flow of words. I even admitted that Alexis was my ex. Jane was enough of a dyke to appreciate the humor of the situation, even saying, "Green? Green food? Just for that we should make out outrageously over dessert." Then she added, with a sly grin, "If you wouldn't feel too embarrassed."

I had to admit I liked the way this woman's mind worked. She already knew just want kind of challenges I am likely to accept. I squeezed her hand. She could get the final answer when the strawberries and whipped cream were within reach.

We turned the corner, now in view of the bright neon lamb chop entwined with a labris that announced we had arrived at Meat Woman.

"Come, let's meet your sister," I said as I opened the door to the restaurant. I am just Southern enough to know that the perfect ending to Alexis's request was to not only find her sister, but to date her, too.

Two Left Shoes

Carole Spearin McCauley

The first time you get kidnapped can ruin your evening. Especially when that evening opens so ordinarily.

In this friendly college town, Ginger—my partner of three years—and I know everyone, at least by sight, and we trust readily. At least we used to . . .

There I was, driving my balky car through plummeting rain. I'd just escaped from the kind of day that rankles an academic press editor enough to contemplate the extreme. By that I mean, quitting editing and embracing graduate school. My a.m. had got eaten by our university press's business manager, prophesying ruin if we don't acquire more books that sell better. My p.m. still lurked undigested under my ribs—a depressing meeting, during which all of us editors rejected a dozen book manuscripts, then more proposals and partials by many writers we'd labored to acquire in the past five years. Especially the scholar-scribes.

Which drove me straight toward Professor Dave Ekberg. He stood at the bus stop, angled away from the wind, trying to protect his briefcase under his flapping coat. Although my intuition whispered, *Don't stop . . . what about his book? . . . don't really know him,* did I listen? It seemed natural to do a favor for a human in distress.

He waved. I stopped. He clutched the door handle and flung himself into my front seat. "Good of you. Thanks." Glancing over the rims of his glasses, he found his handkerchief and mopped rivulets from his face, balding head, and battered briefcase.

"Another flaming January day," I joked, then eased my car into gear. A slipping clutch is a further reason I shouldn't have stopped.

"You live out along Winslow Road? I've seen you getting the bus some mornings."

"You bet. And I just missed it now. Damn annoying on a soggy day. . . You're Ms. Raskin from the press? Thought I recognized you. The answer to a gentleman's prayer." He laughed, then joined his hands in mock piety.

His odd aftershave lotion, which smelled like ferns, seemed to surround me. I ignored his jauntiness. "Oh, everybody calls me 'Racy.' From my mother, Larissa, her nickname. And picking you up is the kind of favor my father liked me to do. He taught history here before the place spread into a university. How we argued about religion and politics." I smiled. "My mother claimed I had two left feet, like, wrong as two left shoes. But Dad and I . . . we got along real well." Why was I babbling like this? Must be nervous. I concentrated on the difficult driving. Because I feared my rear tires would skid on the ice just forming, I braked too suddenly when a bicycle swerved in front of me. Luckily Professor Ekberg now seemed lost in his own thoughts.

Opening his soaked coat, he shifted in his seat. "I've been here only three years. Did you and your father do a lot together?" He sounded so wistful that I stared at him.

I turned up the windshield wipers and the defrost knob. "Well, he's gone now, and I miss him." Dad's image, cheering me on at gymnastic and acrobatic competitions, leaped into my inner eye. How I'd yearned to leap weightless on that balance beam, to overcome my mother's criticism—"so awkward, falling over those big feet. Such feet on a little girl." As if Mother hadn't produced me, and my impediment derived from male genes only.

"What?" I said, suddenly realizing the professor was talking while I'd drifted through Before. I'd now driven to the edge of town and turned automatically onto Winslow Road.

". . . invite you in . . . hot soup, brandy" were the bits I heard. As the professor stared again over his glasses, he deepened the creases that corrugated his long face from nose to necktie. Another image flitted, something to do with the university library, but I couldn't place it.

I enjoy a photographic memory for print and other images, but now I needed my total focus to guide the car between the puddled ruts and the blackness just beyond my headlights. "Thanks for the offer, but this clutch is slipping badly." I downshifted. "See how loose it is? I'm due at Texaco tomorrow for Ed to fix it. But if it dies and I can't shift again, I won't get home at all."

I'd already blabbered too much. To sound less desperate, I bit my tongue. Under my cardigan I shivered. My blouse, miniskirt, and black tights—sufficient for the mild morning—couldn't protect against the sleet now falling.

"Not to worry. I can help," the professor assured, grinning at me. "Such a beautiful young lady."

Get away from him, my innards ordered. Next he'll ask about his book. About which I knew too much. A work on modern freedoms that studied free speech, press, and art media, it also included "forbidden knowledge from Pandora to pornography." According to my boss, Marian, his manuscript was long on footnotes, short on readability. And had been rejected at our afternoon meeting.

I stopped the car before his front gate. "Here you are, Professor."

But he made no move to leave. "I'm not, you know, a full professor. That's why I need my freedoms book published. Or I'm out of a job." In the half light inside the car he looked beaten, his shoulders slumped. Had his previous jauntiness been an act?

Whether he'd visited the press today or not, I knew that I'd also seen him somewhere else. "I'm sorry but, look, I must go. I promised to meet my . . . partner, Ginger. She's at our place, right now."

I inhaled. I now name the truth. Every evening Ginger and I cook together and share our day's events before going to sleep. Beyond that—and including that—our "outing" was my doing. Three years ago, after we'd met at a graduate center women's program, she at first made me agree to conduct ourselves discreetly as a lesbian couple for the sake of her job as assistant to the university president. I saw, however, that we deceived no one, especially during those wannabe-understanding remarks—"Women of your persuasion . . . maybe have not met the right man?" And "it's your choice," or "lifestyle." The first time I heard "lifestyle," while Ginger's boss, the president, stood out of earshot at his cocktail party, I blurted, "It's not a lifestyle. It's our *life!*" Having shushed and pushed me into a mahogany-pan-

eled corner, Ginger whispered the value of discretion. I instantly rebelled. "It's *because* I love you! Trust me." Later we made up—in
bed—and our cumulative years of service to the university have managed to protect our jobs.

"Look, I really must get home," I repeated to the professor. I
reached across his knees to open his door.

"Okay. Thanks for the ride." But having turned toward the night,
he stopped. I groaned inwardly when he continued, "If I can do you a
favor sometime . . . By the way, will you editor folks let me know
about my manuscript soon? I tried to see Marian today. I've waited
more than three months."

Then It happened. I'd hoped that shifting from neutral gear into
first, making the car roll, would scare him into leaving. But if hopes
were horses (not Hondas with 120,000 miles on the clock), editors
would ride. While attempting this nifty maneuver, under my hand I
felt the shift's innards slacken, as if its gears had vaporized. With a
metallic shriek, my car jerked, coughed, died.

I inhaled, then ground my teeth. Next I found the professor's warm
hand on my cold one. He was so close I could taste his ferny odor. He
was laughing.

"It's not funny!" I shouted, surprised to feel cold perspiration run
between my breasts. Somewhere in my throat, I stifled, *Help me.*

"I'm not laughing *at* you." He seemed to apologize. "It's just . . . if
my manuscript affects you and your car that much. You look like—"

"I need to phone the garage," I protested, sounding more curt than
I intended.

"Okay, okay. C'mon in." After we got through the front door, he
added, "Here's a hanger for your coat. Some brandy will warm you
up. Oh, my phone's in the bedroom."

After I found the number for Ed, my mechanic, I heard Ekberg
phone the garage to order a tow truck. If I'd borrowed Ginger's cell
phone that day, I could have used it from outside. Oh well. . . .
Ekberg's living room seemed surprisingly cozy, even elegant. I paced
among tapestry chairs, stained glass lampshades, crystal ware, floral
paintings, and fragrant pine branches at the ready beside the fireplace.

"Here's your hot coffee. Also crackers and cheese. Soup's on." As Ekberg set a tray with two mugs beside the books and journals on his polished coffee table, I pulled my hand from a decanter set on a sideboard. "Ah, I see you've found the brandy. Good. Drink up." He raised his own mug. "Ed says they'll get the tow truck here in about an hour."

"Not before then?" I complained, adding, "Sorry, but I need to get back soon." Nevertheless, I took the mug he held out, cradling my cold fingers around its steaming warmth. Although his brew tasted bitter—espresso with what?—at least I could lean back on a colorful sofa and relax.

"I saw you admiring Mother's things. They're all antique, handcrafted. After she passed away last year, I couldn't part with them. All except the car. It wasn't in much better state than yours." He grinned. "Uh, about my book. You can tell me the worst, you know."

Did he really mean that? Samuel Johnson's remark sprang to mind: "Sir, your manuscript is both good and original; but the part that is good is not original, and the part that is original is not good." Assuming what I hoped was my Sage Editor look, I said, "Your book certainly has merit. The idea of forbidden knowledge is intriguing. And," I lied, reproaching myself, "your book is still under consideration." But my face blushed; I was sweating.

"Damn!" Ekberg exploded. He banged his fist on the table, rattling the mugs and cheeses. "Why is it I don't believe you? You've rejected it, haven't you?" He glared at me. "You have no idea how long that book took to write. Plus teaching, research trips, and caring for Mother."

Startled by his stormy face, I couldn't speak, so I sighed. Too trusting, Racy, bad liar. . . . Just walk out. But I found my legs couldn't move. Next my head drooped and my body went prickly, fuzzed as if floating. My eyesight seemed weird, wandering. With immense effort, I replaced my empty mug on the table. "It's not . . . my . . . fault," I tried to say.

When I could focus again, I felt stunned. I lay on my back in some officelike room with a bright desk lamp beaming down on me. An L of steel bookshelves flanked me.

I tried to move my hands and feet against the velvety thing where I lay. My hands and feet were bound with a Christmas-green satin rope. Stretching from wrists to ankles, it gleamed at me. I was tied up! And locked into this stuffy room that stank of ferns. Looking upward, I saw open rafters. An attic? My throat felt dust-dry, and I coughed. When I raised my head slightly, I saw that my black skirt and ankle boots were missing. I was wearing a lacy negligee and grayish shoes with curved heels and spangled bows. I felt like Ginger Rogers, with a hangover.

And where was Ekberg, the "good" professor? As I realized he must have drugged me, I muttered aloud, "Damn him!" He had said his mother died. Had he also drugged her? On a closed door, next to the desk, a framed photo caught my eye. A moody torso shot of Ekberg, taken from above, while his creased face stared.

Abruptly I knew why he'd seemed familiar in the car. A while ago (October?), while checking some variant spellings on the library balcony, I'd looked down at him holding something black, being escorted from the library by two men. In the next campus newspaper the lead story began "Halloween Prank in Library." A male professor (name withheld) had videotaped the study carrels. The tape contained "only women's feet in shoes." As Ginger had said, "Cra-azy!"

After my mind blended all these bits, their sum chilled me.

Sudden wind whistled through a crack somewhere in the shadows above me. I imagined myself leaping out the desk window into snow, which swirled under the orange street lamp. Despite the tropical heat inside this apartment, my flesh crept with goosebumps; my hands tingled. My wristwatch was gone; what time was it? I stared anew at the gray-green shoes. More Victorian antiques that had belonged to his mother? But they fit me perfectly.

What a trusting fool! With a shock I realized I'd hoped the professor, like my father, would solve my car, dinner, and weather problems. He's not your father. Grow up! Get loose. Out.

To stop the tears rushing down my face, I propped myself on an elbow. Apparently the velvety satin rope looped and tethered me to somewhere in the blackness under this sofa. As I tried to sit up, the negligee opened between my legs. I was relieved to see that my tights, blouse, and pink underwear seemed intact. Now the room seemed to spin. I lay back again. Damn.

Ginger's joke rushed at me. "Racy, where d'you get such sexy underwear?" And I'd answered, "If my car crashes, I'll look good in the ambulance." It wasn't funny anymore. Nor was what Ekberg could do to me. My spirits sank. How I yearned for Ginger's arms around me in our bed.

I dragged my feet in the silk shoes onto the floor, then my hands down near them. As I bent over, I suddenly and unbearably needed to use the toilet. Although Ekberg had done some cat's cradle–type knots that tightened whenever another piece of this drapery cord loosened, I managed to undo my ankles.

As I shook out my hands and wondered whether a toilet stood behind the velvet curtain in the corner, I heard a lock turn and snap. Ekberg walked in, carrying a tray. "Brought you some coffee and a sandwich."

I raised an arm against him. "I—I'm leaving. Bring me my clothes. What did you put in that other coffee?"

"Your skirt and shoes are drying downstairs. Be ready in a bit."

"Why did you tie me up here?"

"You were . . . woozy. What if you hurt yourself?"

What a crock. What to do now? I looked around for something to grab as a weapon. Volumes of *Encyclopaedia Britannica*? Paper knife? I forced my glance away from a pair of bronzed baby shoes on the bookshelf above the desk.

"You look lovely in that robe and the jade shoes. Fit you perfectly. They were Mother's, you know."

My mind screamed. To stifle it, I bit a knuckle. Suddenly I understood why captives wind up joking, agreeing with the creeps who capture them. Anything to postpone violence.

"Yes, they're . . . lovely," I lied. Then wondered, *Why lock me in? And did the tow truck ever come for my car?* "Do you want to discuss your manuscript?"

"Are you saying your company hasn't rejected my book?" Then as if speaking to himself, he continued, "Without a book contract, without tenure, my teaching here ends in May. Forever." He sat down in the leather armchair between me and the closed door.

"I can show you a fine review of my work," Ekberg continued. "In my mail downstairs. Got it yesterday from a respected psychologist. And if he appreciates my manuscript . . . You're well liked at the press, so maybe if I explain to you how it is, I can . . . persuade you."

"And how do you hope to . . . uh, persuade me?" I wriggled at how flirtatious my voice sounded.

"If you can get me a contract—"

"Sure, I'll be glad to show your review letter to Marian and the editorial board." Then I lied, "Your manuscript is under *serious* consideration."

"No! You don't understand." His voice dropped as he enunciated every word. "I'll make it . . . very worth . . . your effort. Racy, you and I have so much in common. I have resources and I know . . . just what a woman . . . needs. Trust me," he whispered. Bending toward me, he reached and grabbed my knee.

Yuck. The next line in films is "And if I don't?" But I didn't even want to breathe that one. No wonder films don't help you more with real life. Catching my breath, I eased my knee from his grasp. "Your resources must come from your antiques and collection of beautiful clothing. And the shoes you have?" I glanced downward toward my antique-shod feet.

"As a matter of fact," he said, pleased, "I have a unique shoe room. I'm negotiating with the university museum to begin an antique clothing wing."

"I'd love to see your items."

"I have one especially precious pair. Three inches long, gold-embroidered. Made by a Chinese foot binder."

I shuddered. "That sounds . . . fascinating. May I see them?"

Suddenly he lunged toward me, extending a thumb and forefinger, his other hand waving before my face. I jerked backward.

"My dear, you're so tense. Please relax." He reached out, placed his thumb and forefinger round the back of my neck, under my hair. Just as my father did, so gently, whenever I studied late. But Ekberg tightened the grip.

Instead of screaming, I just let go inside. I felt the wet ooze travel through my underpants, down my black tights. And onto his mother's negligee! Legs crossed against the warm stream, I stood up, bending from the waist. "Is that a toilet behind the curtain? I need to use it. Please, go outside. Don't want to ruin Mother's shoes or gown."

Ekberg retracted his hands and pointed toward the curtained cubicle. "Yes, I'll get the Chinese slippers. And the review letter downstairs. Oh, don't try to leave." He actually shook his finger at me before locking the door.

I closed my eyes, praying for strength to finish what I had to do. At least my dizziness had passed. Legs still crossed, I hobbled behind the curtain and used the toilet. Having removed his mother's shoes, I placed one in view on each side of the bowl. Then I flung her negligee over the curtained enclosure.

I needed a weapon! I tiptoed to the desk chair, eased open his top desk drawer. And found a photo story that showed a woman strangled, "molested"—and minus her feet. That newspaper nicknamed the killer "Jack the Clipper." My stomach lurched.

Then a page of pasted-up ads for a shop unusual even by Big City standards. "Leather 'n' Lace for Full Figures. Transvestite? Transgender? Just curious? Rubber, leather, fetish goods. Need it for that special evening? We order . . ."

A noise outside! Halting at "Community Service since—" I prayed to whatever goddesses, beginning with Diana of the hunt, to help me Now.

From its book-supporting job I grabbed a mounted brass baby shoe. And stuffed it down my underpants and tights, wincing at the cold metal. My heart banged in my chest. By the door I kneed Ekberg's leather chair directly underneath a ceiling support beam.

With whatever energy I had left, I climbed onto the chair and swung myself upward.

Pretend it's your balance beam. The bookend nearly fell from my underwear, but my body remembered the basic straddle. Just as I stood and balanced myself on the beam, clutching the heavy bronze, wiping the other sweaty palm on my blouse, Ekberg entered. He stopped beneath me and gazed at Mother's shoes, which gleamed under the curtain!

Awareness is all. You bet. Before he could notice me or reach the curtain, I dropped on him. Aiming my knees into his back, I knocked him down. Then brained him with the bookend.

Ekberg lay still, bleeding. Exhausted, I crawled, then hobbled out to the hall, hoping I'd killed him. As I made my way down the stairs, my ankle hurt so much I bit my tongue.

In the kitchen I grabbed my wrist, stopped shaking long enough to phone 911, then Ed's Garage. Ed swore no Professor Ekberg had reported any stalled car on Winslow Road tonight. Last night? Again I hoped I'd killed him. And during college who imagined she was a pacifist?

Awareness is all. Out on the snowy porch, in my blouse and underwear I stood on one foot. Then my knees crumpled. As Jane Austen wrote, "Run mad as often as you choose, but do not faint." I kept repeating it.

The town police arrived promptly. One rushed me to the hospital while the other two radioed. When they entered Ekberg's house, they found him bleeding, but alive, with one helluva headache.

They found his footwear collection. And some nifty business records from that special shop in Manhattan. I hoped its honest patrons, who were not kidnappers or murderers, wouldn't be arrested because one professor was a menace.

Despite my finest efforts, he lived. And claimed he visited the fetish/leather shop monthly—and invested in it—because he was studying "alternate lifestyles" for a new book. Ideally our editors will never see it. . . .

Now, two days later, I'm finally back at our apartment. My bandaged and casted ankle lies throbbing on a pillow. After fixing me some food, Ginger kissed me and left for a class. Already I miss her, despite her parting attempt at humor: "Hey, do you realize Ekberg, your ferny frog, could have become your Prince Charming sugar daddy? Look what you missed."

"No way! Once a reptile, always a reptile. . . . Hey, you call that cheering me up?" Croak. . . . Whether from painkillers for my broken ankle or from posttraumatic shock, I slump in a haze. Trust yourself, and don't do favors next time. Especially when the enemy comes disguised as a friend. Even a Prince Charming. My gymnastics teacher would have scorned my awkward leap from the beam, but he'd never know and I could always claim that hefty bookend had unbalanced me. Besides, wasn't I out of practice?

Forcing myself from my haze, I phone Detective Miller, whom I know from his previous life as head of campus police. Through chatting in his office, adjacent to our publishing area, he and I are good friends. Judy from our office has just delivered to the police the professor's premier opus and his folder of articles. Beyond my headache, I hear Miller say, "Yes, you fractured his skull, but they fixed him up at the hospital. We just got him into a cell here."

I dare breathe again. Do favors, but follow your intuition next time.

"You're one tough gal, Racy."

"It's 'lady' now," I insist. "I grew up fast real fast, night before last. And I got him with both feet. . . . Oh, that poor woman in Massachusetts who lost her feet?"

"We're investigating that one. He did travel to his leather 'n' lace place that week."

"Does that mean he could or couldn't have got to Massachusetts? . . . Uh, will I have to go to court?"

"Depends on what we charge him with."

"Can he get off on some insanity plea?"

"If he's guilty, we'll do everything to see he doesn't."

I can't wait any longer to ask the next question. "Why did he do this to me?"

"All we get is he's nutty about keeping his house, staying at the university, starting his museum. Like, obsessive. . . . And, Racy, he claims you hate men because nobody can replace your father."

Damn. A psychoanalytic fruitcake. The worst kind. "I did tell Ekberg I miss my father, but. . . . Jeez, suppose I drugged *him*? And tied him up? Locked in an attic. Anyway, what's loving about bondage-and-discipline? Or S-and-M stuff from his shop?"

"You really want to know?" Miller laughs.

"No! He's wrong. As wrong as . . ."

"Yes?"

"Two left shoes."

Like a Sore Thumb

Randye Lordon

"Jesus, Rube, it's enough already! No one's gonna see it, nobody," Dominic whispered frantically. He leaned on the shovel and shook his head. Two of his three chins wobbled, as if trying to catch up with the initial movement.

"*I* am, Dom. I'm gonna see it and so are you." Ruby looked at her brother but turned away quickly. Even in the darkness, the resemblance was too close, the eyes, the lips, even the chins. She cleared her throat and whacked her shovel on the fresh mound of dirt. "What do you think, you put a bush on top of it and it just goes away? Well, it ain't like that. Believe me, this is gonna stick out like the biggest sore thumb you ever seen. Mark my words." She slapped his beefy shoulder and pointed to the shovel he was leaning on. "What? I got to do this all by myself, is that the idea?" She paused. "I'm talking to you, Dom." She took a deep breath and mumbled, "I'm getting tired of cleaning up after you."

That was Dominic; he would start something and then just walk away. The next thing she knew her mother would come in, blame her for the mess left behind, smack her around, and make her clean up after him. Mama had it all figured out, right from the start: Dominic could do no wrong and sicko Ruby couldn't do anything right. The good son, the bad daughter. Simple. Easy. Ruby punched him in the arm. He wasn't expecting it, so he didn't have time to tense the muscles. Unaccustomed as she was to touching him, she was surprised at how soft it was.

"Hey, hey, hey, don't hit." He rubbed his arm and slowly went back to the task at hand. "Tell me something."

"What?"

"How do you know?"

"How do I know what?" Her hands were blistered and sore, but she held onto the wooden handle until her knuckles were white.

"How do you know it's gonna stick out like a sore thumb?"

"'Cause I watch movies. And unlike you, I read. I know. That's what they all say. You do something like this," she motioned to the soil, "and it starts to take on a life all its own. That's what everyone says."

Dominic bit his lower lip until he felt the salty, comforting taste of his own blood. He leaned the shovel next to a maple tree and reached for the rhododendron they had bought from the nursery that afternoon. He centered it in the hole they had left and stepped back.

"Wadda ya think?" He cocked his head to see if it was straight.

"It's fine." Ruby took a tissue out of her apron pocket and wiped her neck. Despite the spring chill, the two of them had worked up a good sweat. Once she used to love the sensation that physical exertion would invoke, the stiffness, the sweat, the faint smell from her armpits. Once. But not now. Now she was too old, too tired.

"You sure?"

"I'm sure. It's fine. Now let's just fill the damned thing up." She put the tissue back into her pocket and grabbed the shovel with renewed energy.

By the time they were finished, Dominic was wheezing and Ruby had a blister on her hand that looked like it was ready to pop. The night was clear and as they shuffled back to the house, Ruby looked up at the sky, picked out the first star that she saw, and made a wish.

"Yeah, right." Dominic looked up, unable to see anything more than the lights of a low flying plane headed to LaGuardia. "That'll do us a lot of good."

Ruby glared at her brother and handed him her shovel.

The first thing she saw when she entered the house through the back door was the kitchen clock. It was almost one in the morning. She couldn't remember the last time she'd been up so late. But instead of just walking through the room and turning off the lights, she went to the stove and lit the first burner where the teakettle sat. Then she went to the overflowing refrigerator and rummaged through the contents. By the time Dominic returned there was bacon browning in a pan, maple syrup and butter heating up on a back burner, and a bowl of pancake batter just ready to be spooned out onto a hot skillet. The intoxicating smell of coffee filled the room.

"What took so long?" Ruby asked as she turned the bacon over.

"I washed the shovels and dried them so they wouldn't rust."

"What the hell did you do that for?"

"So no one would be able to tell that we had dug up the backyard."

Ruby shook her head and took a deep breath. "People dig up their yards, Dom. How the hell could we have put in a bush without using a shovel?" She pressed her lips together and reached for the paper towels.

"Yeah, well, if anyone asks, I'll just tell 'em I'm clean. Compulsive."

Ruby turned slowly and looked at her brother, carefully studying him from head to toe. His shirt was stained with sweat and dirt from their nighttime gardening, but that wasn't all. Like all of his shirts there were old food and drink stains spotting the front panel and the sleeves, especially the cuffs. His worn pants were belted three inches below his massive belly and he never seemed capable of zipping them up all the way, as if his hands wouldn't reach. The thick hair in his ears looked like a catchall to Ruby, who often complained that he should clean them out, if only to hear better. "Compulsive? I don't think so." She turned back to the bacon and carefully lifted each browned piece onto the folded paper towels to drain off the grease.

"I can't believe you're fixing breakfast," Dominic whined as he checked out what was in the green mixing bowl.

"Believe it." Ruby poured a little bacon grease onto the pancake skillet and left the bacon pan to cool on the counter.

"I couldn't eat a thing after what we just did. I don't see how you can." Dominic reached for a piece of bacon.

"You don't have to, Dom. You can just go to bed." She poured herself a cup of coffee, deliberately using the mug Dominic had given their mother for her last Mother's Day. *World's Greatest Mom* it boasted in dark red letters. Ruby added three teaspoons of sugar, stirred it in, and took a sip. It was like a drug. She felt her muscles relax and her shoulders ease down. She let out a sigh.

"You eat too much sugar, Rube; it's not good for you." When she ignored him, he groaned, "I can't go to bed. I'm too upset." He plucked another piece of bacon off the paper towel and moved away from the stove. "Besides, you can't eat all that by yourself." He took a glass mug from the dish drainer and sprinkled half a teaspoon of sugar in the bottom of the glass. Then he poured in half a cup of coffee and added heavy cream until it rose to the rim of the mug.

They drank in silence while Ruby flipped the pancakes, stacked them on a plate and kept them warm in the oven. Dominic sat at the kitchen table waiting to be fed. The table was cluttered with a plastic lazy Susan with four salt and pepper shakers, a canister of garlic salt, and two sugar bowls. There was also a basket of fresh and waxed fruits mixed together, newspapers, the model car Dominic was working on, a napkin holder made of Popsicle sticks and filled with blue napkins, and a Tupperware container holding doggie treats. Their dog, Blackie, had died seven years earlier, but Ruby kept buying treats for the neighborhood dogs. Dominic reached for one while he drank his coffee.

"Here." Ruby placed a square plastic plate in front of Dominic piled high with pancakes and bacon. Everything swam in a sea of sweet syrup and butter.

She took a seat across from him and snapped a slice of bacon in half before eating it. "You okay?"

He nodded, his mouth crammed with the warm treat. A thin trickle of syrup inched from the corner of his mouth down a deep line to his chin. Already he had another forkful of hotcakes loaded and ready to jam into his surprisingly small mouth.

Ruby watched him as if for the first time, as if she hadn't been sitting across this very same table from him for the last sixty years. His hands were a blur as he quickly shoveled the food from plate to mouth. *If his hands had moved that fast with a* real *shovel, we would have been done in half the time,* she thought. A drop of syrup flew off his fork and landed on his shirt. He wiped it up with his finger, smearing the sticky brown droplet on his chest, and then brought his finger to his mouth. A half-eaten doggie treat sat next to his knife.

"What?" he asked after he had licked his plate clean. His eyes flickered between her face and her untouched plate of food.

Ruby shut her mouth and released her viselike hold on her coffee mug. "What what?" Her voice cracked.

"I know you, Rube. You're thinking something, something not good. What?" He reached for the doggy treat.

"I was thinking, I think maybe I feel better." She pinched off an end of bacon and nibbled on it.

"What do you mean, better?" He pushed his empty mug toward his older sister.

She looked at the mug, stared at it, without moving a muscle. Then she shifted her gaze from the milky glass and looked him in the eyes. "Better, like I feel like I can breathe. You know?"

"No, I don't know. I feel like shit. Can I have more coffee?" He motioned impatiently to the glass with a fat index finger.

"Sure." She looked away from him. "It's on the stove. Just like it always is." She picked up her fork and squeezed it in her hand.

Dominic's face turned white, but he didn't say a word. Instead, he cautiously reached for the glass mug and dragged it up off the table.

"You wanna tell me what's going on?" Dominic asked his big sister, making sure to keep his back to her. He couldn't watch her face. He didn't want to see that she was looking at him like everyone else did, with revulsion.

"I been your maid all my life, Dominic." She virtually whispered the words. "Ever since I can remember."

"Yeah, so?" He sprinkled half a teaspoon of sugar into the bottom of his glass and reached for the coffee.

"So I don't wanna do it anymore." She set the fork down on the hotcakes.

Dominic paused as he reached for the heavy cream. The cold air from the refrigerator hit him like a slap in the face. He took a deep breath, smelled something stale from the icebox, grabbed the cream, and shut the door.

He fixed his coffee and returned to the table before speaking. The wall clock loudly ticked out the passing minutes. It was 1:47.

"I don't understand, Ruby. You go your whole life with things the way they are and then suddenly you want to change everything? I don't get it."

"We changed everything last week," she reminded him.

He swallowed air and pushed out his lower lip. "That's different." He pouted.

"I don't think so. Like I said before, nothing'll ever be the same after tonight." She started picking the cuticles on her right hand. Large liver spots had started appearing during the last year, one of the few things she had inherited from her mother. Figured.

He downed half of his drink and wiped his mouth with the back of his hand. "One thing has nothing to do with the other, Ruby. You and I have nothing to do with—" The words caught in the back of his throat.

"With what, Dominic? With Mama being dead? What, you can't even say it?" She could feel the familiar sensation of her stomach tightening, gripping until—like every other time—it would work its way up through her body and make her feel like she was choking. Ruby pressed her hands into her lap and exhaled until there was no more air inside her whole body. Then she counted to five before slowly taking a deep, even breath. "Mama's dead." There, she said it.

Dominic flinched.

"She's dead and there's not a thing we can do about it, Dom." Ruby pushed her plate away and exhaled. She couldn't look her brother in the face without seeing their mother, so she looked down at her own lap instead. Her double Ds pulled at the bib of her worn floral print apron.

The plates rattled and she jumped when Dominic pounded the table once with his thick fist. "You can't say that, Rube! You can't say that ever again!" His face was turning a deep shade of crimson. Ruby knew that next would come the rage, then the tears, and finally contrition, childish and always to some extent forced.

She balled her hands into two equally large fists and banged the table right back.

Dominic flinched.

She did it again, and again, and again until the silverware bounced off the plates onto the tabletop. Stunned, Dominic stared in disbelief. She looked ridiculous, sitting there all puffy and pale, beating her hands against the table like a two-year-old in a high chair. She looked crazy, demonic. He grabbed the first thing at hand and threw the dog biscuit across the room. "Stop it," he cried. "Stop it or I'll tell Mommy!"

A palpable silence descended. Without saying a word, Ruby reached into her apron pocket and pulled out a lipstick. She eased off the plastic casing and twisted the bottom once clockwise. Then, never moving her eyes off Dominic, she ran the stump of color—ruby red— along her bottom lip, first to the left, then to the right. One, two. Dominic watched with fascination as she pressed her lips together and spread the color from bottom to top, never going outside the well-defined line of her lip.

When she was done, she reversed her movements; she rolled the lipstick back into the tube, closed it up, and tucked it back into her pocket.

"What are you doing?" Dominic asked in a small, little boy voice.

"I'm going out."

"Where the hell are you going to go? It's almost two in the morning!"

He had a point, but Ruby was up on her feet and headed to the front of the house. "I don't know, but for the first time in my whole life, I feel like I can do anything I want, Dom."

She didn't want to lose the feeling or the cherished recollection of a women's only bar she had known a lifetime ago where they were so friendly she had felt at home for the first and only time in her life. Maybe it was still there. Who knew, maybe Nancy was there, too.

She hurried through the dining room, past the living room, and up the thirteen steps to the second floor. There were four rooms on the second floor: three bedrooms and a bath. Her room was directly across from the staircase. It was small and pink with a lonely, canopied bed. She hated the room. After years and years of wear and tear the furniture was shabby, the carpets were threadbare, and the room had a dingy feel to it, especially at night with artificial light.

Ruby pulled an overnight bag out of her closet and carefully started packing it. Where *was* she going to go? What she was doing was completely irrational, which was anything but like her. If she had to leave so badly, she could just wait until morning, think it through, then do something. But no, it was as if her body had a mind all its own and she didn't have any say. After sixty years of being a slave to her mother, the sudden freedom was exhilarating. She packed underwear, two shirts, a sweater . . .

"Just what the hell are you doing?" Dominic's voice was pinched and winded. He filled up the doorway.

Ruby kept her back to him. "Packing."

He fought for his breath. "I can see that. Where are you going?"

"I don't know," she mumbled. "But I gotta get out of here—"

"And leave me all *alone*?" he screeched. "You can't do that!"

Ruby turned and faced her brother, who was practically drenched in sweat.

"I've never been here alone, Ruby. You can't leave me all by myself. Especially not at night."

Ruby held a pair of blue polyester pants and inhaled. Slowly she folded the pants in half and then in half again. She pressed the slacks to her chest and sighed. "It's okay, Dominic, I won't leave you."

"Promise?" He wiped the perspiration off his upper lip with the palm of his hand and shuffled his feet sheepishly.

Promise? She was sick to death of promises. Promises had kept her tethered to this house and her family for more than half a century. All she had ever longed for was freedom. And tonight, the night she had dreamed of for years—when Mother could no longer watch over her every movement with those hard, inscrutable eyes—she had hoped she would be released once and for all. She hadn't considered Dominic's needs.

"Promise?" he asked again, less urgently.

"Sure." She tossed the folded pants on her bed and said, "Maybe we should just go to sleep."

"But the dishes are dirty." Dominic nibbled on his thumbnail.

"That's okay. I'll do *them* in the morning."

"Mom wouldn't—"

"We made a deal, Dominic." Ruby raised her voice. "No more, 'Mommy would have done this or that.' *You* promised that." She reached for the overnight case and tossed it on a chair. "It's just you and me now and things are gonna change because of that. But they're gonna be good changes, Dom. Trust me."

"Yeah, but—" Dominic started to argue, but knew from the look on his sister's face that she'd do something to hurt him—like leave— if he went on. He took a deep breath and said, "Okay. Good night."

"Good night," Ruby answered, and put the folded pants on top of the suitcase. Dominic didn't budge. "What?" she asked him.

"I don't know." He shrugged.

Ruby untied her apron and draped it over the back of the chair. "Well, I'm tired, Dominic. Let's talk about all this stuff in the morning, okay?"

Dominic nodded, but moved over the threshold into the room, rather than out of it. He sat on her bed, which squealed miserably under his weight.

"What?" She leaned on the dresser and kicked off her shoes.

"I miss her," he said softly.

"Yeah, I know you do, Dom. It's gonna be easier now."

He shook his head. "I want to dig her up."

"No way."

"Come on, Ruby—it won't take that long. We'll be done before it gets light."

"What are you, crazy?" She knew the answer before the question was out of her mouth. They were both crazy. She was crazy to have stayed here for as long as she had, crazy to think that they could bury any part of their past and not cart it right along with them day in and day out. "I'm not gonna do it," she said, and motioned to the door. "Now go to sleep."

"No. I want to do it."

"Then go ahead, but I promise you that when you do that, I'm out of here. We made a deal—"

"Yeah, but I don't like the way it feels!"

"Yeah, but I do!" she hollered right back at him. "Listen to me, Dominic. I hated that old bitch and I'm glad she's gone. I hated her eyes and her sour breath and her scratchy voice, I hated the way she'd squeeze her eyelids and sigh. I hated the way she smelled and how she'd suck on goddamned biscotti before chewing it. I hated the fact that she had so much control over me that I gave up my only chance for happiness or love or even a life! I hated her and I'm glad she's dead and if you think I'm gonna dig up *anything* you're out of your god-damned mind!"

Ruby would have gone on had Dominic not hit her solidly over the head with a lamp that was shaped like a boot to resemble Italy. When Ruby's forehead made contact with Venice, it was all over for her.

Dominic held the lamp squarely over his head and leaned down. "Ruby?" He asked softly. "Ruby, I'm sorry, but you shouldn't say stuff like that about Mom. Ruby?" He put the lamp back on the dresser and got down on his knees to see if Ruby was just kidding. "Come on, Rube, quit foolin' around." He pressed his ear close to her mouth. Then he lifted her eyelids like they do on television, but he didn't know what he was looking for, so he let go. "Oh boy." He got up and wandered nervously around the second floor, trying to figure out what to do. "Mama, what am I gonna do? I just lost my temper, that's all. But she was asking for it, Mom. You heard what she said." After his third pass through his mother's bedroom, he nodded vigor-ously. He hurried back into Ruby's room, grabbed hold of her feet and dragged her down the stairs, through the living room, into the dining room, past the kitchen and the dishes she had left unwashed, out onto the porch, and over to the new rhododendron bush, where he laid her out in the shadow of the maple tree.

He worked feverishly undoing what they had done before. The night was still and the sliver of a moon gave him the darkness he needed. He put the rhododendron half on Ruby as he continued dig-ging. It felt like his chest would explode. His hands and back and arms were stiff and trembling with exertion, but he kept digging until he felt the blade of the shovel meet resistance. "Mama!" he whispered as tears started to dampen his round cheeks. As quickly as he could he unearthed what he and Ruby had so carefully buried. "Mama, I'm so sorry."

Once Mama had been exhumed, Dominic rolled Ruby into her place, wiped his hands on his shirt, said good-bye to his sister, and picked up the shovel.

Though the job wasn't quite as neat as when Ruby had helped, he was finished long before daybreak. The rhododendron was slightly crooked, but he was tired and figured it would settle into the soil and straighten itself out. He brought the shovel back to the garage and then came back, got Mother, tucked her under his arm, and hurried back into the house.

Without missing a step, he swiped a piece of cold bacon off Ruby's plate as he passed the kitchen table and headed to the living room. "It's okay, Mama. It's gonna be fine, believe me." He propped Mama on the sofa and turned to the fireplace. The space above the mantel was empty, save for the outline of a picture frame. The green wall was faded and discolored except where the picture had hung for as long as Dominic could remember. Dominic pushed a worn ottoman in front of the fireplace, stepped up, and wiped off the wall with a doily.

"Okay." He turned and gave his mother a big grin. "It's all ready." With that, he stepped down, lifted the framed picture of his mother off the sofa and very carefully put her back where she could see everything. "That's better, huh?" He studied her stern face with rapture. "You were right about her all along, Mama. I didn't want to do it, but Ruby said she couldn't stand having you look at her all the time. She said she was gonna leave if we didn't do something, so I went along. You know how she is. Always thinking of herself and trying to make me feel bad." He paused. "I know, I know. When you were here, she treated me with respect. But I was scared. I was scared she'd leave me alone. I don't like to be here all by myself. You know how much I hate to be alone."

Dominic went to the kitchen to retrieve Ruby's cold pancakes. As he leaned over to get the plate, he looked out the back window and saw the listing rhododendron. Even in the predawn light, that spot in the garden drew his attention, as if it were lit with neon lights. He forced himself away from the window and brought the food back to the living room. As he ate his sister's meal, he talked happily to the image of his mother hanging over the mantel. When sleep overtook him, he simply curled up on the sofa and covered himself with an afghan Mama had made when he was a boy. "I'll straighten out that bush when I get up," he murmured as he drifted off. "It won't stick out so much when I fix it."

Speeding Cars
Karla Jay

Don't stop reading or tear this up. I'm not writing to you to call you names or reproach you. I just want to set the record straight after all these years, especially since I've been told you don't remember the incident with the car or the weeks leading up to it. I wish I didn't, either. For me, those days play in slow motion in both my waking hours and my dreams.

I know your side of the story. Because I never visited you in the hospital, you told our mutual friends that I had you committed in order to get rid of you, in order to end our relationship. I can imagine my actions seeming like callous abandonment to you. But did you really believe that of me? Did you have to see yourself as the victim? Wouldn't I have found an easier way out, like so many other couples do? Still, it's hard for me to understand how anyone bought such a story, since no one in New York has that kind of legal power. The state could have done it, but not me. Maybe your mother could have committed you. Or you could have signed yourself in. But the other side of queer is that we had no legal relationship that the courts would recognize. Yet, to this day, when I run into some former friends in the subway station, they avert their eyes as if they've seen a rat on the tracks. I wouldn't speak to me either if I thought your version was true.

Until now, my side of the story has been silence. I've been secretive about my pain. I couldn't tell our friends what had happened without reliving the agony over and over. I felt I must have let it happen or somehow caused it. I should have been smarter, or I should have seen it all coming. If I wanted to tell someone, where would I start? And if others knew what happened, they wouldn't understand. I couldn't make credible a sequence of events that made no sense to me either.

And so, I'm writing to you to let you know what I remember as happening. Maybe doing so will clear things up for me, too. I won't try to varnish my actions.

Surely, we were happy for the first three years, as content as any other couple—probably more so. You do remember that we had known each other for four years when Trudy suddenly left me for another woman. And how Benita, my other lover, felt threatened by my sudden intimacy with her and took a hike. Literally. When I last heard from Benita, she was still trekking from mountain to mountain around the world.

I see now that I felt hopeless about my life. I'd tried to avoid the possibility of complete loss by never being faithful to any of my lovers. Every relationship I'd ever been in was open, and though jealousy would strike from time to time, in truth we never did break up over someone else. My relationships ended when they imploded.

All the careful planning I'd put into not getting hurt by Trudy or Benita collapsed along with both relationships. In the few moments that I can laugh at it all, I wonder if that new deodorant I was trying sent everyone packing. That's the sort of minutia that fills my mind. So I know this account is full of both large and small events, and I hope you won't—like some outta control English teacher—mark me down for lack of focus.

Trudy was the love of my life—you knew that—and I made no effort to hide that from you because you were one of my best friends. I knew you wanted me. You never understood why I would sleep with Benita or just about anyone else except you. You'd done your own share of tricking around. If the unknown woman became a friend, that was great, but I wasn't going to risk friendship for a bit of sex. Anyone I knew more than a month was relegated to the "friends" category—permanently. It's just the way I'm made.

Since you were friends with both Trudy and me, you were off limits. Every couple has rules, however odd. Also, you just weren't my type. You were warm and soft, and I lusted after hard, cool, gym rats, triatheletes, marathon junkies, dykes on mountain bikes. Madison Avenue chic didn't turn me on.

Frankly, you scared me. You had a kind of brilliant intensity that made you the most charming of friends. Though you scorned sports, you had an athlete's mind-set: you obsessed about being number one. You stacked up ad accounts as if they were trophies. Your scathing reviews of everything—films, plays, new software, offerings from L.L. Bean—were always hilarious and eerily accurate. Your eyes became brighter, and your jabbing cigarette highlighted your points like a laser pen. But I couldn't imagine living with such profundity, such competitiveness. The very idea seemed tiring, draining. Imagine moving in with Virginia Woolf! I knew my limits.

I was lonely. Perhaps I took unfair advantage of your free time. Maybe you were taking advantage of my vulnerability, my singleness. All I know is that suddenly you turned up with so many tickets to shows and concerts that I thought you'd won some Broadway theater contest, and we were seeing each other every weekend. Though I may not have desired you, I had no time to consider someone else.

I was grateful for your attention. All I really wanted to do was withdraw into the bittersweet brown cave of my room and pull the covers over my head. I wanted to sleep until I woke up and found Trudy next to me in the bed again. Sleep and death are the only worlds without pain. In my dreams I could love in the past and do everything right for once. Going to Broadway musicals, films, concerts, and gallery openings with you kept me moving, and at least I slept from exhaustion, not depression.

You were pretty obvious about desiring me. You'd drive me home in your sweet little Porsche and sigh about having to drive back downtown to your apartment. You were the only person I knew who moaned about going back to Park Avenue, while I cherished the tiny one-bedroom I had once shared with Trudy (okay, and dozens before her).

I don't know why I fought the inevitable for six months. I guess I thought I'd snap out of my lethargy or that you'd meet someone more interesting. Or at least, you'd run into someone in your own tax bracket. You were attracted to the glitter of New York—that's why you'd moved here from South Dakota. I was basically a stay-at-home nerd, a teacher who marked history papers and wrote lesson plans every night until I would find myself staring at the TV in a stupor. In the past I'd joined groups, not because they interested me much, but because they were places to cruise. I'd have probably gone to Sexaholics Anonymous in the hopes of finding a date, except that I would never want to hang out with such people. I liked food and sex, and I'm not even sure in what order. I thought of myself as a foodie and a gourmet vegetarian chef, but you always wanted to eat out. I thought you gallant, and you had a glut of money back then. So we ate out every weekend. You said it relaxed you. The dinner checks made me tense. Looking back, I don't think you enjoyed my cooking. You claimed to have an allergy to tofu. You would have been a total carnivore, had that been socially acceptable. You thought that tobacco and vodka were two of the basic food groups.

Then, after we were watching *A Chorus Line* for the second time, I got looped on some champagne, and the next thing I knew we were lovers. When I woke up to the smells of sex and Marlboros, I knew I had just ruined a good friendship. Women don't like it any better than men when you announce afterward that you don't like them that way; there was no going back. I didn't have the heart to tell you it was the Dom Perignon, vibrator fatigue, and maybe a bit of sexaholism that had landed me in your bed.

Too hungover the following morning, I couldn't even remember whether the sex had been any good. You were beaming. Whatever we had done had worked for you. Sometimes the fulfillment of horny anticipation is enough to charge up a relationship at first, but that kind of sex tends to fizzle out faster than an opened bottle of seltzer.

As we continued to date, the sex was pleasant, though a bit too vanilla for my taste. You seemed ecstatic. I realized that over the years we'd discussed our jobs, our worries, and culture, but never anything intimate. There are no guidebooks for sliding gracefully from one type of relationship into another.

You smoked less, drank less, smiled more freely. I fed off your happiness, your eyes which were now bright, not with determination, but with joy. I loved you more than most of my sex partners. It should have been enough to make a life.

The sex part wouldn't have mattered had you been more like me, but you swore you were faithful to a flaw and demanded the same of me. The polyamorous and the monogamous simply don't mix. At least vegans and carnivores can order food separately. Amy, your ex, once told me how you flipped over a huge bookcase in a fury over her infidelity. She was laughing about it, but still pissed about the crushed early edition of *The Well of Loneliness*. It must have been pretty scary at the time. For someone who never works out, you are amazingly strong.

I knew you'd never agree to the kind of open relationship I'd had with Trudy and every other lover. I wondered whether I could accept a relationship on your terms. Even if I mentally acquiesced, I doubted I could change my inner nature to suit yours. I don't believe in corporate mergers—forget about the personal kind. I had nightmares in which you U-Hauled it over to my place, though I couldn't imagine you living in a building without full services, and a walk up was an insult to your self-esteem.

On the other hand, in 1986, AIDS was starting to make the news daily. Academics, aging hippies, hairdressers, construction workers—the plague didn't discriminate on the basis of class or race. It was only a matter of time until the menace would infiltrate the lesbian community. Trudy used to quip, "What is the name of that nasty disease with purple spots? B-i-s-e-x-u-a-l-i-t-y!" Everyone used to dump on bisexuals, when the real danger was intravenous drugs.

Our male friends dropped like rose petals at the end of fall. Many of them feared saliva, raw food, various forms of sex, poppers, the FBI, pet chimps, cat shit, an antigay conspiracy. The lack of a sure pattern made it all the scarier—Richard lasted eleven days; Mike is still alive.

The time of believing that the worst thing I would ever catch from sex was crabs was over. I had already shown symptoms of a less-than-normal immune system: CMV, fibromyalgia, and any bug that entered the school. You always seemed more worried about my ills than I did. After a while, the fibromyalgia pain was simply part of everyday living, and when it abated on occasion, I felt almost giddy.

I had always said that some lucky woman would be your partner. There didn't seem much out there anymore to interest me, and you'd

always been fun to be with. So when you demanded fidelity, I acquiesced, and six months later, we, like so many lesbian couples before
us, went two-by-two into our new co-op.

Thanks so all those vaginal suppositories and toilet paper rolls you
wrote ads for, we were able to buy Ethan Allen's finest—all the trap-
pings of domesticity, including a fancy black Boston bulldog puppy
with a white streak down his belly. He looked like one of those devil
dog cakes, and the name fit his feisty character. Good thing we didn't
give in to your urge to procreate—or rather, your urge for *me* to procreate.

We did have our roles. Yours was to be the driven corporate execu-
tive while I nurtured my students and grew sprouts under the kitchen
sink. On weeknights, you careened through the door sometime between ten and midnight, your eyes glassy and bloodshot. Otherwise,
you seemed indestructibly healthy. Your body was another co-op to
you, something to be occupied, decorated, and inhabited for your
convenience.

When you started to develop chronic fatigue syndrome, I can understand how freaked out you were. When it came to your body, you
wanted to be the boss. The damn furniture isn't supposed to whine.
Remember how you cursed at your lack of energy and refused to
change your diet, quit smoking, stop drinking, or consider exercising?
You treated your body as if it had betrayed you. I know the feeling,
but maybe the polyamorous take disloyalty more in stride.

Sedition infected our lives. When patriarchal medicine could offer
you little to make things better, you smelled treason all around you.
With your sexual energy often depleted, you convinced yourself that I
was cheating on you. Perhaps that's what you'd have done in my
place. I tried to make a joke of it; after all, this was the first time that I
had been accused of infidelity when I was actually innocent. But, in
truth, your allegations rankled me much more than if I had been
guilty, because they negated my sincere efforts to change my behavior, to respect your sensibilities and our commitment to one another.
When you called me a slut I wished it were still true; the sting would
have been less. I did cheat on you, but only in my dreams where I ca-
vorted with strangers. Perhaps I called out someone's name in my

sleep. I hope not, for they usually had names out of Virginia Woolf's life and novels—Clarissa, Rachel, Vita, Vanessa—or so other women have told me. You couldn't possibly think I had a real lover named Orlando, could you?

When we did connect sexually, you were changed. Your passion re-ignited our relationship. You were fierce to the point of violence. Were you trying to fist me out of love or anger? Both? Your bites were sharper than Devil Dog's. You were also more tender than ever. After sex, you'd hold me and cry that we were going to die together.

The world around us was dying anyway. Worrying about it was an exercise in futility. Since we had no children to protect from our genes, we would take our biological flaws with us to our graves.

I didn't know how to reassure you, to help you deal with illness it-self. You were impatient and angry. You lost your sense of humor. You blamed me for your illness. Somehow, you claimed I had con-tracted HIV from one of my many trysts and then I passed it on to you. You bitterly accused me of waiting for you to die so that I'd in-herit the apartment and share it with former, current, and future lovers.

How was it that monogamy turned out to be less secure than pro-miscuity, that jealousy was so intense in our own closed relationship? Openness is based on trust; monogamy is the product of fear.

I started to stumble upon empty Absolut bottles under the kitchen sink, in the bottom of the laundry basket under the clothes, and even behind your shoe rack. The house was filling up with the fumes of your smoke, your alcohol, your anger. I couldn't breathe. I could think of only one thing that would put your mind at ease.

"Let's get tested for HIV, and then you'll stop worrying."

"What happens when we come out positive?"

"We *won't* come out positive, and then you'll feel better. If through some fluke we do, then we'll deal with it, but it's unlikely."

The following day we trotted down to a city health department clinic. We sat on dilapidated chairs surrounded by depressed, pale men waiting for tests or results. Eventually, we were called in sepa-rately and lectured on the evils of unprotected sex before they took our blood. We left clutching our test numbers, small strips of paper that were supposed to save our relationship.

But deep down, I didn't want "us" to be saved. I wanted that lover I supposedly was cheating with. If I slept with her, I would be free. You wouldn't put up with her, or me.

When you tried to stop me from going to Albany for a teachers' convention because my "other lover" was there, you handed me the perfect plan. After my return home, I announced that at the conference I had hooked up with Artemis, a workshop organizer. How my life had changed! I tearfully confessed the crime I hadn't committed. I knew you'd never consider for a moment that I was making the whole thing up. I couldn't believe I was, either. I was crying not out of some theatricality, but because I dreaded the Absolut mess that was to come. I was prepared with a packed bag and a friend's promise to harbor me for the night should I need a refuge. Remembering Amy's story, I kept away from the tall furniture.

"Our relationship is over, right?" I tried to look sorry for my error, but not sad enough that you'd forgive me and patch things up.

"How was she?"

"Nice. It's not her fault." Heaven help me if she ever found some Artemis's number and called her.

You downed the last of the martini pitcher, then retreated into your bedroom. I sat down wondering whether I should leave anyway. It was your co-op, after all, and I was just the lover-in-residence. I dreaded this part of relationships—trying to figure out who bought the toaster, who'd chosen the bed linens. Why couldn't couples have divorce parties instead of commitment ceremonies? It's the final exit where you need those extra blankets and a second set of china.

But the apartment seemed too quiet. Not a sound from our bedroom, and Devil Dog was snuffling unhappily outside the door. I quietly opened the door and spotted you lying there with the empty bottles of vodka and Vicodin next to the bed.

The next thing I knew I was standing in front of your left headlight as you turned on the ignition, shocked that you made it as far as the car after washing down a bottle of painkillers with an Absolut chaser. Maybe all your heavy drinking had made you immune to opiates, but somehow you had the wherewithal to grab your car keys and shove the medics out of your way as you lunged out our front door and careened past the doorman into the street. Then you beat us all to your Porsche a half-block away. You, the pokey one. Now I wonder whether you had secretly swallowed speed instead of painkillers.

When you raced the engine, I felt glued to the asphalt as if the hot June morning had softened the tar and sucked my feet into it. Yet, I was certain that if I could just make eye contact with you, if you were still there behind the wheel in more than body, then you would see someone you loved—or once loved, at least—and roll down your window to listen to my plea. You glared at me through the windshield. I almost laughed: you looked just like Devil Dog when he's possessed by his bone. He doesn't want to bite me, but he just can't help himself when my hand approaches his favorite strip of rawhide. Only afterward I realize that I'm the one who should know better, the one who is supposed to respect the clenched teeth, the narrowed eyes, the flattened ears. That was you, exactly, except for the ears. So I should have known that you really would hit me with the car and that it never pays to get too close to the possessed.

I wouldn't be writing this account now if the medics hadn't yanked me out of the way when you suddenly hit the accelerator. If the police car hadn't cut you off, you would've killed more than a stray cat. Gawkers crowded the sidewalk for the free show. "I hope she has a gun!" yelled one old guy, waving his cane in a salute.

You forced the cops to bust the side windows and to add "resisting arrest" to the stack of charges they must have been writing up as they pursued you: speeding, going through red lights, driving under the influence, cat killer. If the lesbian community ever finds out about the last, you'll be ostracized.

I couldn't imagine pressing charges against my own lover. How can you have someone arrested after years of intimacy? I understood our battered neighbor—in a flash, I had become her, hadn't I? It was only later that I found out that death was exactly what you had in mind for me, for both of us, really.

It was a good thing you entered the Briarwood Psychiatric Hospital voluntarily. You could have wound up in prison or a state-run snake pit like Creedmore. I doubt you would've made a full recovery at some understaffed place that would've considered you sick just for being queer. No one except zucchinis should be stuck in those facilities.

Maybe a change of scene in a different city would help you get a fresh start. Is it such a good idea to return to your old advertising firm even if they're willing to take you back—the legal aspects of your disability aside? In comparison to your colleague who wrote obscene letters to seven female co-workers and claimed the "devil made him do it," you must seem a relatively minor liability. Like an adder, you had only one enemy in your sights. You emerged from a tight curl to strike the one closest to you—me.

If you ever want to end a relationship, smacking your lover in the hip with a car should be a sure-fire method. But that's not the entire reason it ended, why I couldn't even visit you at the hospital. The pills and the alcohol were an exact replica of my sister's suicide, though, unlike you, she succeeded. Had you died precisely as she had, you would have had your double death wish—I don't think I could have survived that type of loss twice. But you knew how Miranda had died, and I had to wonder whether you plagiarized the moment to torment me. You never intended to die. You were incredibly spry, whereas Valium and bourbon left Miranda in a coma from which she never emerged. I felt enraged at what felt like emotional manipulation, yet profoundly guilty for leaving you, just as I left my sister lying there in a coma for a month. But in the end, those who survive dysfunctional families/relationships often do so because we walk away.

That was one reason I couldn't visit you, but the main reason had to do with those little slips of paper, the ones we got for the HIV lottery. I kept our appointment the following week and found out that I was negative. By now I was suspicious about your obsession with AIDS, so I had a friend pretend to be you to get your results. She was so shocked to hear that you were HIV positive that she hardly had to fool the counselor—she turned white and burst into tears. Then she had to get counseling and referrals. By the time she returned to the waiting room, she almost believed she had AIDS.

I was stunned—and skeptical. What were the chances that you had a false positive? How could I leave you if you had full-blown AIDS?

How could I not leave you if you had betrayed me as you feared I had betrayed you? In my posttraumatic world, nothing was clear nor did I think anything would ever be clear again.

I started therapy the day after I left the emergency room. I hated the very idea of seeing a shrink—it was like paying to have a friend. But I knew, in psychological parlance, that I couldn't "process" any of this by myself. You remember Neela, the therapist. She was the ex of an ex of an ex. In the lesbian community there are only three degrees of separation. She told me right off that I could never see you again, that you were homicidal. Maybe that put it in my mind that this AIDS thing wasn't coincidental. Nor was the rough sex spontaneous. There must have been some reason that you focused on one disease from the vast choices available. Neela suggested that I speak, discreetly, to some of your colleagues. Sure enough, Tim confirmed that you snorted coke, and shot up small amounts of heroin from time to time.

So you knew you were infected, and you planned to take me with you, one way or the other. You said you'd love me forever. But my test turned out negative, so not even the hickeys paid off.

Now you know that I knew. I learned the price of having given up on my own life. Ironically, after I saw death up close, I regained the will to live and thrive, if only to thwart your plans.

Be well, stay safe, be positive emotionally. You don't deserve to die either, in spite of what you tried to do.

HIV is another speeding car, too. Except that it doesn't aim for anyone in particular.

Violation

Victoria A. Brownworth

LAURA RIVERS IS GUILTY.

The headlines are emphatic, definitive, unrelenting. The jury in concerted, inexplicable agreement.

Guilty. On all counts. Murder one. First degree. Premeditation. Planned and executed.

No death penalty; she is a woman, after all. But life. Life in prison, with no possibility of parole for twenty years. Laura Rivers will be fifty-four then. Her life will not be over, but her choices will be. No children, that's certain. No advanced courses of study (impossible to complete one's doctorate in psychological trauma and the complexities of international political torture from prison, although the experience of prison itself might be revelatory). No future, really. Those whom Laura loves are already mostly gone or estranged or . . . she isn't sure about Katrina.

Her mother, Lise, dead a decade earlier from either an accidental or deliberate overdose after years of crushing depression. Her death at forty-six, years younger than Laura will be when she can first apply for parole. Her father, absent, a functional alcoholic until he became totally nonfunctional and disappeared, now no more than a missing persons report and a painful ache of loss each holiday. Her brother, Matthew, born-again Christian in response to their parents dissolution, always seeking order and finding it finally in the tight grip of the Bible Belt where Laura had been squeezed out long before her conviction for murder. And then there was her lover, her beloved. Katrina, Soviet-born, Jewish, Eastern-European-raised expatriate leftist activist against political torture by way of her own brutal teenage prostitution before the Berlin Wall fell and her entire family scattered in a diaspora of their own making and she finally made her way to America, to Brooklyn, and into the arms of Laura, her very own Statue of Liberty, her very own safe haven.

Laura, who no one would ever have considered capable of murder. Laura, who had been everybody's good girl, everybody's rock, support, caregiver. Laura, who had practically raised Matthew, had mothered her own mother, her mother who had been paralyzed by a fear none of them had understood, a fear that hid in the ever-darkening shadows of her own mind. Her mother, whom Laura had spent a lifetime trying to be other than, but who, after her death, Laura had tried hard to deconstruct, to do a psychological forensic study on, to autopsy. Her mother, the ethereal Lise, waiflike yet feral, like a beautiful stray cat who can't quite be coaxed inside. Laura needed a mother now. Needed someone to comfort her, lull her into believing all would somehow be made right.

Of course Laura had friends and colleagues and a mentor here and there. She had supporters throughout her arrest and arraignment and trial and conviction. There was a stalwart group who found it difficult to believe she could commit any crime, let alone one so heinous, one involving torture and mayhem. There were those who found it hard to look at her, the woman they knew, the tall, curvaceous, doe-eyed girl with flaxen hair and a peaches-and-cream complexion, and believe that she could kill, and kill so calculatingly, so pitilessly. After all, Laura had always looked like a sweet Iowa farm girl who had lost her way and ended up in the big city much like Dorothy had landed in Oz, delivered via a bad tornado or some other inexplicable act of God. Laura looked like what she was: displaced, out of her element.

Why hadn't the jury seen it too? Why hadn't the jury seen in her the evocation of innocence? Why was this the one time in Laura's entire life when her soft, good looks had worked against her? For the reality was, Laura Rivers *wasn't* guilty. Not of this crime. Laura Rivers was going to spend twenty years to life in a maximum security prison for a hideous torture murder. A murder she had not, in fact, committed. A murder she had adamantly asserted she had not committed, asserted it over and over, before and during her trial. The jury had been so wrong.

Now Laura was strip-searched and showered and sprayed for all manner of vermin; now Laura was given a dark blue blanket, a washcloth, a towel too small to dry off with from a thrice-weekly shower but not big enough to become a weapon or a means for suicide in the tiny, dormitory-like cell in the women's prison in a state no-where near Katrina or Matthew or any of the staunchest friends—Raoul, Luis, Melinda, Tamika, Serena—who still, perhaps, believed that she didn't belong here wearing regulation navy blue shirt, sweater, and pants (had she ever worn pants except when she was working in the field and needed them for protection? Couldn't pants have saved her if . . .), the garb of some delinquent Catholic schoolgirl.

It wasn't wholly a mistake, of course. Laura had known the man she was convicted of killing. *Intimately,* she thought. Knew Reginald Perry right down to the skin. She wasn't completely innocent of what the prosecution claimed. She was only innocent of murder. Of may-hem. Of torture. Of depraved indifference for the life of another. Her entire career, her entire *life* ever since she was a small child preventing one or another of her mother's suicide attempts (she hadn't been there to intercede in the successful one), had been dedicated to nothing but saving lives.

The predicate of her dark, lurid, endlessly traumatic childhood de-fined her in its otherness from violence. The subsequent work—her trips to Guatemala, El Salvador, and then the long obscenity of Rwanda and later, the Congo—had riven her. The deep, confessional, night-into-day revelations from Katrina as they lay in bed together, barely touching, Katrina's short black hair spiky and sharp against her shoulder, Katrina's inability to cry over all that had happened to her, just like the other victims of torture they both worked with, her inability to cry over what had happened to them both, making Laura's heart pound and her throat constrict and her body shudder in unspent tears—hadn't all of it been the litmus against the crime she had been convicted of?

Why hadn't the jury seen any of this? Why hadn't they understood who she was?

Laura Rivers sits in her small, oblong cell. Sits in the center of her narrow, cotlike bed, which is bolted to the floor to prevent any excitement, any dismantling, any attempts at committing a crime, against others or against one's self, involving a curl of bedspring, a sliver of casement, a shank created out of an unwelded piece of metal. She is sitting in a yogalike position, but yoga and the calm required to practice it are far from her unmeditative mind. Laura is trying to imagine how she will escape before twenty years to life. Laura is wondering if anyone will come to see her, will proffer a plan, will decry the injustice, the *wrong* in her conviction. Laura is considering what else the papers are saying now, what else is being claimed of and attributed to her in publications given to discourse on the kind of work she does and the politics of it. Wondering if there are disbelieving or condemning statements about her in *The Nation* or *New York*. If she has made "The Talk of the Town" section of *The New Yorker*. If *Vanity Fair* will do one of its unpleasant exposés of the totality of her career and its unseaming in her trial, the critique wedged between perfume inserts for Armani and Hugo Boss. If the sweet and compassionate Latina reporter from *Newsday* will remain so now that a jury so completely not of Laura's peers has found her guilty, guilty, guilty with no mitigation whatsoever, no reprieve. For didn't they convict Laura more of a lack of conscience than even of murder? That is certainly how she sees it. She leans back against the flat gray drywall of her cubicle cell, closes her eyes, and begins to cry. Laura has become the prisoner she has always worked to save, the prisoner sentenced to the torture of knowing that they are not guilty as the door slams behind them and the key they can never retrieve turns with finality in the lock.

In Brooklyn Heights it is cold, an almost unbearably windy March day of the sort that reminds New Yorkers of the tenacity of winter, that the presumptive crocus buds and naive snowdrops sprouting in the parks and sporadic neighborhood gardens are mere ephemera. *Spring could be nothing more than delusion. Spring might never come.*

This is what Katrina thinks as she walks and walks, long strides at a pace as brisk as the wind itself on a harsh Sunday afternoon in which snow squalls keep winding up, swirling over her, then abating. It has been decades now since she was in Kiev, years since she was in East

Berlin—not East anymore, she corrects herself, just *Berlin,* as if the grim divide between having and endlessly *not* having weren't still as brutally apparent as the wall itself once was. Those places where winter lasts so much longer than it does in New York. But something about this day reminds her of all those other days in those other places she would just as soon forget, places in which winter never loosed its grasp on any of them, especially not the girls she traveled with.

The girls, in small packs throughout the broken Soviet Union, the shattered Eastern Bloc. Her pack, her best friends Dominique, Lilya, Masha, Eva, and the little twelve-year-old they called Sputnik, with whom she trolled and trolled and trolled the desolate, dirty, moneyless streets, giving hand jobs and blow jobs around the world (as if she hadn't already been there and back at fourteen) for less than it would take to buy a pint of three-day-old borscht or a half-dozen blintzes hardened at the edges, the cheese starting to go off, or a pound of some kind of greenish meat that might have been a brisket once or might have just been a piece of some butcher's old dog.

Katrina stops, looks out over the water. At the park again—Why is she here again?—at the edge of the river, looking down into the water, a dark, impenetrable, bottle green. "Are there fish there?" she would ask Laura who would look at her hard, but never answer. "Bodies, sometimes," Laura said once, her back to Katrina, said this not long before . . .

Katrina does not know what Laura's conviction means. What her sentence means. What Laura's being sent two states away to a small women's prison nowhere near anything—it might as well be in the Soviet Bloc for all she knows about this Muncy—means. Katrina has spent thirty-seven years disbelieving police and courts and judges and all those connected with them. She has spent what seems far more than one lifetime watching the innocent punished and the guilty set free. She knows it is supposed to be different here, that this is not Russia or East Germany. She knows the very fact of her being here signals freedom of a sort she has never fully comprehended. She knows that her sponsorship by the Balinskis, who had once cared for her mother in Kiev and then her in Berlin and her green card, courtesy of Amnesty International, and her seven-year love affair with Laura, testament to their shared convictions, their standard-bearing for justice, their determination to stop at least one torture here or there, are all pieces in the puzzle called freedom that she knows she can never really embrace because it is a language she has never fully learned, an idiom simply beyond her ken.

A flock of geese declares itself above her, loud, insistent as the fog-horn dimly heard a few miles down river. Katrina looks up and feels another shower of late-season flakes upon her upturned face. The V-formation shakes, a little askew, and yet close enough to letter-perfect that she wonders at its instinctual patterning. The sky is a troubled gray, limned with bilious clouds. Fear washes over Katrina as she looks at the geese disappearing into an ill-defined horizon and looks at the clouds, so utterly ominous. Does she believe Laura is innocent, or does she think her lover killed and mutilated the man, Reginald Perry, who beat and raped and tortured them both eighteen months ago in the bedroom that had been Katrina's only sanctuary in her entire life? Katrina turns away from the river. She simply does not know. And since she does not know, neither does she know what her love for Laura means now. If Laura did what they said, should Katrina love her more or less or not at all? She cannot remember details anymore. Details make her anxious, make her reach for the little blue atomizer that sprays a calming tincture of medication into the back of her throat that makes her heart stop beating wildly and makes her thoughts race a little less. Katrina thinks if she sprays the little atomizer enough she will be able to return to work, be able to talk to others about torture and pain and despair, repairing them as she has done for over a decade. Then she thinks maybe not. Maybe she will only ever be able to walk here, here along the water's edge just before you get to the smattering of trees where they found Reginald Perry's body. The *pieces* of Reginald Perry's body. All in place, a butcher's cutout. Spread-eagled on the ground, face down, his underwear stuffed in his mouth, his penis still inside it, splats of blood outlining his body, just like . . .

The conundrum of Laura's crime, of Reginald Perry's crime, swirls around her as a blast of ice pellets spews into her face. She pulls long coat around her slender body, tightens the scarf around and turns toward home. The home she shared with Laur led her away from the courtroom, handcuffed and chained. The home that has felt strange and unwelcoming since the night Reginald Perry rang their bell and sundered their lives for good and all. The home that there are not enough little blue atomizers in the world to keep her sane enough to stay in on her own without Laura.

Rosaria Xavier has been staring at the flashing blue screen for over twenty minutes, twisting the same curl of dark brown hair over and over her right index finger, tapping the same key over and over—delete, delete, delete. It's Sunday, she shouldn't even be here. She's not on deadline. She's not even really plotting out a story, even though she alluded to her editor, Tom Blakely, that one would be in the works in the next day or two. "Follow-up to the Laura Rivers case," she had tossed offhandedly at him. "There's more here than the conviction. We all know that." He had mumbled something to her that had sounded like "Go at it," and she had wondered exactly what it was she was going to go at. She had no idea. But that lack of idea was keeping her up nights—four nights since Laura's conviction, which had stunned the hell out of her and had clearly shocked Laura as well, and Laura's little cadre that had kept a kind of vigil for her in the second row of the courtroom for five-and-a-half weeks, just behind Rosaria, the guy from *The Times,* her friend Nella from the *Village Voice,* that sanctimonious prick Tomlinson from the *Post,* and the little cipher she knew nothing about, Strang, from *The Nation.* Laura Rivers was news. Postconviction, Laura Rivers was *still* news.

Murder isn't that big a deal, Rosaria thinks. There's so much of it. Murd.. n her beat for long enough that Rosaria no longer got the calls to go check out this or that body. She what people could do to one another and why, but churned up by it anymore. She regretted her de- er therapist told her she was reneging on her own ew that a measure of detachment was what al- ep and allowed her to get close to people who red, and tell their stories like they mattered.

That was how she had met Laura Rivers, whom she had liked immediately. Laura, so warm, so welcoming, even her physical presence seemed inviting. Laura and her crisp, cool, Russian girlfriend, Katrina, and Katrina's Russian friend, her *best* friend, the sexy Dominique, had asserted. Dominique, the stripper-cum-prostitute-cum-who-knows-what-kind of troublemaker.

Laura and Katrina had been raped—the scene had been particularly gruesome as Rosaria remembered it. She and a reporter from *The Observer* whom she didn't know and photographers from the *Daily News* and *Post* had turned up a couple of hours before dawn. September, one of those really hot weeks between summer and fall, and the apartment had been stifling. The crime scene guys were just packing up and the PR gal from the Heights PD had been there to orchestrate press. It was one of those dicey cases—race, sexual orientation, some odd political stuff possibly involved, maybe even Russian mob—and the police needed it covered, carefully. It was clear they had picked who they wanted fresh on the scene. Rosaria had been pleased she'd passed the litmus, but hadn't relished the smell of overripe blood so early in the morning. It had been a long time since she'd retched at a crime scene.

The shocker for her was that no one was dead. Because the amount of blood was pretty spectacular. And then there was the bed. Rosaria had called for Jake Phillips, her favorite photo guy, but he'd been late getting there and the light had changed in the room by the time he was taking shots. Rosaria wouldn't forget it, though.

The women's bodies were outlined on the double bed. It was hard to explain to Jake what she meant. Like those chalk body outlines from old thrillers. It looked as if the women had been pressed, hard, like a mold, into the bed. And then their shapes outlined. In blood, and, according to the PR gal, semen. That had shown up with the luminal. In the half light when Rosaria arrived you could see it easily: the shapes of the two women glowed from the bed. Spread-eagled, arms and legs tied to both each other and the sweet little four-poster that seemed so old-fashioned and also so stereotypically perfect for this kind of ritual, S/M crime scene. According to the police officer stationed outside the apartment door who was allowed to answer questions, the perp had tied them both up, one face down, the other face up, and had taken turns doing them—with his dick, his fist, and a double-edged knife. The friend—Dominique—had turned up while it was going on and he'd taken off. Didn't seem interested in her, just them. Part of the ritual. That the women were both expected to survive was, according to the forensics guy Rosaria caught up with later, nothing short of a miracle. "He tried to gut them," Miller told her, his voice low, insinuating, and a little lurid. "There's no other way to describe it. Gut them, you know, like fish."

Reginald Perry had turned himself in. Had confessed to the crime and explained, with an interpreter, a complicated connection to the women involving their efforts to obtain the release from prison of a Haitian political dissident whom Perry, also Haitian, claimed had stolen not just his identity, but his entire life. It had seemed open and shut. Perry was charged, pled out, and about to be sentenced when the feds stepped in and he was released. Just like that. A material witness in something else. Or so they told Rosaria. And Laura. That had been eighteen months ago.

Katrina had been the worst injured of the two women. Her bowel had needed resecting and she'd had to have a hysterectomy. She'd been in critical for two weeks, in the hospital for six. It had taken nearly to the time of Laura's arrest for Katrina to get back to work. That's when Perry—hacked up and mutilated—had turned up in the park near Laura and Katrina's Brooklyn Heights apartment. That's when it was clear the case wasn't over just because the feds said it was.

Laura hadn't been arrested immediately. She'd been questioned, along with Katrina and a few of their friends. She hadn't even been asked not to leave New York. Laura had gone to Haiti to ensure the final release of the prisoner, Pierre D'Alique, the man Perry claimed had stolen his identity. She had come home in time for Katrina's first day back at work. First and last. PTSD—post-traumatic stress disorder—had finally claimed her after years of hovering on the margins of her life, after years of small, grisly tortures at the hands of countless people in several countries. Katrina was now, thanks to Perry, what she had never been before, had never allowed herself to be before: a victim. Laura had driven straight to Long Island, to the small private hospital where Katrina had been scheduled to do reentry with torture survivors. Katrina herself had been sedated with the same medications used to calm those recently released back into the world from hells unimaginable to most others living in the small Long Island community. Except perhaps those in the apartment buildings along the oceanfront who sat and kibitzed in the delis along the Long Island Parkway and who held inside their wrists the faded blue numbers that had once been their only identities in Bergen-Belsen or Treblinka or other circles of hell.

Day had turned to night and Laura had eaten her first meals at Muncy, had gone through her first lights-out roll call. Now she lay under the stiff white sheets that smelled too strongly of bleach and the rough blanket that made the inside of her arms itch if she forgot and laid them outside the covers. Under her pillow were photos: of Katrina, of her mother, of her close friends from work—Raoul and Luis, Melinda and Tamika and Serena, all of whom had stood by her at trial. Another of Matthew, who had been there the day of the verdict, surprised her by coming up behind her and whispering as if they were still kids, "Good luck, Laur. I'm praying for you." She didn't have a photo of her father. Or of Darien, her attorney and once her best friend, who had worked hard at explaining to the numb-looking jury just what kind of work it was that Laura did. Darien, who had looked stunned when the verdict had been read, had grabbed her arm and told her how sorry he was and that he would begin work right away on an appeal. Darien, who had taken the case despite being black, like Reginald Perry, and questioning, she knew, because he had confessed to her one night when it was just the two of them in her apartment— Katrina was out with Dominique—if he was violating some kind of racial code in defending her, a white woman accused of murdering and mutilating a black man. Some of his friends had said the crime was a kind of lynching.

Laura had asked Darien if he needed to quit her case. She had tried to quell her anger, her resentment, but she had instead asked him to look again at the crime scene photos of her and Katrina. Had asked if the sentence Reginald Perry had first received—twenty to life—before he was released, had seemed unjust. Darien had looked away and then back at her and said no. She had asked him if it mattered if she were innocent or guilty and he had said no again, this time without hesitation, but a cloud of something had passed across his face and from that moment on she had known, for certain, that he too believed she was guilty.

The question, of course, was who had actually killed Perry if Laura had not and Katrina had not. Laura was certain Katrina hadn't killed him because of the horror on her face when the police had first come to interrogate the two women and given details of Perry's execution. Then later, the quizzical look Katrina had given Laura when they had arrested and charged her with murder. No, Katrina had not done it.

But who? Laura lay in her hard metal bed and wished for a cigarette for the first time in years. A low hum of noise thrummed just beyond her cell and suddenly Laura wished the cells weren't separate, that she had a roommate, that there was the breathing of someone other than she in the room with her. A thin ochre line of halogen light split the room from the tiny window near the ceiling behind her bed. No light came from under her door. She held the photos of those she loved between her hands like a rosary.

Were there friends of Pierre D'Alique who knew something Laura didn't about his connection to Reginald Perry? Could all of this horror, this unabating pain have been caused by yet another grisly political scheme? Had her work crossed some line, was D'Alique someone other than the fragile, rail-thin prisoner of conscience sick with HIV who had barely been able to walk from his cell to the truck that would take them both to the airport and a flight to New Jersey and a sponsoring family? Had she and Katrina been caught by someone else's secrets and lies? After all, Rudolf Hess and Adolf Eichmann had looked frail at the end, too. Frail for genocidal monsters. Was D'Alique really Macoute, as Perry had told police? Macoute, the zombielike, voodoo-practicing, secret death squads that had run—terrorized—Haiti for decades under the Duvaliers. Or was Perry himself Macoute, released by the feds to lead them to other members of the Duvalier movement still trying to undermine what was left of the shambles of the Aristide democracy? The questions roiled in her head. The only certain answer she could claim as she felt sleep pull her under was that she herself had not killed Perry. All she had done was promised to meet him by the edge of the river on the night he had been murdered.

Dominique Gessen stood at the door of Katrina's apartment, her flamboyantly manicured hand upraised to knock, but hesitant. Katrina had called her, a hysterical edge in her voice that Dominique had heard only once or twice in their more than twenty years of knowing each other, of turning tricks and eating garbage and risking their lives together. When none of those things had caused Katrina to pour out a torrent of Russian in a quavery whisper, what had done so now? Katrina, the one person Dominique loved—had ever loved, really—the one person she would do anything to protect. Katrina, who was all she had left to remind her of what she had survived, what they had both survived. Her knuckles rapped lightly on the door. Katrina let her in.

Dominique had been there that night, of course. Had come, like now, at 2 a.m. She had been supposed to come earlier, but she'd been kept at the new club—she was so glad to be away from Brighton Beach and the old Russian men who never tipped very much despite the show Dominique gave them. Katrina had told her exactly when to come, but she had been late and when she arrived the smell of blood had seeped out from under the door and she had nearly run. She had smelled that smell before, in Kiev. It had been all over her—all over her and Katrina—from the man they had been hired to lure up to an apartment by another man they would later know was KGB, Gorbachev be damned, KGB still there then, rising again, Dominique thought, with Putin. The smell was the smell of that night more than twenty years ago. It was the smell of torture, of killing.

The smell was thick and with the heat it caught in the back of her throat. The door had not been locked—she hadn't knocked, had known not to knock. Inside, mayhem. Blood, gore. And some gurgling sounds she couldn't immediately place coming from the bedroom. She had entered just in time to see the man, Perry. He had been at the new club just a few days before when she was there with Ka-

trina and he had looked out of place and had left. Perry pulled his
bloody fist from Laura's anus. Laura, who wasn't moving, whose eyes
were blackened shut. Laura, who was tied at the ankle to Katrina,
who lay, face down, on the bed. Katrina, unmoving, bleeding, apparently dead.

Perry had turned to Dominique and given her a look she couldn't
quite place. She knew she should have screamed, but no thought of
sound came to her. Her purse dropped from her shoulder to the floor
and he stood up then and walked past her—just walked past her—
into the bathroom. Water ran and ran and still she stood in the same
spot. He returned, drying his hands on a soft green towel now
streaked with bits of the innards of her friends. "Macoute" was all he
had said to her, some French word she did not know. And then he had
pointed to the bed. "They will come back to life," he said, his voice
heavily accented and disturbingly flat. "They will bring others with
them. Macoute always bring others with them."

And then he had gone.

The police and ambulance had come. She had told her story over
and over. No, he wasn't Russian. No, she and Katrina knew no mobsters. That was a lie, because the Balinskis had gotten them here and if
they weren't mobsters. . . . Yes, it could have been revenge. The
women worked for a human rights group, worked with torture victims. Right now? In Haiti. The Congo. No, not Russia. No, she
wasn't sure why Katrina had asked her to come over so late. Maybe
because the two women were going somewhere, to secure the release
of a prisoner, and they always met with her first. Yes, it was late, but
she was a dancer and she worked late and Laura often worked through
the night and Katrina—Katrina didn't sleep very well.

He had called Laura the night of his murder. She had recognized his
voice from the night of the rape, from the lineup. He had wanted to
meet her. By the river. Explain. . . . She had not understood his patois
then, what it was he wanted to explain. Explain why he had tried to
eviscerate her and the woman she loved? Explain why he had tortured
them like they were voodoo sacrifice? Explain why she would never
stop hearing Katrina's screams as he had slid the knife inside her, explain why she could hardly bear her own period now because the smell

of blood sickened her almost to the point of madness? Explain why it had taken her and Katrina nearly a year to be able to touch when they had first met and now it had taken them more than a year to barely touch again? What was it that he could possibly explain, this man who rightfully belonged in a prison cell for life, unlike all the men and women she had tried to free over the years from brutal, illegal incarcerations.

Explain? There were no explanations. None for the beautiful, broken bird that lay, speechless, face to the wall, in their bedroom. None for the images that Laura would never, ever—*"Jamais, jamais—tu compris?"* she had screamed into the phone—blot from her memory. "Macoute," he had told her, his voice high, shrill, a little hysterical. *"Elle est Macoute. Macoute!"* Who was Macoute? And why should she care? With any luck at all, with any *justice* Macoute would take Perry to the hell where he belonged.

He had not been there. *Had she misunderstood where she was to meet him?* She had walked along the river in the chill November night and imagined Christmas a few weeks off. Her father missing, her brother in Iowa, her mother dead, her lover a pale Dickensian wraith.

The air had crackled with cold and her own static fear. The switchblade lay in her gloved hand, her index finger on the little nub that would flick the blade—nine inches, enough to gut a fish or kill a man. Lights twinkled across the river and somewhere nearby Russian music played. She paced for twenty-five minutes, then left. As she walked to her car she thought she heard something—a gurgling noise—but she turned and it was gone.

Katrina had left her a note. She was with Dominique, at the club, a new Russian singer, she felt inexplicably homesick tonight. She wasn't feeling very strong and so she would not be gone long. *I love you.* The only Cyrillic letters Laura knew.

The Balinskis had connections. They had them in Kiev, in Berlin, in Brooklyn. It hadn't taken long for Gregor to track down Perry. Dominique had watched, not quite impassive, while Gregor did what he had learned at the hands of Russia's finest torturers. First there had been the phone call. Then there were no reprieves. Perry had let loose a stream of French babble Dominique recognized as pleas for first his body, then when that was slivered away, his life. And there had been blood to go with it. Lots of blood. Dominique had stood against the wall, her long, russet hair flung back, smoking a cigarette, her perfectly manicured hands little flashes of pink and teal in the half light as Gregor ended by slitting Perry's throat into a gaping howl. They drove him to the river in silence. Dominique explained to Gregor exactly how the body was to be arranged. She closed her eyes and imagined Katrina, face down, covered in gore. Remembered her own inability to move, to go to her, to help her, to save her. *Now* she would save her. One thing Dominique had learned over the years was that everything must be settled. Everything. The unfinished can be lethal. Finality is imperative.

Katrina held Dominique close as dawn crept up behind the thick green drapes she had made after the assault. Dominique thought the curtains were the color of the sea, the color of a dark, cold, winter sea in which food swirled tantalizingly below the surface, but could never be reached, even by the starving. That had been the last time she and Katrina had held each other this close, the night they had stood at the edge of the sea, ready to die together rather than live out one more night of filthy men and desperate hunger.

But now they were in America, where all things were possible and Katrina was holding her again, close enough that Dominique could smell the citrus scent of her shampoo and if she opened her mouth just a bit against Katrina's cheek, she would taste the saline that lined her face from a night of tears over Laura, over her fear that Laura had become what they had spent their lives in concert against: a murderer, a torturer.

Dominique had soothed Katrina, sung her low Russian songs that her mother had sung to her until she'd been killed when Dominique was ten. She had told Katrina she mustn't think about what Laura had done as anything but a service, a quid pro quo, a ridding the earth of evil, of scum. The words had spilled out, in Russian and English. "That, too, is what you want, *nyet*? Removal of the scum? Think, Katya, *what he did to you. Both*. She doesn't deserve prison. She was right and good to protect you. She *avenged* you, *Mishka*. Love her for it." Dominique had tilted Katrina's face toward hers, her pale blue eyes meeting Katrina's. "*Mishka, Mishka,* we will get Gregor and he will take us to see her. Very soon."

Dawn on her second day in prison brought a sullied pink light into Laura's cell. She wasn't sorry Reginald Perry was dead. Wasn't sorry he had suffered as she and Katrina had suffered. This, she knew, was her true crime. She lacked remorse. Lacked "humanity." She might have killed him herself—hadn't she gone there to meet him with a weapon, she who abhorred violence? Hadn't she thought every time she saw the scars on Katrina's body how much she had wanted him dead? Someone had done her the favor she would never have been able to do for Katrina. She was indeed guilty. Guilty of wanting Perry dead, of not caring if he too was a victim of Haitian torture, of caring only that he suffered for making her lover suffer, for making *her* suffer.

Laura knew as she rose to dress moments before the bang on her cell door and the morning roll call that she must stop caring *who* or she would indeed go mad as had so many prisoners of conscience before her. Were they like her? Did they question if some sin of omission had cast them into hell? Had that been true of D'Alique? Or Perry? No, Laura would now do as she had instructed so many others to do over the years. She would cast aside her questionable guilt and concentrate on her incontrovertible innocence. This very day she would begin the campaign for her own freedom. She would ask Darien to help in that endeavor, ask her friends to treat her as they would any other prisoner of conscience, ask her brother to intercede through his church. She would contact Rosaria Xavier—she had been so sweet, so sympathetic—and get her to write about Laura's false imprisonment. She would get herself out of here. She would escape.

Laura knew there was something else she must do. She must tell Katrina the truth. That she had wanted Perry dead, had wanted to avenge them both, but that she had not done it; she was not a killer. Yes, she had gone there to meet him, but at his request, not hers. But he had already been dead then, past help, his femoral artery and his carotid slit by a master of torture which was not she. Laura knew what she must say to her lover. And at the end she would write *I love you* in the only Cyrillic letters she knew.

Murder on Chuckanut Drive

Ouida Crozier

1

Whatcom County Sheriff Department's Chief of Detectives Caitlin O'Shaughnessy pulled her department's unmarked vehicle in behind a Bellingham PD patrol car, edging off the road as far as possible. Traffic crept by, funneling through one lane on an already too-narrow two-lane route, directed by uniformed officers and sheriff's deputies with hooded flashlights. As Lin climbed out of the car, unfolding her long legs, stretching to her full five feet ten inches, she noted with disgust how the drivers and passengers sought to see what it was that brought Bellingham and Whatcom County's finest out so early on a Saturday morning.

Lin had caught the call as she had emerged from the shower. A motorist had reported an apparent hit and run on Chuckanut Drive near Larrabee State Park. It would be treated as a homicide until established otherwise, and she would be closely supervising the investigation for the sheriff's department.

It was with regret that Lin had called her date for the day and canceled their scheduled breakfast, explaining that one of her detectives was on medical leave following a minor surgery. And, if it turned out that the death was in fact a homicide, not an accident, her presence on the case would be essential.

On her way to the scene, Lin had downed a carton of yogurt and a granola bar, mourning the hearty breakfast that she had planned. However, once there, she became the focused professional. Although every law enforcement office in the area knew the county's first female chief of detectives, Lin expected no special treatment. Flashing her badge to an officer at the perimeter, then slipping it into her belt, she stepped across the police line and began her own preliminary assessment.

The fog lingered, though the sun was now above the mountains to the east. *Perversity!* she exclaimed to herself, momentarily distracted. Of course it hindered the investigation of the site. Then, subliminally, she took in the position of the body, which lay in a crumpled sprawl. Next, she noted that someone had marked out something at the east side of the road, and that another spot on the west side had been circled with crime-scene paint.

Spying one of the four detectives she supervised, Lin approached him. Sergeant Karl Johansen was a big-boned, blond bear of a man who might have had a career in professional football. Lin was pleased to see him. She knew Johansen to be a competent, capable investigator, and assumed him to be the officer in charge of the scene.

"Karl—what do we have here?" Lin asked by way of greeting. She took in his rumpled look and surmised he had been roused directly from bed.

Johansen nodded. He likewise respected Lin. Since he had joined Whatcom County Sheriff's Department, the two of them had worked closely on a number of cases. Thorough, detail oriented, she was fair and good to work for. She gave her detectives support and credit for a job well done.

"Looks like hit-'n'-run," he replied. "Passing motorist almost ran over the body, lying in the middle of the road like that. Called it in from his car phone, then waited for the patrol car to arrive. He's over there." He nodded to where a graying man in casual clothing stood talking with a uniformed officer. "The ME says her spine is broken and her skull is crushed, most likely from impact with the pavement. Whoever hit her had to be going mighty fast."

Lin and Johansen exchanged a look. This winding, narrow road had a speed limit of fifteen to thirty-five miles per hour, depending on how many curves there were in a mile and how far down it was to the waters of Chuckanut Bay. Although it was tempting to assume that no one would be foolhardy enough to speed on a road like this, both officers knew that people took incredible chances when sitting behind the wheel of an automobile, particularly if alcohol was involved.

"Who is she?" Lin asked, out of duty, always hating to hear, fearing every time it might be someone she knew. So far, it had not been.

Johansen shrugged. "No ID. She must have been out for a morning run; all she's wearing is sweats and running shoes. No purse, no wallet, no fanny pack—nothing." He shook his head. "These joggers. They don't learn." People without ID peeved Johansen.

While Lin agreed with Johansen's sentiments, it was his peeve, not hers. "Let's go take a look," she said.

As she approached the mangled heap of human remains, Lin steeled herself for the first glimpse. That was always the worst: the shock of death, that recognition of the body as having so recently had life, the awareness of its humanity. She noted the Reebok running shoes, white with teal insets matching the teal of the sweat pants; the horribly abraded left arm, which had bled onto the two-tone teal and white sweatshirt, whose sleeves had been cut off above the elbow. She stood behind the body, memorizing the unnatural twist to the torso, knowing she would use that memory to fuel her search for the hapless woman's killer. Blood had pooled under the head. Lin could see from the exposed cheek that the white face was deathly pale. The dark blonde hair, damp with perspiration and morning mist, had been cut short over the nape of the neck and the ears, and its soft waves now lay matted against the misshapen skull.

Lin moved around to the front of the woman's body. As she took in the face, still and expressionless in death, she was staggered. "Oh my God!" she swore, half to herself. "It's Kathy Kinney!"

Johansen stared at her. "You know her?" he asked with a mix of incredulity and horror. He had yet to find someone he knew lying dead, but dreaded it as much as Lin had.

Dazed, Lin lowered herself to a crouch in front of a face she had seen only last weekend on a dance floor at a women's bar in Seattle. The music had been wonderful, and they had danced, side by side, each with her respective partner, animated by the crowd, the rhythm, the night.

Knowing she should not, nevertheless she reached out and brushed a lock of hair from the dead woman's temple, struggling to make real the death of someone who had—however distantly—been a part of her life. She dropped her hand, fighting a great, welling sadness. Lin knew little of Kathy save that she had been well-liked in the women's community in this part of the state—a natural leader with a winning way that had drawn people to her and caused her to be admired by many. Rumor had it that she had been planning a run for the state legislature next year.

Johansen touched her shoulder gently. "Lin, if you know who she is, we'd better get the word out," he said in a voice made gruff by emotion.

"Hey, Sarge! Look what we found over here!" one of the deputies called.

Spurred by the edge of excitement in the deputy's voice, Lin and Johansen moved promptly to where the woman stood pointing off the shoulder of the road.

"We got us another one," she commented, the excitement in her voice muted by somberness.

In deep shadow, the body of a man lay sprawled on its back on the sharp rocks. It was just now becoming visible as the mist lifted from that particular patch of road. An expression of surprise, perhaps forever frozen on the redhead's freckled countenance, was visible even from where they stood. At their feet was puddled vomit, becoming gelled in the cool dampness.

The deputy went to call the forensic photographer over for pictures while Lin and Johansen puzzled over the significance of this new find.

"Do you suppose this guy was with her?" Johansen wondered.

With a bitter shake of her head, Lin vetoed the idea. "I don't think so. Maybe an innocent bystander—or a witness who had to be disposed of."

"What makes you so sure?" Johansen queried, puzzled.

Lin hesitated only a fraction of a second, yet knew it was long enough for Johansen to notice. "She was a lesbian woman." Lin watched Johansen's face for a flicker of shock, or realization. There was none. Gratified, she went on. "I think the likelihood that she would share a run with this man is very slight." She pointed at the corpse, clothed in slacks, a polo shirt under a lightweight jacket, and a worn pair of tennis shoes. "Besides, he's not really dressed for running."

Johansen put his chin in his hand. "D'ya think this has a bearing on the case?"

Knowing that he was referring to what she had said about the dead woman's sexual orientation, and gratified again that he had not asked how she knew, Lin considered the question seriously. "We can't rule it out," she said with a shake of her head, but to herself added, *Please— let it not.*

A Bellingham patrol officer approached with more information. Lin began adding notes to those she had already made. They were told that, about a quarter of a mile down the road, the imprint of a tire had been discovered in a patch of soft earth at the shoulder. It appeared that a small car, with narrow tires, had turned around there. Perhaps a sports car—one capable of handling the twists and turns of Chuckanut Drive, one powerful enough to have become a high-speed killing machine. The marked area on the west side of the pavement at this location was thought to contain skin and blood from the victim's badly abraded arm. Across the road was a skid mark which may or may not have been from the vehicle that hit Kathy Kinney.

Lin went back and studied the position of Kathy Kinney's body from every angle, making a sketch and detailed notes. Then, after taking in the second scene in its entirety from the roadway, she climbed down and examined the as-yet-unidentified male. He may have had a wallet in his pocket, but no one was permitted to disturb the body until the photographer had captured its position on film, from every angle, and the Medical Examiner had completed his preliminary investigation.

Lin noted the splashes of vomit on the dead man's shoes and inferred the puddle on the roadway above likely belonged to him. If so, what might he have seen to make him throw up? Did the car turn and come back to remove a possible witness? And if he were a witness, did that mean Kathy Kinney's death was deliberate?

Lin was aware of a blossoming suspicion. Although she herself did not take part in gay and lesbian politics because of being in law enforcement, she was aware that Kathy's very openness and active involvement in community politics could have made her a target of someone's violence. Things had recently heated up in the Pacific Northwest around the issue of gay civil rights. She wondered if anyone might have borne Kathy Kinney, in particular, enough ill will to want her dead. She sighed deeply, hoping they would be able to identify the male victim readily and that, more to the point, knowing who he was would produce some answers.

Satisfied that she had seen all she needed to, and trusting in Johansen and the crime scene unit's thorough competence, Lin indicated she would take Kathy Kinney's keys, and arranged for official entry into Kathy's home. Johansen agreed to handle the same task for the male victim as soon as he was identified. Then they would meet to pool their information at their headquarters in Bellingham, the county seat. Given that the deaths had occurred outside the Bellingham city limits, the sheriff's department would be running the investigation.

Lin slid into the car and just sat for a moment, wishing she knew more about Kathy Kinney, knowing she must now go to Kathy's home—perhaps deliver devastating news to a lover or housemate—and invade its privacy, looking for possible clues as to the why of her death. Knowing she must, but hating having to go. Resolutely, she pulled the car out and headed back up the coast toward Bellingham.

2

Kathy Kinney's home sat on a bluff overlooking Chuckanut Bay, one of numerous dwellings along Chuckanut Drive that had been built on the edge of sheer cliff, to the west of the winding, narrow road. Its short driveway angled sharply into the garage. Rustic in design, the structure seemed too insubstantial to weather the fierce storms that sometimes struck northern Washington in the winter. That impression was ameliorated by the thick line of evergreens that stood as a windbreak, obviously planted by earlier owners.

Double-checking the house number with the one obtained from a state database, Lin parked her department vehicle. She and Deputy Pat Knutson got out, looking for signs of life at the modest bungalow. A check of the county records had shown Kathy Kinney to be the only person with title to the property. But Lin well knew that did not preclude that someone else lived there.

Save for the shush of traffic in the roadway and the sound of tires on pine-needle-covered gravel as the accompanying Bellingham PD squad car pulled in, it was very quiet. Lin stationed the Bellingham officer in the driveway with his vehicle. Motioning for Knutson to head in the opposite direction, Lin began to circle to the south, taking in the slight neglect in wilted shrubs and unweeded flower beds. The yard was recently mowed, and everything else about the exterior appeared neatly kept. The drapes were open in all the windows, and the house appeared much as it might on a day when its owner had gone off to work.

Lin sighed. This owner was never coming home again. She observed that the garage door was down, and a made mental reminder to check the garage before they left. When she and Knutson had both returned to the front, Lin first rang the bell, then knocked and called out. When no one came, she fished the keys that had been taken from the pocket of the dead woman's sweats from her own pocket, selected a likely looking key, and inserted it. The door opened easily, into a cool, well-lit interior.

Lin signaled the deputy to cover her. Not expecting trouble but alert to the possibility, she kept her hand on her service revolver as she proceeded. Again, she called out. A small foyer gave way to a large and airy living-dining room combination that opened onto the small deck at the back. The house had a lived-in look: the morning paper, unread, lay on the hassock next to a comfortable-looking armchair; dishes, just a few, were stacked neatly in the sink; the smell of fresh toast lingered faintly in the air in the kitchen. With sadness, Lin observed an array of small dishes, containing several different kinds of cat food, on the floor under the wall phone.

Trailed by Knutson, Lin moved through the home, examining, looking for things out of order, wondering where the animals were for whom the food had been left. The bedroom, on the south end, was bright and inviting. The bed was made up and, from its center, two charcoal grey cats eyed her more with curiosity than alarm. She studied them as they studied her. She would have to see that someone was assigned to take care of them. As her gaze drifted away, she discovered in a corner bookcase what she had expected to come upon sooner or later: lesbian novels, books on lesbian sexuality, biographies of women whom their owner must have admired or about whom she had indulged her curiosity.

On the antique highboy were several expensive items of jewelry. The closet revealed a wardrobe appearing to belong only to one person and whose contents included casual workout clothes, designer jeans, slinky blouses, and conservative business suits complete with several pairs of heeled pumps. Bass loafers and another pair of Reeboks lounged beside the pumps. A purse hanging on the knob of the door contained Kathy's wallet, complete with identification and emergency notification information.

Shadowed by Deputy Knutson, Lin moved back into the kitchen-dining-living area. Everything appeared pretty normal to her. Realizing she had missed the bathroom, she backtracked and inspected, but found nothing unusual there, either. While it appeared that Kathy had lived alone, the extra toothbrush, soap, and shampoo indicated a regular visitor—not out of the ordinary for the single lesbian woman. With a deep sigh, she accepted that there were no immediately apparent clues to Kathy Kinney's death in her home. That meant that she must conduct an intensive investigation of the people and events in Kathy's life. She had unearthed a battered address book in a drawer next to the bed. As she now fingered it where it reposed in her jacket pocket, she felt some satisfaction at having a place to start.

Making sure all the doors were locked, Lin and Deputy Knutson exited the house. While Knutson posted crime-scene tape, Lin headed for the garage. An old Volvo was parked inside. Lin gave the garage a quick once-over, recording the license plate number. Again, nothing struck her as out of the ordinary.

After allowing the squad car behind them to back out onto the congested road, Lin followed. At headquarters, the first call she must make would be to a Mr. and Mrs. George Kinney, of Bryn Mawr, Pennsylvania—Kathy's emergency contacts. Lin did not look forward to it. Informing someone of a family member's death was never pleasant. Assuming that George and Alicia were Kathy's parents, it would be harder still.

3

The Kinneys were not at home. Stressing that it was urgent, Lin left word with the unreceptive housekeeper to have them call her immediately upon their return. In Johansen's continued absence, she began systematically going through Kathy Kinney's address book. Kathy had friends or acquaintances scattered across the country, and Lin surmised that the woman had either done a great deal of traveling in her twenty-nine years or had been involved in something that gave her the opportunity to meet people from a variety of places.

Lin made a careful list, state by state, deciding that she and Johansen would begin with calling those in the Seattle-Tacoma-Bellingham area. She would delegate preliminary calls to the out-of-state and out-of-area numbers to other team members. Technically, she should have waited until the next of kin had been notified, but since the Kinneys were across country, and unavailable, and since what was done in the hours immediately following a murder—if this were indeed a murder, she cautioned herself—was often crucial in catching the perpetrator, she began working through the call list.

She reached a number of answering machines and had not a few no-answers. *People must not be hanging around home on a Saturday at . . . ?* She glanced at her watch and was dismayed. It was three o'clock already—nearly eight hours since she had answered her pager and known she would be out on a call instead of with her date. She had promised to call Caroline Glass to let her know if their afternoon or evening could be salvaged.

Grabbing the phone, she dialed, hoping the psychology professor would still be home. When a quiet, well-modulated voice answered, Lin breathed a sigh of relief.

She apologized for her tardiness and was reassured by Caroline's easy laugh. "I'm fast learning how you are about your work!"

"Thank you for understanding," Lin said. "Especially since I'm not going to be able to get away at all today."

"I guess it wasn't just an accident, then," Caroline replied sympathetically.

Lin hesitated, then remembered she had told Caroline why she was being called out that morning. Suddenly, it struck her that Caroline might know Kathy Kinney. Tersely, Lin informed Caroline of Kathy's death. "I know you'll understand when I tell you that you cannot breathe a word of this to anyone else," Lin cautioned. She went on to impart the basic facts of the case.

Caroline was shocked by the news. "I had never met Kathy—only knew of her. What a terrible tragedy," she said, her voice clouded with sadness.

Lin was interested. "Tell me what you *do* know of her."

Silently, Caroline combed her memory. "Well, she was popular in the women's community in western Washington—had been pretty active in grassroots politics for gay and lesbian causes for the past couple of years." Caroline paused. "I think I heard she had been a whiz-kid computer programmer who quit the business world when she came into some money. There was even some talk of her running for office as an openly gay candidate." Caroline sighed. "I can't think of anything more at the moment."

Came into some money, huh? Lin thought. *From where?* She would have to ask the Pennsylvania Kinneys. She jotted a note.

"Did you see her last weekend, at the bar? While we were dancing—part of a couple next to us at one point on the dance floor?" Lin kept talking in hopes the memory would click for Caroline.

Caroline made a negative sound. "I'm sorry. I haven't the slightest recollection of what she looked like, even though I've seen pictures of her."

Lin thanked her, then said, "Regretfully, I'm not going to be able to see you for a few days. I'm sorry."

Caroline seemed to understand. "I'm sorry, too. Call me when you can—and good luck finding out what happened to Kathy."

Lin sat, her fingers lingering momentarily on the phone. In less that five minutes with Caroline, she had gained more than from the many calls she had made to those in Kathy Kinney's address book. Just as she was concluding her notes from that conversation, Johansen barreled into her office.

They exchanged information. The other victim had indeed been identified by his wallet: as Robert John Smiley, with a Fresno, California, address. Johansen had already put someone on the task of gathering information on Smiley while he had followed the two bodies to the morgue for the initial findings. Since murder was a relatively rare occurrence in Whatcom County, the Medical Examiner had bumped the autopsies on these two victims ahead of those of individuals who were believed to have died of natural causes. Tissue and blood samples would be rushed to the state crime lab in Olympia for further processing, but detailed results would not be back for several days.

Lin gave Johansen his half of the phone list and he headed off for his own desk. Following a second unrewarded call to the home of Kathy's relatives in Pennsylvania, Lin was aware that she and the housekeeper had already become familiar antagonists. Even though Lin stressed the urgency of her call, and that she was a police officer, the housekeeper was tight-lipped.

However, Lin's next couple of hours proved more fruitful. She spoke with several of Kathy Kinney's friends and former co-workers. Although most broke down and wept, some seemed too stunned to express anything but disbelief.

Lin was able to clarify that Kathy had, indeed, come into money—though people's ideas about its source were vague—and that she had been nothing short of a genius with computers. A former business associate informed Lin that Kathy had worked for IBM since before she had graduated from college—achieved at age eighteen—and said that she had left the company because she no longer needed to work for a living.

From what Lin could infer, it seemed that Kathy had wisely invested the substantial salary she had been receiving—and perhaps some of the money she had come into, as well—and had gone into business for herself as a software developer. Many of her friends in the

Seattle-Bellingham area thought of her as being independently wealthy. She had devoted the past eighteen to twenty-four months to lobbying for causes that she believed in, and had, according to one woman, made large monetary contributions to several of them. However, no one she talked with admitted to being the woman on the dance floor with Kathy the weekend prior. All asserted that Kathy had had no enemies.

With the sun sinking in the western sky, Lin reviewed the information gleaned through the afternoon's work. She was not convinced that Kathy's death was an accident, but for now she had nothing more than intuition to go on. Until there was some hard evidence to back up her hunch, she was in limbo. Stretching her tired muscles, she picked up her notes and left the tiny space that was her office to see what luck Johansen may have had.

She learned that, so far, everyone they had talked to had a pretty uniform view of the dead woman. There was no info yet on Smiley. Lin shared her failure to reach Kathy Kinney's relatives.

Johansen shook his head. "You should just call the local PD and let them handle it," he advised. "Save your energy for the work here."

Lin nodded. "I should. I just . . . I just thought maybe they could tell me something useful."

There was a tired silence. Then Johansen stood. "Let's get something to eat." He glanced at his watch. "Did you even have lunch?"

Lin reviewed her day and shook her head.

"Well, then! You call the Kinneys—or their PD—and I'll run out and grab us some food."

Glancing at her own watch as Johansen left, Lin calculated it would be nearly 10:30 p.m. in Pennsylvania. Debating about calling so late, she decided she might actually have a chance of catching the Kinneys at home at that hour.

She placed the call, heard the noises in fiber-optic space, and listened to the unanswered multiple rings on the other end. Sighing with frustration, she hung up, then dialed the number for the Bryn Mawr Police Department. Following her conversation with the detective on duty there, she sat tiredly for a moment. When Johansen returned a bit later, she was resolutely working her way through the local call list again, trying people who had not been home earlier in the day.

4

The initial autopsy report on Kathy Kinney came back Sunday morning as confusing as it was clarifying. Lin, working on too few hours of sleep, struggled over it. The injury to Kathy's left arm and the massive bruising under the right portion of her rib cage were consistent with someone or something having struck her and knocked her down, most probably before she was hit by the automobile that had caused her death. However, the injuries sustained when she was impacted by the automobile indicated that she had been on her feet when the vehicle had struck her.

The ME's preliminary report on Robert John Smiley indicated that he appeared to have been struck by the same vehicle: both bodies had minute particles of similar automobile paint ground into their clothing. That he had had bodily contact with Kathy was almost certain: her blood was on his right hand, and fibers apparently matching her clothing were found under his fingernails.

Had they collided in the fog, a runner with a walker? Had both subsequently been struck by the vehicle, simultaneously? Given the positioning of their bodies relative to each other, this seemed impossible. Had Smiley first knocked Kathy down, then lifted or helped her to her feet, at which point first she, then he, had been hit—accidentally—by the automobile? Again, the positions of the bodies made this unlikely.

Perhaps he had knocked her down, lifted her to her feet, then thrust her into the path of the oncoming vehicle. That scenario would imply that Smiley had colluded with the driver of the automobile. If so, it would make sense that that person would have wanted the only witness to a murder out of the way. Was that why Smiley had been killed as well?

And just who was Smiley—and what was he doing in Washington? The query to the law enforcement authorities in the Fresno area had produced the information that Smiley was a former star athlete who, after a knee injury during his second year at college, had gotten so heavily into drugs that he had lost his athletic scholarship and flunked out of school.

Lin speculated about why he had ended up in northern Washington. There had been a huge influx of drug trafficking in the past few years. It was easy to think he may have been involved with that. Easy—but not necessarily true.

Midday on Sunday, Johansen fielded a call from the Bryn Mawr police, who had paid a visit to the Kinney home. The recalcitrant housekeeper had been far more cooperative with the local authorities, especially when she had learned that Kathy had been killed. In shock, she had divulged that the Kinneys were Kathy's aunt and uncle, not her parents, and that they were out of the country. The BMPD officer assigned to the task had assured Johansen that he would contact the Whatcom County Sheriff's Office as soon as the Kinneys had been notified of their niece's death.

By Sunday afternoon, Lin's team had secured Smiley's local address, where it was not hard to see from his spartan living quarters and minimal wardrobe that Robert John was down on his luck.

People in such a situation get desperate, Lin thought, as she surveyed the tacky efficiency which Smiley had rented near Western Washington University. *Maybe someone took advantage of his desperation to enlist his help in committing a crime.* Maybe he had not known that murder was to be involved. Or maybe he had—and it had not mattered to him. Perhaps he had trusted someone he should not have. Or, if he were somehow involved in drug trafficking, perhaps he was the target of the murder, not Kathy Kinney. Perhaps *she* had been the innocent victim; perhaps *she* had witnessed *his* murder. Except the positioning of the two bodies and Kathy's blood on Smiley's hand did not support that theory. Lin's head spun as she once again attempted to consider all possible scenarios.

Careful questioning of Smiley's neighbors in the apartment village yielded little additional information. He was new in the area, had supported himself, it was commonly believed, with odd jobs, conveying the impression that he was just passing through. His month-to-month rental agreement supported that view.

On Monday morning, while following up on a report of a car abandoned at a used car lot, a Bellingham PD patrol unit was taken to a sports car with scuffed and dented fenders whose paint seemed a possible match for that found on the clothing of the two victims.

The county crime lab was called. Of the numerous sets of fingerprints lifted from the vehicle, the only matches made were those of the salesman who had talked to the man who had left the car, and of the business owner himself, who had called because of the peculiar circumstances under which the automobile had come into their possession.

On Monday afternoon, Lin and Johansen interviewed the salesman, a beefy, red-faced man in his forties named Duff. "This guy came onto the lot on Saturday, midday, saying he wanted to look at cars. I talked with him a few minutes, then went to answer a page. When I came back, he was gone. I didn't think much of it until later in the day when I realized his car was still parked over there on the edge of the lot. I told the boss, and come this morning, when it was still sitting there, he phoned the police." The salesman shrugged. "We checked the glove box—there was no vehicle registration. How were we to know it was involved in a murder?"

"We don't know yet that it was," Johansen demurred.

Duff shrugged again and went on to furnish a fairly complete description of the man who had left the car. In retrospect, Duff judged that the man had seemed a bit on edge.

By Tuesday morning, a composite drawing of the suspect was being circulated: a white male, about six feet two, hefty but not overweight, with very light brown hair and several days' growth of beard. Duff had thought the man's hair had seemed bleached out from chlorine or salt water.

The abandoned auto's registration data indicated that the sports car belonged to an Edward Browning of Spokane, who was a student at Western Washington University in Bellingham. The vehicle had not been reported missing. A patrol car was dispatched to Browning's local address, but he was not at home and none of his neighbors knew where he was.

Although Browning's state driver's license photo showed him to be of African ancestry, thus not fitting the description of the man who had abandoned the vehicle at the car sales lot, the Spokane police were asked to locate and contact his family and inquire as to his whereabouts. All the Brownings could tell the Spokane police was that their son had planned a long camping trip in the North Cascades during the summer break. They did not know exactly when or where he had gone or when he would return. Neither could the Brownings provide any information about Ted's acquaintances or friends in Bellingham. It seemed that Ted, being in his mid-twenties, did not see fit to report to his family on the details of his college life, although they were supporting him while he was in school.

By Thursday of the week following Kathy and Smiley's deaths, Lin's team had all the evidence needed to link the two and prove that the automobile was the single instrument of death: matching traces of flesh and blood had been identified on the impounded vehicle, and fibers matching those of the victims' clothing had also been recovered. One of the tires had been matched to the imprint of the track at the scene.

What Lin lacked was a plausible explanation of the deaths and an identifiable driver of the apparently stolen vehicle.

On Thursday evening, as Lin was home readying herself for a long-awaited supper date with Caroline Glass, the dispatcher called to tell her that a woman had just phoned the Bellingham police station demanding to know why Kathy Kinney's home had been sealed. She had refused to identify herself, insisting that the officer in charge call her at Kathy's residence. Obviously the woman had pulled off the police tape.

Wondering if this was the frequent visitor suggested by her earlier inspection of the property, Lin pondered her options. If this woman was willing, Lin knew she could be there and have conducted an interview in the space of an hour and a half. The question was, should she bring Caroline along, and perhaps forego having a deputy meet her there, or pick Caroline up afterward? She determined she would let Caroline decide for herself. First, she called Kathy Kinney's home.

The woman who answered still refused to identify herself. When Lin refused to give out any information over the telephone, the woman agreed to Lin's coming by.

Lin called Caroline and quickly outlined the situation. Caroline elected to accompany Lin. Thinking that having the psychologist along as an observer might be of value, Lin decided against arranging to have a deputy meet her at Kathy's house. She said good-bye to Kathy's cats—she was the person chosen by default to care for them—and breezed out the door.

Half an hour later, when Lin turned her Camry into Kathy's sharply angled drive, she noted that every window was alight behind the drawn drapes. She and Caroline approached the house, but before she could ring the doorbell, the front door opened.

A small woman of Asian ancestry, whom Lin estimated to be about twenty, stood in the doorway. Lin realized two things instantly: First, that the young woman must at least already suspect the truth of the empty dwelling and the yellow banner proclaiming an investigation site—her ear-length dark hair, cut in a short pageboy, was in disarray, and her dark-irised eyes were red-rimmed and anxious; and second, that this was *not* the woman with whom Lin had seen Kathy Kinney on the dance floor two weekends ago.

Lin introduced herself officially but simply gave Caroline's name, making no statement about her presence there.

The young woman motioned them in, not pausing to close the door, which Caroline shut as she entered. "Where are Kathy's cats?" the woman was asking in a ragged voice.

"I have them," Lin replied quietly.

"You?" The woman turned back to her in surprise.

Lin nodded. "No one else was available." She took a chair without being asked and noted that Caroline followed suit. "Why don't you have a seat and we can talk."

The woman seemed about to say no, but then lowered herself to the love seat. "What happened? Where's Kathy?" she demanded.

Lin eyed her for a moment, sizing her up. She countered the demand with one of her own. "Why don't you tell me who you are."

The ebony eyes fixed on Lin's with cold hostility. "I'm Anna Kushima. And if you're wondering why I'm here, it's because—" Her voice broke and her struggle to keep her walls of denial from collapsing was evident on her face.

While she waited for Anna Kushima to recover herself enough to speak, Lin unobtrusively slipped a small tape recorder from her purse and turned it on, then placed it on the coffee table in front of them.

"Why *are* you here, Anna?" Lin prompted softly.

Anna raised her head and took a deep, unsteady breath, wiping at her eyes. "I came to see Kathy, because Kathy and I are . . ." She faltered again. This time her gaze was uncertain as it sought Lin's, and she seemed afraid.

Lin supplied the word she thought was missing. "Lovers? You and Kathy were lovers?" Anna nodded, relief and anxiety mixed on her face. She apparently did not notice that Lin had used the past tense in referring to the women's relationship.

Lin leaned forward. "You needn't tiptoe around it, Anna. I know Kathy was lesbian-identified."

Anna's expression suddenly became wary. "'Was'? What do you mean 'was'? What's happened to her?" she demanded angrily as tears began to seep from her eyes.

Lin took a breath. "Kathy was struck and killed by an automobile last Saturday morning while she was out running along Chuckanut Drive." She paused a moment before offering softly, "I'm sorry."

When Caroline rose to go and sit supportively for a moment next to the stricken young woman, Lin was momentarily startled. She had been so focused on Anna, she had forgotten Caroline's presence.

"Where have you been this past week?" Lin asked when Anna was calmer.

Between Anna's bouts of crying, the history of the women's relationship emerged. A little more than three years ago, Anna had been a student intern in an office in San Francisco where Kathy was a software consultant. Anna had found herself strongly and inexplicably attracted to the handsome, slightly older woman, and had pursued a nonbusiness relationship with her. When Kathy had come out to her, Anna had, at first, been very frightened, having realized at the moment of Kathy's disclosure that her attraction to Kathy included a strong sexual element. She had withdrawn for a few days, but eventually had invited Kathy out for dinner and a walk. After a short period of dating, they became lovers. According to Anna, halcyon days together had been interrupted by Anna's father, who had learned of Kathy's sexual involvement with his daughter after having them followed by a private investigator.

"Then, he engineered Kathy's termination at her work," Anna spat disgustedly. "I moved away from home and refused to have anything further to do with him. Kathy moved to Bellingham shortly after being forced out. A few weeks later, I followed as far as Seattle and enrolled at the University of Washington to complete my degree in business."

"Did your father have any idea where either of you were living?" Lin asked.

Anna shook her head. "Not once we came to Washington. And we were very discreet—when we saw each other, we stayed in hotels or motels all around the area, sometimes used false names, all so his private dicks couldn't find us, if they were still looking."

Lin had listened to the tale with growing interest, thinking that if a man were vicious enough to have Kathy fired from her job for her involvement with his daughter, he might also be vicious enough to have Kathy killed, or to kill her himself, if the involvement persisted. Another part of her mind was remembering the former business associate of Kathy's who had implied that Kathy had left of her own accord.

"And so, where have you been during this past week?" Lin asked, repeating her earlier question.

Anna blinked at her, coming from a haze of memory into the present. "In California, visiting my mother. She had surgery a few days ago. I went to stay with her when she came home from the hospital."

"I thought your parents didn't know where you are."

"My father doesn't," she corrected. She gestured woodenly. "My parents are divorced."

Lin paused. More and more questions were piling up. "What kind of man is your father, Anna?"

Distaste rippled across the smooth features. "He's an angry, hateful man," she replied, her voice flat and hard. "He ruined my mother's life and tried to ruin mine." She wrinkled her nose. "But neither of us would let that happen."

When Anna did not go on, Lin prompted, "Let what happen?"

"Let him run my life like he did my mother's. She encouraged me to follow my heart and stay with Kathy if that's what I wanted." Her mouth drawn in a bitter line, she added, "You see, my parents' marriage was arranged by their parents during World War Two, when the Japanese living in this country were put into internment camps like the Jews in Germany." She brought her eyes to Lin's, her expression clearly accusatory. "My parents were merely infants, betrothed according to a way of life that had originated in Japan. My mother had no love for my father, but married him out of duty. My father was interested in wealth and status—these things are very important in Japanese culture. Children are important, also, but for many years, my mother had no children. When I was born, my father treated me like one more of his possessions.

"When I turned fifteen, my father tried to marry me to the son of one of his business associates in exchange for a large 'loan.' My mother finally rebelled. She left my father and took me with her, filing for divorce under California law. That was more than ten years ago."

As Anna faltered and looked down at where her hands lay clenched in her lap, Lin again revised her estimate of Anna's age. When Anna raised her head, tears had begun to trickle down her cheeks again.

"So when did you last see your father, Anna?"

"Two, two-and-a-half years ago," she said vaguely. "When he came to my apartment in San Francisco to threaten Kathy. I had already moved away from home so he wouldn't bother my mother. I had no idea how easy it would be for him to find me there. I was certain that when I moved to Seattle he would leave all of us alone." She shrugged. "As far as I know, he has."

Lin reflected on all she had been told. She thought Anna's mother a very unusual woman—not only for having gone against her cultural heritage in leaving Anna's father but also because the majority of the gay and lesbian people Lin had known had been thrown out of their parents' homes when their sexual orientation became known. She wondered what Kathy's parents had thought of her, if they had even been aware that their daughter was lesbian. Drawing herself back to the situation at hand, she formulated the question she knew she must ask. "Was your father angry or hateful enough to kill Kathy—or to hire someone to kill her, Anna?"

The dark eyes clouded over, filling again with tears. Her hand to her mouth, Anna whispered, "Kill her? I don't know." Her eyes beseeched Lin for the requested answer. "How could someone do that?"

Lin could see that Anna's resources were nearly depleted. She decided that any further questioning could wait until tomorrow. She said as much, then, standing, offered a rare piece of advice.

"If I were you, I wouldn't stay here tonight. Check into a motel. Go to a friend's."

Some of the hostility returned to Anna's face. "Why not? You can't think my father would try to hurt me?"

"I don't know that your father hurt *Kathy*, Anna. But someone did, and that someone might want to hurt you, too." She added gently, "Besides, I don't think Kathy would want you staying here alone— not the first night."

"How do you know what Kathy would want?" Anna parried tiredly, sounding now more petulant than hostile.

Lin laid a card with her phone number on the table and, signaling Caroline with her eyes that it was time to leave, turned away. Anna sat frozen in the numbness of a shock too great to bear.

5

Friday morning, Lin phoned Kathy Kinney's home, certain that Anna would be there in spite of Lin's having urged her to stay elsewhere.

When Lin and Johansen arrived at the bungalow a little later, Anna appeared more haggard than she had the night before. Her hair was a tangled mess, her face was swollen from crying, and she remained in the clothes, now rumpled and wilted, that she had worn the previous evening.

Lin asked Johansen to have a seat and sent Anna, who was now less resistant to suggestion, off to shower while she busied herself in the kitchen. She had no idea if Anna drank coffee or not, but she knew she could use a cup herself, having had a late night with Caroline. She and Caroline had devoted at least half an hour to discussing Anna and the possibility of her father's involvement in Kathy's death.

When Anna was seated, in robe and wet hair, steaming cup in hand, Lin began to probe her for further information. She had decided against the tape recorder today and had asked Johansen to take notes while she interviewed.

"Tell me about Kathy, Anna. Please."

Anna worked to dredge herself up from her exhaustion. "What do you want to know?" she asked hesitantly.

Lin shrugged. "About her family. Her interests. What she'd been doing for a living. Who the people were in her life. That sort of thing."

With detachment, Anna began to relate what she knew of Kathy Kinney. From Pennsylvania originally, Kathy had moved to San Francisco when she had finished graduate school, at twenty, and had gone to work full time. Several years ago, Kathy's parents had been killed in an automobile accident on the Pennsylvania Turnpike. An only child, Kathy had inherited a fortune in cash, property, and investments. The Kinneys were old money back East.

"About six months after her parents' deaths, Kathy decided to quit her job and go to work for herself—"

"Wait," Lin interrupted. "You said last night she was fired."

Sipping her coffee, Anna hesitated. "Well, technically, she was. Kathy and I had—" She cast a self-conscious glance at Johansen, who had done everything he could to fade into the background.

Lin shifted, drawing Anna's attention again. "Go on," she prompted gently.

Anna dropped her eyes and gathered herself. "Kathy and I had become lovers not long before her parents were killed. When they died, she needed a lot of emotional support. She took some time off work, and I was spending a lot of my time with her. My father realized it and questioned me about it. He was always questioning me about my life, my relationships," she said acidly, seeming to have gotten beyond her earlier reserve. "Then he hired a private investigator to follow us around until he had photographic proof that we were lovers.

"When he had his sordid pictures, my father went to Kathy's supervisor and showed the photos to him, alleging that she had seduced me. He said I was a minor—which was not true—and he demanded that Kathy be fired. He threatened a lawsuit.

"Kathy's supervisor called her in and showed her the pictures. She denied nothing except the seduction, informing him that I was of age and that our involvement was mutual decision." A grim but appreciative smile found its way to Anna's mouth. "How like her to mention nothing of the fact that I was the initial pursuer." She shook her head and the enveloping sadness returned to her face.

"Anyway, he told Kathy that her personal life was her business and that he had nothing but respect for her professionally but he couldn't allow the company to be dragged into court over such a thing. He said he expected her resignation, but would give her an excellent reference when she wanted it.

"She informed him at that time that she had planned on leaving the company to start her own business in a few months, anyway." Anna sighed. "A few weeks later, she moved into this bungalow." She drifted into silence, staring at the by now cold coffee in her cup.

"Anna, I'll need the name and address of your father and his place of business. I'll also need to call your mother and verify that you were with her last week."

"Why?" Anna replied sharply. "Am I now a suspect, too?"

Lin reacted to the challenge in Anna's voice with an unflinching gaze. "Should you be?"

Anna flushed and hurried on. "Please, don't disturb my mother with this news. She was very fond of Kathy. She's just had major surgery. It would only make her recovery more difficult if she knew Kathy had been k . . . was dead," she finished weakly.

Intuition told Lin that Anna was concealing something, but she decided to play along for now. "All right, Anna, I'll respect your wishes about your mother for the time being." She noted the relief behind the nervous eyes. "But I do still need the information about how to contact both of your parents."

Later in the day, a Bryn Mawr police detective informed Lin that the Kinney family had finally been notified of Kathy's death.

It turned out that George and Alicia Kinney had left strict instructions with their housekeeper about taking any calls from out-of-town police. Someone claiming to be a police officer from the West Coast had called them two or three times several months ago, determined to obtain information relating to Kathy's whereabouts. Suspicious of the man's manner, they had made inquiries about him. The caller's identity could not be verified, so they had directed the housekeeper not to accept calls from anyone other than their local police department, who had assured the Kinneys that they would be notified by out-of-town authorities in any case of emergency.

Lin took down a bit more information from the Bryn Mawr detective, then thanked her colleague for his help. She was excitedly relaying the information about the suspicious inquiries to Johansen when her phone rang again. It was a strained George Kinney, calling from overseas to find out about Kathy's death, and asking for help with funeral arrangements. Lin informed him that his niece's body was being held at the morgue and referred him to Anna Kushima. She made no attempt to explain who Anna was, figuring it was up to Anna to disclose whatever she wanted Kathy's relatives to know. Furthermore, Lin had no knowledge of the provisions of Kathy's will; according to the Bryn Mawr detective, the will was on file in Pennsylvania where Kathy's aunt and uncle lived.

Regarding Kathy's death, Lin gave him only the essential facts. To her surprise, he seemed satisfied with that. People often wanted to know everything there was to know, in some effort, she supposed, to make sense of it all.

Lin wanted to make sense of it all herself. She sat back in her chair and began to lay out to Johansen just what the investigation had so far turned up: Kathy Kinney and Robert John Smiley had been killed by the same automobile. Although they did not know why, it appeared from the premortem bruising on Kathy's body that she had been physically assaulted—likely by Smiley—prior to being struck by the car. Smiley's presence at the scene made him a witness to Kathy's death—one to be removed.

They now had a murder suspect in the person of Anna's father, who had, according to Anna, amply demonstrated his capacity for intervening in both Anna and Kathy's lives. What did not fit the picture was that the man who had abandoned the car that had killed both victims at the car lot was of European extraction. Anna's father, Yoshiro Kushima, was of Japanese ancestry. Had he hired someone to murder his daughter's lover after locating her in the Pacific Northwest? Not Smiley—he was dead when the car was dropped off at the used car lot. And, Lin believed, not a professional hit man. A pro would never have allowed himself to be seen and later described by the used-car salesman, would never have made the car so easy to find, and would have wiped it completely clean of prints.

"And just how was the car obtained?" she posed. Too many things did not add up. Lin told Johansen she was going to contact a professional acquaintance with the San Francisco PD and enlist help in collecting information about Anna's father.

By Monday at noon, they had a fairly complete picture of Yoshiro Kushima's recent activities. Airline records showed that he had flown to Fresno the day before Kathy's death and returned to San Francisco the day after her death. Members of the board with whom Kushima had met that weekend had placed him in Fresno well after midnight on the Friday before Kathy's death, and at midmorning on the day of her death. There was no way he could have gotten to Bellingham and back within that short window of time.

A disappointed Lin was forced to accept the evidence that Anna's father had not, himself, killed Kathy. Now the question was, did he have anything to do with it?

Lin kept coming back to Anna's nervousness about Lin's desire to call Anna's mother. With Johansen on the extension, Lin picked up the phone and dialed the number Anna had so recently given her on Saturday morning.

A frail-sounding voice answered on the second ring. Lin identified herself briefly and explained that she merely needed to inquire about Anna's whereabouts during the past two or three weeks. She assured Mrs. Kushima that Anna was in no trouble and this was just part of a routine investigation.

Keiko Kushima nervously confirmed that Anna had indeed flown down to be with her during and after her surgery, nearly three weeks ago now. Mrs. Kushima believed that Anna had returned to Seattle ten days ago. If not, she could not say where her daughter might have been during the time since Anna had left California and the time Lin believed her to have returned to Kathy Kinney's home.

Lin thanked Mrs. Kushima and hung up without telling her about Kathy Kinney's death. Grimly, she eyed Johansen. "Time for another visit with Anna," she stated. "This time, I'm not phoning ahead."

6

Anna stopped in mid-greeting when she realized it was the two sheriff's officers who stood on her doorstep. "Oh, it's you," she said, clearly taken aback.

"You were expecting someone else?" Lin asked, pushing past her into the foyer of the bungalow.

"Well, yes, actually, I was," Anna admitted, shutting the door slowly behind the two officers.

Lin showed herself into the living-dining area, scanning her surroundings for new clues as to what was going on. "This shouldn't take too long," she promised, plopping down on the love seat, arms folded.

Anna had followed uncertainly and remained standing in the middle of the room. She glanced questioningly at Johansen, who likewise had not seated himself and whose expression remained neutral.

Lin had noted a bulging soft-sided weekend bag on the floor near the foyer. She saw now that Anna's purse lay open on the dining table, keys and wallet strewn out beside it. Anna wore tight-fitting designer jeans and a casual cotton blouse. Her sandals were laced with thin leather straps and had only a thin sole—not constructed for much walking. "Were you going somewhere?" Lin asked, her eyes holding Anna's, daring her to lie.

Anna seemed flustered, but demanded hostilely, "What do you want?" She folded her arms, imitating Lin's posture.

Lin stood, wanting to use her height to intimidate. "I want to know why you lied about where you were during the week Kathy was killed."

Anna looked as if she had been slapped. Her arms fell to her sides. "You—you called my mother?"

"Yes. Your mother informed me that you had left San Francisco to return to Washington ten days ago." She took a step closer to Anna. "Where *were* you the Friday evening before Kathy's death until I spoke with you?"

Anna's face reflected her struggle with fear, anger, and tears. "It's none of your business where I was. I had nothing to do with Kathy's death. If my father didn't kill her, I have no idea who did." Her voice was angry, but shaky.

"It *is* my business—this is a homicide investigation," Lin snapped. "Tell me the truth right now, or I'll haul you in for questioning." There was no mistaking the promise in Lin's voice.

Anna sagged. "You can't do that. You have no reason to question me."

"Try me."

Anna collapsed into a chair. She buried her face in her hands and began to cry. "I didn't want Kathy to know," she wailed.

"Know what?" Lin pressed.

Anna raised tormented eyes. "That—that I'd been seeing another woman."

Lin sucked in a breath, feeling the betrayal as keenly as if it had happened to her. Both surprised and dismayed at the strength of her own reaction, Lin maintained her professional demeanor. Deliberately, she took out her notebook. "Who, where, and when?"

With much reluctance, Anna gave the name of a woman, Sharon Monaghan, who lived in one of the wealthier areas of Seattle. "Sharon's husband is a prominent businessman there. We've had to be very discreet." The two had met at a women's business conference in Seattle in the early spring. They had seen each other only four or five times prior to their longer tryst during the week after Kathy's death. That week, they had gone to a resort out on the Olympic Peninsula and, as was their custom, had registered under assumed names. Unprompted, Anna volunteered the names.

"You were together all that week?" Lin asked, jotting the pseudonyms in her notebook. Anna nodded as Lin glanced up. "Who can verify that?"

Anna looked at her hopelessly. "Other than Sharon, I don't know," she whispered.

Lin moved into Anna's space and leaned over her. "Anna, while you were off cavorting with some heterosexual woman who wanted a fling with a dyke, someone ran down your lover of three years. It looks more and more like calculated, cold-blooded murder." Nodding almost hysterically, Anna had begun to cry again. "I'm going to find out who it was, with or without your help. But believe me, if I have to do it without your help, you'll wish I hadn't."

Lin let the threat linger, then straightened. "You have my card. Call me if your memory improves."

Turning on her heel, she made for the front door, Johansen trailing in her wake. She yanked the door open to find a petite but full-breasted white woman with frosted blonde hair in the act of reaching to press the doorbell.

Startled, the woman drew back.

"And who might *you* be? Mrs. Monaghan?" Lin spat caustically.

"Well, yes, but how—" A deep Southern accent was evident in the smooth voice.

"I'm sure Anna will explain," Lin muttered as she pushed past Anna's paramour.

Then, thinking better of it, Lin turned abruptly and closed in on Sharon Monaghan, who still stood staring at Lin and Johansen, a hand at her throat. "Where were you week before last?" Lin demanded.

By now, Anna was at the open front door. Sharon glanced at her, then said, "Why, Anna and I were staying out on the Peninsula for a few days." She looked questioningly at Anna, who was stone-faced, then back to Lin.

Lin bit down on a retort, turned again, and stalked to her car, her anger multiplying with each step. Controlling it with an iron will, she took leave of Johansen, who, arriving separately, had left his department vehicle parked on the shoulder of the road. He was now on his way to check out another lead on Smiley.

Carefully, Lin drove to a lookout point a little farther down Chuckanut Drive and pulled in. Cutting the engine, she slumped against the wheel and gave vent to her rage by slamming a fist against the padded dash. She knew the anger was out of all proportion to present events, knew it was rooted in events from her past that she never willingly thought about. Wrenching open the car door, she bolted from its confines.

From what she had learned of Kathy Kinney, the woman had deserved much better of her significant other than Anna had delivered. After calming herself by standing gazing over the quiet bay, Lin climbed back into the car to return to her office. There, wanting some solace, she called Caroline and arranged to see her that evening at Caroline's apartment.

That done, Lin forced herself back to the mystery of Kathy Kinney's death. She telephoned a journalist she had met during a two-year stint in law school down in Seattle and explained what she needed. Scarcely three hours later, she held a copy each of a photograph of Sharon and Sean Monaghan.

"Ain't technology wonderful," Johansen remarked with a smirk when she handed the facsimiles over to him. "I'll get on this right away." He nodded and was off to canvass the neighborhood where Robert John Smiley had lived, this time hoping to find someone who recognized either Monaghan or his wife. He would also talk with the salesman at the used car lot, and he would contact local authorities on the Olympic Peninsula and ask them to verify Anna and Sharon's alibi.

Meanwhile, Lin got on the phone and began her own inquiries as to the whereabouts of Sean Monaghan during the weekend that Kathy was killed. She also initiated a complete background check on him.

By the time Lin parked her car shortly before nine thirty that night in the lot of Caroline's building and began to munch on a double cheeseburger and french fries, she had learned that while Sharon Monaghan and Anna were at their resort, Sean Monaghan had flown to Bellingham in his private plane and spent the weekend that Kathy was killed somewhere in the Bellingham area. She had yet to learn where, and whether or not he had been alone.

Johansen had called in to report that no one in Smiley's neighborhood had recognized either of the Monaghans, though one man thought Sean vaguely familiar and that he might have seen his picture in the Seattle paper, which was entirely likely, given that that was where the picture had come from. Duff, the car salesman—so far their only firsthand witness—could not make a positive ID from the fuzzy facsimile. Without that, they did not have enough to authorize picking up Sean Monaghan for questioning. The salesman's offer to view a lineup would have to wait.

Lin sipped her Coke. Had Sean Monaghan harbored reason to want Kathy Kinney dead? Could he have hired someone to kill her? Might he have done the killing himself and lined someone else up to get rid of the car? And if he knew of his wife's affair after all, why would he want to kill Kathy when it was Anna that his wife was involved with?

The glare from a pair of headlights turning into the lot interrupted Lin's musings. Caroline pulled up beside her and waved.

Putting down the remains of her soft drink, Lin disengaged her lanky frame from behind the steering wheel. She greeted Caroline quietly and trailed her into the building, then into the living room of Caroline's apartment without saying anything further. She had no notion of what to say, really; she had merely known when she had called earlier in the day that she needed some comforting, and had waited for hours now to get it. Anna's betrayal of Kathy had stirred up memories too painful to endure alone. The healing balm of touch was what she sought here tonight.

7

It was Tuesday afternoon, ten days since Kathy Kinney had been run down on Chuckanut Drive. Lin had been called into the chief deputy's office for a status report. The department was getting pressure from members of the area's gay and lesbian community who were becoming impatient that Kathy's killer had not yet been found.

"Now you and I know," Chief Deputy Wilson began, "that Ms. Kinney's being gay has nothing to do with the progress of this investigation."

Lin stiffened; of course it did. Wilson simply did not understand that there was more than one way it could have bearing.

Oblivious, he rumbled on. "I know Karl Johansen is the best field man available."

Lin nodded.

"And, I trust that you have been at this like a dog with a bone."

Inwardly, Lin cringed. She counted at least three offenses already committed by the chief deputy. She hated doing "het-education," but knew that sometimes it was unavoidable. She mentally gritted her teeth preparatory to interrupting the paunchy, fifty-something white man with the thinning gray hair. "Chief," she said with a large measure of resignation.

He lumbered to a surprised halt. "Yes?"

"Chief, I think you should know that I have a vested interest in solving this case—not just because it fell to me, but because Kathy Kinney was an acquaintance of mine." Wilson's eyebrows shot up as he gathered the direction of her speech. "She was a highly respected member of the lesbian community."

There, she thought, watching his face take on the pinkness of slight embarrassment, *I've supplied him with the right word.*

"And," she continued, "I've begun to suspect that she may have been killed *because* she was a lesbian woman." Ignoring his discomfort, Lin directed the full force of her gaze into Wilson's muddy brown eyes. "If that's true, and her killer gets away, it says to the world that it's all right to brutalize homosexual men and women. And you and I, Chief, know that it's not." She paused for effect, expecting, and receiving, no response before she went on. Hands together, elbows on her knees, she leaned toward the chief deputy. "I'm going to find the person responsible for her death and bring him—or her—in. If it's the last thing I do." She drew her final words out, emphasizing her determination, then leaned back.

For a few moments, Wilson seemed at a loss. Lin waited politely until he collected himself enough to ask her to fill him in on the details.

That evening, the five, six, and eleven o'clock local news broadcasts aired a taped interview with Whatcom County Sheriff's Chief Deputy Laron Wilson and Chief of Detectives Caitlin O'Shaughnessy, the law enforcement officials overseeing the investigation into the murder of Kathy Kinney, resident of the Bellingham area who had been a prominent and respected member of the western Washington lesbian community. Photographs of the automobile that had killed her were shown, along with a composite drawing of the man who had left the vehicle at the used-car lot where it was found. County officials were calling for assistance in identifying the person who had abandoned the automobile.

Within minutes of the conclusion of the eleven o'clock newscast, a call came in from a student at Western Washington University. Identifying himself as Edward Browning, from Spokane, he stated that the car shown on the television broadcast might be his. He had just that evening returned from an extended camping trip in the North Cascades to discover his car gone from its parking place. But since his girlfriend had a key and sometimes borrowed the car when he was away, he had thought nothing of its absence. After listening to the broadcast, however, he had tried to call Colleen, but had gotten her answering machine.

Lin immediately dispatched a patrol unit to Colleen O'Brien's address—on the block behind the apartment building where Robert John Smiley had been living. Roused from sleep, O'Brien confirmed that she had a key to Ted's car and said she vaguely recognized Smiley from a photograph she was shown, but she claimed to have no knowledge of the whereabouts of Ted's car or of Smiley and his doings. Smiley was someone she might have seen at the bus stop or talked with in a neighborhood laundromat. She did not know his name or exactly where he had lived, though she acknowledged that she might have given him that and other information about herself.

Regarding Ted's car, she stated she had not seen or driven it for several weeks. She, too, had been out of town. An archaeology student, she had been on a dig. This statement was corroborated by her next-door neighbor, an elderly man charged with tending to O'Brien's cats and mail in her absence. Neither the neighbor nor O'Brien recognized Sean Monaghan from the photo they were shown.

When asked, O'Brien could not produce her copy of the ignition key for Ted Browning's car, but indicated it had been on the key ring she had lent her neighbor so he could access her apartment. She always took just one spare apartment key with her when she traveled. The neighbor sheepishly confessed that he usually left the key ring hanging in the door while he was in Colleen's apartment so he would not lock himself out. He admitted to finding the keys lying on the floor once during her most recent absence when he went to lock up, but he assumed they had merely fallen.

Lin felt a grim satisfaction at the news that Smiley had lived in the same neighborhood where O'Brien's apartment complex was located. Smiley had somehow, she now was certain, been involved in acquiring the car for the use of the person who had later run him down with it. Perhaps he had observed the distinctive ignition key on O'Brien's key ring when he happened upon it in the door, known what it was, and removed it.

Lin called Chief Deputy Wilson at home, having been ordered to do so "no matter what the hour." His sleepy wife answered the phone and Lin could hear it being fumbled before Wilson came on the line. Lin brought him up to date, and reminded him that they had initiated a background check on Sean Monaghan, but that the complete results of that effort were still not available.

When Lin went to bed, her mind was too wound up to shut off. She lay wide awake for a long time, tossing and turning, before eventually sliding into fitful sleep less than two hours before her alarm was set to wake her.

The Fresno connection proved to be a valuable link. When interviewed again by the San Francisco police, and asked specifically about Robert John Smiley, Anna's father said that the young man had played football at the private college where Yoshiro Kushima now served as a member of the board of advisors to the college's athletic programs. Kushima, a martial arts champion in his younger days, was a graduate of the college. Apparently, when Smiley had ended up in northern Washington, broke and out of work, he had remembered Kushima, for whom he had once been a "gofer" at an advisory board function. Smiley had called Kushima from Washington and asked for help. Flattered by the request, Kushima had given Smiley the names of several of his business associates in the Seattle area, including Sean Monaghan. When pressed, Kushima swore that that was the extent of his connection with Smiley, and maintained that he knew nothing of Kathy Kinney's death until he had learned of it from the Fresno police. He also denied recognizing that this was the same Kathy Kinney whom he had contrived to have dismissed from her job some years earlier.

Lin had her doubts about the truth of Kushima's profession of ignorance of either Kathy's death or her identity, but she was gratified to have another link between Smiley and Sean Monaghan. Sean had been in the Bellingham area the weekend Kathy was killed. Could he have capitalized upon Smiley's dire straits and enlisted his help in murdering Kathy? If so, she could well understand why Sean would want Smiley dead. But why would he want to kill Kathy? That was the knot she could not unravel but which seemed at the heart of understanding the puzzle she was trying to solve. Could Monaghan have owed Kushima a favor? Had Kushima put Monaghan up to killing Kathy? Had either or both seen a chance to use Smiley to help, and thus divert suspicion to someone else?

As she was pondering, Johansen appeared in her doorway. "I've got the results of the background check on Sean Monaghan."

Materials split between them, the two detectives soon sat quietly in one of the interrogation rooms, engrossed in absorbing the various details of Sean Monaghan's life. Suddenly, Lin gasped. "Here's something," she said excitedly. "An intake from a psychological evaluation ordered by a judge. Monaghan had just turned eighteen and was a freshman in college."

She began to summarize. "Monaghan was severely castigated verbally as a young boy by both his father and his stepmother when he several times took garments from his stepmother's closet and hid them under his bed. He told the psychologist that they didn't understand his sadness about his mother, who had left him and his father when he was very young.

"Apparently the boy's father had told Sean repeatedly that his mother had left because she had become involved with one of her *female* professors at the community college where the mother was enrolled. Dad said that the professor had seduced Mom, otherwise she would never have left them." Lin glanced up. Johansen was listening carefully.

She went on. "Sean said that, as he grew older, he forced himself to 'forget' his sadness at his mother's abandonment. However, the psychologist thought that the sadness had been transformed into anger." Lin lifted her eyes to Johansen's. Her voice was vibrant with intensity. "It was Sean's assault on another student—whom he perceived to be lesbian—that got him into trouble and ultimately led to his psych referral.

"Listen." She began to quote directly. "'I broached this notion to the young man, and he seemed open to the idea that his assault on the other student was connected with his mother's abandonment. But, he emphasized that the young woman *deserved* his anger because she had publicly humiliated him by taunting him about his being jealous of the time his girlfriend was spending studying with her.'"

Lin and Johansen locked eyes.

"What kind of conference did Anna Kushima say it was where she met Sharon Monaghan?" Johansen asked.

Lin thought for a moment. "A business conference?"

He had begun flipping through his notes. His face lit up with satisfaction. "A *women's* business conference," he reported.

Wheels were turning in Lin's head, too. "What if Monaghan found out his wife had been seeing someone she met at a women's conference, and that someone was a woman? Was he still angry enough—

decades after these events—to have conceived a plan for punishing the woman he believed had seduced his wife?"

Johansen listened interestedly, but Lin grimaced. "Something still doesn't add up. Why wouldn't he go after *Anna?*" She shook her head. "We're missing something."

Johansen nodded. "But what?" He puffed out his cheeks in bafflement, his chin in his hand. "Anna told us she and Sharon Monaghan used fake names. What if he thought Anna was Kathy?"

Lin shook her head again. "I thought of that, but the names she gave me were 'Mary Smith' and 'Nancy Ito.' There's no way he could arrive at the conclusion that Sharon was seeing Kathy through those names."

"Did they always use the same names?" he persisted.

Lin realized that, distracted by her anger the day Anna had revealed her duplicity in seeing Sharon while still involved with Kathy, she had assumed that the names Anna had given her were names the two women customarily used when they were trysting somewhere. "I don't know," she said, feeling herself flush as she admitted her gaffe to Johansen. She swore, slapping the flat of her hand against the table.

Johansen already had his prized new cellular phone out of its holster and was looking expectantly at Lin. "Well, what's her number?" he prompted.

He punched in the numbers as she read them to him from her notebook, then handed the bulky gadget to her.

Lin allowed it to ring a dozen times before closing the phone and handing it back to Johansen.

Johansen accepted it noncommittally, then seemed to think better of his silence. "Look," he began.

Lin shot him a look that said, *I don't want to talk about it.*

He weighed her silent injunction, but forged ahead anyway.

"Look," he said again. "So *we didn't* think about it. I was there, too, remember?" He reflected for a moment. "There must have been something about what she said or the way she said it that made us think they always used the same names."

Lin probed her memory. "It was the offhanded way she gave them to me." She shook her head ruefully. "It doesn't matter. I still should have asked," she declared bitterly.

Johansen sighed. "Spilt milk." He glanced at his watch. "Don't you think it's time for a little talk with Mr. Sean Monaghan?"

Lin agreed. Shaking off her dissatisfaction with herself, she retrieved Johansen's phone and dialed Chief Deputy Wilson's office and asked to see him.

A few minutes later, the chief deputy was deliberating over their request. Stepping out of his own jurisdiction made him nervous. "Let me call the deputy chief of police down there and talk it over with him," he said.

Lin rose, handing over a piece of paper with the phone number on it. She had anticipated him. "We'll be in my office," she said.

Ten minutes later, Wilson came into her eight-by-eight and closed the door. He sat on the rickety chair next to her desk. "Seattle PD's chief of detectives, a Fred Townsend," he said, glancing at the note he had made, "and one of his detectives will accompany you to interview Mr. Monaghan."

Lin maintained a bland expression. She had also anticipated that the Seattle chief of detectives would not be warm to someone from outside his department interrogating a prominent local. "When do we leave?" she asked.

Wilson pushed himself to his feet. "You—not Johansen," he replied, ignoring Johansen's grimace of disappointment. "You leave as soon as you're ready. I already signed the papers. And O'Shaughnessy." His brown eyes glittered. "If you're right about this, and you can nail that bastard, you're going to make me a very happy man."

The implication that, if she were wrong, it would make him a very unhappy man, did not escape Lin.

8

To Lin's surprise, Wilson had authorized use of the department's little Cessna to fly her to Seattle, reducing the hour-and-a-half drive time to a mere thirty-minute flight.

Shortly after 5:30 p.m., Lin was met at the airport by someone she had not seen in more than a decade: Detective Antonia Gianelli. The two women had met when Lin was in law school and Gianelli was still a uniformed patrol officer. Lin shook hands warmly with the shorter, stockier woman. They agreed it was good to at last be working together.

Lin was introduced to Gianelli's chief of detectives—a man of about Wilson's age, but who had clearly taken better care of himself—at the Seattle PD headquarters. She also met several officials from various precincts in the metro area.

She began to feel uneasy. She did not want to see this operation bungled, like a pot of stew with too many cooks. After the introductions, however, Toni took advantage of a short lull to whisper that the others had been invited as a formality. Only she and Lin were to accompany COD Townsend to Monaghan's home.

The Monaghan estate, as Lin immediately described it to herself, was located in an expensive section of greater Seattle. The sprawling house was situated on a spacious lot and was made invisible from the roadway by artful landscaping. Dusk was near and the front of the house and the drive were already lit, as if company were expected.

A middle-aged Chicana woman dressed in a maid's uniform answered the door and ushered them into the foyer. The inside of the home reflected the same aura of comfortable wealth as had its exterior. Townsend identified himself to the maid, who left to convey the information to her employers that they had unexpected guests.

In a moment, Sharon Monaghan appeared, dressed in a stunning cocktail gown whose champagne hue warmed her pale complexion without clashing with the rosy highlights in her hair. Without exception, the three visitors took note of the generous cleavage exposed by the low-cut bodice, and of the shapely legs encased in shimmering stockings. "How may I help you, officers?" she warbled, faltering as she recognized Lin.

Townsend glanced from Sharon Monaghan's flustered expression to Lin's smug one. "I see you two have met," he commented, his deep baritone bouncing off the tiled floor of the entryway.

Lin kept quiet, wanting to see what Sharon would say for herself, and still trying to place Sharon's Southern accent.

"We've, uh, met in passing," Sharon replied, attempting to recover her composure. A perfectly manicured hand at her throat, she asked again, "How may I help you?"

"Well, actually, ma'am, we're here to see your husband, if we may," Townsend replied.

"Oh—well, he's not in at the moment. We're expecting guests, you see, and he ran out on an errand." Her smile seemed forced and Lin could see that the woman was very uneasy.

Townsend seemed to deliberate over his fedora, which he had removed when Sharon Monaghan had entered the foyer. He said diffidently, "Perhaps we could have a word with you, then, while we wait for Mr. Monaghan to return." He finished with a dazzling smile that, Lin suspected, was equally as false as Sharon's.

"Uh, yes," she agreed reluctantly. "Well, why don't we step into the great room here." She gestured to a set of double doors behind the three officers.

Townsend nodded and turned, motioning Sharon Monaghan to precede him. "Ma'am." As Sharon walked past him, he said, "Gianelli, you wait out here for Mr. Monaghan." He smiled again as he followed Sharon into the great room, his hand on Lin's elbow, lightly guiding her along with him.

Under questioning, Sharon Monaghan declared she knew nothing of her husband's activities on the specified weekend. She said that she had, herself, been out of town the week inclusive of the date Townsend had cited.

"You recall that exactly, now do you?" he asked quietly. As she nodded her reply, he went on. "With whom, ma'am?"

"Why, with one of my friends," she answered smoothly.

Equally smoothly, Townsend asked, "Can you prove that, ma'am?"

Taken aback, Sharon Monaghan sputtered a bit and went on the offensive. "Now see here, officer . . . er, Chief Townsend. What do my whereabouts have to do with anything? I thought you wanted to talk with my husband."

"We do, ma'am. But we are investigating a murder. We have reason to believe that the victim was well acquainted with the 'friend' you were staying with at the Oceanside Resort during that week you so clearly remember."

Neither he nor Lin had missed her blanching. "And who might that be? The murder victim, I mean." Her hand was at her throat again.

"Kathy Kinney."

Sharon Monaghan's eyes and mouth went wide with shock. "Oh my God, that was Anna's friend!" she exclaimed.

"Yes—but you already knew that, didn't you?"

"Well, no—I—I—"

"Isn't that where you recognized Chief O'Shaughnessy from? Ms. Kinney's home?"

"Well, I, uh—I—"

Lin stepped forward. "Don't lie about it, Mrs. Monaghan. We very nearly collided with each other in the doorway last Monday. I questioned you on your whereabouts, as Chief Townsend has just done. Surely you know why Anna was so upset." Lin's voice held an edge.

"She—she called me, said she needed to get away for a day or two. We—we went to a friend's bungalow. She didn't tell me what had happened. I had no idea—"

A sudden knock on the door was followed by Gianelli's dark head poking through it. "Mr. Monaghan has arrived, Chief," she said quietly.

"Good. Gianelli, why don't you finish taking Mrs. Monaghan's statement while Chief O'Shaughnessy and I talk with Mr. Monaghan?"

While Townsend shepherded a disconcerted Sean Monaghan, who was carrying two shopping bags from an upscale wine and spirits shop in downtown Seattle, into the den on the opposite side of the hall, Lin was busy noticing that he perfectly fit the description given them by the used-car salesman. Pulling the double doors shut behind them, Townsend introduced himself and Lin. Monaghan set his packages on his desk and nervously assumed a placating expression. "Chief Townsend, couldn't this wait until later? I mean, I have guests coming—"

"No, Mr. Monaghan, it can't. I'd consider it a great personal favor if you would answer some questions for my counterpart from Belling-ham. Chief O'Shaughnessy?" he said, turning to Lin.

Lin was ready. She carefully and thoroughly proceeded to interrogate Monaghan regarding his whereabouts on the weekend that Kathy Kinney had been killed. He admitted to flying to Bellingham that weekend for a combined business and pleasure trip. No, he had not spent the weekend with any one person. Yes, he could produce business acquaintances who could verify his whereabouts. No, he had never met anyone named Kathy Kinney. No, he had never heard of anyone by that name.

Something about his denial, particularly of having heard of Kathy Kinney, made Lin think he was lying. She pressed him.

"You're sure you never heard her name—perhaps in the TV news? Saw it in the newspaper? She was a well-known lesbian activist—"

"No," he said again, quickly. "And why would I have an interest in such a person?" He smiled in a way that seemed to imply how ridiculous, even preposterous, such a notion was.

Lin paused for a moment, noting the throbbing pulse in his throat, then lobbed out her next question. "Did you know your wife was having an affair with another woman, Mr. Monaghan?"

He stared at Lin, speechless, a look of horror on his face.

"What are you implying?" he finally managed.

"I'm not implying anything, Mr. Monaghan. We have it as fact. Your wife has been romantically involved with Anna Kushima."

A look of panicked confusion crossed his face. "No! She was—" He broke off.

"She was what, Mr. Monaghan?" Lin prodded relentlessly.

His mouth worked but nothing came out. His eyes were those of a bewildered, stricken animal.

Lin's jumbled puzzle segments suddenly began to coalesce, and she was certain she had found the missing piece. A shudder ran over her.

Slowly and deliberately, she closed the distance between them. Her voice, when she spoke, was quiet and menacing. "You suspected your wife was seeing someone. You had her followed, perhaps, confirming your suspicions." Lin's eyes, as she brought her face close to his, were

emerald hard. "Why did you think it was Kathy Kinney she was seeing, Mr. Monaghan?"

She straightened, stabbing at him with her finger as she continued.
"You thought it was Kathy Kinney your wife was seeing and you set
up her murder. In fact, you may even have done it yourself—and
murdered another person to cover it up. Why, Monaghan? Why
Kathy Kinney? Why not Anna Kushima?"

Monaghan fell back under Lin's onslaught, knocking over a pen
holder and picture frame on his desk, tipping over one of his shopping
bags. His face crumpled. "I—I—The investigator I hired last spring
said her name was Kathy Kinney. He—He told me that was the
name of the woman my wife was spending nights in hotels with. He
said . . . it was . . . Kathy Kinney." He lowered his head into his hands.

Lin felt rage well up again. "You killed the wrong person, Monaghan. The woman your wife was seeing was Anna Kushima. They
must have 'borrowed' the name of Anna's lover, who is now dead because of their cowardice and your—your—" She could not find the
right work for what he had done. In revulsion, she turned away.

"You don't understand," he protested plaintively to her back. "I'm
making a bid for a state senate seat next year. I couldn't have it known
that my wife was running around on me—especially with a—
a *bulldagger*." As he uttered the final word, his voice contorted violently.

Lin had not heard the vicious epithet for a long time. She resisted
the urge to spit at and pummel him by keeping her back to him.

"Don't you see? Don't you see?" he pleaded.

"Read him his rights, Chief," Townsend instructed quietly, replacing his fedora firmly. "I'll call for a squad car."

Numbed by the knowledge that Kathy Kinney's death had been
completely without reason, Lin recited the Miranda warning, then
cuffed the prisoner to his heavily padded leather desk chair. Blindly
then, she exited into the foyer, where she literally ran into Gianelli,
who, by the look on her face, had figured it all out from questioning
Sharon Monaghan.

Her hands on Lin's arms, Gianelli steadied Lin. "I'm so sorry," she said quietly, empathy evident in her dark eyes. "I know how you must feel."

"I'm sure you do," Lin whispered hoarsely, tasting the bile burning in the back of her throat. Breaking away from the kind grip, she stumbled out onto the portico, sucking in the cool night air, trying not to give in to the urge to vomit. She needed Caroline's arms around her right now. Caroline could help her to make some sense of the senselessness.

She did not know how she could ever stand to lay eyes on Anna Kushima again. She realized now that the anxious look behind the dark eyes, once Anna knew that her own father had not killed Kathy, must have been fueled by guilt—guilt and fear, inspired by the suspicion that something she had done might have contributed to Kathy's death. Lin hoped fervently that Anna would carry that guilt—reinforced with the knowledge that she had, indeed, done something to contribute to her lover's death—with her to the grave.

Unbidden, her own specter rose to haunt her: her mother's death when her father had learned that she had wanted to divorce him and start anew with someone else. Fourteen-year-old Lin had stood helplessly by, paralyzed with fear and shock, while her drunken father had beaten her mother senseless, then choked the life from her when she was beyond response to his rage. In her head, Lin now knew there was nothing she could have done to prevent what had happened, that her inability to act had been a natural response to the horror of the violence. But in her heart, she would always harbor an unremitting guilt that she had not at least tried to stop him before it was too late.

Yes, she definitely needed Caroline's arms around her.

Clinging carefully to the vestiges of her control, she hunkered down to bide her time until she could return to the haven that awaited her in Bellingham.

Phantoms

Ursula Steck

After it was all over I tried to remember when I had seen them for the first time. At the parking lot, where we unloaded our backpacks, changed from sneakers into hiking boots, put sunblock on our faces, made sure we had locked the car? Had I caught a glimpse of them there, without really noticing them, while Julie took her time to adjust her right boot so that it would not give her trouble on the trail? Was it that early that the young men had picked us out among the groups of hikers getting ready to swarm out into the woods? Or was it pure coincidence that they selected the same trail we had chosen?

Later I wondered about many things. Why, to begin with, these kids in their tight jeans, canvas shoes, and polo shirts even showed up at a place where all there was to do was hike up a mountain, look at a hidden canyon, and march back down. Two women in their late thirties, city-professionals with an insatiable longing for fresh air, the perfumes of herbs and pine trees, and some time together, alone with each other in beautiful nature, Julie and I were a more likely species to be found here. But maybe we were exactly the lure that drove these guys to this place, a starting point for a variety of walks into the forests of the national park—a starting point for them to have whatever they considered was "a whole lot of fun."

The first time I consciously noticed the three was about an hour into our hike. Julie and I had set out on the trail at ten in the morning, having arrived from San Francisco the day before. Our guidebook recommended the trail we had chosen: *Two-day nature adventure for the medium-experienced hiker. It will lead you up to awesome sights of Mount Marga, Viper Canyon, and through woodlands of divine beauty. Expect some steep ascents but nothing that cannot be managed by the well-trained city folk.*

Beware of bears, make sure to read the ranger's warnings, and stick to the rules.

Medium-experienced hikers—exactly what Julie and I were. We had come up to the mountains about three or four times annually for the past twenty years. Almost always they had been pleasant, sometimes wonderful weekends.

Our hike up to Mount Marga and Viper Canyon had begun without any problems or bad omens. It was a warm, sunny day, a few scattered, round white clouds high above us in a clear sky, signs of stable weather. Julie had managed to fit her new boot onto her foot just right, and her limp was almost imperceptible even to me, although I am used to noticing the slightest change in her walk, and measuring it on my inner scale for the degree of her pain.

It seemed that we were the only people on this particular trail. As usual Julie and I had left a plan of our route at the lodge: If we did not come back the next evening, we would be searched for. I felt comfortable, happy, and safe on our trail. The first two or three miles it was not steep, and led us through a glade of high-stemmed flowers so tall they reached almost up to our shoulders, and that sent sparks of pink out of the dark green brush.

"Foxglove," said Julie, "gorgeous, toxic, and a lifesaver. What a wild combination."

"In the true sense of the word," I agreed.

Julie is a doctor. I am used to her view of nature as a huge pharmacy. For me a flower is a flower is a flower. I like them, and admire their beauty, but I do not even know their names or their medical potential.

I reached for Julie's hand. She closed her long fingers around mine, and we swung our arms a little as we walked. Her skin was dry and warm, and touching it felt like plugging into an energy source— a source I had known almost forever, although I could not recall us ever having walked hand in hand when we were girls, or even touching at all, for quite a long time.

Julie and I met when we were twelve. The day I walked into the classroom—I had just moved with my family from St. Louis to San Francisco—she sat in the very back of the room, the only kid alone at

a desk, and the teacher placed me next to her. She was a lanky girl
with short hair, glasses, and a rather big nose. At twelve years old, she
was already five feet eight. "Tall for a Chinese girl," her mom often
said, who is as short as I.

As forest closed around the path, voices sounded behind us. We let
go of each other's hands, slowed our steps. A woman and a man in
their forties, and a teenage girl passed us. The woman wore a khaki
baseball cap over her short blond ponytail, the man, similar headgear
in red over an equally red, wide face. The adults appeared highly mo-
tivated, walking as if to break a record. The smile with which the man
greeted us did not seem particularly joyful, especially when compared
to the expression of the girl. Sullen, head hanging down, brown curls
falling into her eyes, long legs in a tight denim miniskirt and hiking
boots, she stumbled over the uneven ground of the trail. But despite
her display of opposition, she kept up with the adults.

Once the little group had passed us, Julie and I picked up speed
and entered the forest. The orchestra of the meadow, the humming of
myriad insects was now overpowered by the tweeting, and shouting,
and cackling of all kinds of birds in the branches all around us, but
which we could not see. It was cooler here; the earthy, humid smells of
tree bark and decaying leaves surrounded us.

"How did it go in LA last week?" Julie asked.

I am a photographer, and had come back from a work trip the day
before. We had been too busy getting ready for our weekend to exchange news. I looked at her. There it was, that familiar little smile in
the corner of her eyes. I stopped, waited until Julie came to a halt too,
and slung my arms around her. The warmth of her skin underneath
the T-shirt seemed to melt into mine, our bodies trembling a little,
from the movement of the hike, from our heartbeats that were like
big tumbling machines slowly calming down. We kissed.

Then we heard the giggle. It came from right behind us. We let our
arms fall, turned around, and saw the guys standing there. They began to laugh. Their voices were so loud that it seemed suddenly impossible that we had not heard them before. How could they have just
sneaked up on us like this? There were three young men, aged somewhere between sixteen and nineteen. One was a bit bigger, heavier set

than the other two, but not particularly fat. He had short brown hair, was tall and broad-shouldered, and had a square face. The second one was skinny, with dark curls, with a narrow, pale face that could have been handsome if not sprinkled with pimples. His eyes looked like big black moles, round, and implacable. The third one seemed to be cloned for a boy band: the blond cute kid, for whom whole populations of young girls would scream their souls out if he ever stepped onto a stage.

I remember thinking that their gear looked very urban. No multifunctional hiking pants or shirts from one of the many outdoor shops in the city. No boots or orange sun-protection caps, such as Julie and I wore. They only carried little backpacks, which made strange clinking noises when they moved. But I did notice that one had a rolled-up tent dangling from his pack.

Julie just stared at them. We did not move, and a moment later the guys had passed us, almost ran around the curve of the path, and were gone from our sight.

"Kids," Julie said. There was a little laugh in her voice, but it was very short, like a breath you take with somebody sitting on your chest.

The path became steeper. I tried to synchronize the length of my steps, and my breathing. I could see that Julie was testing out her foot. The best length of step, the ideal spot to put weight on, the perfect balance between pressure and release. The toes on Julie's right foot are missing, due to a childhood accident. She once explained to me that it is an intricate and unpredictable pattern of phantom pain and nervous signals in the scars that pulsates in her foot. Walking on it mostly relieves it, but she needs very well-fitting shoes, and a careful gait. At night, when she lies besides me, I can often feel her moving her leg around, trying to avoid the burning and stinging that sets in when the ghosts of her long lost toes show up.

Sun rays broke through the ceiling of trees, and it felt as if we were walking among happy little phosphorescent creatures. Julie asked again about my work, and I described the women I had portrayed in Los Angeles for a book project, undocumented immigrants who had worked all their adult lives and had become old in a country where their lives were never acknowledged in terms of statistics, health care, and retirement income. It had not been easy to find women who agreed to have their pictures taken for the book, and those who did wanted to be disguised. There are photographic methods to do this and still create pictures that tell a story. I was looking forward to working in the darkroom the following week, to watch the silhouettes of the faces appear on the paper when I developed the photos.

Julie listened with concentration, and focused on the path before her. "I wonder how many people's survival depends on the secrets they keep," she finally said.

I knew she did not expect a response to this comment. I studied her profile—a face I knew so well I could have painted it in photo-realistic quality if I were a painter. It still seemed to be new whenever I could look at her unobserved: the generous mouth, the funny, round, rather big nose, her black hair. She was like a benign panther—self confident, graceful, and secretive.

I was just about to reach for her hand, when we heard another giggle.

"Not them again," Julie whispered.

This time they were blocking the path. The broad-shouldered one stood on one side, the pimply one on the other, while the boy-band star occupied the center. Each had a beer can in one hand, and a kind of bat—at closer look they were thick gnarly tree branches—in the other.

"Just keep on walking, Diane," Julie said to me.

Until the very last second it looked as if we would collide with them. They stood there motionless, laughing a bit, checking out how we would react. Then the big guy stepped to the side, and we slipped through the gap between him and the boy-band star. I tried not to gasp when we arrived on the other side of this male roadblock. Julie stared at the ground while we walked on.

"Don't you wanna say thank you?" a high-pitched, loud, sarcastic voice sounded behind us.

It struck me like a shot in my back—an attack I had waited for without knowing it.

"Don't turn," Julie warned me.

"Next time we won't be so polite to let you ladies through," a second voice lit up.

"Ladies? Come on! That's not what I would call them!" the first voice again.

I could not help myself, and looked back.

"Hey dyke, wanna know what a dick feels like? Then you'll change your mind." The same nasty voice. It was the kid in the middle. The blond boy-band charmer. He swung his tree branch, grabbed his crotch, and swung his pelvis back, and forth.

"No thanks," I bellowed.

Julie touched my arm. "Don't!"

"I bet you'd love it," Blondy yelled, and cackled. "A whole ass full."

Julie was walking very fast. I picked up her speed. Our pace was so quick that we even caught up with the family with the teenage girl. A little later they appeared before us, and this time we passed them. I thought I heard the three right behind us all this time, giggling and hitting the grass at the side of the path with their bats, but when I looked over my shoulder they were gone.

"Let's turn around and go back to the car," I said to Julie.

"Why?" was her response.

"Honestly, I don't really want to see them again."

"They are somewhere behind us. So we would run into them. Anyhow, why let them ruin our weekend?"

She proceeded to tell me about a patient she had operated on two days ago, a five-year-old boy with appendicitis. "He tried to give me his favorite teddy bear when I came to see him after the operation."

I tried to concentrate on her story, on her eyes that had the shape of two half-moons as she squinted against the sun. The treetops were slowly becoming lower, and the path lighter. As Julie talked she looked relaxed again. Even the little smile crept into her eyes once more.

Julie did not always have this readiness to laugh in her eyes. When I first met her in grade seven, she had already been singled out by the three meanest bullies. I entered the class four months into the school year, and the whole hierarchical system was firmly established. Julie had been selected as the lowest member of the pecking order. As a kid

I never tried to analyze what it was about her that got her into this position. Much of why somebody gets trampled on and humiliated is an arbitrary thing, a random choice by those who are looking for a punching bag. If Julie had been in another class among another group of children, maybe she would have been left alone or have even become popular. But she was cornered almost every recess by Bill, Dan, and Bob, three boys as witty and colorful as their names who had nothing that made them special but their cruelness and childhood brutality. They would stand around Julie, call her names, tell her she was the most ugly and despicable girl in the whole school, and the moment she tried to get away from them, they would grab her, shove her around, and sometimes beat her up. During class they threw empty soda cans at her, sent little notes from one kid to the next containing dirty jokes about her. They would tear up her homework, break her pencils, and smear dog shit over her textbooks.

Julie would bite them, pinch them, scratch them, but they were stronger, and they always fought three against one. The more she defended herself, the worse her injuries became. Black eyes, bruises everywhere, and the occasional blow to the stomach that sent her vomiting into the girl's bathroom.

Bob was the meanest of the three, but he also had a blooming kind of good looks, a certain boyish handsomeness—brown spiky hair, symmetrical face, cutting blue eyes—and the self-confidence of the born majority that attracted many of the preadolescent girls. The other boys stayed away from the bullies, knowing they would be left alone as long as they did not provoke them, and as long as Julie was there as a whipping "boy" for all of us. The teachers did not seem to notice what was going on, or they just did not care. And why Julie's parents did not intervene—after all, they must have seen that their daughter was in some sort of distress—I never found out.

And where was I during all of this? I was the new kid on the block. I was small, and red-haired, and quiet, and my instinct told me that I would be the next in line if the three ever lost interest in Julie or if my existence ever entered their conscious minds. So I did nothing. I did not help Julie fight, or comfort her, or even offer friendship. We were both shy kids whose strategy was to remain silent so that as few people as possible would notice we were there. This way we would be left alone. It worked for me. Not for Julie.

Then the accident happened. My mother picked me up after school on Wednesdays and took me to guitar lessons. I was not there, did not wait at the streetcar station on Church Street together with Julie, and the bullies, and many of the other kids of our class. I heard later that the three boys had shoved Julie around, and then they had pushed her in front of a Muni train. They wanted to frighten her, was what they had to say in their own defense later, as if wanting to frighten somebody could ever be an excuse, but had underestimated the velocity of the vehicle. So Julie's foot got crushed between the metal tracks and the wheel of a mega-ton streetcar train.

She had to stay in the hospital for the whole summer. What the boys had done finally touched my by now thirteen-year-old heart, and I went to visit her. When she came back to school in the fall she was still walking with crutches, the three bullies had been expelled for good from Castro High—I never saw them again—and Julie and I had become friends. That we would later become most secretive teenage sweethearts and eventually life partners was something I did not ever imagine. But that summer, when our friendship began to develop, I felt as happy and excited as if I were falling in love.

Julie never talked about what had happened at the streetcar stop. We never spoke about the three boys, and how she must have felt all of those months when they were after her. The few times I tried to bring up the topic she merely said that she was happy it was over, and she did not want to think of it anymore.

The accident changed her. It was during her first weeks back to school when I realized the way her eyes could smile. A smile that became stronger, more steady over the years, ready to take over her mouth, turn into a sarcastic grin, but also into pure, heartfelt laughter. And as soon as she could walk without too many problems again, she began to practice martial arts. She learned karate, tae kwon do, kung fu, and many more. She never tried to take part in any competitions or to win belts. Even today she leaves our house two times a week to practice the art of self-defense and attack. I sometimes used to worry that she might get hurt, but she assured me it kept her body flexible and fit, and she knew all the tricks to protect her foot from being injured.

About two hours after our second encounter with the young males, the trees became sparser. Big rocks rose up to the right side of the path, and we climbed onto a smooth boulder to eat our lunch. From here we could already see the western flank of Mount Marga. A distant rock face, several thousand feet high, at whose bottom, still invisible from here, Viper River ran. Julie and I ate our roasted veggie sandwiches in silence. Then we stretched out on the stone's warm surface for a short rest. Our shoulders touched lightly, and I felt one of Julie's fingers on my thigh, a swift warm lizard. I let my index finger stroke her bare arm. Something touched my other arm. I turned to see what it was and shot up. Next to me was a black, bulging, ripped-open shape, inflated, and sunken-in looking at the same time. Maggots in bright-white, lumpy formations crawled in its decomposing guts. Hairy pieces of skin were stuck to purple-colored, almost liquid, rotting flesh under which bones shone; and then my nose caught the smell. Foul, weirdly sweet, and instantly nauseating. I choked.

"What's the matter?" Julie asked. Her eyes were still closed, her long limbs stretched out in the sun.

I grabbed my backpack. "Let's go!"

Julie rose, saw the rotting carcass. "A dead raccoon," she remarked. "Particularly dead," she joked.

I did not laugh. She followed me off the rock. When I heard the giggle again, I knew what had happened. Almost at the same moment as we did, the three males stepped onto the walk, a little further uphill. They must have crawled through the underbrush over to our resting place, and placed the stinking animal corpse practically on my arm. Why had we not heard them? Were they experienced creeps? Or did we have to become more careful, less visible to them?

They were waiting for us in the same order as the last time, swinging their makeshift bats.

Julie walked up to them without changing her trajectory or her speed. I had to fight against the impulse to turn and run. But I stayed in tow. None of them moved to let us through. But when Julie was close enough she shoved aside pimple-face just as if she were pushing her way through the crowd at a street fair, and made the next step. Then she tripped. I was close enough to catch her arm. She regained her balance and went on. I saw the bat that the blond one stuck between my legs before it could make me fall, jumped over it, and followed Julie. The three closed up quickly. Now they were all around us, pushing at Julie, who expertly avoided their touches by stepping around them, and punching me with light but already powerful little hits of their fists. I was not as trained as she, and it seemed that strong, knuckled hands were everywhere. *We have to get away from the edge of the trail,* I thought. On the right side of the path was a steep slope, almost a precipice that led far down.

The big male had a stern look. He managed to take sips from his beer can while he punched me on the back, the ribs, the upper arms. Pimple-face had acquired red patches all over his skin, from the sun or the alcohol, and his face looked as if it would explode any minute with all its craters and inflammations. But the boy-band star had changed the most radically. His skin was sucked back over his cheekbones, corpselike, induced by the wide grin stretching out his mouth.

Julie's steps had gotten very long and fast, and I had to jog to keep up with her. But the three matched our speed, still dealing out their punches, which became harder, and more painful, their bats constantly between our legs, in front of our feet. I saw Julie trip again. One of the sticks had caught her right leg, and with her next step she landed hard on the front of her vulnerable foot. I could almost feel the pain that shot through her. A sudden pallor covered her face, and her gaze seemed to go into the distance. She stopped. I stepped close to her. We had made it to the far left side of the path, with our backs to a high rock wall.

"Why don't you just leave us alone," Julie said. She sounded calm.

All three were taller than me. Julie could look the two smaller ones in the eye but the third one towered over her.

"Piss off," I yelled at the one with the vacuum smile.

Julie stood very close to me. I could sense her physical warmth, but we did not look at each other. Then I felt her hand. It lay calm on my shoulder. "Don't . . ." she whispered.

"What did the bitch say?" Vacuum-face's voice overpowered not only the noises of nature but our surroundings altogether as if the beauty of the land around us and the colors and scents of the plants were only pictures on a screen. The alcoholic breath of the guy washed over me in a wave.

"The lady's wish is our command," he said.

His friends looked at him.

"Come on," their spiritual leader said, and unzipped his pants.

He unwrapped his reddish, hairy penis, and aimed it toward my hiking boots. His companions continued to stand around with zipped-up flies, but they moved up to Julie, and to me. One more time Julie tried to push them away, to clear the path for us, but this time the three did not move an inch. The big one caught Julie's arms, and the pimply one mine. The first drips of the blond guy's urine started to wet my shoes. My knee jerked up without me thinking about it. But before my kneecap could smash into the guy's pecker, the broad-shouldered one pressed it down with his own leg, and I had to watch my boots being sprinkled. Vacuum-face did not aim very well. Before more than a few drops could touch the leather of my shoes, voices approached from down the trail. The three stepped back from us in one fast movement, and Julie pulled me away, and up the path.

It was the family again. They had finally caught up with us, and now came unsuspectingly to our rescue.

"No, we cannot go back now!" said the man, his head turned to the girl. "We've already walked too far. We'll set up camp before dusk as planned. It's only two more hours to go."

"Isn't it wonderful up here?" the woman remarked when she saw us.

"Beautiful," Julie answered. Her voice was very calm—and very serious. Unusually serious for the content of her comment.

"Gorgeous," the woman continued, without a sign of puzzlement.

We walked beside the couple. The three males were a little bit ahead of us, their backs to our group, the blond one's arms moving in a way that told me he was zipping up his pants.

"It's always great to get away from the city for a day or two, even if our daughter doesn't share my opinion," said the red-faced man, and pointed at the teenage girl. She walked between us and the three males. Vacuum-face, who had closed his jeans, turned around and gave the girl a little smile. I could not see her expression, but she walked even faster, and left her parents behind.

"Yes. That's true," Julie said in response to the woman's last remark.

Soon we were behind the family, and they disappeared around one of the path's many bends ahead of us.

Again I suggested we turn around and head for the car. But Julie said: "It's true what the man told his daughter. We have come too far. It'll get dark soon. We can't make it back before that; and it's dangerous walking around here at night."

For the rest of the hike we were left alone. Insects began to hum, in the far distance we heard the call of an animal, a low, hoarse sound. Julie and I did not talk. I could see she was hurting. Her limp quite distinct, she marched on without complaint.

"Is it bad?" I finally asked.

"Don't worry," she answered. Her eyes looked into the distance; her mind seemed to be walking through a very far terrain.

I was trying to keep my own fear from surging up in my stomach like a geyser. I was shivering a bit. The canyon's depths had fully opened up right next to the path. I tried not to look down into the gorge, although this view was what we had come up here to see. My feet seemed to be losing their grip on the uneven rocky surface, I began to imagine trying to hold Julie, who dangled over the abyss, but then having to let her go because our hands slipped.

At last we reached the campground. We were not yet above the tree line. Low but dense conifers covered the vast platform where we were allowed to put up tent. We found a spot where we could see no other campers in the immediate vicinity. Julie is the expert in erecting our tent, and I set out with a pot to find the brook, which our guide mentioned, to scoop water. I had to walk about three hundred yards through the woods and arrived at a clearing. I crossed it and saw the little stream. I passed only two other tents, both were set on the edge of the glade. One was quite large, a green thing almost hidden in the brush. The other one was the tent of the three males. It was low, and yellow, with beer cans littered in front of it. Only one of the three was visible. Pimple-face sat in front of the tent, sipped beer, and gave me an empty stare, so drunk that not even a menacing little smile crossed his features. He looked as if he had just seen me for the first time, and I felt something like relief. Fortunately they had set up camp as far away from us as possible. When I came back to Julie I did not mention that I had seen the three, nor did she ask me.

We did not finish the small pack of instant cream of portabella-mushrooms-soup that Julie had prepared on the gas cooker. I managed to swallow half of it, while her cup seemed to be full. In the slowly vanishing daylight she looked very pale.

"Coffee?" I asked.

She shook her head.

We pulled our supplies up into a tree, fastened the rope around the tree trunk the way we had learned it, and hoped for the best with the bears. The sun had sunk behind the mountains. Neither of us had noticed any particularly impressive sunset. Neither of us had been in the spirit to give our surroundings a closer exploration. The campground was situated on a natural platform with a fabulous view of the canyon, but I knew it only from what I had read.

In the beam of our power flashlight Julie took a closer look at her foot while I put on a thick pair of jogging pants, wool socks, and a sweatshirt, rolled out the mats and sleeping bags in the tent, and crawled into mine. Julie came in soon after me. She brought her first-aid kit, the flashlight, and carefully zipped up the tent flap. Then we both lay in our sleeping bags. It was absolutely dark. I rolled over so that I could embrace Julie, and she moved into my arms.

I do not know if we ever fell asleep. It seemed as if I had closed my eyes only seconds ago when they opened up again. I did not consciously hear a sound but I knew a noise had torn me out of the state of dozing or presleep. Julie had come out of her sleeping bag. She switched on the flashlight, and opened the tent.

"Wait," I said. Panic wrapped its fingers around my throat. "It could be a bear."

"This was no bear," Julie said. "Bears don't giggle."

I followed her out of the tent. She let the beam of the flashlight roam over the ground, and illuminated a little galaxy of scattered items. Our food container was among them, the lid taken off, and the soup spilled on the ground. Chocolate bars lay around with torn wrappings, the contents broken up and strewn all over the place. Mashed peaches, and a number of bananas with the peel ripped down littered the forest floor. Whoever had done this had even made sure to lay out a neat little track of breadcrumbs and salami slices up to the entrance of our tent. A food court for every bear passing by, together with a tempting olfactory guide to the even bigger sleeping goodies contained in the nylon wrappings of our tent.

As quickly as we could we collected everything, stuffed it into our zipper bag, and threw it and the supplies far into the underbrush. That was all we could do for now.

Back in the tent I could feel Julie shaking when I touched her. "Who knows who did this," I said, trying to sound lighthearted. "There are a lot of weirdos in these campgrounds."

She did not answer. I wrapped my arms around her. After a while her breath calmed, and I felt her become heavier as her body relaxed. And, as if somebody were stripping me of the armor that held my body upright and covered me with a dark blanket, I fell asleep.

And dreamed. In the dream I stepped out of the tent into the gray light of dawn, and into a puddle of blood. It was huge and toxically red, and I knew I only had to follow the red footprints that led away from it to find the body that had lost all this fluid. I walked and walked, following the glowing marks that were splattered over the pine-needle-covered ground. Then I saw the great pile: a naked human body, still bleeding from many wounds. I wanted to see who it was, tried to see the face. But it was buried in the ground. I would have had to touch the corpse, and roll it over. I tried to move my hand but could not. I was standing in the middle of the forest with a dying person, and had turned to stone.

When I woke up I felt heavy as a rock, and it took me an unbearably long time to realize that I could move. I tried out my fingers, then my feet, and finally was awake enough to distinguish that I had surfaced from a nightmare. Julie was gone. Her sleeping bag was empty when I touched it, no breath, and no body's heat in the tent but my own. It was still night, still so dark that my eyes had nothing to process. I searched for the flashlight, but could not find it. In a sudden realization I also tried to find Julie's first-aid kit. She is a doctor. It contains more refined equipment than the regular shop-bought kit for the layman. She usually carries a whole number of drugs around, such as painkillers and emergency heart medication, along with everything that she would need to take care of a heavily bleeding wound, and an assortment of disposable scalpels—to take a bad splinter out of somebody's flesh or to cut open a piece of cloth and examine the wound underneath. After all, she is a surgeon.

I stumbled out of the tent, tried to see if Julie was out there, close by, catching fresh air, as unlikely as that may have been, considering the nightly dangers of the forest. Under the canopy of trees I could not see the ground before my feet or the next tree. With every breath I sucked in the darkness. It spread inside of me, a glutinous black stream, flowing into my arteries, inhabiting me like the paralysis I had felt in the dream.

I managed to lift my feet. I wanted to run into the woods, into the darkness where Julie was somewhere. And I wanted to hide, creep back into the tent, curl up until she came back. I walked. Into the direction where I thought the brook was; and the tent of the three young males. I remembered the little flashlight on my key chain, the key chain I wore around my neck. I grabbed it, sent its weak beam over the forest floor before me, a small dancing dot that did not show me much more than that there was a floor. I walked and walked and stumbled, sometimes ran into a tree. I had also become deaf. Not a sound was there around me. No bird's cry, no distant howl or even tapping of big animal paws. No human voice, no giggle. Nothing.

But I reached the open space, the clearing at whose edge the bank of the creek lay. The moon was a thin white stripe high above. Its light painted the world in nuances of dark-gray shadows, enough to make out the edge of the tree line where I had earlier seen the lonely green tent, and farther up, the tent of the three. Following an inner radar I never knew I possessed, suddenly I was there. My little glowworm lamp caught some green nylon: the edge of the first tent. I tried to produce an inner map. Where was the camp of the three? I had to turn about ninety degrees, move along the trees, but remain on the clearing, and after about fifty yards turn left again.

Their tent was gone. My light did not touch a small roof-shaped structure. But I could easily make out where it had been. Bright yellow rags littered the ground. The tent floor was still there. It was orange. Two of the young men lay on it: the broad-shouldered one, and his pimply, mole-eyed companion. They were both naked. Nothing was there that they could have wrapped around themselves. No sleeping bags, no blankets that were not cut to shreds. Their clothes were equally cut up as was the tent. The only undestroyed items I could make out were two canvas sneakers, and they did not match. To take all this in I had to move my flashlight up and down and left and right numerous times. The thin guy had vomited all over the floor, and gazed up at me with the expressionless stare of an animal in shock. The broad-shouldered one looked mainly drunk. He seemed to be fast asleep, snored a bit. His penis lay limp on the ground, a thin long piece of skin that gave the impression of being unattached to him.

But it was still connected to his body. Neither of the two appeared to be injured beyond what the nakedness and the act of somebody cutting up their tent had done to them. There was no blood, and no sighs or screams of pain from either of them. The third guy, Mr. boy-band–vacuum-grin, was gone. The beam of my light did not hit him anywhere near.

"Where is he?" I inquired.

Mole-Eye continued to stare at me, but did not answer.

"What happened?" I tried again, raising my voice.

"He went with her," the guy finally said.

"Where did they go?"

He shrugged, only then seemed to realize in which unprotected state his genitals were, and grabbed for a piece of cloth lying next to him. It was very small, not much bigger than my hand, and it looked as ridiculous as a fig leaf when he held it over his penis.

I stumbled through the forest for a long time. First I made it to the path that led back to our tent. But then I heard something. A sharp

whining sound, somewhere in the distance. From the direction where
the canyon lay. When I had tried to recall the location of the clearing,
the map from our guidebook had popped up in my head again. So our
tent stood not far from the edge. Maybe thirty yards away. That was
where the sound came from. I broke into the brush again. The darkness that surrounded me was eternal.

At one point the sheer loneliness of my expedition became the
source of my despair. I only wanted to find Julie. The picture from my
dream flashed up before me. Suddenly the bleeding body had Julie's
face. But then there was somebody standing next to the body, a knife
in her hand. The person turned around. It was Julie too. I started to
cry. Sobs shook me so hard, my legs bent under them. My tiny key-
chain light went dead.

I realized that I was possibly moving around dangerously close to
the edge of the canyon. I shouted. "Juuuuuliiiieeee!" No answer! No
sound at all. I had to turn around. From then on I aimlessly walked
through the night.

I wandered on, and on, and on.

And then I stood in front of our tent again. Instinct or mere coincidence had brought me back. I tripped over one of the strings, felt for
the entrance in the dark, zipped up the flap with hands shaking like
sparrows' wings. I could not recall if I had closed it earlier. Maybe I
had not, and maybe Julie had made it back, and was lying in there
now sleeping. But my hope was in vain. The tent was empty as I had
left it. I could not get myself to crawl in. I had to find her. I set out to
look for her again.

In this moment Julie came back. There was the cracking of dry
branches, and the rustling of clothes, and the woman I love broke
from the underbrush, a foggy circle of light hovering before her. She
did not come from the direction of the glade but from the side of the
canyon.

"What are you doing out here?" she asked.

"Looking for you. Where have you been?"

"Somebody needed a doctor."

"You were gone a long time," I said shakily.

Julie looked at my face. Only when I saw myself in a mirror the next day, did I find out how scratched up it was.

"Let's put some disinfectant on that."

We entered the tent, crouched together on the floor. Julie positioned the flashlight so that it comfortably illuminated all that she needed to see. She set down her first-aid pack, which she had carried over her shoulder. When she opened it, I tried to look inside, but she quickly got out a small bottle and some cotton pads, and closed the bag again. I could not make out any of the other contents.

Julie cleaned my wounds. It should have stung, but I was so drunk with the relief of having her back that I did not feel it. I studied her face while she examined each of my scratches. The smile was back in her eyes. Her strong hands worked expertly and fast—they looked very clean.

I tried again to find out what had happened. "Who needed a doctor?"

"A young girl," Julie answered.

"The kid we saw on the trail?"

"I can't tell you. You know that."

"Even when it is a nighttime emergency you can't?"

"No."

"How did they find you? Who knew you're a doctor?"

"I heard a shout. It sounded like somebody was seriously in trouble. I went to look."

Before I could ask the next question Julie embraced me, and kissed me. Her lips were soft and hard at the same time. They tasted salty. I responded. First with hesitation. Then Julie became slower, gentler. I opened her mouth with my tongue, and breathed her in. We had kissed each other for the first time more than twenty years ago. But it felt as if I had never kissed her before. She tasted all new; and still familiar. Her mouth was deep, delicious, and oozing with flavor like an oyster that melts on your tongue. The skin of her face stroked mine. Softer than anything I knew. I let my head sink onto her shoulder. I had her back. Happiness opened my chest until it was so wide that

I started to laugh and cry at the same time. Julie's mouth was at my ear. She said, "It's over. Don't worry."

She kissed my neck, moved down in my arms, and said, "Let's get some sleep. I'm so tired."

The sun was up and the weather beautiful again when we awoke. We retrieved our food bag from the brush—it had remained untouched—prepared coffee, checked out which of our supplies were still edible, decided that one of the apples and a small bag of cereal whose one corner was only torn up a little bit were okay, and had them for breakfast. Then we inspected the campground. The green tent was gone. The spot where the boy's tent had stood was unpopulated. The remains of the tent, and of their clothes, were still strewn around.

"Wow, that looks bad," said Julie.

I tried my luck. "Yeah, I wonder what happened."

"I wonder how they got back to the parking lot," she answered.

I wanted to ask the question. Wanted to know if she had done this to the tent. But then I saw her expression. She looked so relaxed and content—her skin was smooth, her eyes smiling. I could not do it. I could not say anything that would change the way her face beamed back at me when I smiled at her. I wanted her to always look like this.

She reached for my hand, and we walked on to explore the edges of the canyon. The view was as gorgeous as the guide had promised—it was the sheer vastness between the giant walls of rock. Mount Marga on the other side of the canyon looked as if it were floating above the ground, ready to rise into the sky and disappear. We stood at the very edge of the canyon, which fell down in terraces of gray and rusty-red stones. Below us was only air, and far, far down was the river that looked like its namesake, a tiny green snake, lingering in the sun. I felt a twitch between my shoulder blades, as if something there wanted to spread.

The peace of the scene was interrupted: first by the sharp sound of rotor blades, then by the sight of a white helicopter that came up from the bottom of the canyon, something hanging from its belly. An orange, elongated package—and a man holding the wrapped-up, body-sized load, preventing it from dangling, while the aircraft rose.

"Somebody needed to be rescued," Julie said. She looked seriously worried this time.

When we started out for the walk down the mountainside, and back to our car, I saw that Julie's limp had become almost invisible again. This time we were not interrupted. We walked for many hours without encountering anybody. The foxglove clearing was right before us when we saw two male rangers coming up the path. They looked very young, in new uniforms, almost like action figures. Both were small and wiry. Both black-haired, one had curls, the other one thin, straight hair.

"Hi," the curly one said.

"Hi, how are you?" I responded.

Julie only looked at them. Nodded a greeting, walked on.

Something in me wanted to wait. Wanted to chat with these guys. Ask them what they were up to. If they were walking up to the campground. If they had heard news of anything that had happened there last night. Of course I did not. I continued to walk, following my partner.

"Have a good day," the noncurly ranger said with a friendly smile.

"Did you see the guys last night?" I eventually asked Julie after the men were gone.

"I did. They were drunk. The blond one had tried to rape a girl."

"Tried?" I asked.

"Yeah, he did not succeed."

"What happened?"

"The girl got away. That's all she would tell me. I found her in the woods. I took her to her parents."

"Somebody should notify the police."

"That's up to them."

"Where is the boy? Did he get away?"

"Let's not talk about the guys. I'm happy it is over."

And so I did not ask again. Julie and I walked back to our car. Our hands never separated. Even when we got hot and sweaty our palms remained dry. We did not speak for the last hour of the hike. In my head thoughts and images tumbled around. We had left the forest and were hiking through grassland, but the woods I had walked the night before continued to pop up in front of my eyes: snapshots of trees, strange and ghostly in the dark, that my little flashlight had illuminated. I would not be able to tell Julie all of what I had felt. And I did not want to. It had been humiliating to feel so utterly lonely, a side of me I had never seen before. Julie and I had known each other for twenty-seven years, had lived in the same house since we had become adults. Still, most of our lives happened in spaces where we were not together—work spaces, airplanes, conference rooms, operating rooms, the spaces of our minds. We had been together during the encounter with the three males yesterday, but I did not really know what it had done to Julie, and I could not bring myself to tell her what it had done to me.

We never saw the three again. At the parking lot Julie laughed at me and said, "Hey, my sweet brooder, are you ready to come back to me?" When I looked around I saw the family with the teenage girl. They were talking to another ranger, this time a sturdy woman. When the young girl recognized us, her face twitched in a quick, shy smile. Julie gave her a wink. The kid smiled again, and then turned back to her parents and the ranger.

In the week after our hike I spent hours in the darkroom watching the silhouettes of women's faces—round shapes, profiles with noses like birds' beaks, among them a face with a forehead as high as Nefertiti—appear on the photo paper like mirages. And I listened to the radio news constantly. There was no report of a missing person in a national park, an attempted rape, or a story of somebody having fallen into a canyon, not even a little joke of some young men having turned up stark naked at a parking lot in a popular hiking area.

Julie did not have any night shifts that week so she picked me up after her workday, freed me from my red-lit confines, and we went for dinner. I showed her the new pictures, listened to the parts of her job that she wanted to share with me, and we made plans for our next hiking tour. My curiosity about the three—their motives, their character, their fate—slowly subsided, fading like the images of their faces in my head. As did the urge to ask Julie about them. Whenever I looked into her eyes I found that smile there; and that was all I was searching for.

About the Editor

Katherine V. Forrest is twice winner of the Lambda Literary Award for best mystery and the Pioneer Award from the Lambda Literary Foundation. She is the author of numerous novels, including the popular Kate Delafield Mystery series and the classic romance *Curious Wine*. She has been profiled in *USA Today, The San Francisco Chronicle, The Bloomsbury Review,* and most major lesbian/gay publications in America, including *The Advocate, The Book Report, Curve,* and *Visibilities*. Ms. Forrest teaches classes and seminars on the craft of writing and lives in San Francisco.

Contributors

J. L. Belrose's short fiction can be found in *Queer View Mirror I*, *Skin Deep*, *Pillow Talk II*, *Best Women's Erotica*, *Uniform Sex*, *Set in Stone*, *Body Check* and *Hot & Bothered 3* and *4*. She was born in Toronto, Canada, attended the Ontario College of Art & Design, then traveled through Britain and Europe, living for several years in London, then Paris. She's now resettled in Toronto and shares her home with a lazy pitbull named Onyx and a kick-ass Muse. She is in the revision stage of her first novel, which she refers to as "the beast," and dreams of visiting New York and California. "House Built of Sticks" is her first venture into the mystery genre.

Victoria A. Brownworth is a political and social activist, and the author of ten books, including the award-winning *Too Queer: Essays from a Radical Life*. She is the editor of twelve books, including the Lambda Award–winning *Coming Out of Cancer: Writings from the Lesbian Cancer Epidemic*. A Pulitzer Prize nominee, she has been a longtime columnist and reporter for numerous queer and mainstream publications, and her critical essays have appeared in newspapers, magazines, and journals throughout the United States, Canada, Europe, and Australia. Her monthly column on queer politics appears in *Curve* magazine; a weekly column on national and international politics is syndicated by the *Journal-Register* newspapers; and her biweekly TV column, "The Lavender Tube," focuses on queers and politics. She is also a book critic for the *Baltimore Sun*. She teaches writing and film at the University of the Arts in Philadelphia, the nation's largest college of the creative and performing arts. She lives in Philadelphia with her six cats.

Ouida Crozier is currently the Coordinator for Diversity for the Minnesota Department of Human Services. She was born and raised in

Florida, and lived in South Carolina for ten years. She has lived in Minnesota since 1981, where she was licensed and practiced psychology for fourteen years. She is the author of poetry, essays, short fiction, and a novel, *Shadows After Dark.* She resides in Minneapolis with her partner and their animal companions.

Joan M. Drury is lucky enough to be engaged in a number of activities that primarily have to do with women and words. The author of four novels, including the celebrated Edgar Award finalist, *Silent Words,* she has just finished her fifth novel, *Looking for Lonnie.* She runs Drury Lane Books, a bookstore in Grand Marais, MN; Norcroft, a writing retreat for women in Lutsen, MN; Drury Enterprises, a development company that specializes in affordable housing; and a number of other commitments that focus on feminist social change and peace. She dedicates her life to her family—both biological and chosen—and to making a difference. Most of all, she reads.

Jeane Harris's previous fiction includes *Black Iris* (Naiad Press, 1991), *Delia Ironfoot* (Naiad Press, 1992), and *The Magnolia Conspiracy* (Chennault and Gray, 2004). Her short fiction includes "Walker Among Us" (*Sojourner,* 1983), "Peace and Quiet" (*The Romantic Naiad,* 1993), and "The Road to Healing Heart" (*The Erotic Naiad,* 1994). *A Grave Opening: A Delia Ironfoot Adventure* is forthcoming. She grew up in Illinois and Colorado and attended Colorado State University on a creative and performing arts scholarship, receiving her master's in education in 1975 and her PhD in rhetoric and composition in 1986 from Texas Christian University. She is a Professor of English at Arkansas State University in Jonesboro, Arkansas. She lives with her dog, Sweetie, and her feline, Señor Lucchi.

Karla Jay is Distinguished Professor of English and Women's and Gender Studies at Pace University in New York City. She has written, edited, and translated ten books, including *Dyke Life: From Growing Up to Growing Old, a Celebration of the Lesbian Experience,* which won the 1996 Lambda Literary Award, and, most recently, *Tales of the Lavender Menace: A Memoir of Liberation.* She has written for many publications, including *Ms. Magazine,* the *Village Voice,* and the *Gay & Lesbian Review Worldwide.* She reviews books for *The New York Times, The*

Women's Review of Books, and *Girlfriends.* Her short stories and satires have appeared in *The Chronicle of Higher Education* and *Harrington Lesbian Fiction Quarterly.* She is currently at work on a mystery and on a collection of satires titled *Migrant Laborers in the Fields of Academe.* She lives in New York City with Karen, her life partner, and their two Maltese dogs, Felix and Beanie.

Lisa Liel was born and bred in Chicago, but has spent sixteen of her forty-one years living in Israel, Manhattan, and the beautiful mountains of Santa Cruz. She works as a programmer, reads voraciously (mostly science fiction, fantasy, and mysteries), and watches far more television than is good for her. Among other sites, Lisa owns and maintains http://www.orthodykes.org, a Web site for Orthodox Jewish lesbians. She lives in Chicago with her partner and their four-year-old daughter. "The Last Minute" is her first published work of fiction.

Randye Lordon departed from Chicago several days after her eighteenth birthday and headed for Manhattan and the American Academy of Dramatic Arts. By her mid-twenties, having grown tired of hearing what a fabulous living she would make as an actress once she hit her fifties, she began writing a mystery series. The series debuted in 1994 with *Sister's Keeper,* followed by *Father Forgive Me* (1997), *Mother May I* (1998), *Say Uncle* (1999), *Brotherly Love* (2000), and *East of Niece* (2002). *Son of a Gun* (2004) is the latest in her Lambda Literary Award–winning series. She has published short stories, stage productions, radio plays, and computer games. She now lives happily by the sea.

Carole Spearin McCauley is a medical writer, editor, and novelist. She lives in Greenwich, Connecticut. Her twelve books include titles from Women's Press (UK) and Daughters, Inc. (USA). The first of her series, *Cold Steal* and *A Winning Death,* appeared in 2004 and 2005 from Hilliard & Harris. Nearly 200 pieces of her short work (stories, articles, poetry, satire, reviews) have appeared in periodicals, including *Self, Omni, Family Circle, Child, Mystery Time, Gaysweek, Lesbian Short Fiction, Harrington Lesbian Fiction Quarterly, Bay Windows,* plus anthologies *Women: Omen* and *Suspense of Loneliness.* Nine pieces have won prizes in contests, including *USA Today,* Radio Netherlands

Worldwide, Contemporary Connecticut Writers. She works with Sisters in Crime and Women's National Book Association.

Diana McRae lives in Oakland, California, where she works as a writer, political activist, and librarian. She graduated from the University of California at Berkeley with a degree in rhetoric and began her writing career with a small newspaper in Contra Costa County. Among her published fiction is the novel *All the Muscle You Need: An Elsa Pirex Mystery.* Her family includes her life partner, Carolyn Moskowitz, and their three children, Wilder, Jaslo Eliza, and Harper.

Martha Miller is a middle-aged, Midwestern writer whose short-fiction has been widely published in literary and feminist anthologies and periodicals. She teaches writing at a local community college. Her latest book is *Dispatch to Death,* published by New Victoria Press. Other stories featuring African-American-lesbian-attorney-heroine Bertha Brannon are the mystery novel *Nine Nights on the Windy Tree* and *Skin to Skin: Erotic Lesbian Love Stories,* both from New Victoria Press. Her novel, *Tales from the Levee,* was published by The Haworth Press. She has two grown sons and lives with her partner of many years, their two dogs and two cats, in Central Illinois.

J. M. Redmann has written four mystery novels. The most recent, *Lost Daughters,* was published by W. W. Norton; the first two, *Death by the Riverside* and *Deaths of Jocasta* have been recently reissued. The third book, *The Intersection of Law and Desire* (W. W. Norton) won a Lambda Literary Award and was an Editor's Choice of the *San Francisco Chronicle;* and *Lost Daughters* and *Deaths of Jocasta* were both nominated for Lambda Literary Awards. In her copious spare time, she, along with writer Marianne K. Martin and publisher Kelly Smith, have founded Bywater Books (bywaterbooks.com). A Mississippi native, J. M. Redmann now lives, works, and frolics in that city in a swamp: New Orleans.

Ursula Steck was born in 1964. She grew up in Germany and the United States, and received a master's in English literature and philosophy from the University of Cologne. She has worked on a farm and also as a singer, parking lot attendant, teacher, and journalist. She has published three mystery novels: *In a State of Flux* (1999), *Fire Signals* (2000), and *Attack!* (2004), all from Grafit, Dortmund, and has published various short stories in German. She is currently at work on her first mystery novel for an American publisher.

HARRINGTON PARK PRESS®
Alice Street Editions™
Judith P. Stelboum
Editor in Chief

Zach at Risk by Pamela Shepherd

An Inexpressible State of Grace by Cameron Abbott

Minus One: A Twelve-Step Journey by Bridget Bufford

Girls with Hammers by Cynn Chadwick

Rosemary and Juliet by Judy MacLean

An Emergence of Green by Katherine V. Forrest

Descanso: A Soul Journey by Cynthia Tyler

Blood Sisters: A Novel of an Epic Friendship by Mary Jacobsen

Women of Mystery: An Anthology edited by Katherine V. Forrest

Glamour Girls: Femme/Femme Erotica by Rachel Kramer Bussel

The Meadowlark Sings by Helen R. Schwartz

Blown Away by Perry Wynn

Shadow Work by Cynthia Tyler

Dykes on Bikes: An Erotic Anthology edited by Sacchi Green
and Rakelle Valencia

Order a copy of this book *with this form or online at:*
http://www.haworthpress.com/store/product.asp?sku=5371

WOMEN OF MYSTERY
An Anthology

_____in softbound at $19.95 (ISBN-13: 978-1-56023-543-9; ISBN-10: 1-56023-543-8)

Or order online and use special offer code HEC25 in the shopping cart.

COST OF BOOKS_____

POSTAGE & HANDLING_____
(US: $4.00 for first book & $1.50
for each additional book)
(Outside US: $5.00 for first book
& $2.00 for each additional book)

SUBTOTAL_____

IN CANADA: ADD 7% GST_____

STATE TAX_____
(NJ, NY, OH, MN, CA, IL, IN, PA, & SD
residents, add appropriate local sales tax)

FINAL TOTAL_____
(If paying in Canadian funds,
convert using the current
exchange rate, UNESCO
coupons welcome)

☐ **BILL ME LATER:** (Bill-me option is good on
US/Canada/Mexico orders only; not good to
jobbers, wholesalers, or subscription agencies.)
☐ Check here if billing address is different from
shipping address and attach purchase order and
billing address information.

Signature_____

☐ **PAYMENT ENCLOSED: $**_____

☐ **PLEASE CHARGE TO MY CREDIT CARD.**

☐ Visa ☐ MasterCard ☐ AmEx ☐ Discover
☐ Diner's Club ☐ Eurocard ☐ JCB

Account #_____

Exp. Date_____

Signature_____

Prices in US dollars and subject to change without notice.

NAME_____

INSTITUTION_____

ADDRESS_____

CITY_____

STATE/ZIP_____

COUNTRY_____ COUNTY (NY residents only)_____

TEL_____ FAX_____

E-MAIL_____

May we use your e-mail address for confirmations and other types of information? ☐ Yes ☐ No
We appreciate receiving your e-mail address and fax number. Haworth would like to e-mail or fax special
discount offers to you, as a preferred customer. **We will never share, rent, or exchange your e-mail address
or fax number.** We regard such actions as an invasion of your privacy.

Order From Your Local Bookstore or Directly From
The Haworth Press, Inc.
10 Alice Street, Binghamton, New York 13904-1580 • USA
TELEPHONE: 1-800-HAWORTH (1-800-429-6784) / Outside US/Canada: (607) 722-5857
FAX: 1-800-895-0582 / Outside US/Canada: (607) 771-0012
E-mail to: orders@haworthpress.com

For orders outside US and Canada, you may wish to order through your local
sales representative, distributor, or bookseller.
For information, see http://haworthpress.com/distributors

(Discounts are available for individual orders in US and Canada only, not booksellers/distributors.)
PLEASE PHOTOCOPY THIS FORM FOR YOUR PERSONAL USE.
http://www.HaworthPress.com   BOF04